AWAKENING THE SENTIENTS

AWAKENING THE SENTIENTS

THE CHRONOTRACE SEQUENCE VOLUME 2

DJ EDWARDSON

GIRAFFIX

Dedicated to my wife Maria.
Thank you for reading my stories and
believing that they were worth sharing.

S.D.G.

"Man's conquest of Nature, if the dreams of some scientific planners are realized, means the rule of a few hundreds of men over billions upon billions of men. There neither is nor can be any simple increase of power on Man's side. Each new power won *by* man is a power *over* man as well. Each advance leaves him weaker as well as stronger. In every victory, besides being the general who triumphs, he is also the prisoner who follows the triumphal car...

For the power of Man to make himself what he pleases means, as we have seen, the power of some men to make other men what they please."

—C.S. Lewis, *The Abolition of Man*

NOTE ABOUT TERMINOLOGY

The world of the Chronotrace series is very different from ours. As such, the units of measure, time, and especially the technology used by the characters in these stories may seem unfamiliar to new readers. For this reason a glossary has been provided at the back of this book should a particular term need further explanation.

CONTENTS

ONE

TABULA RASA

Two men sat across the table from each other in black polymeric chairs. They had met countless times before, but never in this place. The room was old, but it was new to them.

One of them had thick, dark hair and a short beard. He wore the gray robes of an assessor, the security force which monitored the Collective. His robes had black accents on the shoulders and the hem, denoting him as the Assessor Primary.

The other man was unremarkable in appearance. He wore the same silver lab coat all scientists in the Collective wore. His most notable thing about him was the knowing look in his plain brown eyes. Those eyes had seen much, but they were seeing things in a new light since the destruction of Oasis.

"My men found a ship in the desert, in sector seventeen," the dark-haired assessor said, preferring not to use his bioseine, despite the speed which such mind to mind communication afforded.

"You're sure the ship belonged to a scout?" The scientist's

face remained impassive. It had never displayed emotion as far as the assessor knew.

"It was a radial jaunter, the kind typically used by the Delegation for interstellar travel. It was severely damaged, but the pilot was not found."

"That would be the second one. It is only a matter of time before one of them discovers our presence here and constructs a beacon portal."

The Assessor Primary nodded gravely. "With the anti-orbital battery down, we won't be able to stop them from doing so. The only question is why they haven't done so yet. Our only hope is that the pilots died from the injuries sustained in their crashes."

"Highly unlikely. They are escalons, after all."

"All this cursed biological tampering," The assessor rubbed his forehead. "Darius should have finished off the Delegation when he had the chance. He should have known they would come after us. And destroying the Nebula—how did we ever sign off on that? That was our only advantage over them, militarily."

At the mention of Darius' name, the scientist's eyes fogged over as he struggled to recall details about the past, details that were slowly trickling back now that the lead memorant in the Collective was gone. "Darius was an idealist. He must have had his reasons. But that does not matter now. We must prepare as best we can. How close are our forces to being field ready?"

"They are still unproven when fighting in large numbers. The simulators can only test so much."

"So send some to the surface and test them there."

"On what? The sand?" the assessor scoffed.

"The andros, of course."

"That would hardly be a test." The desert natives may have had numbers, but their weapons were far too primitive. His eyes lit up with a thought. "Why not send the somatarchs against the renegade? We know where his base of operations is now."

The scientist regarded him with an austere expression. "We might want to wait until we're fully ready. He has managed to build up quite a little army in the desert."

The assessor's frame shifted uncomfortably beneath his robes. He didn't like getting military advice from this walking test tube. "Who do you think crashed the energy mesh? The longer we leave him out there, the more time we're giving him to augment his forces. They've already attacked us once."

"You're giving him far more credit than he deserves," the scientist responded coolly. "His forces would have been annihilated if it had not been for that storm. He could not have predicted when it would hit or that it would be of that magnitude."

The assessor set his jaw the way he did when his mind was fixed on a certain course of action. "True. But the renegade would be more of a test than defenseless andros."

"You're certain this isn't personal?" asked the scientist. It was a rhetorical question.

The Assessor Primary's eyes flitted about the room for a moment, lost in thought. He would never have put up with these sorts of questions from non-military personnel when he was still serving the Delegation. But here, things were different. They had so few resources left at their disposal. He could not afford to alienate the chief scientist in the Collective. They had to work together if there was any hope of survival.

"So what if it is?" the assessor asked at length, "Tactically it's still the best decision. His presence at Landfall can mean only one thing."

The scientist retreated inside himself, hiding behind his tightly drawn expression.

Though he would never have admitted it, the assessor feared whatever calculations his colleague was pushing through that organic computer inside his head. It was like facing a hidden enemy on the battlefield. The only thing he feared more was the mind reading memorants. But all but one of them had perished in the storm.

"I still think you overestimate him, but I'll defer to you in this matter." The scientist relaxed his expression and dropped the mask. "Now tell me what our course of action will be. And let's dispense with this inefficient verbal chatter."

The dark-haired man gave him a wary look. He didn't like having anyone inside his head, but this meeting had gone on long enough, he supposed.

"*Very well.*" He reluctantly switched to the bioseine connection, "*We should be able to deploy the first wave within three days, sooner if the storm lets up.*"

"It can't go on forever."

"*As if you and your scientists knew anything about this accursed atmosphere.*"

The scientist's mind bristled at the assessor's reminder. The storm which had destroyed Oasis had been a singular event. Nothing even close to it had ever been recorded before or even thought possible. It was highly unlikely anything like it would ever happen again.

"*You take care of your responsibilities and we will take care of ours,*" came the scientist's terse response. "*Just send me the tactical data so that I can make sure your forces will have what they need.*"

In acquiescence to his companion's request, images, diagrams, terrain maps, and equipment lists came pouring out of the Assessor Primary's mind. Deep down inside, the old soldier felt a sense of relief. He didn't like being holed up in this underground facility. He was looking forward to doing what he did best: going to war.

Pock marks scoured the walls of Will's abandoned compound. Chips and pebbles flew off on the wind as Adan and Gavin approached. But at last they were free from the storm.

A mixture of emotions seized Adan as he staggered into the small patch of sand surrounded by four char walls: relief they had made it, hope for what they might find, but above all the hollow reminder that he would never see Will again.

"Where did he keep the extractor?" Gavin asked. Some of his lost memories were stored in this device and it was for this reason they had come all this way.

"In the shelter," Adan said.

They passed by Will's barrels and sacks of scrap and into the small enclosed room in the corner, the only part of the compound which had a roof.

Lighting up one of Will's lumins after shutting the door, they hunted through the menagerie of storage compartments and spare parts jammed into every corner. After checking all the containers they could find, they came to the conclusion that the extractor must have been left outside. But with the wind still blasting sand over the crumbling walls, all they could do was hole up and wait for it to die down.

"That's fine. I'm exhausted anyway," Gavin said, but Adan could tell he was disappointed.

They stretched out as much as possible in the cluttered enclosure, but Adan couldn't sleep, afraid the storm might get worse again.

The journey back from Oasis had been far more difficult than he had imagined, harder than going hungry when the shifter broke, harder than being captured by somatarchs, harder even in some ways than Will's death. It wasn't just the grueling ten-day trek through sand and storm; that had certainly taken its toll; it was not knowing whether Gavin was going to live or die.

The after effects of the solec drug had caused Gavin's muscles to seize up with cramps. After a few microslices, he couldn't move at all. Knowing that Gavin never would have taken the drug if he hadn't needed it to rescue Adan only made matters worse.

After sitting out in the open desert for half a day, waiting for Gavin to recover enough to be able to move again, another storm swept in across the desert. Adan dragged Gavin's paralyzed body into a dip in the dunes and used his friend's unfurled garrick as a makeshift tent to protect him. Then he battened down his own and prepared to wait out the storm's fury. Throughout the howling assault. doubts about whether they would survive beat against Adan's mind, every bit as fierce as the winds threatening to carry them off into the Vast.

The only way he had gotten through was to pray. Perhaps that decision had been brought about by the memory he had received from the remin fluid. Will had given it to him just before they parted, and the vision it had shown him—part real, part synthetic—had been of someone in prayer to Numinae, the mysterious being spoken of by the Welkin, the people who dwelt beneath the Vast.

Adan knew he couldn't save Gavin on his own. But Numinae, who somehow transcended space and time, had the power to do anything. He was bigger and stronger than anything Adan could imagine.

Even though at first, Numinae seemed not to answer Adan's pleas for help, those prayers sustained him somehow. They gave him hope when he had no other reason to hope.

Microslice by microslice, Adan's lonely vigil passed, one hundred microslices in a slice, twenty slices in a day, until a sense of peace came over him, and he knew, he just somehow knew, that Gavin would get better.

For two days Gavin's health shifted like the wind. One moment he would open his eyes and manage to look like himself again, the next his face would turn ashen and his skin go cold.

But on the third day Adan's prayers were answered. Gavin started breathing normally again. By the next day he had recovered enough to walk. At that point he insisted they resume their journey. Though Adan thought he could have used another day of rest, Gavin said that walking would help work out the stiffness in his limbs.

They made steady progress from that point on, weathering a few minor storms, but nothing like the first one, and certainly nothing like the one that had destroyed Oasis.

They arrived back at the compound six days later, disheveled and exhausted, but alive; alive and with new hope for the days ahead.

———

A feeble light filtered through the cracks around the shelter door. Gavin, oblivious to the new day, slept on. Adan, who had fallen in and out of sleep all night, waited until the winds settled down to the occasional murmur before rising and stepping outside into the haze-filled air.

Dust floated by on a few stubborn currents. The barrels, crates, and walls lay coated under a thick layer of the stuff. They resembled a sort of bumpy, odd shaped dune. In several places the char walls had crumbled and left holes to the outside world.

Images from the storm in Oasis flashed through Adan's mind. Black walls of silt pounded his memory and the tangled remnants of the Institute swirled inside his thoughts. He could almost feel himself falling again through that tempest until something caught him. Then the memory faded and he was back in the compound again.

Adan wandered about, searching for the extractor with his mind. That would be the quickest way to find it now that the storm could no longer suppress bioseine connections. After several microslices of mental probing, it became clear he was not going to find it that way. The extractor had either lost power or been blown outside the range of his bioseine. Either way, finding it would take a lot more work than he had first hoped.

He started sifting through the containers. He removed the lids, pulling out every last piece of scrap he could find. To Adan's anxious mind, a great many of the metal bits looked like the silvery torc at first glance, but in the end, none of them were. He rifled through the canvas sacks, but again his search came up empty. By that time it was late afternoon. Weary from picking through the piles of scrap, he walked outside the compound. With all the holes in the walls it was possible the extractor might have been swept outside. If that were the case, the likelihood of finding it was slim.

At first he walked around the compound, trying once again to sense it with his mind. He found no trace, but did spot something he had forgotten about: the lev, the hover vehicle Will had used to bring him back from Oasis. Will had shown it to him before they were carried off by the somatarchs. It was still parked out behind the compound, covered by a large tarp. Adan could sense with his mind that it was still functional.

He stood staring at it for a moment, wondering whether he should uncover it and see if for some reason the extractor was hidden beneath the tarp. In the end he decided to unfasten the pins on one of the corners and take a peek. All he saw was the empty metal platform with handles around the edge and a steering column up front.

Dismayed, he wandered back inside. As he entered, the shelter door scraped open across the sand and Gavin emerged.

"I see you've really fixed up the place," he said, rubbing the sleep from his eyes and surveying the upended barrels and emptied sacks. He gestured towards the disintegrating walls. "And the windows are a nice touch. Should let in a nice breeze in the evening."

"I'm glad you're finally awake," Adan said. It was nice to have Gavin back in good spirits. "I've been looking for your extractor. So far, I've found nothing."

Gavin's expression turned serious. "We'll just have to look harder, then. Let me make some atol first and then we'll start looking again."

A pleasant sensation spread through Adan's memory at the mention of the warm, grainy drink Will had introduced him to not all that long ago.

"I'll get the shifter," he said, licking his lips.

The shifter had been the one bright spot in their return. They found it tucked away inside the shelter the night before, and the cutter along with it. The cutter was what Will used to chop up the nearly endless supply of scrap from the barrels. He fed the resulting 'plugs', as he called them, into the shifter, transforming them into any elemental compound he wanted. That was how they got their food and water, as well as char to repair the walls.

The kern they'd salvaged from the Waymen in Oasis was getting old. The desert dwellers may have been tenacious when it came to surviving storms out in the Vast, but they were not much when it came to culinary skills. After eight days of the sinewy fare, Adan was more than ready to try something different.

Gavin set about making plugs with the cutter and Adan dropped them into the shifter. In little time at all they had hot, thick liquid swishing down their throats. The grainy drink was just as satisfying and tasty as Adan remembered.

Refreshed, they resumed their hunt for the extractor. They searched for most of the day, but never found it. They went through all the piles of scrap Adan had previously searched through and even a few barrels and sacks he'd missed.

"You said you looked outside earlier?" Gavin asked as the daylight began to fade.

"Yes, but only a little. I didn't think there would be much chance of finding it out there."

"Stumbling across it out in the dunes would take a miracle, but I don't see what choice we have."

Adan nodded, his head heavy with exhaustion. They set out into the desert surrounding the compound, splitting up.

The sand near the compound was almost completely free of the metal scraps which littered most of the Vast. It made sense that Will would have already picked the closest areas clean. A few small rocks, flecks of metal, or bits of char were all that was left. They were on their fourth sweep, increasing the distance each time, when Gavin's voice came to Adan from the other side of the compound.

"Adan," he shouted. "Come here. There's something you have to see."

Adan rushed towards the sound of his voice, connecting to Gavin's bioseine once he got within range.

"*Did you find the extractor?*" Adan asked, his thoughts brimming with anticipation.

"*No, it's something else.*"

The image of what Gavin saw appeared in Adan's mind.

He was staring at an open metal container, half buried in the sand. The elongated, opaque tube was a little wider than a man and a little taller, like a giant pill. The opened lid had exposed the interior, now coated in a thick layer of sand.

"*What is it?*" Adan asked, coming up alongside his friend. When Will had initialized Adan's bioseine, he had implanted a great deal of information inside of it, but nothing matched what he was looking at now.

"*A stasis capsule. They are used for keeping someone alive in long term storage.*"

"*Do you think it belonged to Will?*" Adan shared the question both of them were thinking. If it did belong to him, Adan didn't see how he could have failed to see it when he was here before. Perhaps the desert storms had uncovered it; it was buried rather deep.

Since it was an esolace enabled device, Gavin mentally searched the capsule's activity log. "*It doesn't list any details about whether or not there was ever anyone inside, but the capsule was timed to open fourteen days ago. That would have been the day after I left for Oasis.*"

"*I can't imagine it being set to open if someone wasn't inside.*"

"*I agree.*" Gavin's mind worked quickly, analyzing what possible reasons there might be for such a device to be planted out in the Vast. "*I'd say there is a distinct possibility that you weren't the only one Will freed from Oasis,*" Gavin concluded. "*And I'm guessing that whoever was in this capsule is the person who took the extractor.*"

Adan's insides felt as hollow as the capsule. If the extractor was lost, that meant Gavin's memories were lost as well. "Oh Gavin," he said, "I'm so sorry."

TWO

ITERATIONS

"So what do we do now?" Adan wondered as they trudged back to the compound. Night was coming on and they had learned all they could from the capsule.

Gavin stared up at the cloud-choked, swirling green sky.

Despair crept in with the encroaching dark. Had they come all this way for nothing? No, there had to be some way of recovering those memories.

"*Didn't you say the Developers kept the memories they erased somewhere in the Institute? What if we went back? Do you think they might have survived somehow?*" He stared expectantly at Gavin, waiting for his reply.

Gavin's face remained impassive. "*Yes, the Repository would have contained our memories. We stored them there in memory arrays. But it was destroyed, along with everything else in the Institute. There's no way it could have survived the storm.*"

"*The Repository.*" Adan held the name in his mind for a moment, as if that would somehow bring it back.

Gavin was right. There was no way anything could have

survived that storm, but something inside Adan refused to accept it. Until he saw Oasis again with his own eyes, he could always hope.

Gavin stopped in front of the door to the compound, a look of resolve on his face.

"Our only hope of finding the extractor is the chronotrace."

"The chronotrace? How could that help us? Whoever was in that capsule might have taken over a ten span ago. The chronotrace can't go back that far."

Adan's mind flashed back to the trace he'd created in Oasis. Reconstructing the past with Gavin's invention may have led them to Darius, but it had taxed the energy mesh of the city to the point of it crashing. If the mesh hadn't been enough there was no way they'd be able to the kind of power they needed out in the desert.

"You're right. The device doesn't have the functionality we need—yet." Gavin glanced at him, a gleam in his eye. *"But there was a saying we had back at the Institute, 'expand what's possible today and you'll shatter tomorrow's impossibilities.'"*

"Did you learn that from Darius?"

"Not everything he taught me was a lie," Gavin replied.

Adan recalled Darius' cunning eyes and the way he had spoken to him, as if Adan were just a thing, another piece of technology to be managed the way Darius managed the rest of Oasis. But he was dead now, taken by the storm which destroyed the city.

"So, you really think you can improve the chronotrace quickly enough to find the extractor?" Adan asked.

"No," Gavin admitted. *"But I have to try."*

"Well, I don't suppose I'd be of much help with something like that."

Gavin gave him a thoughtful look. *"Perhaps not. But there are plenty of other things which need to be done."*

"Like what?"

"Well..." Gavin gazed around the compound. *"Fixing these walls would be a good place to start. I won't be able to accomplish much if this place crumbles to the ground around us."*

Ah, well, that was something he could do, he supposed. Adan nodded and the two of them headed for the shelter to get some rest. It looked like tomorrow would be a long day for the both of them.

The next morning Adan began repairing the walls. He made plugs with the cutter, created char with the shifter, and spread the rocky paste over the walls, just the way Will had taught him.

It felt strange being back in the compound without him. So much had changed since the two of them had left a few short days ago. In some ways, though, Adan felt closer to Will now than he had when he was alive. Will had always been somewhat of a mystery when they were together, even before he had taken the remin fluid and recovered the plans to overtake Oasis. But watching Will die had changed the way Adan saw him. Will's vision of the mysterious messenger of Numinae the Welkin called an 'eidos', just before he died, had affected Adan in a way he found hard to explain. Though he hadn't seen the otherworldly being himself, the change that had come over Will in those last few moments had been undeniable. *Restoration* was the closest word Adan could find that seemed to fit. There was a kindness in his eyes when he died, a humility and a peace that Adan had never seen before.

But there was something else about Will's death that kept coming back, something Will had said: *"It wasn't my idea..."* He had been referring to the virus that was supposed to destroy

Oasis and kill Adan as well. But, if it wasn't Will's idea then whose was it? No one else knew about the virus besides Gavin, Will, and Adan, as far as he knew.

"Impossible!" Gavin exclaimed, pulling his head out of one of the barrels and interrupting Adan's thoughts. He had already thrown about half the scraps from inside onto the ground and was presently holding in his hand a chunk of raw metal covered in grime.

"What do you mean?" Adan asked. Like most of the scrap in the Vast, the piece had no doubt been part of some machine at one point, but in its present state there was no telling what purpose it had once served.

"I don't believe it," Gavin muttered, "It looks like...celerium."

The word didn't register with Adan. "Celerium?"

Gavin rubbed away some of the grime with a rag, revealing a dark metal cylinder with blue flecks running through it.

"There was some information about this material in the Developer archives. It's an energy amplification agent. But it was just a theory. It doesn't occur naturally and all attempts to synthesize it have failed. Or so I thought."

"What's it doing in Will's barrel?"

Adan stared at the dark piece of scrap. It looked fairly useless despite Gavin's wide-eyed look.

"I don't know. That's another thing they never told us about —all these machines out in the desert. Who knows how long they've been buried out here or even what they were for. If there's celerium out there, there could be anything."

"So can we use it?"

"I don't want to get your hopes up," Gavin answered, "but if it does what I think it will, I may be able to resolve the energy efficiency issues with the chronotrace. The energy amplification coil was always its weakness. That's why it had to draw in so *much extra power to compensate. But if I could improve the amplification process, the device could run on a tiny fraction of what it used before."*

Adan accidentally dropped the glob of char he had on his trowel into the sand. *"Then what are you waiting for?"*

―――

Gavin worked nonstop on the new energy amplification coil, barely sleeping over the next two days. The hardest part had been finding a way to mold the celerium so it would fit inside the chronotrace. The cutter's bright, triangular energy blade had no effect on it, which puzzled Gavin to no end. It should have been able to cut through anything.

In the end, he was forced to create a set of calibration controls for the cutter and use an additional power source in order to adjust the frequency of the beam. The cutter normally had two variations in the beam it projected: yellow for cutting inorganic material and red for cutting organic, living things. The beam that Gavin finally got to work was blue in color, something the cutter had been incapable of producing before the modification. This new cross stream blade could cut through both living and non-living material and even energy fields, but it drained the power considerably. Even then, the celerium resisted the blade so that Gavin had to work it back and forth for a long time to shape it how he wanted.

Once he finished, he was finally able to fashion the celerium into the form he wanted, a kind of ribbed wafer, which he inserted into the expanded energy chamber inside the lower section of the chronotrace. The new chamber also had space for more bismine chips to boost the device's power.

In the meantime, Adan continued the grueling task of patching up the char walls. His arms grew sore and heavy from lifting so much of the gray, goopy rock to fill in the gaps. On the second day, though, he was able to rest for the better part of the morning when a storm swept through and forced them back inside the shelter.

Adan tried to follow what Gavin was doing, but even when Gavin shared information through his bioseine, there were too many unknowns for Adan to fully grasp what was going on. Gavin himself barely seemed to understand everything fully. He was going mostly on hope and hunches.

"How do you manage to do all those calculations and iterations of your algorithm so quickly?" Adan asked as they finished off their cups of atol.

"That's another benefit of being a memorant. We do not just process other people's thoughts quickly, but any type of information."

Adan was still unsure about whether or not he wanted to develop his own latent memorant abilities, but this certainly sounded useful.

"How close are you to being able to test the modifications?" Adan asked.

Gavin set down his empty cup. *"Tomorrow."* His eyes glinted with expectation.

"I can't wait," Adan replied, catching his friend's enthusiasm.

Unfortunately, the weather did not accommodate Gavin and Adan's eagerness. A storm raged over the compound all the next day. Gavin worked on what refinements he could, but the shelter was cramped and even though the storms were outside, the bioseine interference it caused affected the shelter as well, cutting off Gavin's ability to connect with his device.

After a while, Gavin gave up and they decided to wait until the storm blew over.

"Well, since we've got some time on our hands," Gavin said,

"perhaps you'd like to learn a few things about being a memorant?"

Adan paused, caught off guard by the suggestion.

"Um..." he said, hedging. Was he ready for this?

"You know, if we ever do find your memories, being a memorant will help you absorb them much faster."

This was something Adan had not considered. What was he really afraid of anyway? Perhaps it was just a leftover reaction from the time Gavin had used his abilities to read Adan's thoughts without him knowing. He wasn't sure he wanted that kind of power. Still, he supposed there was a way to control it or turn it off somehow when he didn't need it.

"Okay, just go over the basics," he said.

Gavin studied Adan's face, looking him directly in the eye. "One of the first things you must do is quiet your own thoughts and notice everything you can about the person whose mind you are attempting to read."

That seemed easy enough. Adan stared back at him, trying to see if he could tell from Gavin's expression anything about what he was thinking. He looked serious, but Adan thought anyone would have been able to tell that.

"And the way you must begin to do that is by closing your eyes," Gavin instructed.

Adan let out a short laugh. "Close my eyes? But didn't you say I was supposed to—"

"Just try it," Gavin said. "Close your eyes and try to remember what my face looks like. Study it from your memory."

Adan rolled his eyes, but did as he was told. He tried to picture Gavin's face. At first all he could see was a static image of what it looked like, but then dozens of expressions began to flash through Adan's mind. He was surprised to find that Gavin's relatively plain face was capable of such a variety of emotion. He was equally surprised that he could recall his expressions so clearly, but he didn't see how this would help him guess what Gavin was thinking at that particular moment.

"You may open your eyes again," Gavin said. "Now tell me what I'm thinking."

Adan opened his eyes to the same serious expression Gavin had been wearing before.

"You're pleased with my effort?" he ventured.

Gavin shook his head. "Don't just guess."

"Wait, wasn't that my intuition?" Adan said, confused.

"Yes, but you can't always trust your intuition."

"But I thought—oh, never mind." Adan shrugged and Gavin made him repeat the process again: closing his eyes, watching the parade of expressions rush by, and then opening his eyes again to try and divine what Gavin was thinking.

After the fifteenth time, Adan said, "You're just looking at your own reflection in my eyes. You're not thinking about anything, are you?"

Gavin cracked a smile. "Well done," he said. "That's the first thing you have to learn about reading people's thoughts— how they can mask them. You have to know what the false readings look like before you can ever figure out what the real ones are."

"I can't believe you were just tricking me this whole time," Adan said, chagrinned. Gavin was generally so forthright, but when it came to his memorant side, he could be extremely enigmatic. "So are you going to stop masking your thoughts now and let me really try to read them this time?"

"I don't know," Gavin replied, still smiling. "You tell me."

"You're not going to make this easy, are you?"

"You see, you're reading my thoughts already." He laughed.

Adan shook his head, both amused and frustrated by Gavin's evasiveness.

"Maybe I'm just not cut out for this," Adan said.

"Just because you have the ability doesn't mean you don't have to put in the work to learn how to use it. Any skill worth doing well is worth banging your head against until you break through."

Adan nodded. He knew Gavin was right, but he was still a little leery of this memorant business. Part of him wondered if he should just stay the way he was. He wondered if knowing the sorts of things Gavin seemed to know might not be more of a burden than a benefit.

"You are right to worry," Gavin told him, picking up on what he was thinking. "Sometimes knowing what others think is painful. And it's tempting to use it for selfish reasons. I have certainly done that many times in the past. But if Numinae granted you this ability, you can be certain that it must be for some purpose."

Adan regarded him thoughtfully. "I suppose you're right. I guess I shouldn't let myself get frustrated. So what else do I have to learn?"

Gavin gave him a sympathetic nod. And with that he resumed expounding on the subtle and difficult art of being a memorant.

THREE
MINING AND CRAFTING

THE INITIAL TESTS OF THE CHRONOTRACE WENT BETTER than expected. Will had left behind ten bismine crystals in a box in the shelter and Gavin inserted these into the new energy array to work with the celerium. That was enough to make a trace which ran back almost a full day, with plenty of power left when Gavin brought the test to a halt.

"Why did you stop?" Adan asked.

"Because I don't want to burn out the crystals. Bismine recharges over time, but if you drain it too far down the crystals become useless."

"Do they really recharge on their own? Where does the energy come from?" Adan watched Gavin slide the array out from under the shiny black chronotrace and open it to examine the chips. The yellow crystals were arranged in two half circles spread out around the celerium wafer.

"The energy comes from a mixture of the light that filters through the clouds and the locus energy field which surrounds all matter," Gavin explained.

Though Adan had never heard the term 'locus field' before,

Gavin didn't have to explain it to him. The information was already in his bioseine. The field was akin to the zoetic energy which permeated the universe. However, whereas zoetic energy held living things together, the locus field did so with inorganic matter. But the fields could interact with each other and locus energy could be harnessed to disrupt both living and non-living matter. The cutter used locus energy in this way.

"*So, how long will it take before those chips fully recharge?*" Adan asked.

"*About two days.*"

"*Then how are we ever going to trace back to when the extractor was taken? The capsule opened seventeen days ago.*"

"*Since the trace has already started, when we do the next run we will pick up from where we left off.*"

"*But how? I thought the chronotrace always had to trace back in time from the present.*"

"*That's the way it works right now, but I'm working on some adjustments that might change that. We'll see if I can pull it off.*"

Gavin's thoughts turned back to his work, but Adan allowed his hopes to rise ever so slightly. For the first time since discovering the capsule, he felt there was an actual chance of finding Gavin's memories.

Over the next few days, Adan continued to improve in his ability to read Gavin's surface thoughts. With the walls patched back up, he shadowed Gavin as he worked on the chronotrace, studying him as often as he could and asking him from time to time what he was thinking. Adan was getting to where he could guess without even closing his eyes, but he was still wrong most of the time.

"*Even I don't always get it right,*" Gavin assured him. "*And you are picking it up far more quickly than I did.*"

"*I suppose that's because I have a good teacher.*"

Gavin laughed. "*We'll see if I'm as good an inventor as I am a memorant. The bismine chips will be fully recharged in less than a slice. Let's grab something to eat while we wait.*"

They whipped up a batch of atol and mosh and had a quick bite before heading out to the stasis capsule to test the chronotrace. The grainy drink and the bluish green paste made a wonderful combination, gritty and salty with a hint of sweetness.

The winds kept quiet all afternoon. Even the sickly green sky seemed to swirl less than usual. It looked like perfect conditions for the test.

After placing the chronotrace next to the capsule, Gavin went over the improvements he had been working on.

"*I was able to further increase the power efficiency, as well as the range of effect, yesterday, to the point that I could test the new modification: downtime tracing.*" Gavin's eyes glowed with excitement. He often got that way when sharing about his invention. "*You see, after the initial sample, all of the variables the chronotrace needs for its calculations have been recorded. I just had to implement an efficient way to store them. With that in place I was able to continue the trace all yesterday with five of the bismine chips while the others were recharging.*"

"*How far back did you get?*"

"*Almost five days,*" Gavin effused. "*And I think the array will have enough to get us back to the point when the extractor was taken.*"

Tiny needles of anticipation pricked Adan's skin as the chronotrace fired up. It let off its usual shower of light and then faded from view, replaced by the whirling desert winds and restless sands of a swiftly changing landscape. Inside the temporal bubble everything was a blur until it reached the time when the capsule was supposed to have opened. Then Gavin slowed everything down.

From his connection to the chronotrace, Adan could see the energy array was down to sixty-five percent. That would still give them plenty of time to finish the trace.

The desert winds swirled inside the temporal bubble. With time flowing in reverse, from beyond the edge of the trace Adan noticed a figure walking backwards into the scene out of the corner of his eye. But the figure only got half-way into the projection when everything winked out of existence. The chronotrace flashed and went dark and the energy levels took a sharp drop, dipping suddenly below thirty percent.

"What happened?" Adan asked.

Gavin growled in frustration. "It was the thought-mapping algorithm. I shouldn't have tried to test it so soon. It caused a power spike and crashed the system."

"You're trying to get the chronotrace to map a person's thoughts as well? I didn't know you were working on that."

"I wanted to find out who this person was, not just follow the trace to see where they went. It would have saved us a lot of time if it had worked, but it looks like I was overly ambitious. I didn't tell you about it because I didn't want to get your hopes up. I knew there was only a slim chance of it working. I'll need a lot more time and much better equipment to get that running, I'm afraid."

"Don't be so hard on yourself. At least you got far enough back to see the event. A few days ago that wasn't even possible."

Adan brought up the memory of the last scene from the chronotrace in his mind. Whoever was walking away from the capsule had dusty brown hair and wore the nondescript robe of a patient from the Institute, identical to the one Adan had worn. He was walking towards the compound. Unfortunately his face was still hidden beyond the edge of the temporal projection.

"*We may not know who he is, but he was headed towards the compound. He had to be the one who took the extractor,*" Adan commented.

"*Probably, but even if that's true, we won't know where he took it until the chronotrace can backtrace the days after this event occurs.*"

"*Wait, isn't the chronotrace limited to depicting the events at a given location? If he headed out into the Vast, wouldn't we have to do a separate projection for each location he traveled to?*"

"*Not if the downtime processing works as expected. I configured it so it can follow an event sequence over space, as well as time, after it maps the initial conditions.*"

"*And the bismine array?*" Adan asked. "*It can't recharge now. The chips are drained.*"

Gavin picked up the chronotrace and pulled out the array. The color of the crystals was fading, more brown than yellow now.

"*I guess we'll have to find some more,*" Gavin replied stoically.

"*How?*" Adan had no idea where Will had gotten the bismine, and he had never seen any of it out in the Vast.

"*I'll tell you.*"

And with that the details of bismine prospecting came racing in.

Adan ran his finger along the edge of one of the lentes he wore. The green lenses over each of his eyes let him see through the dust-choked winds surrounding him as though it was a clear day.

He stood atop a long slope of rock gazing down at the exposed bismine vein at the base. It peeked out from a small depression, a little nub of orangish rock, nothing more. He might have mistaken it for a piece of rusted metal if he hadn't been tracking its location.

The vein was just where he had expected it to be, based on the locus field emanations coming from the bismine shard he held in his hand. The emanations themselves were invisible, but Adan's bioseine was able to read the otherwise imperceptible vibrations in the chip whenever he pointed it towards a large enough source of active bismine. In this way he could tell which direction he needed to go and the proximity of the nearest vein. From what Gavin had shared with him, all bismine shards functioned this way as long as they had at least some amount of energy left.

Adan made his way down the slope, nearly losing his balance when a sudden gust of wind blasted him from behind. He caught himself and managed to skid down the dune without falling.

Stopping at the yellowish patch of crystal embedded in the ground, he reached back and loosened the cutter strapped to his waist. He yanked the device over his forearm, then twisted his wrist. A bright slice of yellow light appeared at the end of the tube just beyond where his hand would have been. Because the cutter didn't use esolace technology, he had to adjust a dial inside the housing with his thumb. He increased the blade to its maximum length, almost twice the length of the cutter itself.

Better hurry, he told himself. *Might be a storm coming.*

He sliced out large chunks of rock surrounding the glowing vein. He was careful not to cut the bismine itself yet because he didn't want to kill the vein off completely. Bismine required light to grow. The vein might extend for a great distance below the ground, but if the surface crystals were ever covered or destroyed, the rest of the vein would slowly lose its power over time and become dead rock. It seemed odd to think that rock could grow in this fashion, fed by light, but that was how it worked according to the information that Gavin had given him. Adan recalled that the Welkin people who lived in the caverns beneath the desert had several rocks which they used for food and other materials. He wondered if those rocks grew as well.

The work with the cutter was practically effortless. Adan simply waved his hand and the gray bedrock fell away. Once he got knee deep in the ground, he shrunk the blade down to about the length of his hand and carved out two dozen shards from the lower parts of the vein. He placed the shards into a satchel he wore at his hip.

Once his work was finished, he stepped up out of the pit and headed back towards the compound, muttering a quick prayer of thanks to Numinae that they were one step closer to finding the extractor and Gavin's memories.

Adan got safely back to the compound without running into any storms.

Gavin wasted no time in putting Adan's bismine chips to use. After he inserted them into the chronotrace's energy array, the device sprang back to life. Its yellow light reflected off the compound walls.

It was almost evening by the time Adan returned, so the two of them turned in for some much needed rest. The combination of the celerium coil and downtime tracing allowed the chronotrace to work for much longer periods of time, so they left it running through the night.

The next morning when they checked on the chronotrace's

progress, everything seemed to be going as planned. They made some atol and let the trace run its course.

Gavin said the trace would last all day. With nothing else to do, they decided Adan should head back out into the Vast to see if he could find another deposit of bismine. Gavin would stay behind and pack what they needed for their trip across the Vast, tracking down whoever had the extractor.

Adan did not return to the previous vein for fear of tapping it out, so he was forced to start his search afresh. It was a long, dreary day, walking up and down seemingly every dune within half a day's walk of the compound, but he failed to find any more bismine.

When he returned to the compound, light was streaming out from beneath the shelter door. It was far too much for a simple lumin. Gavin was probably making a few last minute adjustments to the chronotrace.

When Adan opened the door, instead of seeing Gavin, he found himself face to face with a brown-haired man about his same height. His hair was short, like the style worn by the scientists at the Institute and his face was like theirs as well. But he wore a garrick instead of a lab coat, and his kaff hung loose at his throat. The most striking thing about him was what peeked out from underneath his scarf: around his neck he wore the silvery extractor containing Gavin's memories.

FOUR
FOLLOWING A PHANTOM

THE STRANGER STARED STRAIGHT THROUGH ADAN. HE walked towards the shelter door as if he meant to leave whether Adan moved or not. It reminded Adan of the way people in Oasis looked at him without even acknowledging he was there.

He started to back out of the shelter, but at that moment, the stranger froze in mid-stride. That's when Adan noticed Gavin watching the scene from the corner of the room.

"It's only a trace," Gavin said.

Adan felt foolish for having been taken in by the projection, but Gavin's recent traces looked uncannily real.

"Who is he?" Adan wondered, studying the stranger's face. He looked exactly like all the other people he'd seen from Oasis except for the eyes. There was an unusual intensity there.

"Hopefully we'll find out soon enough." The projection faded and Gavin rose to his feet. "Time to get on our desert gear. Are you ready for another journey?"

"I think so. At least this time we won't have to walk." Looking into Gavin's strong, honest face Adan saw his own smile reflected there.

Although Gavin looked exactly like the scientists in Oasis, with their fine brown hair and cold gray eyes, there was a gentleness about him that put Adan at ease. Though their friendship had gotten off to a rough start, he now felt around him much the same way he had felt around Senya, his Welkin friend.

Senya...I wonder if she and her children are safe? Or if I'll ever see them again. They had been forced to flee their underground home, but he had no idea where they had fled to.

The fate of his Welkin friends lay heavy upon him as he and Gavin strapped on their garricks and kaffs.

"I'll meet you around back at the lev," Gavin told him as he finished. He headed towards the door.

"Do you think the extra bismine chips will be enough?" Adan asked. He was still fixing his kaff.

"Yes," Gavin's thoughts continued as he walked out of the shelter, *"They should last us a few days and we can always mine more if we run low."*

After Adan finished wrapping his kaff snugly, he helped Gavin load the supplies onto the lev: the shifter, the cutter, and of course, the chronotrace. They also brought along some tumblers of atol and canisters of mosh. Since they would likely have to make more slugs for the shifter on the journey, they also packed two small barrels of scrap. There was plenty of castoff machinery in the Vast, but they didn't want to have to waste time stopping to collect it. They rolled up the tarp and put it on board to protect their gear—and themselves—during storms. Lastly, Gavin brought along a pair of lentes. They were only able to scrounge up the one set. The stranger had taken the other pair, along with the extractor and some desert gear.

"So what are we going to do if we actually find this person?" Adan asked as they stepped up onto the platform.

Gavin considered the question for a moment. "We'll ask him to give us the extractor, I suppose."

"Somehow I don't think it will be that easy."

"Somehow I think you're right," Gavin said. "But you never know which way the wind will blow until you're out in the storm. We'll figure it out when we find him."

Gavin connected his mind to the lev and engaged the power. The platform rose gently off the sand. The desert winds wafted across them, spraying sand on their kaff-covered faces as the lev rotated away from the back wall. In no time at all, they were rushing across the dunes, the compound lost in the distance.

Though the terrain rose and fell, Adan had little difficulty in keeping his balance. The lev kept itself as steady as if he'd been standing on solid ground, compensating for the dips and irregularities of the rolling dunes, always keeping about a body-length between them and the ground.

Following the stranger's path as it had been mapped out in the chronotrace, they headed in the opposite direction from Oasis. This gave Adan mixed feelings. Part of him still wondered if the Repository had somehow remained intact, but another part thought it might be best if he never returned there at all. Right now, it didn't matter, though. They had to find the extractor first.

They had intended to use the lentes to navigate through the night, but when a storm blew in close to dusk, they decided to wait it out. The lev was heavy, but riding high in the air it was vulnerable to under-drafts and risked being upended if the winds got too strong.

They fashioned a makeshift tent by attaching the tarp to the bars of the lev on one side and spiking the other into the ground.

The winds swirled around them as they consumed their

evening meal. The gusts never grew strong enough to dislodge their makeshift shelter, but the constant fear that it might turn worse made for a night of uneasy rest.

Long before the morning light came they set off again, as soon as the storm died down enough to safely pilot the lev. The chronotrace continued to track the stranger's journey, but it would take several more days before they'd be able to pinpoint his current location. Adan and Gavin had already traveled about the same distance as the stranger had over the first three days. From the trace, they could see he had traveled both day and night, only resting once for a few slices, but as he had been on foot and they were not, they would catch him eventually.

"*He must have a bioseine,*" Adan observed as he reflected on the incredible pace the man had kept. Adan had used his own bioseine in the same manner to keep up with the Waymen when he'd run with them, though never over such a long period of time.

"*That would stand to reason,*" Gavin replied.

Why had Will brought this man out into the Vast and left him in the capsule? Had he been part of the plan to destroy Oasis as well? It seemed like the only possible explanation, but Adan could not imagine what the stranger's role would have been. Perhaps, since he wasn't headed back to Oasis, the Developers had another city somewhere out in the Vast? That was an unsettling thought, but the longer the journey wore on the more Adan's mind returned to it.

Late that afternoon they noticed a pair of storm cells forming, both ahead and behind them. They were separate systems, but they looked to be converging on their position. Even if they turned the lev from its present course, it looked like the storms would be too large to avoid.

The stretch of desert they were traveling across at that point was no place to be caught in a storm. The sand was strewn with gigantic pieces of machinery, some three times higher than the compound walls, far higher than the lev could fly. This would greatly reduce their maneuverability, forcing them into paths they might not want to take. Besides that, panels, rivets, and gears from the surrounding wreckage shook in the wind, ready to be set free once the wind gained enough strength. Spindly, wire-like tubes of metal lay scattered across the plain, like rusted grass. These broken needles swayed and creaked in the desert gusts, waiting to snap and be done with the long, slow, ache of decay. If the storm caught Adan and Gavin inside the ruins, the torquing winds might soon be filled with enough scrap to rip them both to shreds.

As they crested a dune between a pair of enormous rusted metal drums, Gavin pointed towards the storm off to their right.

"We're not alone," he informed Adan.

Adan stared into the sandy jumble of onrushing air, but without the benefit of Gavin's lentes, he could see nothing but billowing sacks of dust. He reached into Gavin's mind to look through the eyes of his friend.

Still some distance away, and shrouded in the massive dust clouds, were several figures. It looked like they were skating through the air, a short distance above the ground. Little trails of white light marked the path they had taken, but they lasted only a little while before fading. He could make out a dozen of them at first. Soon twice that number emerged from the dust clouds, several of them riding small floating vehicles.

Adan had never seen ships like these before. They were triangular platforms with sides that flared out and slightly upwards, forming an aerodynamic lip. Each also had a large, elongated black weapon mounted on the front. Whisper cannons. The echoes of their deadly blasts resounded in Adan's memory. Two figures dressed in white rode on each of the vehicles, one seated behind the enormous weapons, the other standing behind a narrow column behind that.

Though Gavin had the lentes on maximum zoom, at first the figures were too far away to tell what they were. But from the color of their robes, Adan guessed they must be somatarchs, the empty, soulless servants of the Developers who looked human, but possessed no will of their own.

Gavin sent the lev swerving in the opposite direction. There was no way they could take on a force of twenty-plus somatarchs with whisper cannons. The approaching storms suddenly seemed like a safe haven.

"*Somatarchs on attack skiffs and skimmers. What are they doing out here?*" Gavin wondered. "*This is completely against the Xenon protocol.*"

"The Xenon Protocol?"

"*Darius wanted to keep the presence of Oasis secret from the indigenous population of the Vast. Whenever we sent agents outside the city, they had to dress like the Waymen or Welkin and avoid any interaction with them. Barring that, they would eliminate anyone who saw them, ensuring that no witnesses survived.*"

As the lev ate up the ground before them, Adan's gaze remained fixed on the clouds behind. It was not long before the terrible creatures burst through and he could see them with his own eyes. It looked like they had spotted Gavin and Adan's transport because they were headed straight for it. Gavin had the lev going so fast it was all Adan could do to hold on now, but still the somatarchs were gaining—rapidly. Their only hope seemed to be to lose them in the oncoming storm.

Gavin's thoughts sounded another warning in Adan's mind. *"Look up ahead."*

Adan wheeled around to face the oncoming storm. He didn't need to borrow Gavin's eyes this time; the force ahead had already emerged from the swirling clouds.

This new contingent consisted of three groups of thirty or forty figures each, packed onto massive, elongated transports. The floating ships had slanted grills in the front and an open bay in the middle. These ungainly contraptions were in much worse condition than the small ships coming from behind. Their grime-covered fuselages looked pieced together from cast off machinery. They moved ponderously across the desert, as if doing so with great effort. Each had half a dozen guns mounted along the sides in haphazard fashion, shoved into odd orifices or soldered on precariously in unexpected positions. Though the weapons were quite large, they didn't look anything like the deadly whisper cannons. The barrels of these weapons were blunt and much wider. Yellow lights ran in dotted lines along either side of the barrels, making them stand out amidst the dust clouds of the storm. Adan ran a quick check with his bioseine, but found nothing to tell him what sort of weapons they were.

Unlike the forces behind them, the figures on the decks of these new ships were dressed like Waymen, wearing faded khaki-colored garricks and kaffs. But they could not be desert warriors. Waymen never used any kind of technology whatsoever, in fact they were afraid of it. They had to be somatarchs in disguise.

Adan and Gavin were now pinned on either side. The only question was which group they would have to face first. The one ahead of them had at least three times the number of warriors, but they were concentrated on only three ships and their vehicles looked to be far less maneuverable.

"We've got no chance against that force behind us," Gavin explained, *"They're too fast and too spread out. We've got to try and get around that line of ballast cruisers and hope we don't come into the range of their pulsers."*

Gavin didn't bother going into any more detail before veering the lev to the left. Darting in and out of the taller mounds of scrap, he tried to pick the best path to get past the ships. But with so much salvage to avoid, they veered too close to one of the cruisers and it opened fire on them.

Beams of intense yellow light blazed across the desert, slicing through the scrap around them. Four or five rays swept over their heads, forcing Gavin to plunge the lev downwards so that it skipped across the sand. Though the lines of energy were constant, concentrated pulses zipped along the beams like tiny balls of light.

Adan and Gavin's ship dove behind a box-like hulk of metal giving them temporary cover. Their concealment only lasted a moment. Beams sliced the giant piece of scrap into smaller chunks which tumbled to the sand.

No doubt the ship firing on them would have sliced the lev to pieces a moment later if Gavin hadn't steered sharply back to the right. The turn was a blind one, swerving around a pile of wreckage. Gavin had no way of seeing the pile of machinery waiting for them on the other side. They came in too fast. Even the avoidance technology on the lev couldn't stop them from colliding with the twisted metallic wreckage that rose up before them. Gavin veered hard to the left so that they avoided a direct hit, but they clipped the side of it. The lev flipped forward, launching Adan and Gavin skyward.

Everything twirled past Adan in a dream-like haze. Then the world came rushing up from below. His body crashed into the scrap-filled sand. The last thing he saw was the swift chaotic sky descend upon him, burying him in darkness.

FIVE

BETWEEN TWO STORMS

Adan came to a short time after the crash. The storms were nearly upon him. Visibility was down to a couple hundred paces. The lev lay bent and in ruins close by. Gavin was nowhere to be seen.

The left side of Adan's head was splitting with pain. When he touched it his hand came back splotched with blood. But the pain and his injuries did not occupy his mind long. An enormous ballast cruiser floated towards him not fifty paces away, loaded down with figures in garricks.

Adan reached out with his mind to Gavin, but sensed nothing, not even the minds of the figures on the ship. They were either the same kind of somatarch that had captured him and Will in the compound or the storm was interfering with the connection.

The ballast came to a stop in midair. Several figures leapt from the deck onto the sand, rushing towards him. Adan shot to his feet, pain slicing down the side of his head. He was about to take off when something caught his eye in the sand: the cutter. He scooped it up and shoved it on his arm as he ran towards the oncoming storm. He thought he could spot bits of shiny debris flashing in the dust clouds ahead—scrap from the ruins most likely, but it didn't matter; he would have to go through it.

The somatarchs were running hard to close the distance, sand flying up from beneath their feet. They already had metal pinions in their hands. These short javelins were the favored weapon of the Waymen and in the hands of a somatarch they rarely missed.

Adan stumbled over some pipes jutting out of the ground, but caught himself before he fell. A pinion thudded into the ground next to his foot. He ducked as another shaft whizzed over his head. Because of his misstep, his pace fell off. The three somatarchs closed to within thirty paces. He sprinted towards some hunks of abandoned machinery, hoping he could lose them there. But he was nowhere close to reaching them when he felt a terrible pain stab through the back of his calf. He went down in a tumbling heap.

He rolled on his side and saw one of the pinions jutting out from the back of his calf, his blood trickling into the sand. He tried to get up, but the movement lit up his leg in searing pain. He screamed and fell back to the sand. He had no choice; he suppressed his senses with his bioseine and the pain disappeared.

He reached down and slid the pinion from his leg. Though there was no pain, his hand came back solid red. He would have passed out had his bioseine not been in control of his body. Even with the bioseine, he had to staunch the wound quickly or risk losing too much blood.

Frantically, he unfurled his kaff. His hands were a blur as he set to wrapping the wound. He was pulling the cloth tight just as the first of the attackers closed in and dove on top of him; two more joined in, pinning him to the ground.

"I told you he wasn't a gear-head," sputtered the first one in the Wayman tongue. He was panting heavily. His voice sounded incredibly human for a somatarch.

"But he was on one of their ships," said the second.

"It doesn't matter, whoever he is—let's finish him," said the last one.

While the others held Adan down, the first one pulled out a shiv from his belt. Adan struggled to free himself and avoid the death stroke, but the blow never came. Instead, he heard an awful sound, one he had hoped to never hear again—the whispering blast of an oscillathe.

Two of the men vanished, their garricks deflating beside Adan. The shiv thudded into the sand. The third attacker hurled one of his pinions back across the desert before he turned and ran. Adan followed its trajectory and watched as it clattered harmlessly off the attack skiff heading straight towards them. The man sprinted across the sand to avoid the skiff's deadly weapon, but a moment later the unnerving whisper caught him and he vanished as well.

The skiff, bearing two somatarchs, sped past Adan before turning and doubling back around. Adan jumped to his feet and darted into the maze of machinery nearby. Another whisper streaked past, incredibly loud and incredibly close, but it shot out beyond the machine in front of him. More whispers came on all sides. His enemies were firing randomly now, hoping to hit him with a blind shot. The ruins offered no actual protection from the whispering blasts, but they kept the somatarchs from knowing where he was. Adan heard the whispers, sometimes close, sometimes far, but he ran off in a random direction after each shot, managing to stay out of the oscillathe's path.

He could hear the hum of the skiff closing in. He was still hidden by the wreckage, but once the somatarchs passed over, they would spot him.

Just as the ship was about to fly overhead, a wild notion seized him. He spun the cutter dial to full and leapt on top of a nearby hunk of metal, thrusting his arm as high in the air as he could.

The skiff passed right through the energy beam. The blade sliced one of the wings clean off and sent the ship spiraling out of control. The two somatarchs shot from their ship, their bodies crashing into a metal monolith jutting out of the ground. The ship itself careened past them, burying itself in a thick bank of sand.

Adan took off running again, away from the crashed ship and away from the ballast cruiser, still hovering in the same position, firing its guns in all directions in a tapestry of light. They were not firing at him. They were targeting the white-robed somatarchs with their hover skates and small ships. The somatarchs were swarming around the larger ship, firing their whisper cannons at the figures on the cruiser in synchronized fashion so that it looked more like they were engaged in a performance than a battle.

Both sides suffered in the exchange, but the white-robed somatarchs took the worst of it. Every time they vaporized one of the gunners, another appeared in his place. And the regularity of their attack patterns made them predictable and easy to target. Though most of the attacks got absorbed by the skiffs' invisible shields, the skaters got picked off quickly and eventually, one by one, the yellow pulse beams sliced through the somatarchs' ships. They could not last long, and yet they showed no signs of retreating.

Adan realized another thing then. The men on the cruisers must be actual Waymen. Somatarchs would never attack each other like this.

Whatever the result of the conflict turned out to be, Adan did not plan on staying around to find out. He took off across the dunes, his bioseine allowing him to continue on his wounded leg, though he couldn't run as fast as before. He did not look back, running with reckless abandon away from the fray. The storms closed in on him from both sides. For once, he prayed they would overtake him. Getting lost in the storm was his only hope of survival.

His gait unsteady, he fought for every step in the shifting sand. If he still had the lev, he would have already been safe by now, but all he could do was ramble forward, hoping his injured leg would hold up.

Thankfully, the Waymen and somatarchs were more interested in killing each other than in hunting down a lone straggler fleeing the battlefield. Unpursued, Adan plunged into the wall of billowing sand and lost sight of the battle.

Bits of sharp debris tore into his skin from the moment he entered. He held his arm in front of his exposed face and tried to find a large piece of machinery to block the wind, but the storm was too fierce. Without lentes, he could only see a few paces in front of him. As he crested a dune, several lights materialized out of the storm off to his left. The swirling metal shavings cut into his forehead. They threatened to slit open his eyes, but he risked a glance to find out what was happening.

The lights grew brighter and larger. He saw now that they were the lights which ran along the barrels of the guns of the ballast cruisers. They weren't firing at him yet, but that was probably because they hadn't seen him. He took off down the opposite slope, but his foot slipped on a piece of smooth metal scrap. He tumbled down the sandy dune, a human piece of scrap himself, about to join the others. He banged his head on something as he fell, but his bioseine blocked out the pain.

He slid to a rest at the bottom of the slope. Rolling over and looking up, the enormous outline of the ballast cruiser emerged from the chalky clouds surrounding him. He rose and started up the new slope, but the sand was too thick to build up any speed. The ship, unhindered by the desert terrain, easily overtook him. As he turned, four Waymen leapt out of it, landing almost on top of him. Adan stumbled forward on his bad leg, but only got three steps before the Waymen caught him.

They dove on top of him, driving his face into the sand. He lifted his head, spitting the grit from his mouth and struggling to get free. One of the Waymen yanked off his cutter and tossed it aside while the others wrestled his arms behind his back and bound him with metal clamps.

Adan could offer no real resistance as they tossed him up and several hands pulled him onto the deck of the cruiser. At least twenty other Waymen were present on deck, but only a handful paid any attention to his arrival. Two men dragged him into a cramped compartment at the back of the ship. Inside, they chained his bonds to a ring in the floor. This forced him to sit next to it. They disappeared without a word, bolting the door shut behind them.

The small room had two round pillars in the middle, making it seem even more cramped than it was. The metal walls looked old and cobbled together, just like the outside of the cruiser. The place reeked so strongly of sweat and flesh that even with his bioseine dulling his senses, Adan got some sense of how awful it must have been.

A few moments later the door opened again. Three new Waymen stepped inside, slamming the door behind them.

Their khaki garricks were in better condition than most of the Waymen he'd seen, and looked to be better made. They wore their kaffs unwound, revealing their close-cropped hair and surly, stubble-ridden faces, though one of them, the tallest, had a short beard that was more well groomed. The same man also had a purplish scar that looked like a jagged knife running beneath his right eye. The eye was also a little swollen so that it bulged, augmenting the effect of his glare.

He looked Adan up and down as if trying to place him from somewhere. The longer he stared at Adan without speaking, the more unsettled Adan became. He began to wonder if the man was trying to decide whether he should kill him or interrogate him.

"You know we almost killed you," the man said in the Wayman tongue. His tone was accusatory, as if he were attempting to blame Adan for his recent brush with death.

"Who are you?" Adan asked, but the man just stared back at him with that bulging eye of his.

"Lucky for me those first shivs botched the job," he continued, failing to acknowledge that Adan had spoken. But at least it didn't sound like he wanted him dead—for now. He had some purpose in capturing him, though Adan couldn't think what that might be.

"What do you want with me?" Adan asked.

"Our Reeve has been looking for you. He says you know what's happening out in that machine city," the man answered sharply, continuing to bore into Adan with his lopsided gaze.

"And?"

"And he wants to know what you know." The Wayman gave him a look as if Adan owed him an explanation by virtue of the fact that the Waymen hadn't killed him.

"What makes you think I'll tell him?" Adan asked.

"Oh, it doesn't matter if you want to tell him anything or not," the man said. "You can't hide anything from the Reeve. No one can." He gave Adan a sneering smile and his scar seemed to glisten, as if it were about to come to life.

Adan's hopes withered beneath the man's long, intimidating glare.

"And who is your Reeve?" Adan asked, his voice muffled by the tightness in his throat.

"You'll meet him soon enough, shim. Soon enough. That's all for now." With that the Wayman turned and rapped on the door.

The bolt slid away and the thick metal portal swung open. The group exited into the sand-filled winds on the deck and the scraping bolt went back into place.

Adan surveyed his wounded leg, knowing it would only get worse with time. He had a deep gash on his forehead and a dozen small nicks over the rest of his face from the storm. He needed medical attention, but he had been so pre-occupied with the Waymen he had forgotten to ask for it. He called out to them several times, but no one answered.

As the day wore on, his wounds, and the bleak outlook of his situation, drifted to the back of Adan's thoughts. Instead, he wondered what had happened to Gavin. A sickening feeling welled up inside him. If Gavin had not died in the crash, it was likely he'd been killed either by the somatarchs or the Waymen.

Despair worked on his heart, greasing the bolt that held back his panic, but then he checked himself. In the midst of the dank, unclean room, he remembered there was one thing he could still do. He closed his eyes and began to pray.

SIX
HULL

DURING THE NEXT TWO DAYS, ADAN SURVIVED ON KERN and the brackish water which the Waymen brought to him twice a day. Though he still thought often about Gavin, he had placed the fate of his friend in Numinae's hands and it no longer tempted him to despair.

What did worry him were the wounds to his face and leg. Not because they were getting worse, but because they were getting better. When the Waymen brought him his cup of water and three strips of kern on the first morning, he had begged them to bring a healer to take a look at his wounds, but whether because there was no healer on the ship, or they didn't think it worth their time, all they brought him was a fresh scrap of cloth to bandage his leg around midday. He braced himself for a gruesome sight as he unraveled the original bandage, but instead found that his wound had closed up completely. Some reddish discoloration and puckered skin around where the pinion had pierced his calf were the only signs the injury had even occurred.

He checked his bioseine to see if it had done anything

while he slept, but it gave him no explanation as to why the wound had healed so dramatically. He couldn't see the wounds on his face, but his bioseine informed him that those were rapidly disappearing as well. Clearly, something unnatural had happened inside his body, and not knowing what it was frightened him.

Worried that the Waymen might notice and ask questions if he removed the bandage entirely, he wrapped his leg with the new cloth anyway. Of course, he couldn't do much to hide his face, but it was coated with enough dust and grime that he hoped they wouldn't spot the change.

As much as the sudden improvement in his health troubled him, he was glad to be able to disengage his bioseine. He never liked the dulling of his senses which the pain suppression caused. The reek of the cabin was hardly a welcome change, but he preferred to have the full use of his senses.

On the third day, the gentle gliding of the ballast stopped with a shudder, as if the ship had bumped into something. A commotion erupted outside the compartment. Were they being attacked again? Was the ship malfunctioning? Adan couldn't tell, but all sorts of terrible possibilities ran through his mind.

A short time later, the door to his room opened and two Waymen stepped inside.

"Time to move," one of them said.

One man stood watch by the door while the other unchained Adan from the ring in the floor. They led him out onto the deck. As Adan blinked away the bright lights, he could see that the ship was docked next to a long platform with a ramp leading down to the ground. At least half the Waymen were already off the ship, milling about below and talking amongst themselves.

All around lay a sprawling city. Hundreds of buildings the size of Will's compound could have fit inside of it, perhaps more, for in some places Adan couldn't see the end of it. It was surrounded by a continuous, haphazard-looking, metal wall. The wall was higher than the cruiser in most places, but lower in others. Its patchwork metal paneling had been soldered together in rudimentary fashion. In several places the exposed inner framework was visible, but around every such breach, crews worked on creaky scaffolding to fill in the gaps. At the top of the wall, naked beams stretched skyward, leaving open the possibility of expanding the structure even higher.

The outer wall was connected to the interior buildings in many places by sectioned walkways. Other walkways connected the buildings themselves. Some of these were completely enclosed, while others consisted of nothing more than a few exposed planks, similar to the bridge system Adan had seen in the Basin, the enormous cavern within the Viscera where the Welkin lived.

Most of the inner structures were in far worse shape than even the walls or walkways. Crews labored to repair these as well; almost every structure had some level of damage to it. The entire settlement looked like one enormous piece of scrap salvaged from the desert.

Scattered amongst the buildings were groups of tents separated by sandy paths. Given the unfinished state of the buildings, Adan guessed that was where most of the city's inhabitants actually lived.

"Where are we?" he asked, but the men with him just shoved him towards the ramp. A lev hovered at the bottom. It was half filled with crates and barrels, but there was still plenty of room for passengers. They herded Adan onto it. His escorts boarded after him, and the transport lurched into motion with a sudden jerk.

The lev was far more beaten down than the one Adan and Gavin had ridden in. A pair of Waymen stood next to the thick steering column, attempting to drive it. They didn't seem to know exactly what they were doing. At any given moment, one or both of them took hold of it and twisted the column in a different direction so that the transport swerved wildly from one side of the path to the other. Though they weren't going much faster than a brisk walk, the city was so packed with buildings, tents, and people, chaos broke out wherever it went. Weaving in and out of the crowds, people dove out of the way to avoid being run over. The pilots nearly came to blows several times over their inability to control where the ship was going. Adan had to concentrate to keep his feet steady and avoid being mashed by the shifting crates and supplies stacked at the back of the vehicle.

By the time the raucous ride finally came to an end, Adan was standing in puddles of sweat. He let out a long exhalation as he placed his feet on solid ground once again.

The lev had stopped in front of an enormous, elongated building with a rounded roof. It was one of the few structures in the city which actually appeared finished. Two enormous metal doors, at least twice as tall as Adan and wide enough for five people to enter abreast, marked the entrance.

The Waymen steered Adan towards the building. After several moments of standing, the enormous doors swung open slowly, revealing a contingent of Waymen on the other side.

Of the six men in the party, four wore simple vests and, judging by the pinions strapped to their backs and the way they never took their eyes off Adan, were guarding the two men standing in the middle. One of the two was the Wayman who had interrogated Adan on the cruiser, his prominent purple scar shone even brighter in the light of day. The man who stood beside him did not look like a Wayman at all. He wore a full beard and had thick, dark hair that went down to his shoulders. He walked with a long metal staff set with a translucent spike on top. His beige robes were trimmed in gold. The clothes contrasted sharply with his eyes, which were as cold and gray as the metal walls surrounding the city.

This last man stepped forward, his arms sweeping wide.

"Welcome to Hull, Adan," he said. His voice had a slightly melodic quality to it.

Adan stared at him in disbelief. "You know who I am?"

"It is my business to know what happens in the Vast," the man said, "It is how I survive. But even I do not know everything. And one thing which I do not know is how you made it out of Oasis alive."

This man not only knew about Oasis, but he knew that Adan had been there. How was that possible?

"What do you mean? What makes you think I was there?"

The man drew back into the shadows of the doorway. "Come to the control deck and we will talk there." He turned and walked into the building.

The Waymen behind him gave Adan a shove before he even had time to follow. As he passed inside the well-built structure, the temperature dropped noticeably. The doors closed behind them on their own with a quiet click. Lumins lined the walls. Just inside the door, a Wayman was attaching a metal plate to the wall with self-drilling bolts. He tapped them with his finger and they sunk into the walls on their own. It was not anything approaching the technology of Oasis, but Adan could not understand how desert dwellers like the Waymen could be using such things. They feared and even hated technology, treating it with suspicion and superstition.

After making their way down an arched hallway, they arrived at another, smaller set of doors in the interior. These parted automatically as they approached. The passage beyond was lined with doors along both walls.

A wave of weakness sunk down Adan's throat as they

entered this new hallway. It looked just like the Institute and the Annex. What was going on? Were the scientists and the Waymen in league together? But then why were they fighting each other?

At the end of the hallway another set of double doors opened into a semi-circular chamber. They proceeded down a curved ramp until they reached the floor. At the bottom rested a long oval table surrounded by a dozen black, polymeric chairs.

"What is this place?" Adan asked "And who are you?" His clamps started itching his wrists like mad. He had to get out of this place.

"I am the Reeve of Hull, the largest, and most powerful of all the thrals in the Vast." The man handed his staff to one of the guards and motioned for Adan to sit.

Adan took a chair and the Reeve sat down across from him. His slimy, sweaty garrick squelched in the soft chair.

The Wayman who had interrogated him on the cruiser sat in the chair next to the Reeve. The guards remained standing.

"But what is your name? It only seems fair that you tell me yours since you already know mine." Adan asked, secretly trying to slip his hands out of the clamps under the table, hoping the sweat would help, but his hands were just too big.

The Reeve gave him a nod. "You may call me Nolan if you like." He gestured to the man seated next to him. "And this is Mok, the high sunder."

The Wayman gave Adan a nod, but Adan did not return it. He had known another Wayman who held the rank of sunder. If this man was anything like him, he had little desire to afford him any kind of respect.

"You'd best watch yourself around the Reeve," Mok warned. "Like I told you on the ship, you can't hide anything from him. He sees it all."

Adan ignored the comment. The Waymen were a superstitious lot. This was just naive boasting or an idle threat. But there was *something* unusual about Nolan, that much was obvious. Was he from Oasis? He certainly didn't look like a Wayman.

"So you said you'd talk to me about what's going on." Adan said.

"First, I want you to tell me how you survived," Nolan replied.

"I—but I still don't understand how you seem to know so much about me." This conversation was starting to feel like Adan was back in Oasis, being asked questions that had some undisclosed purpose. Something in Nolan's words told Adan he was not *meant* to survive what had happened in Oasis.

"You are in no position to be looking for answers," Nolan said, his manner turning brisk. "I, however, am. Now tell me what happened. Everyone in Oasis should have been killed, and yet it seems that is not the case."

Mok's words echoed back through Adan's mind: *you can't hide anything from him*...Suddenly Adan remembered his own abilities as a memorant. Was Nolan one as well? He had to find out.

Recalling Gavin's lessons, Adan stared into the Reeve's face, but found it hard to concentrate with the Waymen all staring at him. Nolan gazed back at him, his face as expressionless as the canvas of a Wayman tent. There was nothing there for Adan to latch onto. Nolan's mind was blank.

"You know about Will, don't you?" Adan blurted out in a panic. He had no idea where the question came from. It simply popped into his mind out of desperation.

The corners of Nolan's lips crept upwards in a knowing smile. "Yes, I know about your friend. I know about the virus, about the attack, about everything—except what went wrong. That is what you're here to tell me."

Adan's whole body tingled with foreboding. "You knew what Will had planned?"

"Tell me what happened in Oasis," Nolan demanded.

Adan gripped the seat of his chair with sweat-greased fingers, as if Nolan's words were threatening to knock him out of it.

The Reeve's presence seemed to fade into the background. The events in Oasis came rushing back: the whisper cannon, the somatarchs, the remin fluid, the truth about the virus. But of all the terrible things he had experienced there, the image of his dying friend gripped him the most. Will's words blazed through his mind, *"It wasn't my idea."*

Adan's eyes twitched as Nolan came back into focus, sitting in the chair across from him. Was this the person who had planned the attack on Oasis? If Nolan had been responsible for sending him to his death, now more than ever Adan knew he was not safe here; he had to leave this place, and he had to leave now.

"Why should I tell you anything? I don't even know who you are," Adan said, stalling.

"Perhaps you don't remember me, but we have met before," Nolan replied, his voice rising promisingly, as if he had a secret to share. "In fact, there are some things I could tell you about yourself that you would find rather interesting, if I were so inclined."

Adan sensed Nolan was toying with him, that this whole interrogation was a ruse. It was the Institute all over again, questions upon questions, and just like the scientists, what Nolan really wanted to know had nothing to do with what he was asking.

"Where is the man who took Will's extractor?" Adan

demanded, but the moment he said it, he wondered if it had been a mistake, if he was letting on too much.

"So you've been back to the compound. If you expect to find who you're looking for here, I'm afraid you're too late. He left several days ago. He's back in Oasis by now." The look of self-satisfaction on Nolan's face deepened, as if Adan's attempts to avoid telling him what he knew were what Nolan actually wanted. "There, I've told you something," he said, "now it's your turn to answer my question. Why are the somatarchs roaming freely over the Vast? Why wasn't Oasis destroyed?"

Something in Nolan's voice triggered more memories of Oasis. They came swirling in, swarming his mind whether Adan wanted them there or not, like a desert storm pushing sand inside his clothing and there was nothing he could do to keep it out. His mind hurtled back to Oasis. He found himself in the wreckage of the Institute. The leader of the Waymen was screaming for his death. He watched Sparc's body disappear with a whisper from Will's oscillathe. Then a terrible pain pierced his heart as a pinion flew from Nox's hands into the belly of his friend.

It was one of the curses of the bioseine and his latent memorant abilities that he could remember everything in perfect detail. The memories were so vivid it felt as if they were happening all over again. The clouds swirled high overhead, the storm gathering strength until it could return and finish off the city. He looked down and there was Will in his arms. The light in his eyes had gone out.

It wasn't my idea, the words kept echoing in Adan's mind over and over again.

"You sent Will to Oasis," Adan said at last, certain that it had to be true. "It was your plan."

Nolan nodded, his eyes fixed on Adan. That little gesture

was like the opening of a latch inside Adan's mind. Little by little things began to fall into place.

"The Waymen—you sent them as well, or you had something to do with it. I saw the aftermath of the battle. Hundreds died, maybe thousands. Did you know about that, too?"

"That part, at least, was expected. The promise of power can be an effective motivator. But you still haven't answered my question. What I want to know is how the plan failed. Did the Developers stop you? Or did you find out about the virus before you got to the Annex?"

Adan locked eyes with the Wayman leader. Nolan's question was too close to the truth to have been a guess.

"*Yes, I'm a memorant as well,*" came Nolan's thoughts into Adan's mind. "*And apparently more skilled at the art than you.*"

Adan attempted to sever their bioseine connection, but there was nothing to sever. He wasn't sure how Nolan had gotten inside his mind, but he knew that he had to get him out. He averted his gaze and closed his eyes.

"*So Gavin was your teacher, then?*" Nolan continued.

Panic gripped Adan. He hadn't even been thinking about Gavin. How was this man inside his head?

"*Apparently, he didn't tell you how to force yourself inside someone else's thoughts. Or perhaps he didn't want you to know that.*"

Adan leapt up from his chair. He dashed towards the exit ramp, but the guards were on him in a moment. They wrestled him back into his seat and two of them remained standing on either side of him.

"I told you," Mok said, shaking his head, "You can't hide anything from the Reeve of Hull."

SEVEN
FRIENDS AND ENEMIES

Adan now realized that Nolan's mind had been pressing against his mind the entire time. And once inside, Nolan was not going to leave until he had the information he wanted.

Adan tried to cloud his thoughts, the way he might when someone was connected to his mind via the bioseine, but found there was always some part that escaped. He couldn't catch hold of it long enough to keep it hidden.

And then, without knowing how it happened, his mind slipped free once again.

"I should have suspected it was Gavin who stopped you," Nolan said, "It was his virus, after all." He turned to Mok. "Are you certain this was the only survivor from the wreck?"

"We didn't find anyone else," Mok said. "But then again, we had our hands full scrapping with those gear-heads. They might have got him first."

Nolan gave him a look of displeasure. "Ready the ballasts. Take half the fleet, as many men as you can spare. This man's friend knows a great deal about our enemies. If we can capture him, it might shift the wind in our favor."

"I shall do all that is in my power, oh Reeve." Mok rose and bowed low. He then left the way they'd come in.

"You know, Adan," Nolan said, leaning forward with his elbows on the table, "you and I have something in common. The Developers took my past from me as well."

"Do you mean you were part of the Remapping Initiative?" Adan asked. He wasn't sure he could trust anything this man said, but it certainly would explain the fact that Nolan was a memorant.

"Oh, no. I was before that. I suppose in some way I was merely a failed attempt for what they ended up doing with the remapping. But for both of us, the result was the same."

"But if you lost your memories, there may be a way of getting them back," Adan said tentatively. He wasn't sure he should try to help this man. He was clearly dangerous. But if Adan could somehow bargain with him, maybe Nolan would let him go. "Gavin said there was a place called the Repository in Oasis and that all the memories of everyone, even those from the Remapping Initiative were kept there."

"We may have one thing in common, but not everything." Nolan's voice had a sharpness to it which severed Adan's slim hopes. "I have learned to accept my fate. You would do well to do the same."

I'd say we have nothing in common, Adan thought to himself, wondering if Nolan was still reading his thoughts. "So why did you send Will to destroy Oasis? That doesn't sound like you're accepting your fate."

"You think I'm motivated by revenge? Have you considered that perhaps I seek to destroy them for other reasons? There is such a thing as justice in this world, Adan. Have you ever thought of that?"

"For most people, justice is just another word for revenge. I don't think you're interested in real justice." Adan felt backed into a corner, but his desperation gave him surprising courage. "I think you wanted Oasis for yourself, that's why you tried the virus."

Nolan chuckled quietly to himself.

"You have promise, Adan. And you've been helpful to me in more ways than you know. Normally, I would kill you since I already have what I need from you, but you may yet prove useful to me."

Adan glared at his adversary across the table. "I'll never help you. You sent me to my death."

"There are worse things than death," Nolan said.

Adan had no idea what Nolan meant by the remark, but he didn't care. "Whatever you want, I won't do it."

Nolan leaned his chin on his hand and regarded Adan thoughtfully, but it was a sleepy sort of attention, as if he had grown tired of the conversation. "You've already done what I wanted once before. There are many ways to get someone to do something, especially if you know what they want. You simply have to make it so that the thing you want and the thing they want are the same thing."

Adan tried to read more deeply into the expression on Nolan's face. The Reeve was not the only one who could read people's thoughts, after all. But Nolan's eyes stared back into his in a lazy, dream-like way and Adan could get nothing.

"Who are you, really?" Adan asked, resorting to a more direct approach. "Waymen don't use technology like this. And they certainly don't have memorants or know as much about Oasis as you do."

"*This is Thral Hull,*" Nolan replied with his thoughts. "*Under my leadership, the Waymen have learned to cast off some of their superstitions, though not to the degree that it would be wise to speak of these matters openly."*

"Are you afraid of what would happen if you told them the truth? Are you afraid they wouldn't follow you if they knew you were just an experiment like me?"

"They will still be following me long after I'm done with you," Nolan shot back.

The Reeve motioned to the guards who grabbed Adan and yanked him out of his chair.

"The interrogation is over," Nolan declared. "Take this prisoner to the pits so that he can have some time to think. But first see that he's fed. I don't want him dying on me." He paused, as if a thought had just occurred to him. "In fact, take him to the dispensary on your way."

"You will serve me, whether you choose to or not," came Nolan's last thought as they dragged Adan from the room.

Outside the building, the Waymen loaded Adan onto another lev. The ship shuddered into motion and began zigzagging its way through the city on another tilting, jostling ride. By the time Adan dared open his eyes, he was in a section of the city he had not seen before. It was a wide open space filled with people and a few small tents scattered here and there. Almost everyone present was engaged in some form of manual labor. Some mended or washed clothes or tent fabric while others tinkered with various rundown machines.

Located more or less in the middle of the sprawling bustle was a tent that was easily ten times larger than any of the others. It was towards this structure that Adan's lev made its way.

A long line of people stretched out in front of the opening, waiting to get in. The line doubled back and forth in random fashion, winding its way through the other workers like a giant scribble. The tent looked like it would fit at least a hundred people, perhaps more. Set up near the entrance was a long metal table with four large bowls on top of it. Four women were serving the contents of the bowls to the people in line. Once the recipients received their portion, they passed inside the tent.

The lev pushed its way through the crowd and straight to the front of the line, sending the masses scurrying. There had been a sort of subdued chatter as they approached, but it died away completely with their arrival.

"Give us some of your slop," one of the Waymen at the front of the lev ordered.

"Certainly. Where is your container?" the first of the serving women inquired. Though her voice had barely been audible, it sent a shock of recognition through Adan.

He rushed to the front of the platform so he could get a better look at the woman's face. It was covered in grit and her hair was coated in sand, but he recognized her at once. It was Senya. She still carried herself with that same quiet strength she'd displayed back at her home in Aldea.

"Senya? Is that you?" Adan asked, though he knew it was.

She said nothing, but the tears welling up in her eyes were all the answer he needed.

"I don't need a container. Just give me the whole pot," ordered the Wayman in the front, interrupting the reunion and shoving Adan aside. "You—stay back."

"Are the boys safe? And—and Lila?" Adan asked, pressing forward despite the Wayman's words and his restraining arm.

Tears streaked through the grime coating Senya's face. "Yes. The boys are here with me and Lila is safe with—"

The Wayman let out an angry shout and shoved Adan into the arms of two of his companions. Their hands clamped onto his shoulders, holding him fast.

"Haul this onto the ship," the lead man said, pointing at the massive bowl. The stuff inside seemed to be the color and consistency of mosh, though the smell was less pleasant than Adan remembered.

"But we won't have enough to feed the others now," one of the women beside Senya protested.

For a reply she received a back-handed blow from the lead Wayman. "Give them some of that," he said, chuckling. The other Waymen joined in, laughing and mocking the serving woman who had been knocked to the ground by the vicious blow. Senya knelt down to help her to her feet.

"We'll make do," she told the woman. "Numinae always provides. He'll watch over us." She caught Adan's eye. He could see in her look that she meant the remark for him as well.

The Waymen heaved the bowl onto the lev as the laughter died down.

"I'll come back for you, Senya," Adan called out to her as the lev jerked backwards and pivoted away towards the city.

One of the Waymen struck him in the chest, sending a sharp pain slicing through him. He would have doubled over if he hadn't been held fast by two others. "Quit your jawing." The man snarled, his eyes burning with malice that showed he would have liked to have done much more. "Come on, let's drop this scrap off at the pits."

Leaning out over the edge of the transport, Adan got one last glimpse of Senya as they pulled away. She was dusting off the other woman's clothes, but their eyes met one last time.

We'll be all right, her look said. *All things, in the end are passing.*

And yet as Senya's face became lost in the crowd, Adan wondered how either of them would ever be free of this place.

The name "the pits" turned out to be quite literal as Adan found out when they dropped him into a hole in the ground. It was about three times as deep as he was tall and wide enough to sit in, but not to lie down. A metal door with a piece of smoky glass embedded into the center covered the opening above. It let in just enough light for him to see that there was but one way out of his prison.

At least they had unshackled his hands and feet before dropping him down the hole. He tried a few times to work his way up the sides of the pit, but the walls were a mixture of rock and sand that made it impossible to climb. Each attempt only stirred up a cloud of dust at the bottom and sent him into fits of coughing, so that he soon gave up.

With nothing else to do, he untied the bandage on his leg and examined where his wound had been. There wasn't a scratch. He stared at it for the longest time, still finding it hard to believe it had healed so quickly. He had been wounded before and had never made such a rapid recovery. But the more he thought about it, he had always received some form of medical treatment in the past soon after hurting himself, whether almamenth or solec. He had never been left to heal on his own. Perhaps the Developers had done something more to him than he knew, but if so, why didn't his bioseine seem to know anything about it?

He stuffed the bandage inside his garrick and gave up trying to guess what had happened to his leg. His thoughts turned to Senya. Watching her feed the haggard workers out in front of the tent, he could see that she suffered far worse than him. They were both captives, but Adan, at least, was not being forced to serve the people who had captured him. Or was he? Nolan's final thought continued to haunt him: *you will serve me, whether you choose to or not.* He wanted to believe that statement wasn't true, but he'd been manipulated before. Will had used him without Adan realizing it and he had no guarantee it would not happen again. All he could do was stay vigilant and try to discover whatever plans Nolan might have for him. That might prove harder than he thought. He knew so little about the mysterious Reeve.

He rubbed his back against the wall to relieve an itch. He was tired of always being one step behind, of not knowing what was going on. He thought the Welkin had evacuated to some place safe, but Senya was here instead and there was no telling where the rest of the knit had ended up. Now that the somatarchs seemed to be moving openly in the desert, perhaps the rest of the Welkin had already been killed or carried off to wherever the Developers fled to after the storm. And then there was Nolan and this strange city of Hull. That was perhaps the most disturbing development of all. Waymen were frightening enough with their handmade weapons. Now that they had begun to use technology, there was no telling what atrocities they might commit.

He tried to stifle such thoughts, but they consumed his mind long after the little window of light above had gone dark. Unable to put his mind at rest, he let his bioseine put him to sleep, instructing it to wake him should the Waymen return in the middle of the night.

When Adan awoke the next morning, pangs of hunger spasmed

inside his stomach. The Waymen had given him some of Senya's mosh before dropping him into the hole, but he'd had nothing since.

He stared up at the little cube of light above. The assurance that Numinae was with him, which had been so palpable on the journey back to the compound had completely deserted him. *Why did you save me from the storm if you meant to abandon me down here?*

Of course there was no answer. He was beginning to doubt there ever would be any more answers. Gavin may have been healed in the desert, but Adan had been given no assurance that his prayers would be answered in the future. Here, in the bottom of this pit, nothing seemed certain, not his foolish hope of finding his or Gavin's memories, not the possibility that he would find a way to escape and free Senya, and certainly not the existence of a distant being who could somehow intervene and make everything right.

Adan passed the rest of the day fighting off despair. He stood on the edge of a great void, staring down into it. All it would take was a gust of wind to push him over. And yet, somehow he clung to the tiniest hope that tomorrow something would change.

As darkness descended once again over the tiny window, Adan considered using his bioseine to send himself back to sleep. There was no point in staying awake. The Waymen never came. There was no food, no sign of activity above, though the wind did rattle the cover over his hole from time to time. It seemed to be picking up. He wondered idly if a storm was on its way.

At least I'm safe from the wind down here, he thought, though just now, he would have preferred to take his chances with the elements.

He had just resigned to put himself to sleep when he heard

a soft thump above. A few moments later it came again. He stared up at the door, but he could see nothing through the window. Another thump sounded, slightly louder, and then another and another. Each time they seemed to come a little louder and a little faster.

The thumps turned to shuffling and sliding sounds and then everything went quiet again. Adan thought about calling out to see if anyone was there, but decided to wait and listen a little longer.

A few moments later, he heard a click and the round covering began sliding away, barely making a sound. As the opening got wider and wider, a gust of air swirled angrily down the side of the pit, kicking up dust.

The door slid away entirely and a large, dark shape filled the opening. Bits of rock and sand skittered down the pit as the figure descended.

Adan gripped the sides of the pit. "Who's there?" he whispered, but there was no answer. The figure kept coming.

A thought seized Adan's mind: *Nolan's decided to kill me after all.* He clenched his teeth and prepared to fight. He would not go down easily.

As the figure got closer, it became clear that a rather heavyset man was making his way down into the cell. When he hit the ground, Adan was forced to press himself against the wall just to accommodate the stranger's substantial girth.

The man had his back to him and as yet had made no move to attack, but Adan remained tense, waiting to see what he would do.

Standing so close to the stranger, Adan was overwhelmed by the man's unpleasant odor. Finally, the man turned around and Adan could make out the details of his face. He possessed a wildly curly beard and bulging jowls which parted in a hideous grin.

"Nox." Adan gasped, too stunned for the moment to say anything more. He felt a tremble run through him as he stared into the face of the man who had murdered Will.

"Just dropping in for a visit," Nox said in a hoarse whisper. "Did you miss me?"

EIGHT

THE SAND DUSTER

"What—" Adan began, but Nox clamped a meaty hand over his mouth.

Adan was certain Nox meant to kill him. But then why had he gone to all the effort to climb down into the pit? It would have been easier just to hurl a pinion down from above.

"Quiet or you'll spoil the whole batch of kern," Nox warned. "I'm here to get you out."

Adan pried Nox's hand away. "You're crazy if you think—"

Again Nox silenced him with one of his ample hands.

"Shh!" Nox put a finger to his lips. "Now for the last time, shut your horn. We only have a moment before the next set of guards comes around." He grabbed hold of one of Adan's hands and forced it towards the thick cord dangling against the wall. "All right, now shimmy up."

Adan stared at him in disbelief. Nox was a killer. Adan had watched him murder Will and he would not hesitate to do the same to Adan if he were so inclined. And yet here he was, claiming he was here to help Adan escape. Adan couldn't read the Wayman's expression in the darkness, but he couldn't help but sense he had something terrible planned once they got out of the pit.

Adan took hold of the rope Nox had used to climb down into the pit and the Wayman removed his hand from Adan's mouth.

"There's no way I can trust you," Adan said, careful to keep his voice down. "Tell me what you have planned and maybe I'll go with you at least out of this pit, but I won't do a thing until you tell me what you're up to."

Nox snorted impatiently, "Trust? Who said anything about trust?" He shot a feverish look up towards the hole. "I need your help and you need mine. That's all that matters. Now get up that rope if you want to cheat the wind for another day."

He grabbed hold of Adan's other hand and placed it on the rope, but Adan promptly let go. "Help with what?" he demanded.

"Getting out of this city, what else? I'm not here for the kern and the company. I got captured, same as you. Now hurry up before someone finds the guards I gutted."

A cold shudder ran through Adan. Nox was a killer, yes, but Adan couldn't get over how bluntly he treated it, as if murder were something common and insignificant, like mentioning what sort of food he had eaten at his last meal.

Adan glanced up at the opening. It went against his better judgment, but Nox and his rope were probably his only way out of this pit. Hopefully he could get free from Nox after he was out, especially since Nox was letting him go first. He shook his head and started up the rope.

As if reading his thoughts, Nox grabbed Adan by the shoulder.

"Now don't go slinking off when you get topside," he said, leering at him. "I'm saving your life, you hear? And I expect you to pay me back in kind. You owe me." He planted a plump finger square in Adan's chest.

Adan sighed and began his ascent. He supposed that he did owe the Wayman enough to at least help him escape. And he doubted he'd be able to sneak out of Hull on his own anyway.

I hope I don't regret this.

The rope rubbed Adan's hands raw as he struggled towards the top. He sent showers of dust raining down on Nox as he half climbed, half walked up the side of the wall. He almost slipped off the rope twice during the ascent, but in the end, his arms aching and his hands throbbing, he crawled over the edge of the pit. A dozen other pits lay nearby, surrounded by char walls. A single barred gate was the only exit. A lumin dangled from a rod embedded in the wall beside it, but it provided little light. No guards were visible. He felt like lying flat on his back and taking a moment to catch his breath, but Nox had said a new set of guards might come at any time.

Stepping around the other pits, Adan padded over to the gate as quietly as he could and peeked through. A narrow passage ran along the outside of the pits, the opposite wall was made of metal. Two Waymen lay slumped against the char wall to either side of the gate. Dark pools of liquid glistened beneath them in the dim light, seeping into the sand and dirt. Nox should have at least pulled them inside the gate to avoid the bodies being discovered, but then again Nox was not the brightest person in the Vast.

Adan tried the gate but it held fast. A rusted metal padlock hung around the latch on the other side. In a way, he was relieved to find it shut; it made his decision to stay with the Wayman that much easier.

A few moments later, Nox heaved himself over the edge of the pit, grimacing or grinning from the effort, Adan could not tell which. Nox yanked up the rope, wound it into a loop, and snuck over to where Adan crouched near the gate.

"I suspected you might have an eye for the road," Nox said, pointing at the padlock. "So I left it shut. You'll need Nox's skill and cleverness for this next bit." He whipped out a pair of thin metal needles and began to work them in the lock. The old device gave way with a loud click and the gate swung open with a groan that Adan was sure must have been heard if anyone was close by.

Suddenly, Adan remembered Senya.

"Wait," he whispered, pulling at Nox's coat before he could slip through the gate. "I'm not the only prisoner in this city. I have some friends here who—"

Nox snickered and cut him off. "Friends? Well, a whole lot of good they did you, eh? Let them find their own rip in the tent. I'm the only friend you've got now—the only one that matters anyway. And I'm not about to risk my life for a few hangers on."

The Wayman gave him a dismissive look and started to push through the gate.

"If you don't help me free my friends, then I won't help you," Adan said. At his words the Wayman stopped and spun around. Before Adan knew what had happened, he felt the jagged edge of a metal shiv pressing against his neck.

"You'll help me get out of here or I'll lay you on the ground with these two," Nox threatened, nodding in the direction of the dead guards. Adan had seen that murderous look in his eyes before.

Adan gritted his teeth and nodded in silent assent. Maybe Nox was just bluffing since he seemed to need Adan so badly, but with Nox, you never knew what he might do next. Best not to test him and find out. Still, Adan's insides went cold at the thought of leaving Senya and her children.

Nox pulled him through the gate and pointed down the shadow-filled passage. Pushing Adan in front, they crept along the wall. Adan was only slightly more afraid of being caught by the guards than he was of Nox.

They soon emerged into an area packed with tents and surrounded by the dilapidated husks of buildings. Low voices and shuffling feet drifted in from up ahead, but Adan and Nox skirted the edge of the area and managed to avoid encountering anyone.

Once they left the tents, they emerged onto a wide path bordered on either side with large, run-down buildings. Lights shone inside, but Adan couldn't see anyone moving along the path. A strong wind whipped up the sand, obscuring what lay at the other end.

Nox paused before stepping out onto the path.

"At the other end is what they call the docking bay," he said, pointing towards the haze. "That's where they keep all their ships. We swipe one of those and we should be able to slip out of here."

"But they won't let us just take one. They'll be guarded. And if this involves more killing, I don't want any part of it," Adan said.

Nox let out a muffled chuckle. "Don't worry," he said, "The winds have been kicking up sand all night. No one will see us. And if we do run into anyone, I brought these."

He opened up his garrick and pulled out a handful of dark round objects and placed one in Adan's hand. It was small enough so that three or four could fit in his palm.

"These are sopor pods," Nox explained. "We also call them nap-traps. There is a powder inside that'll knock a man out for a good long while. Just toss these at any shims that give us trouble. Aim for the chest."

He shoved a few handfuls at Adan, who reluctantly

inserted them into the compartments of his garrick. "All right, but do your really think if we take one of their ships they'll let us just fly off into the Vast? They'll try and stop us."

The Wayman scratched at his scraggly beard. "It's a risk," he said, shrugging, "but I don't see any other way."

Adan took a deep breath, wondering how Nox had managed to get as far as he had if he was so terrible at planning.

"There is no way this is going to work," Adan said. "We might as well turn back—"

Nox grabbed him by the collar of his coat and jerked him in close, giving him a blast of fetid breath. "Come on," said the Wayman with a malevolent grin, "The wind will blow our way. Haven't you ever heard of improvising?"

Nox rushed ahead and Adan lost sight of him in the haze. From out of the dust clouds came shouting and the sound of padding feet on the sand. Adan had no idea where he was going. He shambled forward, scanning his surroundings for any sign of the Wayman. Suddenly, he spotted the silhouettes of two ballast cruisers looming up ahead in the mist. For a moment Adan froze in panic until he realized that the ships were still docked. Just in front of them stood Nox, stepping over the last of three bodies lying in the sand. In one of his hands was a bloody shiv which he wiped against one of the fallen men's garricks.

"Nap-trap didn't work on that one," he said, nodding towards the man. "Had to do him the other way."

Adan averted his eyes and pointed towards the cruisers docked behind him. "Those ships are too big. They'll spot us for sure if we take one."

"Right," Nox squinted at them, as if noticing the size of the ships for the first time, "We need something small and fast, but mostly just fast." He took off without warning again, racing towards several dark shapes in the haze.

They soon stumbled across a row of box-like ships docked on an elevated platform. They had plated sides made of scrap metal fused together. The front end sloped slightly downwards and housed a pulse gun like the kind Adan had seen on the ballasts, only this one was about half the size.

He ran a check with his bioseine to see if he could tell what kind of ship it was. The closest match he could find was a combination assault transport called a 'sovos' or 'sand duster'.

"If this is what I think it is, it should be fast enough," Adan said. "Let's just hope I can make it work."

"I thought you were machine-wise. Was the seer lying about that too?" Anger sparked in Nox's face and Adan was once again reminded that he needed to stay on his guard around this man.

"These ships are more primitive than the ones I'm familiar with," Adan explained. "But don't worry. I'll figure it out."

Their conversation was cut short by the sudden appearance of half a dozen Waymen out of the haze.

"What are you two doing in the bay?" one of them asked.

"Just came by for a surprise inspection." Nox hurled a nap-trap into the group along with his reply. It caught the lead man in the shoulder, exploding in a puff of greenish dust and what sounded like a loud exhalation. The guard staggered forward and fell face down into the sand. Adan fumbled for one of the pods as the others surged towards them, but Nox yanked him back towards the platform before he could throw it. A pinion thudded into the ground near his feet.

Nox managed to fling another pod before heaving Adan up onto the platform and leaping after him. Another Wayman fell to the sand. A barrage of pinions clattered against the structure, narrowly missing Adan as he leapt from the platform into an opening in the side of one of the sand dusters.

There was no door to close, but behind the thick walls of

the ship, they lost sight of the Waymen for a moment. Adan could still hear them racing towards the platform, though. He had to figure out how to get this ship started fast.

The sovos didn't have many parts, but he had no idea what any of them did. He tried yanking on an arrangement of levers jutting out of the floor near the gun but they were all locked in place.

"Hurry up," Nox yelled as he tossed another pod through the opening in the side of the ship and then ducked as a pinion clanged against the ship's outer wall.

Adan moved to the back where a closed compartment was embedded into the floor. He flipped it open, but all that was inside was a bundle of pinions and a few boxes.

Nox cried out and Adan spun around in time to spot one of the Waymen leaping onto the duster. Nox flicked his wrist and the man went down in a cloud of powder, falling backwards off the ship.

Another man burst onto the deck. Adan froze, forgetting all about starting the ship. Nox wasn't quick enough to get off another pod this time. The Wayman rushed at Adan with a drawn shiv.

Nox leapt forward, wrapping him up before he could strike. Both went crashing to the floor. The attacker flailed wildly with his shiv, attempting to plunge it into Nox's throat, but Nox dug his teeth into the man's wrist. The assailant cried out and dropped his weapon. But before Nox could go do anything else, another Wayman rushed onto the ship and dove on top of him.

Finally, Adan came to his senses and pulled out one of his sopor pods. He hurled it at the two men attacking Nox. They were all so close together that instead of hitting the attackers, the pod hit Nox in the back of the head.

When the Wayman's hefty frame slammed onto the deck,

the air around him erupted into a cloud of green smoke accompanied by a whoosh of air. Adan felt himself start to lose strength in his knees as the cloud washed over him, but the sensation quickly passed and, to his surprise, the sopor had no further effect upon him.

As the dust cleared, Adan spotted dozens of pod husks scattered around the bodies of Nox and the two Waymen. Nox's garrick had ripped wide open.

Adan rushed over and shoved the bodies of the two Waymen off the ship. Two more lay motionless just outside the opening. Adan gave Nox a quick glance to make sure he was still breathing and that's when he noticed two translucent panels on the floor near the pulse gun. Examining them more closely, it looked like they could be moved. He tried shoving them in all directions with his foot, but they wouldn't budge. Finally, he stamped on them out of frustration. One of them sank slightly into the floor and began to glow with a soft yellow light. At the same time, yellow channels lit up along the levers and the ship floated gracefully upwards.

Keeping his foot on the panel, he felt the levers and noticed they were now loose. He pushed the first one gently and felt the ship drift forward. Encouraged by this discovery, he pulled the one to the left of it and the ship pivoted. Thus experimenting, he pushed and pulled the various levers until he had a rudimentary understanding of how to maneuver the ship. Pushing down on the one that made the ship rise, he fought his vertigo as the duster floated past the other ships docked next to it.

Pushing the velocity lever, the duster picked up speed. With Adan and the unconscious Nox on board, the ship left the platform and flew towards the docking bay exit.

Floating above the dust clouds, at or near maximum altitude for its lev thrusters, Adan had a clear view of a set of massive doors at the far end of the docking bay. A series of beams and ramps cobbled together formed two makeshift towers on either side. Lights glittered feebly along the walls and Adan spotted several Waymen scattered on top. Some stood near large pulser cannons while others patrolled along the walkways.

For a moment he contemplated heading back into the sprawling city to find Senya. Nox was unconscious and the ship was his to command. But even if he didn't get shot down, he had no idea where she might be. Flying blindly through the city would most likely get him captured again and do nothing to save her.

He would have to come back for her after he found Gavin. He knew Gavin would be able to come up with a plan to save her and the boys. Finding him had to come first.

He turned his attention towards the massive gates and once again his resolve faltered. There was no way he was going to get through those with Waymen manning the walls and towers. Nor could the ship fly over the walls; Adan may not have known much about this ship, but hover class ships couldn't fly very high.

He glanced down at the pulser. He'd have to cut his way out. But he'd have to find the right spot to do it. If they saw him, he'd be shot down. Dust clouds covered most of the docking bay, but thinned as they rose and disappeared before they reached the higher platforms which ran along the walls.

Out across the bay, a ballast cruiser rose up out of the mist and began heading his way. Adan let out a frustrated grunt. He must have been spotted. He rammed the altitude lever forward, sending his craft diving back down into the sand clouds.

The sovos swiveled back towards the nearest wall. At least his time above the dust clouds had given him a way to locate his position inside the bay. Though he couldn't see more than fifty paces inside the dust, his bioseine told him exactly where he was. All he had to do was get to the closest wall and cut his way out before they could get to him.

Racing through the dust-filled air, he heard several monotone hums fire up off in the distance. More hovers were powering up. But he was too busy dodging ramps and platform struts to worry about them.

His hand bounced back and forth across the levers, coating them in a layer of nervous sweat as he tried to maneuver through the nearly invisible maze. Platform posts flashed up at him out of the dust clouds like immobile sentries. Swerving to avoid one he invariably steered himself towards another. He reacted too late once and the side of the sovos listed into it. But the ship was sturdier than the platforms. All he did was bend the post badly and tilt the edge of the dock. He rotated the duster away and plunged back down the path.

At last the outer wall loomed up out of the haze. He couldn't fly directly up to it because the platform running along its length topped out above the dust clouds; he would have to cut through the platform supports in order to get to the wall.

Placing his hands on the pulse gun, he felt around for its controls. After a moment, he spotted a glowing yellow dial on the right side and a small lever on the left. Since these seemed to be the only moving parts, he spun the dial until it would no longer go any further and the dial's glow intensified.

He thought the lever would fire the weapon if he pushed it, but instead it tilted the barrel so it pointed at the ground. Playing with it some more, he found that he could tilt the gun in practically any position he wanted.

The dial looked like it could be pushed as well as turned and so he tried that next. The barrel of the gun sung in low vibration and lit up along the side with yellow lights. A bright yellow beam shot out from the end, slicing through the legs of the platform. Pellets of light lined the beam, scattering the darkness.

The platform quickly caved in on itself and toppled to the ground. Adan began tracing a hole in the wall large enough for the ship to fly through. He was about three quarters of the way done when another locus beam lit up the air around him, crossing his own beam and just missing his ship.

Adan glanced back and saw the shadow of a long ship drifting towards him. He shifted the sovos to the side to stay out of its line of fire while maintaining the bead he had on the wall, but the sudden movement caused him to slice wide of his target.

Flicking his wrist in the other direction, he overcorrected and sliced into the circular shape he was trying to cut out. The wall panels around where he was cutting were starting to bend and groan, but held together.

The shape behind him loomed larger and larger until it took the form of a massive ballast cruiser. Whoever was piloting it had maneuvered it out of position for the moment. It no longer had a direct shot, but Adan saw one of its guns swiveling back around towards him. He could not afford to wait until it got into position. He shoved on the forward levers as hard as he could and rammed the sovos into the unfinished hole. The duster pummeled the wall and the flimsy metal went flying, but then the ship stopped, caught underneath on a section of the wall.

Adan yanked back and forth on the forward lever so hard he thought it might come off, but nothing happened. He flicked his eyes frantically between the giant ballast bearing down on him and the stubborn lever in front of him.

"Please, please, please," he said over and over, his heart threatening to leap into his throat.

Then, with a jerk, the duster shot forward and out into the open night.

Adan glanced back at the mangled hole he'd escaped through. The wall panels and platform struts lay in a jumbled heap. The opening was far too small for a cruiser to fit through, but even if the cruiser could, he was confident he could outrun it in the open desert. They'd have to find another ship if they wanted to catch him and by then they would have lost sight of him.

He shoved the velocity lever forward as far as it would go and the duster whipped across the dunes. There was almost no light left in the sky, but he could see enough to know that he was free again. Glancing down at the slumbering Nox, he wondered for how long.

NINE
THREE JAUNTS AWAY

Adan did not engage the guide lights for the ship until the city of Hull was out of sight. To make sure they didn't run into anything, he kept the ship flying as high as it would go, about two full body-lengths off the ground.

He was grateful when daylight broke forth at the edge of the horizon and no sign of pursuit could be seen. His heart warmed with gratitude to Numinae, certain that it was he who had delivered Adan out of the city, though the instrument he had chosen to do his work was certainly an unexpected one.

Nox remained passed out on the deck of the duster, oblivious to their success. As far as Adan was concerned, the longer he stayed down, the better. But he would wake up eventually. Once the light got strong enough, Adan stopped the duster and did a quick search of his unconscious companion. He found a full water pouch, some kern, a few metal spikes, the long cord Nox had used to get down into the pit, and three shivs hidden in the pockets of his garrick. Adan wondered how Nox had managed to scavenge so many supplies, but then the Waymen were quite adept at looting.

As a precaution, he decided to relieve the warrior of his weapons and tossed them into the sand, hoping Nox would not be too angry when he found them missing.

Searching inside the Wayman's garrick, he found around his neck a silver circlet with a little bauble on it. The pendant had a yellow crystal embedded inside a notched wheel. This seemed odd. Adan had never seen Waymen wearing jewelry or other adornments before. He also found a strange black disk hidden inside one of Nox's inner pockets. It was not much larger than the palm of Adan's hand and had four small pieces of glass embedded into its surface on the top. It looked like some form of technology, but a check with his bioseine failed to yield any information as to what it was.

He searched the ship as well, finding the pinions he had found earlier in the supply compartment in the back. He threw those out beside Nox's other weapons. The plastic boxes inside the compartment were all empty, but underneath them were two spare sets of desert clothing. He gratefully donned the kaff to replace the one he'd used as a bandage. To his surprise, tucked inside the folded up piece of cloth was a pair of lentes. He placed these over his eyes and found they were fully charged. Sliding his finger along one of the rims, the faraway dunes zoomed into view.

He remembered the first time he had used lentes, when he and Will had descended into the Viscera, searching for food and water. He had found water that day, but more than that, he had been introduced to the world of the Welkin and to Senya's family. Again he considered briefly going back for her and again decided against it.

Gavin will know how to save her, he told himself. *Besides he may be in even greater danger than Senya and her children.*

Re-engaging the duster, he glanced down at one of the black crystal panels on the side of the steering column. It showed the status of the vehicle's systems in a schematic composed of glowing white images. The only one Adan really cared about was the power level and that looked good; it showed they had seven days of flying time left.

As the journey wore on and Nox continued to remain unconscious, Adan began to wonder whether or not he had been hurt more seriously than it appeared. Adan hadn't seen him stir for so long that when he finally caught Nox moving out of the corner of his eye he gave a start.

The Wayman sat up and patted his coat several times, a questioning look on his face.

"So, you lifted my shivs, eh?" Nox said at last, his expression shifting to a dark brooding. Adan tensed, gripping the controls and trying to think what he would do if Nox attacked, but the Wayman's eyes sparked with cruel mirth as he let out a full-bellied laugh. "Well done! Now you're thinking like a Wayman. Never trust anyone."

Adan concentrated on steering the sovos and tried not to appear too nervous. "You won't need your weapons around me," he said. "I'm no threat to you."

"Everyone's a threat." Nox reached into his pockets, no doubt to see what else Adan had taken. "But I don't need my shivs. I can kill just as easily with my bare hands. It just takes a little longer."

Adan fastened his eyes on Nox. He half expected the man to lunge at him. But the Wayman just stood there, smiling to himself and fingering the silver chain which hung around his neck.

"Nice shards," Nox remarked, nonchalantly, as if he hadn't just made a veiled threat on Adan's life.

"What?" Adan replied, trying to steady his nerves.

"Those things on your face." Nox pointed at the lentes,

flashing his decaying teeth. "How can you see where you're going with those things on?"

"They actually help me see farther than normal," Adan said, still eyeing Nox warily. "I could let you try them on if you'd like."

Nox gave him a startled look. "Oh no. I'm just an empty shaft. Relics aren't for me. Too many parts, too many things to go wrong."

"Fair enough." To be honest, Adan would not have been all that thrilled with using the lentes again after they'd touched Nox's grimy face. "What's that necklace you're wearing?" Adan asked. "I didn't know Waymen wore that sort of thing."

Nox promptly shoved it back inside his garrick and gave Adan a suspicious look, as if he expected Adan had designs on stealing it.

"I guess you don't know much about Waymen," was all he had to say. He wandered over to the edge of the duster. The wall of the open-topped ship went up to about his shoulder and he peered over the side at the sandy floor whisking by. The land was relatively free of scrap, but rock formations loomed in the distance. "So where are we?" he asked.

"Three jaunts from Hull," Adan said, glancing down at the status screen. A jaunt was about how far a Wayman could travel in one day.

"You're twisting my gears," Nox said in disbelief. "How long have I been out?"

"More than half a day."

Nox glanced towards the horizon. "Well, I guess we're clipping along at a pretty good rate, then." He reached into his garrick and pulled out a few pieces of kern. "That would explain why I'm so gut-quivered," he said, taking a bite out of one of the tough strips.

"So, why were you at Nolan's camp?" Adan asked, eyeing the kern and feeling his own gut quivering.

"Ah, the shim caught me in a raid," Nox said, scowling and spitting on the deck as if the kern had left a bad taste in his mouth. "He's been swelling his ranks like mad ever since the attack on that fake Tasada place you and your friend drug us to."

Adan shifted uncomfortably at the mention of Tasada, the name some Waymen used to refer to Oasis. Dark memories flitted through his thoughts. He would never be able to forget that the man in front of him had killed his friend there.

Nox chattered on. "After I made it back to Thral Gyre, my tyranny as the new Reeve lasted all of three days before I was captured," he said, shaking his head. Then he burst out laughing. "Killed an awful lot of us, but they captured even more—that was what they were after—warm bodies; fit as many of us as they could onto those floating crates of theirs."

"So you're saying Nolan forced you to serve him?" Adan studied the Wayman, trying to gauge what was really going on inside his head. Nox's thoughts proved impossible to unravel. He seemed to be both afraid and seething with anger at the same time. The impressions were too vague, too unreliable, as if Nox himself had no idea what he was thinking either.

Nox shrugged. "It's part of the Wayman life—you get captured and pressed into a new thral from time to time. Nolan was different, though. He tried to force that gear tech on us. It blew by me like the desert wind, though. I'm too empty up top to learn that gimcrack stuff. So they put me on latrine cleanup instead." He spit on the ground again. "Bah! That's Welkin work, not something for a well-built Wayman like myself."

"Well, at least you're free of him now," Adan said.

Nox shook his fists at the air as if the invisible Nolan were standing in front of him. "Ha! We sure showed those hollow skulls back there how it's done, eh? A little nap-trap is worth more than those death relics when it comes right down to it, I say." He gave Adan a hearty slap on the shoulder, causing his hand to slip on the steering lever and forcing the transport to dip to the left. Adan jerked it back to center before the vehicle could descend too far and collide with the dunes.

"So where are you taking us in this desert loper? Not through those rocks, I hope?" Nox asked, gesturing at the landscape ahead.

"Yes, through those rocks," Adan replied. "I lost a friend a few days ago on the other side of them and I have to find him." Adan knew from his bioseine exactly where he and Gavin had been separated. The auto-map screen of the sovos indicated that it wouldn't be long before they arrived back there.

Nox let out a loud cough and cleared his throat. "Now just set your heels in the sand a moment, gear-head. I was the one who dragged you out of the pit. I'm the one that says where you're running this wreck to."

Adan had wondered how long it would be before Nox unveiled his true intentions. Even though he no longer had his weapons, the Wayman was still a threat. Adan had little doubt Nox would turn on him if he wanted to, the same way he had on Will.

"Well, where is it you need to go?" Adan asked tentatively, looking away as if he were focused on piloting the duster, and scrutinizing the auto-map even though he already knew their exact position. "Perhaps we're headed in the same direction."

Adan's remark caught Nox off guard. He scratched his beard and sputtered out mono-syllables as if he had suddenly lost the ability to speak.

"Go-off-um, oh, uh-er..." he sputtered. "Yes, that's a very good question. Where am I going?"

"I'll make an agreement with you," Adan said quickly,

taking advantage of Nox's confusion. "If you'll let me look for my friend, after I find him I'll take you to wherever you want to go—or I can even drop you off on my way if you like," he added hastily, hoping the latter would be the case.

"Well..." Nox continued mumbling to himself, making odd faces as if the kern wasn't sitting all that well in his stomach. "I suppose that suits me fine enough. My thral is gutted. I just wanted to put as much distance between me and Hull as possible. I hadn't really spiced my kern enough to think about where I was headed once I got out."

Without warning he backhanded Adan in the face, sending him stumbling.

"What was that for?" Adan shot back as he hurried to grab hold of the steering column again, his cheek stinging like mad.

"That's how we make agreements in the thrals," Nox said. "Now you slap me back and we'll call it a deal."

As tempting as Nox's offer was, Adan shook his head. "No, that's all right," he said, massaging his throbbing cheek. "I don't need to hit you back. I'll keep my word. You can count on that."

"Fine, suit yourself," Nox said, wagging his head from side to side and grinning so that his ragged teeth poked out from behind his lips. As always, the Wayman's smile gave Adan an unsettling feeling.

Adan was not entirely sure he had made the right decision in agreeing to stay with Nox, but opposing the Wayman didn't seem like a very wise choice either. He only hoped his decision would not come back to haunt him. In the meantime, he kept an eye on the Wayman, wary of any sign that Nox might change his disposition.

And so, uneasily, their journey continued, sending them

into the rock fields. The formations were mostly low enough for the duster to fly over. If not, Adan simply swerved around them. He didn't bother using the lentes during the day to conserve their charge, but towards nightfall they were still in the rocks and the shadows began to lengthen so he slipped them back on to better navigate the treacherous terrain. Nox, who did not have the benefit of such vision became increasingly anxious whenever they passed close to the dark shapes looming up at them. After a time, his fitful exclamations became so distracting Adan used his bioseine to turn down his hearing so that all he could hear was a low murmur in the background.

Focused as he was on piloting the duster, he gave a startled shout when Nox grabbed him by the shoulder and spun him around. Nox glared at Adan as if he had done something terribly wrong. Adan felt certain the Wayman was about to lash out at him, whether verbally or physically. He re-engaged his normal level of hearing in hopes that it would be the first of the two.

"What is it, Nox?" Adan asked.

"It's pitch dark!" Nox shouted. "We're going to crash if you don't stop this ship. And if you don't, I'm going to throw you off and then jump myself. I can't take any more of this!" Though the temperature in the Vast never changed much, even at night, Nox's kaff was soaked clean through with sweat.

"We're almost there," Adan assured him, but Nox refused to calm down, screaming as they passed beneath the shadow of an enormous rock.

"You're trying to punish me for what happened in Tasada, aren't you?" Nox cried, grabbing Adan's arm and wringing it with both hands, like he was desperate to get them clean.

Adan winced and tried to pull away, but Nox held him fast. "No, Nox. Forget about that. Just hold on a little longer. These glasses let me see as if it were midday—better actually. I wouldn't continue if it wasn't safe."

Nox let go of his arm and kicked the side of the ship. "A curse on all relics. If it were up to me, we'd drop all this gear into a vat of taline and be done with it."

Nox quieted down after that, but not much, continuing to bellow and curse until they arrived at the crash site. He jumped out of the duster the moment it stopped and threw himself face first into the nearest dune, blubbering about how unfair life was for ignorant "shafts" like himself and how men were never meant to fly. Eventually his ravings petered out and his grumbling turned to snores, echoing across the desert like a distant avalanche.

But Adan couldn't sleep. He could not rest until he found Gavin. Every moment he delayed, his friend might be closer to death or further away if he'd been captured. He doubted Gavin would still be at the crash site after so much time had passed, but it was the only information he had to go on. If he wasn't near the wreck of the lev, Adan hoped to at least find some indication as to where he might have gone after the crash.

He was nearing exhaustion, but if he had to, he could use his bioseine to keep going without sleep. He intended to go on looking until his system shut him down. The only thing that mattered was finding Gavin.

Adan found the remains of the lev with little difficulty. Even though the crash and his ensuing capture had been chaotic moments where he'd been running for his life, his bioseine led him to the exact spot.

Most of the scrap from their ship was covered in sand now. He pulled away the smaller sections, but the larger ones were far too heavy. If Gavin was trapped underneath any of them, Adan doubted he would still be alive, but he decided to check there first. He looked around for a long bar or something similar to wedge under the panels and perhaps lift them using leverage. He wandered around for some time, but found nothing.

Then he remembered the cutter. Running over to the spot where he'd been captured by the Waymen, it only took a moment to find it. He shoved it onto his arm and headed back to the crash site. His feet were dragging now; he wasn't sure how much longer he could hold out. When he arrived back, he started slicing up the larger pieces of the lev with the yellow blade, but found no sign of Gavin.

His searching was not entirely in vain, though, for he managed to salvage two important pieces of equipment from the wreckage.

The first item was the shifter. It was battered and scuffed, but amazingly, still powered on when he turned the dials. With it, he could at last make something to eat.

The other item gave Adan mixed feelings; it was the chronotrace. It had actually been lying out in the open, all by itself, but he didn't notice it until his work with the cutter was finished. It, too, was badly dented, but still in working order. The bismine array had separated from the rest of the device and some of the chips were missing, but after a long search, he found all of them and reattached the array and restored power to it.

But the fact that Gavin's precious invention was left lying out in the middle of the desert only confirmed what Adan feared most: Gavin was no longer there. His friend would never have abandoned the chronotrace on his own; he must have been captured. And if that was so, the chances of finding him were bleaker than ever.

TEN
A NEW TRACE

TWO FORCES HAD BEEN PRESENT WHEN THE LEV CRASHED.
Adan was certain the Waymen hadn't taken Gavin since Nolan
sent his own men to find him; that left only the somatarchs. As
far as Adan knew, most of them had been killed in the fight
with the Waymen, but Adan had not seen everything. If some
of them had survived, they could have easily captured Gavin
and carried him off under cover of the storm.

Adan was tempted to despair at this thought until a realization flashed through his mind: he had the chronotrace. That
could tell him Gavin's fate.

He set to work at once, powering on the device and
instructing it to begin its initial scan of the area. Since the crash
had happened several days ago, he would have to let it run for
some time, but once it had gone back far enough, he could run a
backtrace to find out where Gavin had been taken, following
him in the same way they had followed the stranger who had
taken the extractor.

Adan left the softly glowing device to run its course and
picked up the cutter. He slid it onto his arm. There was plenty

of abandoned machinery nearby so it wasn't long before he had a few dozen plugs for the shifter. His eyes drooping and his limbs heavy, he slid the plugs into the black box and watched as first the ingredients for mosh and then the those for atol dropped out into a pair of containers he found in the wreckage of the lev. He quickly mixed them together, then gobbled down half of what he'd made and sealed up the rest for later.

After placing the cutter and shifter in the storage compartment on the ship, he found a clean stretch of sand and collapsed. Giving the snoring Nox one last wary glance, he let sleep overtake him at last, instructing his bioseine to wake him if it perceived a threat or when the chronotrace finished, whichever came first.

By the time Adan stirred, Nox was already up, staring at the pulsating chronotrace, grinding his decayed teeth so loudly it sounded like they were made of metal. He looked both mesmerized and apprehensive at the same time, and barely gave Adan a glance.

The glowing ring around the base of the chronotrace dimmed until it was barely visible in the pale light of the morning. The spinning half-sphere slowly wound down as the trace completed.

"When can we leave this place?" Nox asked. "These relics give me the shivers."

"Soon. I just have to find out what path my friend took."

"Who is this friend of yours, anyway?" Nox asked. "Is he a gear-head, too?"

"Yes. He was the man Will rescued in Oasis—the city your people thought was Tasada."

"Ah, of course. The one who threatened to kill me and my men." Nox gave Adan a sinister look. "I do hope you find him."

Adan turned away and tried to forget the dark look on Nox's face. He hoped Nox would be long gone by the time he found Gavin.

"You can probably go ahead and wait for me on the ship," Adan told him. "I just have to check to see that there weren't any problems with the trace. It will only take a moment."

Nox perked up at Adan's words and shuffled off towards the duster.

Adan closed his eyes and connected his mind with the chronotrace. He instructed it to begin playback at the crash scene four days ago.

The trace began to play just before the lev flipped. Adan saw his body flying through the air in slow motion. He winced involuntarily as he watched himself slam into a sandbank. Seeing how far he'd been thrown, Adan marveled that he had not received any major injuries.

Gavin had been thrown in a direction perpendicular to where Adan landed, but he had not been thrown nearly as far. From the trace, Adan could tell that Gavin's zoetic pulse was still active and that the crash had not killed him, though his garrick had been torn in several places and he lay face down in the sand.

Adan sped the trace forward one microslice until Gavin stirred. Gavin rose to his feet and walked towards the remains of the lev. Adan began to hope that perhaps his friend had walked away on his own power, but Gavin noticed something beyond the edge of the trace and began to run. He only got a short distance before a white-robed somatarch on skimmers swooped down and picked him up under its arm. Adan froze the trace. The creature looked as soulless and inhuman inside the projection as it did in real-life. It was bleeding in several places, but nothing severe enough to hinder it since somatarchs felt no pain.

There was no point in watching the rest of the trace play out. It would use up unnecessary amounts of power and, more importantly, it would take precious time. Adan could always pull it up later if he needed to. With every passing moment, Gavin got further and further away; Adan had to start after him at once.

He disconnected his mind from the chronotrace and headed towards the duster, picking up the precious device as he went. Nox was sitting in the doorway of the ship, his pudgy legs dangling over the side. When he saw Adan heading towards him he jumped to his feet and clapped his hands.

"Finally!" he blurted out, his eyes aglow.

"I've locked onto Gavin's trail," Adan said as he stepped onto the ship. He set the chronotrace down beside the steering column and engaged the duster's power. In a few moments they had risen once again above the grayish sand of the Vast. "We should find him soon."

That moment could not come soon enough for Adan. Shoving the velocity lever forward, the ship surged into motion, sending them hurtling out across the field of ruined machines.

The duster zipped across the desert, careening above the sand like the shuttle of a loom, leaving behind a thread of displaced dust and debris in its wake. Nox, for all his anxiousness to resume their journey, soon dropped off into a dead sleep. He lay at the back of the sovos, propped up against the outer wall, snoring away. He could not have been all that tired, having slept the better part of the last two days, but whatever the cause of his drowsiness, Adan was glad to have the ship to himself.

As the duster sped along Gavin's trail, Adan checked the chronotrace from time to time to get a snapshot of how the trace was progressing. He saw that the somatarch was using skimmers to cross the desert, carrying Gavin on its shoulders. The sovos was about twice as fast as the air skates so Adan was steadily gaining ground. Even so, because he had started a few days behind, he knew he would not be overtaking Gavin anytime soon. One thing he did know, though: the somatarch was headed in the direction of Oasis.

While Adan had little desire to return to that city, there was nothing he could do about it; he had to follow the trace. He kept the velocity lever in full forward position, using the lentes to travel through the night, knowing that any delay might mean the difference between finding Gavin dead or alive.

On their second day of travel, Nox, in one of his rare waking moments, seemed at last to realize where they were headed.

"You're taking us back to that machine city, aren't you?" he said.

"Yes, that looks like where my friend went."

Adan expected some sort of protest from the Wayman, knowing how much he seemed to fear technology, but Nox was strangely silent and a short time later the sound of his snoring could be heard once again above the wind. Adan wondered why the Wayman chose to stay with him. Even if his own thral had been destroyed, there had to be others he could join somewhere in these lands. But perhaps Nox didn't want to go back. Perhaps he preferred the freedom of striking out on his own. Adan didn't know enough about him, or about Waymen in general, to understand what his motives might be. Whatever his intentions, he hoped they would not involve traveling with him much longer. Adan would never feel completely safe in Nox's presence. Even in sleep, the Wayman's face often formed itself into unsettling expressions, as if he were intending some malice even in his dreams.

On the third day after finding the crash, they arrived at a familiar place: the Desiccant Flats. Marked by a stretch of black nidor rocks which the Waymen feared to cross, the flats were a pale stretch of sand that occupied the hills surrounding Oasis. Though Adan knew where they were from his bioseine and the enhanced vision afforded by the lentes, a sand storm racing across the landscape obscured the terrain to the naked eye. It wasn't until Adan landed the sovos on the edge of the field of flat black rocks that Nox became aware of where they were.

"The blood rocks again. Are those weapons out there?" Nox asked, referring to the whisper cannons which protected the outer perimeter of Oasis and had killed so many Waymen during their previous journey here. He had to shout so his voice could be heard above the winds whipping across the flats.

"I can't say for sure," Adan said, "but unless they replaced the one we destroyed last time, we should be safe. I'll drop you here and make sure, though."

"What?" Nox blurted out, obviously alarmed. "Leave me? How do I know you won't run off with the ship into the dust clouds and disappear forever?"

"I promise I won't leave you," Adan assured him.

"Ha!" Nox laughed. "Promises are empty wind. You'll have to give me something more tangible." Nox looked down at Adan's feet where the chronotrace rested. "That's what you're using to track your friend, isn't it?"

Adan nodded, wary of where Nox was headed with his question.

"Leave it with me," the Wayman said, "as proof you'll return."

Adan did not like the thought of leaving something so valuable in the hands of this unpredictable Wayman, but Nox did not trust him any more than Adan trusted Nox. He picked up the device and reluctantly handed it over. If for some reason Nox took it into his head to run off with it, Adan would be able to track him down with the duster.

"Don't do anything to it," Adan said.

Nox's face broke out into one of his unsightly grins. "Oh, don't worry," he said, gripping it with his thick fingers. "I can be quite delicate when I need to be." He let out a raspy chuckle, clearly enjoying Adan's anxiety.

Nox hopped out of the ship and onto the sand.

"I won't be gone long," Adan told him, both as an assurance and a warning.

Nox pulled out a piece of kern from one of the pockets of his garrick. "Take your time," he said, yanking down his kaff so he could take a bite. Though he got a mouthful of sand from the storm along with his food, it didn't seem to bother him. "I'll be waiting."

Adan engaged the forward lever of the sovos and launched into the surrounding clouds. The billowing debris was almost invisible seen through the lentes. It looked like a thin film shifting this way and that in front of him.

He soon passed over the cracked, windswept sections of the flats and the ground became more sandy. In a short time he reached the remains of the whisper cannon. It appeared almost exactly as it had when they left it, a charred out hulk of ebony metal. The only difference was that the base was now coated in several layers of sand.

Adan circled around it one time just to be sure it was no longer a threat. Satisfied, he thrust the forward level to full again and sped back towards Nox.

When he arrived at the edge of the flats, he found Nox some distance beyond the place where he'd left him.

"I didn't like being near the blood rocks," the Wayman explained once he had boarded the duster again. "I know they're not enchanted, but old ways are hard to shake." He fingered the pendant he wore at his neck, his eyes darting about, as if expecting something to rush out at him from the dust clouds.

"We'll be across the flats soon enough," Adan said as the ship ramped back up in speed. "And the cannon is still down so you won't be in any danger."

"Good. I'm looking forward to seeing the mess." Nox scanned the shifting walls of dust around them. "Maybe one day the same thing will happen to Hull," he added. "Unnatural, that place is."

"How long has Nolan been the ruler there?" Adan asked. He knew Nolan had left Oasis at some point, but he had no idea when.

"No one knows for sure," Nox said, "but we started hearing about a Wayman who'd mastered the ancient relics quite a while ago. That was the reason Sparc wanted to capture Oasis, so that he'd be as powerful as the Wayman we were hearing about."

Adan could see why Nolan would have been a threat to the other thrals, but he still wondered how he had created the walled city and all of those ships and weapons in the first place.

A sudden dip of the sovos startled him out of his thoughts.

"What was that?" Nox shouted, his face brimming with a sort of bewildered rage.

Adan checked the topography of their location via the map displayed on the instrument panel.

"We're in the foothills surrounding the ridge," he said. "Get ready for a bit of a rough ride."

"More rocks! And we're heading deeper into the storm,"

Nox bellowed. "You're trying to kill me again, aren't you? What an empty shaft I was for agreeing to ride in this death trap."

He moaned and complained all the way up to the ridge, but Adan soon forgot he was there. He was too busy maneuvering around the rocks, pressing and pulling on the levers to keep the sovos from crashing. He wished the ship had an esolace connection; that way he could have controlled it with his mind instead of through these clumsy controls. If Adan hadn't been wearing the lentes they would never have been able to make it. The storm got worse the further they went until the winds beat so fiercely against the fuselage that only the ship's massive weight kept it from being blown away.

As they wound their way through the maze of Virid Ridge, Nox gestured wildly and dashed around the ship, hollering about the evils of machinery. From the way he talked, it sounded like he was blaming the storm on the very thing protecting them from it: the ship itself. The demons were mad at him, he said, because he was riding around in one of the relics, as profane an act as possible in the mind of a Wayman. Adan was grateful when his squeals eventually got drowned out by the wind.

As the gusts rattled the ship's paneling, Adan wondered how much longer the duster would hold together. He didn't even feel safe after the ship left the ridge and plunged over the far side and down towards Oasis, though the storm did let up some as they flew towards the edge of the city.

With the diminished force of the wind, Nox's squealing rose above the storm's racket once again. Adan tried several times to get him to calm down and be quiet, but he wouldn't listen. Up until now, Adan had always assumed that Oasis would be utterly abandoned, but at that moment a thought occurred to him. *If there are somatarchs here, that must mean some of the Developers survived. They're going to know we're here if Nox doesn't keep quiet.*

As they entered the city and Nox kept spouting off doom and woe, Adan scanned their surroundings. With his lentes he could at last see the full extent of the devastation. Oasis was almost unrecognizable from the ordered metropolis it had once been. Nothing in the city had been left untouched. The buildings were either piles of metal and debris, empty husks, or were gone altogether. Even the pavement was in shambles; it looked like a giant army of Waymen had hacked it to pieces with their weapons.

Nox continued to wail that the storm had come back to the city, bellowing that the end was near.

Finally Adan had had enough. He pulled the duster to a stop just inside the remains of The Service Ring, halfway to the center of the city. He let the ship hover in place over a debris-strewn street and turned to face Nox. For the first time since he'd met the murderous Wayman he was not afraid of him. Better to risk the wrath of Nox than to attract the attention of somatarchs or Developers.

"Stop it!" Adan ordered, rushing at Nox with the intention of clamping his hand over the hysterical Wayman's mouth. But as he reached for him, Nox, whether from shock at Adan's reaction, or because of his own mad gyrations, slipped and fell backwards. Adan, already committed to his forward movement, fell along with him, landing on top of the startled Wayman. "You're going to get both of us killed," Adan said angrily, struggling not to yell and draw even more attention.

Nox went dead silent. He stared up at Adan, his eyes wide with disbelief, as if he could not fathom a world in which someone like Adan would do what Adan had just done.

Adan was breathing heavily. A rush of adrenaline flooded his head. Finding his feet, he rose to stand over the prostrate

Wayman. With newfound boldness, he pointed his finger
threateningly at the stupefied man. But the words of admonish-
ment he had intended to say never left his lips.

At that moment a bright light flashed all around them and a
deafening blast rocked the sovos, shooting Adan straight out of
the vehicle. There was a brief sensation of movement, an
instant of confusion, and then nothing.

ELEVEN
A FAMILIAR STRANGER

THE WORLD CAME BACK ONLY HALF A MICROSLICE LATER.
Pain washed over Adan. The wind pelted the multiple cuts on
his hands and face with debris, but the worst pain came from
his leg. It was the same one that had just healed. This time the
wound was not in the calf, but in the thigh. A sheet of metal,
about the size of his hand was buried deep in his upper leg. The
terrible stinging felt like his leg had been thrust into a fire. He
shut off the pain with his bioseine before it became too much.

The shrapnel was a jagged, irregular metal sheet. Slowly,
mechanically, he worked it back and forth until it popped free.

Blood welled up from inside the wound, seeping into his
clothes, but his bioseine kept him from passing out. He ripped
off his kaff and fashioned a makeshift tourniquet. Sand raked
across his face.

Once he finished the grisly work, he surveyed the wreck of
the sovos. It lay about a dozen paces away, a mess of warped
metal, flipped upside down from the blast. It looked like a
beaten up, metallic version of Will's shelter, with the floor now
forming the roof. The lentes had flown from his face in the

crash so he could no longer see through the swirling dust clouds, but he could make out the skeleton of destroyed buildings to either side and several piles of rubble which obstructed parts of the street in front of him.

There was no sign of Nox, but debris was everywhere. He must have been lying somewhere amongst the wreckage. Adan had no great attachment to the Wayman, but he was not about to abandon someone who might be injured or dying. Whatever had destroyed the duster was no doubt still out there. Adan had to find Nox and get out of this place as soon as possible.

He rose to his feet, but as he placed weight on his injured leg, it felt unsteady, as if he were standing on a layer of gel. Checking his bioseine, he realized that he had sprained his ankle as well. Because he felt no pain, he could still walk on it, but it did not support him well enough to move very quickly. He had to limp in order to avoid putting too much weight on it and injuring it further.

The large sheets of metal which littered the scene made him remember the cutter. That would make the task of searching for Nox that much easier. Rifling through the wreckage, he soon found the tube poking out from under one of the metal panels that had flown off the sand duster.

He shoved the cutter onto his forearm. At that moment there was a break in the wind and sounds of movement came down the street from behind. Thinking it must be Nox, he turned and looked in that direction. All he could make out were piles of rubble. Was Nox behind one of them?

Adan hopped back to the overturned sovos and squeezed inside. If it was Nox, he would find out soon enough. If not, he could only hope they wouldn't come inside the ship.

He fingered the controls of the cutter nervously, hoping he would not have to use it. He thought he caught the sound of voices on the wind, but couldn't be sure. Still, the possibility did give him a spark of hope. Somatarchs rarely spoke; if someone was talking, it was most likely not one of them. But it could still be an assessor, another part of the Oasis security detail, which would be just as bad.

Peeking through a chink in the duster's outer wall, he stared down the ruined street. He thought he saw a pair of round shapes pop up over a pile of debris. They might have been heads, but were nothing more than silhouettes. They quickly disappeared.

"It's all right," came a man's voice, shouting from down the street, "We don't mean you any harm if you don't mean us any."

Adan pulled away from the opening, his heart pounding, certain he'd been spotted. The words were followed by more muffled conversations and then the same voice spoke again, louder this time.

"Come out and show yourself," it said. "We aren't going to hurt you."

Adan had no way of knowing whether or not the man was lying, but he wasn't going to outrun anyone on his bad ankle and he couldn't stay inside the sovos forever. Still, how could he trust them? He could almost hear Nox's voice inside his head, *"Now you're thinking like a Wayman. Never trust anyone."*

Risking a look through the chink in the wall, he spotted, half-shrouded in dust and haze about thirty paces away, the figures of four men emerging from behind a large pile of rubble. They approached the ship slowly. Soon Adan could make out a few details. Three of them had on tattered gray jumpsuits with canvas hoods and scarves that covered their mouths. The fourth wore Wayman gear: a garrick and kaff that had seen better days. Each of them had pinions strapped to their backs, but none were drawn to strike.

Adan did not duck away this time, but kept watching them as they drew steadily closer.

"We're sorry we shot down your ship," said one of the men in the jumpsuits, the one in the middle. He wore a metal band with a lit screen around his wrist as well as a pair of green-tinted lentes. "But we didn't know anybody else in Oasis had ships and we couldn't take a chance that you were working for the Administrators." The man's voice sounded calm, but firm. Adan was encouraged by the fact that whoever he was, he didn't claim to be on the side of the Developers.

Adan swallowed hard and called out through the opening, "Who are you?"

The men stopped advancing.

"We call ourselves Sentients. We're survivors of the storm that hit Oasis." The man who spoke was the one in the Wayman gear. His voice was deeper, with a gruff edge to it.

Inside the remains of the sovos, Adan bit his lip, unsure of what to do. So there had been survivors? If so, maybe they'd be able to help him find Gavin.

Adan decided to take the chance. He hopped out through the doorway and stood looking at the four men standing outside his ship. From the haggard looks on several of their faces, they looked as relieved as he was that the situation hadn't turned violent. Adan sensed in that moment that they were people just like him, trying to survive in a dangerous and turbulent world.

"It's a shame about your rig," said the man in the jumpsuit who had been doing most of the talking. "I tried to tell Bryce that the hollow men don't float that kind of boat, but he didn't trust my specs." He tapped the lentes and tipped his head toward the man in the Wayman gear. His companion just cleared his throat.

For the first time Adan caught sight of the other man's eyes. There was something familiar about them. They shone with an intensity that could be made out even in the midst of the swirling sand. And all at once Adan recognized who it was—it was the man from the chronotrace, the one who had taken Gavin's extractor.

Adan felt suddenly light-headed, but he caught himself on the wall of the ship before he stumbled.

"This man needs medical attention," said the one who'd taken the extractor. He waved his companions forward.

The two men who had yet to speak hurried towards Adan. One of them pulled out a crumpled piece of cloth from inside a slit in his jumpsuit.

"That looks pretty bad," he said, taking a look at Adan's leg. He had a look of resignation in his eyes, as if he'd seen injuries like Adan's many times before.

The man set about wrapping his wounded leg at once. Adan was grateful for his help, but he couldn't keep from glancing back at the man in the Wayman gear. Whatever else these Sentients were doing here, that person's presence cast a shadow over the rest of the group. Adan didn't trust him, and that suspicion spread to his companions.

"You're favoring your other leg pretty heavily," observed the one who was wrapping his wound. "Are there any other injuries you suffered?"

"The ankle," Adan muttered distractedly. "It's sprained."

The man started digging around in the debris until he found a couple of long, flat pieces of metal. Then, along with the other man attending him, they set those on either side of his ankle and wrapped it with more cloth to give it some support.

"My name is Von," said the man who had been asking about his injuries, "and this is Nance." The other man nodded. His eyes were the same plain brown as Von's, but much less grim.

The other two men came up behind Von and Nance, observing as they finished wrapping Adan's ankle. The one wearing the Wayman gear glanced several times towards the dust clouds, his brow a stiff line of concern.

"I'm Raif, by the way," said the man with the lentes. "And this is Bryce." He pointed to the one who had taken the extractor. Adan met Bryce's gaze and gave him a searching look, but Adan's emotions were running too high to be able to read his thoughts. "We have a shelter we can take you to," Raif continued. "There are other Sentients there. It's not much, but we'll be able to treat your injuries."

Adan glanced back towards Raif, unsure of what to say. He wanted to ask about the extractor then and there, but it didn't seem wise to confront Bryce in front of his friends out in the middle of a ruined street.

With the ship destroyed and the wounds he had suffered, he didn't see what choice he had but to go with these men. At least he had found Bryce. Once they got out of the storm, Adan would find a way to talk to him about the extractor.

"Thank you," Adan said at length. "But there were actually two of us on the ship. The man traveling with me has to be close by."

"Strange. We only picked up a single zoetic signature," Raif said, confused.

"What do you mean?" Adan asked.

Raif held out his arm so Adan could see the screen on his wrist. "My variance modulator would have picked him up if he was there. It can detect zoetic sources, bioseines, all sorts of things."

"Couldn't it have malfunctioned? I mean, maybe the storm disrupted the signal."

"I suppose you're right. It's kind of a hacked together piece of equipment. For a while I did actually lose the signal," Raif said. "But look, it's working right now."

Adan glanced at the screen and saw five red dots in the same arrangement in which all of them were standing.

"He was probably killed in the crash," Bryce said. "I'm sorry, but we don't have time to look for him now. We've been out for too long as it is. Somatarch patrols run all over the city. Either you come back with us now or I'm afraid we'll have to leave you to look for him alone."

The other Sentients shuffled nervously, waiting for Adan's response.

Adan scanned the surrounding area one last time. He couldn't see much. The only thing that was moving were the swirling dust clouds. Perhaps Bryce was right. If the modulator didn't pick him up, then Nox must have died in the crash. "All right, then," he said, "Let's go."

As much as he'd been hoping to get rid of Nox, this was not the way he wanted to do it. But the decision had been made. Adan hobbled down the street along with the Sentients, a mix of conflicting emotions swirling inside of him. In death, as in life, Nox was an enigma. If anyone deserved death it was him, but somehow dying in a crash like this did not give Adan any sense of peace or closure.

It soon became obvious that the boot they'd thrown together was not going to be enough for the long walk back. Von came alongside him and Adan put his arm around his shoulder. He found he could keep up a decent pace with the extra support. In his other hand, he still wore the cutter. It gave him a small measure of assurance since he was not entirely ready to trust these men until he knew what Bryce was up to.

Raif pointed to the device on his forearm. "Is that what I think it is?" he asked.

"It's a cutter."

"Well, sparks and smoke," Raif said, admiring the banged

up tube, "I didn't think anything like that was still around. That's vintage, man. Vintage."

"It belonged to a friend," Adan said.

"The one you lost in the crash?"

"No—I..." Adan found himself unsure of how to answer. His thoughts vacillated between telling him about Will and saying nothing. Bryce's presence scrambled his thoughts. He must have had some connection to Will since he'd been in the compound, but Adan had no idea how much he knew. "It belonged to someone else," he said, avoiding Bryce's gaze.

"I used to collect old technology when we were, well, you know, part of the Collective. Where'd you get that ship, by the way?"

"I sort of borrowed it, I guess you could say." Adan gave him a nervous smile. "What was it like, being in the Collective?"

"What do you mean? Weren't you part of it too? Or did they erase that from your memory?"

"I don't know," Adan said. "Maybe I was, maybe I wasn't. I've been out in the Vast for a while, but I was here before the storm hit. I got out just before Oasis was destroyed. How did you survive anyway?" Adan studied Raif's face, exhilarated to actually be able to talk with someone from the Collective. He could already sense this man was different from the scientists who ran the city. There was an alertness, a curiosity to him that was almost infectious. Adan could tell he was eager to learn and fill in the missing gaps in his knowledge.

"Dumb luck, I guess," Raif said, "Some of us woke up in the middle of the storm, some didn't wake up until it was all over, some didn't wake up at all. But those of us who did think for ourselves now—and that's what matters."

"Things haven't been easy," Von said, his gritty tone

contrasting sharply with Raif's animated manner. "But none of us wants to go back to the way things were."

Whatever Bryce's view was, Adan couldn't tell. He kept his thoughts to himself and Adan was too distracted trying not to aggravate his ankle to get a sense of what he felt.

Who are you? Adan wondered. *And what are you doing in Oasis?*

At that moment Bryce gave him a stern look. Adan didn't think he had been listening in on his thoughts, but after his experience with Nolan, he could not really be sure.

TWELVE
MANY KINDS OF WOUNDS

"Get down," came Raif's sudden warning. Adan dropped awkwardly to one knee along with the others, behind a pile of rubble.

They were walking through the hollowed out ground floor of what had been one of the massive skyscrapers of Oasis' central district. Though the floors were now little more than a twisted lattice of metal beams, some of the ceiling on the ground floor still clung to the framework. It was one of the more intact buildings left and gave them some measure of shelter from the storm.

"What did you spot?" Bryce asked, glancing at Raif.

Raif looked up from the modulator on his wrist and pointed into the billowing haze outside the building. "Hollow men. Two of them."

"Hollow men?" Adan asked, puzzled by the unfamiliar term.

"Somatarchs," Bryce said. "Everyone, get ready."

Bryce motioned for them to split into two groups: Raif and Nance in one, Bryce, Adan, and Von in the other. Adan's group

hurried over to a section of support beams that were still standing, each of them taking up position behind a different beam.
Raif and Nance ducked down behind a large pile of rubble
about twenty paces away.

Adan clenched his fist around the handle inside the cutter,
terrified by what was about to come out of the storm.

"You better take one of these," Bryce said in a low whisper
and handed Adan a pinion.

Adan took the weapon without noticing what it was at first.
When he felt the rigid metal in his hands and realized what it
was, his first impulse was to toss it away. Seeing it brought back
memories of the slaughter he had witnessed in the Viscera. The
first time he had seen someone die was from one of these
weapons.

"Aim for the heart, otherwise you'll only slow it down,"
Bryce told him.

Adan swallowed the lump rising in his throat. The cold
smooth metal slid back and forth beneath his sweaty hands.

"What if the somatarchs have oscillathes?" Adan asked,
remembering the battle at Virid Ridge and the hundreds of
Waymen who had died there at the hands of the somatarchs.

"Don't worry, Raif will take care of their weapons."

"But—"

Bryce signaled with his hand for Adan to keep quiet.

At that moment Raif popped up from behind the pile of
debris and tossed a small black ball towards the wall of dust
blowing through the streets. Adan saw nothing at first, but as
the ball hurtled towards the street it grew in size until it was at
least twenty paces in diameter. Then it burst in an explosion of
white light.

As the light faded, from inside the billowing dust, a white-
robed figure rushed towards them. It held a small silver oscillathe, but instead of firing, it simply slid the weapon into a clip

on its belt and sprinted forward. It closed as though borne on the wind. Bryce hurled his pinion. Von's shot followed. Both of them had good aim, but the somatarch dodged Bryce's pinion so that it lodged into its left shoulder. Then, using Bryce's pinion, it deflected Von's stroke with the weapon already impaled in its body.

It happened so fast, Adan had no time to react. The somatarch only slowed down enough to yank the pinion out of its shoulder before rushing on. That was enough for Bryce and Von to get off two more pinions. Adan hurled his as well, but the somatarch swatted Bryce's down with the spear as before and both Von and Adan's throws went wide to either side.

By then the creature was upon them. Discarding the spear, it slammed into Bryce's body, pinning him to the floor.

The wound to the somatarch's shoulder seemed to have robbed it of the use of its left arm, otherwise, it might have gone worse for Bryce. As it was, all he could do was fend of its attacks with one arm, while simultaneously trying to shove the creature off him with the other.

Bryce could not deflect all the blows, though. The somatarch landed two quick jabs to his head before Von could reach him. When the creature landed a third blow to Bryce's temple, his head dropped to the ground and he went still.

Von was going to suffer the same fate if Adan didn't do something. He rushed towards the somatarch as it rose to face Von. Adan forgot all about his ankle and closed the distance in three stuttering steps, arriving just as Von dove towards it.

The creature shrugged off Von's attack and sent him tumbling to the side. His head connected with one of the intact vertical beams and he rolled onto the ground, dazed.

The somatarch regarded Adan with empty, dead eyes as he pulled up in front of it. For a moment his mind went blank. He had no idea how to fight this creature. He had been so focused on what was happening to Bryce and Von he was completely unprepared for the somatarch's blow.

All he saw was a blaze of light and the world turned upside down.

A thunderous boom shook through his senses and his vision returned. He thought he was looking back out across the building to where Raif and Nance had been, but there was nothing but dust and debris drifting down from above.

He whipped his head back around and saw Von fall to the ground from a vicious blow to the back of his neck. The somatarch who gave it was bleeding from another wound in its side, but that didn't stop the creature from finishing Von off.

The Sentients immobilized, the creature turned its lifeless gaze towards Adan.

Adan hobbled to his feet, hoping the creature's wounds would slow it down enough for him to have a chance, or that Raif and Nance would appear from somewhere to help.

As the creature stepped towards him, Adan remembered—the cutter!

He flipped the controls to extend the blade and swung it in a wide arc. The somatarch twisted away, but it was too close. The beam of light passed right across the center of its chest.

The creature paused for the briefest of moments, glancing down at its own body in a detached way. There was no sign of any damage. That was when Adan noticed that the cutter's blade had been set to yellow—it would only cut non-living things. Adan had missed his one chance.

Before he could switch it to red and swing again, the somatarch knocked him to the floor with a crippling kick to the abdomen. Adan went pinwheeling backwards, landing hard in a heap of rubble next to another one of the support beams.

While Adan scrambled to rise, a loud crack reverberated overhead. Looking up Adan saw the ceiling start to cave in.

The last thing he saw before the building came down on top of him was the support beam next to the somatarch slamming into the ground, cut clean in two by the cutter's brilliant yellow blade.

Adan was lying on a bed of rubble. Voices, low and serious, hovered somewhere nearby. Light seeped in around the corners of his vision. As his eyes came into focus, he could make out dark figures leaning over him.

"He's coming around." It was Raif's voice. "Are you all right?"

"I'm not sure," Adan said. Since he felt no pain, he checked his bioseine and saw that he had two cracked ribs, a dislocated shoulder, and a broken collarbone. Besides his internal injuries, he had a finger-sized gash on his upper arm, but someone had already wrapped that up. His bioseine had been able to stop any internal bleeding, but he would need serious medical attention.

Adan informed Raif of the extent of his injuries, wondering privately if this ragtag band of survivors would even be able to help him now.

Raif leaned down so Adan could see his face better. It was still covered by his scarf, but it didn't look like he'd been injured in the fight. "Well, it looked like half the ceiling fell in on you. You're lucky to be alive."

Von was kneeling beside him. "I don't have the resources to deal with these kinds of injuries in my field kit, Raif. We need to get him back to the shelter fast."

"Right. We'll have to jerry-rig something to carry him on."

"Just hurry. Another patrol could come at any time." Bryce's voice came from somewhere off to Adan's right. He glanced in that direction, but it was too dark to see more than the outlines of two figures standing in the shadows.

"Did everyone make it, then?" Adan asked.

Raif nodded in response as Von disappeared back into the shadows.

"How did you stop them?"

Raif gave him a satisfied smirk. "A little recipe I cooked up. One part energy disruptor to disable their oscillathes and another part chemical frag bombs to finish the job. My signature move. I brought down half the building and it looks like you brought down the other half."

A few moments later Von returned with Nance and they began to wedge a makeshift pallet underneath him. It was made of a large piece of silvery scrap metal. Raif lent a hand and through careful effort, they managed to slide Adan onto it.

Von and Nance grabbed the pallet at either end and lifted him off the ground. They trudged slowly through the rubble so as not to jostle him too much, but Adan couldn't keep himself from sliding around on the rigid metal sheet.

Neither Nance nor Von looked like they'd been seriously injured, but when Adan finally got a look at Bryce, the effects of his clash with the somatarch were clearly visible. His kaff was ripped and dangling from his head so that his face was now exposed to the elements. Scratches crisscrossed his skin in patches like threadbare fabric. Dark red splotches sprinkled one side of his face. Despite this, he marched resolutely ahead, showing no signs of pain.

Masking it with his bioseine, Adan thought.

They left the building and made their way onto the debris-filled street. Explosions echoed off in the distance.

When Adan asked what it was, Raif answered, "Another Sentient cell fighting the somatarchs, probably. There are four other cells scattered across the city that we know of. We stay separated to keep ourselves spread out. We've been fighting the Administrators ever since the storm destroyed Oasis."

The Administrators. That was what the assessors called the Developers. "Do you have any idea where they are?" Adan asked.

"The Admins? Not a clue. But I suppose if things keep up the way they're going we'll all end up there soon enough. They capture some of us every day, seems like. We've lost close to half our cell already."

"Why don't you just leave this place—go where the somatarchs won't find you?"

"We've been trying to," Raif said, "but the storm hasn't let up since the day the city fell. Today's one of the few days we've even been able to move around on the surface. The only thing we can do for now is try to survive and find out where they're operating from—find out a way to stop them. So far we're not doing all that great at either."

The storm hadn't let up since Adan left? That had been twenty-three days ago. He'd never heard of a storm going on that long.

"We'll find the Admins," Bryce stated confidently, "and stop them for good this time."

The winds picked up as they made their way down the street. The further along they went, the more anxious Adan became about Bryce. He needed to talk to him, to find out about the extractor, but he was afraid what his reaction might be. He seemed like a person it would not be wise to cross. If he really was associated with Nolan as the Reeve had suggested, that might be doubly true.

By the time they arrived at the shelter, the winds were blowing so hard Von and Nance could barely keep the pallet from tipping over. Raif and Bryce had to come alongside to keep it steady. They lowered Adan into a depression, shutting out the winds. Continuing down, they brought him into a dimly lit tunnel. A thick, round door shut behind them and the wind's roar finally died away.

They placed Adan on the floor and Raif informed him that someone would come soon and take a look at his wounds. The passage they set him in was a long shaft with two circular doors, one on either end. Both had a large wheel-latch mechanism to keep them shut, but the one Raif and the others went through, opposite the one they'd come in, stayed open. Voices conversed in low tones on the other side.

A woman dressed in a tattered jumper entered through the open door. A plastic bottle hung from the belt she wore, and she was carrying a large bowl of water as well.

"Hello there," she said in a quiet voice. "You don't look so good."

She knelt beside Adan and looked him up and down, studying his injuries. Her clothes were covered in dust, but he could still make out the original pearl blue color of the fabric. Her fine brown hair came down to her chin and she had a thoughtful, concerned look in her gray eyes. Adan's mouth fell open as he stared at her.

"I know you," he said.

She stared back at him. "You what?"

For a moment, Adan could not bring himself to respond. He was too overwhelmed by the fact that he was looking at the woman who had been his handler at the Institute. Though they had met only briefly, she had left an indelible impression on him, the one person in all his time there who had treated him with some measure of kindness. Her hair was longer now and her face looked sadder, but there was no mistaking it was the same woman.

"How do you know me? I thought Raif said you came from out in the desert," she said when he didn't reply.

Adan could see her thoughts working even though he had no direct connection to her mind. She was anxious and excited all at once, wondering who he was and what he knew, but most of all wondering if he could tell her anything about the world outside of Oasis. She was much like he had been when he first woke up in the Institute—confused, scared, and desperate for any information about her past.

"Yes, but before that I was in the Institute," Adan said. "You were my handler there."

She blinked several times. "So, you were a patient?"

"We met only once. You probably don't remember me."

"No, I...I'm afraid not." She pulled out a cloth and dipped it in the bowl of water. Besides his broken bones, Adan had numerous nicks and cuts on his hands and face which she began to gently clean with the rag. "We only learned enough to take care of the patients we were handling. Once they left our care, we...forgot about them. I'm not sure how the Administrators did it, but they made sure we didn't remember very much." She paused, holding the rag in her lap. Dim glimpses of her memories floated through her mind. They were disjointed and incomplete and Adan couldn't say exactly what they were about.

"I'm sorry, but you never told me your name the last time," Adan said.

"Oh, of course. We never did that. My name is Sierra." A smile flickered briefly across her face. She dipped the cloth in the water again, but instead of wiping Adan's wounds she wrung it until all the water went out.

"I'm Adan."

"Yes, Raif told me."

"So you don't remember me. What do you remember?"

"Hardly anything. I have images, flashes, but none of them

are connected. It would be easier to go on if—if I knew more, or even if I could just meet someone who knew me."

Adan had thought that exact same thing hundreds of times.

She looked down and noticed the dry rag. Her cheeks flushed and she dipped the cloth back into the basin and resumed cleaning his wounds.

"I heard the Developers kept a backup of our memories in something called the Repository," Adan said, trying to offer some hope. "I can't help but think that somehow, somewhere, we'll find our memories again."

She gave him a half-hearted smile. "Maybe," she said quietly, but Adan could tell she put little faith in his words.

When Sierra finished with the rag she reached into a small pack she wore on her hip. She pulled out a clay container and removed the lid. Though his bioseine dulled the smell, Adan could see from the greenish color and thick texture that it was almamenth.

"Do you think that will be enough to heal my broken collar-bone and cracked ribs? Is almamenth really that powerful?"

"No, but it will make you stronger. We'll cover the injured areas with yeso. That will help set your bones, though it will take a long time for you to fully heal."

"I'm not familiar with that. Yeso?"

"It's a paste that hardens on your skin," she explained, beginning to rub some of the almamenth near the wound on his arm. "You'll see how it works when I put it on. But first, let's finish this."

The way Sierra applied the almamenth so gently reminded him of Senya. She had the same worn look to her face. Though obviously younger than Senya, in some ways Sierra's face was even more troubled. She had the haunted look of someone who has not yet had time to recover from a tragedy, where the hurts are still fresh and the pain still lingers.

After she finished applying the paste, she pulled out a silver rod not much longer than her hand and pointed it towards him. Yellow lights emitted from the end of it, sending shifting patterns across his shoulder and chest. Adan remembered seeing one of those devices back in the Institute.

"Does that help to heal me also?" he asked.

"No, it's just an activator. We use it for diagnosis."

"I could let you connect to my bioseine," Adan said. "It would be quicker." Now that he was out of the storm, he could sense the presence of her bioseine as well as several other Sentients in nearby rooms.

"No, that's all right," she replied, "I prefer to use the activator."

Adan nodded and said nothing more, watching as she completed the scan.

"We're going to need a lot of yeso," she said, shaking her head. "We may have to make a fresh batch."

"Where do you get supplies in these ruins? Do you have a shifter or something?"

"A shifter?" Sierra asked, scrunching up her nose so that for a moment the sorrow in her face disappeared. She actually looked a bit funny. "No, we don't have access to anything like that. We just make what we need from the powders in the rocks."

The last time Adan had heard anything about gleaning material from the rocks he was with the Welkin. He wondered if Sierra was talking about the same thing.

"So you mix them with water?" he asked, recalling the methods he had heard about.

"Yes," Sierra said. "There's a large vadi that lies just beneath the surface of Oasis. None of us knew about it before, but when the storm came through, it exposed some of it to the open air again. We found tunnels like this one that were used to tap into it. We came down here at first just for shelter, but we also found food and water."

"Wait, why do you call them 'vadis'?" Adan asked, giving her a curious look. "Where did you learn that word?"

"Oh, those are large rocks the Waymen use to gather water from. Sorry, I don't know any other word for them." Sierra said. "The Waymen taught us the word, as well as how to use them."

"You know about the Waymen?" It felt like the wind had just blown away sand from some hidden object, buried in the desert. The Waymen were here?

A hint of life glimmered in her eyes. "Of course. They're the only reason any of us are still alive."

THIRTEEN
RETHINKING

ADAN STARED AT SIERRA, HIS MOUTH GONE SLACK.

"What's wrong?" Sierra asked.

"The Waymen—they're helping you?" he finally stammered. "But...they came here to attack you, not to help."

Sierra put away her activator rod and pulled the clear plastic bottle off her belt. "Here, take some water. You need it." Placing her hand beneath his neck, she tilted his head up so that he could take a drink.

As he drank, she talked. "Some of the Waymen did attack us at first, but we met others who helped. It was hard to trust them at first, but we were desperate and hungry. They taught us how to survive."

Adan took a breath after having gulped down close to half the bottle.

"That's hard to believe," he said.

"The Waymen told us about raiding and fighting each other," Sierra said, "But I think the battle affected some of them. I don't think they were prepared for what they saw when they came here. It made them rethink things."

He handed her back the bottle with a thank you. She stared at it for a moment as if she were somehow sad that it was empty, but Adan saw her thoughts turning back to those first few days after the Wayman attack and the storm that destroyed Oasis. Like the Waymen, she was navigating a new reality as well, one where her life was no longer controlled by the Developers.

"You were happier the last time we met," Adan said. "At least you seemed to be."

"You think so?" she paused, considering his words for a moment. "I don't know. Sometimes I wish I could go back to the way things were. But then I realize that it wasn't really me, that wasn't really my life. It was more like a dream. We were happy because anything that threatened our happiness was taken away."

"How did you figure out what was going on?" he asked.

"The assessors told us. A few of them survived. I think most of them stayed with the Administrators, but some joined the Sentients. They're the other reason we've been able to survive —them and Bryce."

Adan's heart quickened at the mention of Bryce's name.

"Can I ask you something?" He looked her directly in the eye to make sure he had her attention. "What do you know about Bryce? What's he here for?"

"He came to stop the Administrators. He also told us about how they were controlling us and manipulating our memories. He knows even more than the assessors. He says no one will be safe in the Vast until the Admins are dealt with."

"I've heard words like that before," Adan said. "I wonder how he knows so much."

"He says he came from here. That they did some experiments on him," she gave a trusting shrug. "Maybe you should talk to him yourself. Most of what I've heard comes second hand from Raif and Von. I spend most of my time in the shelter, tending to the wounded and making supplies."

Adan cleared his throat. For some reason he was glad Sierra didn't know much about Bryce. "Maybe you're right. I need to talk to him."

Her face shifted, becoming suddenly thoughtful. "What's it like out there in the Vast? I've talked to some of the Waymen about it, but they have an odd way of describing things."

"It's mostly sand and scrap-filled ruins—and lots of storms," Adan said, "You never really feel safe there. It's like the desert is just waiting for the right moment to bury you beneath the sand."

Sierra sighed and reached into one of her pockets, pulling out a resin tube. Twisting off the top, she shook a little white gel onto her fingers. "This is yeso," she said. "It's made from cretan powder and umor oil."

"I'd love to see how you make it sometime," Adan said.

"Sure. I could take you to the cavern and show you how we get the powders."

A thrill of memory ran through Adan's mind as he recalled the beauty of the tunnels and caverns below the surface of the desert. The glowing neophosphorous veins and the cool feel of moisture in the air lifted his spirits just thinking about them. He wondered if Sierra's cavern would be anything like that.

Raif passed into the room, pulling Adan out of his thoughts.

"How's it going, Sierra? Miss my scintillating conversation?" Raif asked, cocking his head mischievously.

"Um, no, not really." Sierra gave him a weary look which said she wasn't in the mood for joking. "I'm going to need some more yeso, though."

Raif's face turned into a giant pout. It reminded Adan of Lila, Senya's playful daughter. "You need to get out of this hole sometime. Fresh air might do you good, lighten you up a bit," he teased. Getting nothing more than Sierra's flat stare, he gave up. "Fine. I think Zain was making some more anyway. I'll have him bring it in as soon as it's ready."

"Did you say, 'Zain'?" Adan asked, pulling himself up onto his elbows. The movement caused Sierra to place a hand on his good shoulder, cautioning him with a concerned look against rising any further.

"Yeah, why?" Raif asked.

"Is he one of the Waymen Sierra was talking about?" Adan asked anxiously. The face of the noble Wayman he'd met before the attack on Oasis rushed back to him.

"Yes." Raif's face morphed from rascally to reflective. "In fact, he's their leader."

Adan could scarcely believe what Raif was telling him. Zain was not only alive, but had somehow become the leader of his people. It didn't seem possible.

"You said he's coming here?" Adan asked.

"You know Zain?" Sierra interjected.

"Yes. I thought he died out on the ridge with the rest of the Waymen. I don't see how he survived." Despite his bioseine-dulled senses, Adan thought he had never breathed sweeter, more refreshing air.

"It's a miracle any of us are alive, I suppose," Sierra said.

"Tell me about it." Raif rolled his eyes. "I haven't eaten a thing since this morning. I've got to go score some of that gravel paste the Waymen are cooking up or they're going to have to bury me in the ruins." He patted his stomach, then, with a wave of his hand, he disappeared through the door.

"I can't believe Zain is here." Adan shook his head.

"There's a lot about life that's hard to believe," Sierra said. "Every day something unexpected seems to happen. Though it's usually the bad sort of unexpected."

Adan's mind brimmed with anticipation at the thought of seeing Zain, but looking at Sierra, his mood sobered.

"Not in a thousand years would I have ever imagined this was what life was really like." Sierra pushed her hair back over her ear and looked into Adan's eyes, as if inviting him to tell her the world was not as harsh and brutal as it seemed to be.

"A friend once told me that everything, every problem we face, only endures for a while. In the end, all things are passing. The important thing is to never give up." Adan sensed that the words did not resonate with Sierra the way they had with him.

"It's a nice thought," she said softly.

"What was it like, waking up for the first time?" Adan asked, trying to bring her out of her melancholy by some other path.

Sierra bowed her head and glanced toward the opposite doorway, the one that led outside. "I don't think I even knew I was awake at first. I couldn't see hardly anything. People were running everywhere. Some got swept off into the storm. Something must have hit me in the head. When I woke up again I remember the sky looming over me. There was a break in the storm, but it was still mostly black. I should have been terrified because the building I ran out of was gone. There was just a pile of scrap standing where it had been. But in those first few moments, all I could think of was, 'that's the real sky', because that was the first time in my life I'd ever seen it."

Adan stared at her, remembering clearly the first time he woke up in the Vast and saw the sky for himself. It was something he would never have been able to envision before that moment. He could see the same awe and fear playing through Sierra's mind as she recalled the experience.

He found it almost effortless reading her thoughts. She was more open than any other person he had ever met. For the first time he began to get a sense of what it was like to be a memorant. It was as if he couldn't help but notice what she was thinking. Though they were only surface thoughts, their meaning was as obvious as if she had spoken them out loud.

And yet, the ease with which he could decipher what she thought also made him uncomfortable. He remembered how he felt when Gavin first told him that he could read his thoughts. Adan was invading her privacy and it didn't feel right, but he wasn't sure of the right way to tell her about it, or what effect it might have if he did.

"I don't know why I woke up," Sierra continued. "Not everyone did. Bryce says we were supposed to be in something called a 'flat-line'—that we shouldn't have been able to wake up at all. But the ones who didn't wake up..." The innocence in her expression faded and her eyes dimmed. "I saw them die. So many of them. I can never forget that."

Her voice broke and whatever wall had been holding back her emotions broke as well. Her memories washed over Adan like wave after wave of buffeting winds. Tortured faces, agonizing screams, chaos in the streets. Much of it was obscured by whirling, debris-filled gusts that drowned out the death and destruction, but even so, Sierra had seen more suffering and slaughter on that day than any person ever should.

Tears coursed down her cheeks. Without thinking, Adan reached up to brush them away.

Sierra grabbed his hand and held it there for a moment. She closed her eyes and rocked back and forth.

Adan searched her face, wishing there was some way he could ease her pain. "Tell me about Zain," he said, trying to take her mind off the memories. "How did you meet him?"

She let go of his hand and wiped her tears. Though her eyes remained full of sorrow, his concern had not gone unnoticed. She breathed deeply and did her best to dry her face.

"We found each other inside one of the buildings in the Service Ring," came a familiar voice at the entrance.

Adan's eyes darted to the door. Zain passed through the opening, his face radiating with a tender smile. Sierra erased the last of her tears with her sleeve and turned to face the Wayman.

"Zain!" Adan said. Sierra's sadness had dampened his excitement, but it could not hold back the surge of joy at seeing his friend. The short man had his customary burgundy sash wound around the top of his head and dropping to the side. He also had a newly grown beard, but otherwise looked the same as when Adan had last seen him on Virid Ridge.

Adan sat up impulsively to greet him, but Sierra once more placed a hand on his shoulder to keep him down.

"Listen to your nursemaid," Zain scolded gently as he squatted beside him. He did not use the Waymen language, but spoke in the dialect used by the Collective. Most Waymen did not know how to speak it, but the Welkin seemed to, and Zain's parents had been Welkin.

"I'm so glad to see you." Adan lay back down, but he grasped Zain by the arm and squeezed, as if to make sure it was really him. "When I saw the remains of the battle on Virid Ridge, I thought perhaps you didn't make it."

"I feared the same had happened to you, my friend. Master Will told the Reeves you'd been killed. But death cannot find you if you are resting in the palm of Numinae's hand. Seeing you now, my heart is fuller than it has been for a long, long time."

Adan beamed up at him. "And now Sierra and Raif tell me that you are the leader of the Waymen? How can that be?"

Sierra regarded Zain with endearment as well. His presence seemed to have a calming effect upon her.

"Life is full of mystery. Many things seem impossible until

they come to pass," Zain said. Adan noticed for the first time that he was carrying a large bundle underneath one arm. He set it down between himself and Sierra and proceeded to unwrap it, revealing a lump of white, chalky gel. "But first the yeso. I will tell you my story while I work."

He opened Adan's garrick and pulled up his shirt. Taking a handful of the pasty white material, he smeared it over Adan's mid-section. As their conversation wore on, the yeso grew harder and harder until it formed a light-weight, but extremely stiff, protective coating. Near his skin, however, it stayed smooth and supple, as if it sat on a thin layer of gel.

"There are only a few of us left," Zain said, "but those remaining are of like mind and have chosen to defer to my counsel in important matters. Not like the old ways under the Reeves, more like warriors in need of a sunder to direct them in the storm."

"How *did* you survive the storm and the battle?"

"Providence. What else?" Zain said in warm tones. "I came down with Master Will and the rest of the Waymen who survived the attack on the ridge. We took control of the first floor of the building he said contained the leaders of Tasada. But when he went down to find them he didn't come back. We waited a long time, but were forced to leave once the storm hit and seek shelter in other parts of the city."

"You understand now, what I was trying to tell you on the ridge—that this isn't the eternal city," Adan said.

Zain nodded sagely. "Yes, I know that now. Sometimes truth must be swallowed slowly and it takes time to reach our bellies, but sooner or later, it nourishes us all the same."

"How many were left when you took the Institute?"

"No more than a thousand, perhaps," Zain said as he finished applying the yeso over Adan's ribs. "Even so, the Reeves were overjoyed. We thought we had won. But I think

less than a hundred survived the storm. I was knocked unconscious. When I awoke, the city was gone."

"I think Numinae wanted you alive," Sierra said. "We
would not have made it this far without you."

"His ways are deeper than than the deepest wells. I thought
it was the storm to end the world, but here I am." He placed a
hand on Adan's shoulder. "Are you ready for me to put it back
into place?"

Adan nodded. "It's okay, I can't feel anything," he said.

Zain raised himself up and came down hard and fast on
Adan's dislocated shoulder with his knee. The shoulder popped
back into place in one swift jerk. Once again, Adan was
grateful for his bioseine.

"Better?" Zain asked.

"Yes, thank you," Adan replied, looking up at the Wayman
in disbelief. He still found it hard to believe they had found
each other. "I am glad Numinae spared your life, my friend."

"Yes. We survived by his mercy. Every day is a gift," Zain
said, his eyes shining with a sure and steady light, "and now
that we have you, perhaps the winds will begin to shift in our
favor."

FOURTEEN

EVEN A MEMORANT CAN FORGET

Adan dropped his chin and looked away. "The last time I was in Oasis things didn't turn out all that well."

"But you're a survivor—like us," Zain countered, "and Numinae has you here for a reason."

Adan wished he could echo those words. But doubts and questions riddled his thoughts. He could barely move. It would take days to recover. And meanwhile Gavin was still at the mercy of the somatarchs and probably the Developers. They might erase his mind completely this time and he was helpless to do anything about it.

"I wish I knew what that reason was," Adan said. "I don't understand why, if Numinae gives us life, he allows so many of his creations to suffer and die. Look at what happened in Oasis. You believe he caused that storm, don't you?"

"Yes," Zain said, carefully unwrapping the makeshift splint Von had placed around Adan's ankle.

"Then what makes you think he won't just send another storm instead?" Adan knew Numinae answered his prayers, but the character of this being remained largely a mystery.

Zain paused, reflecting for a moment as he finished removing the splint. Then he scooped up another handful of yeso.

"You see this yeso here?" he said, applying the paste around Adan's ankle. "The Waymen did not invent it, neither did the Welkin. We only discovered the knowledge of its healing properties through trial and error. But who really made the yeso? The same one who gives the storms. If we will refuse one gift, we must refuse the other. Everything comes to us from the hand of our Creator."

"But why doesn't he give us only good gifts? If he created us, why would he also want to destroy us?" Adan glanced at Sierra, who was watching and listening to Zain just as intently as he was, if not more so.

Zain's face glowed with kindness. Adan sensed that his words came not merely from his mind, but from somewhere much deeper. "I understand your confusion, my friend. For it is the way of men to think of themselves as deserving of all good things. Few consider rightly the weight of their own actions. It is the nature of man to want to rule over his own life as if he were somehow self-created. I am no different in that respect. When I look inside myself, I see a man who wants to rule his own soul, but that will often mean I must put others beneath my feet to get what I want. But for the restraining hand of Numinae upon my heart, I cannot say that I would be any different than the most murderous and cruel of men."

Adan failed to see what he was getting at. Zain was entirely different from the other Waymen like Sparc and Nox. They cared nothing for the lives of others. Zain was one of the most compassionate people he had ever met.

"There is a darkness in our hearts which no one escapes," Zain continued, "We have rebelled against Numinae, and we have taken up arms against his most precious creation: each other. And by doing so, we have taken up arms against him. He alone holds back the storm inside us from breaking out and joining the tempest We have been going on like this, slaughtering each other, or teetering on the edge of the conflict, from time out of mind. The question is not, why does he not give us only good gifts, but why does he give us any good gifts at all?"

Adan still wasn't sure he understood what Zain was saying, but Sierra nodded in silent understanding. He studied her eyes, but for once could not make sense of her thoughts. The one thing he could see was that a peace had settled over her mind that wasn't there before.

How could someone like Senya or Zain have the potential to act like Sparc or the other Reeves? And even if they did, did they deserve the sort of devastation which had been wreaked upon Oasis?

"Perhaps we will talk of these things more after you have had a chance to consider them," Zain said, rising to his feet, his work apparently done, "but I am still wondering how and why you have returned, my friend. You have not yet spoken of that."

Adan folded his arms over the newly dried yeso band around his middle.

"It was Gavin," he said, his mind running back through the events of the last few days. "He is a friend of mine who was captured and taken to this place. I was searching for him when my ship was—oh no—"

"What is it?" Zain asked, his normally smooth brow creasing.

The image of the overturned sovos lying in the cluttered streets of Oasis burst into Adan's thoughts.

"The chronotrace—I left it on the ship."

It took some time for Sierra and Zain to get a clear idea of exactly what the chronotrace was. Once they did, Sierra called in Raif, Bryce, and several other Sentients while Zain put Adan's arm in a sling to help his collarbone heal.

Sentients, many of whom Adan had never seen before, soon began filtering into the narrow tunnel which served as a makeshift infirmary. There were two or three who looked like Waymen, and five or six others who were former Collectives. By the time everyone had crammed inside, there was hardly room to move without bumping into someone.

"So this device—can it really see into the past?" Raif asked, his eyes sparkling with the possibilities the chronotrace presented.

"Yes," Adan said. "I have to get it back if I'm going to find my friend."

"Incredible. But how does it work?"

"I can explain everything more clearly if we connect through our bioseines."

Raif nodded enthusiastically, but the others exchanged nervous glances, reluctant to open up their minds.

Bryce, who stood with his arms folded near the back, spoke up. "Even if this device does what you say it does, I don't think we should send anyone out just now. The storms have picked up since we brought you inside."

Von, who stood next to Bryce, cleared his throat. "I'll go," he said, his face grim as always. "If the device really does what he's claiming, it could be the break we've be looking for."

Bryce gave Von a searching look. Adan could tell the two shared a mutual respect. "I don't like it," Bryce said after a long silence. He gave Adan a dark look. "But if what you say is true, I suppose it might be worth the risk. Tell us everything you know about this device."

Raif pumped his fist enthusiastically. "All right, then. Rip us off a connection."

Adan smiled at Raif's eagerness. One by one, the minds of the Sentients opened around him.

As you wish, Adan told the others once they had joined their minds together. Sierra was the only Sentient present who did not make the connection.

Adan shared with them the details about the chronotrace and even some of Gavin's background; including how the two of them had escaped from the storm which destroyed Oasis. He stopped short of sharing about their search for the extractor and Gavin's memories. He was not yet ready to confront Bryce.

The revelation that Gavin had been a Developer had a strange effect on the Sentients. Adan could sense that it raised suspicions in some, but most seemed to regard it as a positive thing. They realized that Gavin must be one of them since he had defected and left Oasis. Though their thoughts were mixed about Gavin, when it came to the chronotrace they were of one mind. Once they realized what it was capable of, everyone agreed that it must be found. If they could retrace the past and find out where the Developers were located and what their plans were, that would change everything. Bryce, in particular, latched onto this idea. More than anyone, he wanted to put a stop to the Developers' control over Oasis. It reminded Adan of Will, and not in a good way. Adan had seen what could happen if such desires were pushed too far.

"If the chronotrace really does everything these schematics say it does," Raif said as they disconnected from Adan's mind, "then we have to find it. Having a former Admin on our side would be huge as well—ace prime level huge."

"Though I was not able to see this vision Adan showed you, I respect your thoughts in this," Zain said. "But what about the storm? Should we not wait a little longer until it dies down?"

Von regarded the Wayman respectfully, even if his tone was a bit stiff. "Normally I would agree with you, Zain, but the last scouts who came back reported an unusual amount of somatarch activity on the surface today. We can't risk them finding it first."

"I don't mind volunteering," Raif offered. "Finding the chronotrace is worth the risk. I've been out in the elements more than anybody here and my specs are probably the only chance we have of spotting the device in this weather."

Raif pulled the tinted lenses from one of his pockets, flipped each of them in the air with his thumbs, and caught them with a smirk when they came down.

Bryce moved up towards the front. "I'd rather you let someone else borrow your lentes, Raif. You're the best tech we've got."

"It'll be a quick operation," Raif said. "In and out. We already know where the ship crashed. I'm ready to go right now." He gave the exit a meaningful look.

Bryce's mouth was a thin line of disapproval, but he nodded at length. "All right. I suppose if anyone could weather the storm it would be you. And Von can go with you in case you run into trouble."

"I'll go get my gear," Von agreed, taking off at a brisk nod from Bryce.

"I'd like to go with them," Nance volunteered. Bryce gave him an uneasy look, but nodded all the same. Nance followed Von out of the tunnel.

"As for the rest of you," Bryce said, "with the increased somatarch activity, we'd better be packed and ready. I think we've worn out our welcome in this section of the city."

"I'm in the mood for a change of scenery, anyway," Raif said. "I never really liked the decor in this place."

"Decor? But the tunnels all look the same, Raif." Zain gestured towards the surrounding environs.

Raif clapped him on the back, flashing another grin. "It's a joke, Zain, a joke."

"Ah, I see." Zain nodded slowly, forcing a smile.

"We have everything but the medical supplies packed and ready," Sierra said.

"Good." Bryce turned to go.

At that moment something else occurred to Adan. "Wait. I also had a shifter on the ship. That would be very useful to have as well."

"Wow, you must have gotten hit harder than I thought," Raif said.

Adan smiled, his mood lifted by Raif's humor.

As the Sentients filed out, Adan beckoned Raif aside, remembering one more thing. "And be sure to look out for the man who was traveling with me—he's a heavy-set Wayman, with crooked teeth."

"Are you speaking of Nox?" Zain's eyes narrowed with suspicion.

"He saved my life and helped me escape from one of the thrals," Adan said. "It's a long story, but we ended up traveling together. I couldn't find him after the ship crashed, though. I don't think he survived."

"If he did survive, be extra cautious, Raif," Zain warned. "Nox is as dangerous as any hollow man."

Raif turned serious for once. "We'll be careful, Zain," he said, then he followed the others out. With his departure, all the excitement and anticipation drained from the room. Sierra and Zain stared wordlessly at the exit to the outside. A terrible time of waiting lay before them.

"What's on your mind?" Sierra asked.

Adan's thoughts returned from their wanderings. He had been staring at the door again, wondering when Von and the others would be coming back. Two long slices had already come and gone since they had left. Bryce had informed them that the rest of the Sentients could only wait one more slice before beginning the evacuation.

Zain had stayed talking with them for a while, but he eventually went off to check on the other Waymen.

"I could let you connect to my thoughts directly," Adan said, in answer to her question. During the long wait they had shared a great deal about their struggles: not knowing who they were, their doubts about what was happening in Oasis, and whether or not they would ever find a place where they belonged. Adan felt drawn to her more and more as they talked, and yet he sensed she was holding part of herself back.

Sierra winced at Adan's suggestion. "I'm sorry, but I'd rather not," she mumbled. "It's not you, though. It's just..."

She didn't have to say what she was thinking; he knew she preferred to remain blank. Even more than the rest of the Sentients, she had an aversion to anything to do with the esolace or her bioseine. That was how the Developers had controlled them, and many of them now feared using it.

"That's okay, but there's something I should probably tell you." He paused then, unsure whether or not to go on. Looking into her eyes, though, he sensed that somehow she would be able to accept what he was about to tell her. "You know how we can read each other's thoughts when we connect through the bioseine? Well, I can do that even without a bioseine. Gavin taught me how."

Sierra sat up straighter, crinkling her lips as her thoughts churned inside her.

"It's fairly limited—and it's not always accurate," he said, trying to assure her.

"You can read my thoughts right now?"

Adan nodded, searching her face to gauge her reaction. He feared that knowing he was a memorant might push her away.

Her face grew unusually tight. "I don't understand..." she began, but then her expression softened and she nodded to herself, as if resolving some puzzle inside her. "But thank you for telling me."

Adan lost the thread of her thoughts. He could no longer tell what she was thinking, but he didn't think she sounded upset.

"You know, though, I don't really think it matters," she continued. "Maybe I'm foolish for doing so, but I trust you, Adan. You don't seem like the kind of person who would use an ability like that for bad things."

"It's not that I'm really trying to do it," he said, "Sometimes it's hard not to—at least with you."

"Women have that ability too, you know," she said with a grin. "We call it intuition."

They both laughed at her remark and then laughed at the fact that they were laughing. It felt wonderful and helped evaporate the tension that had built up over the long wait.

Finally the laughter died down and Sierra rose, grabbing the empty plate of food she had brought to Adan almost a slice ago. "I should pack up these dishes," she said. "I'll be back soon." She made her way out the door.

She was gone far longer than Adan expected. When at last he heard her footsteps coming back, she was dressed in a coat that looked like it had been stitched together from old rags. A tattered scarf waved limply at her neck.

She carried the cutter under one of her arms. Reaching down, she handed it to Adan.

"Here. I believe this belongs to you."

"But I can barely walk," Adan said.

"Bryce thought you might need it. He said it's some sort of weapon." She turned to go, but paused at the door. "It's been three slices. We have to leave. We can't wait for them any longer."

Adan swallowed hard, wishing he had never remembered the chronotrace.

FIFTEEN

THE PORTAL

SIERRA FINISHED APPLYING THE SYNTH METAL SEAL around the portal. Bryce had ordered her to seal it only a few microslices ago. It was time to leave.

Adan twisted back so he could see the exit. Between his sling and the yeso cast around his ribs he could barely see it.

"What's going to happen to Raif and the others?" he asked.

"If they've been gone this long, they've probably been captured, or killed." Sierra stared at the door also, but he knew she wasn't checking her work. She was looking beyond it, the same way he was.

Zain entered the room, accompanied by two Waymen, and handed Sierra a pack. She slung it over her shoulder lethargically, as conflicted about leaving as Adan. The two Waymen with Zain had a cloth stretcher which they laid on the ground. The stretcher was little more than strips of old clothing lashed around two long metal shafts which served as handles.

"Do you need us to lift you onto the carrier?" asked one of the men. Like Zain, he also spoke in the language of the Collective.

Adan shook his head no, but instead of sliding onto the stretcher he caught Zain by the hand. "Can't we wait just a little longer? They went out there because of me. I wouldn't want to think..." Images of the three Sentients dead in the rubble seared his thoughts. When he realized his fingers were digging into Zain's sleeve he let go and sank back to the ground.

"I don't want to lose them anymore than you," Zain said, "but we've delayed the evacuation as long as we can."

Adan could see people gathering in the next section of the tunnel through the opposite doorway. They were loaded down with packs of supplies slung over their shoulders. A chromium cart hovered beside them, covered with boxes and bulging sacks.

Bryce stood at the far end of the tunnel.

"That's everything. The outer door has been sealed. It's time to go." Bryce's voice boomed down the tunnel.

Zain nodded to the two Waymen beside Adan. They knelt down and helped Adan slide onto the cart. Zain passed through the doorway and moved towards the front of the assembled Waymen in the next tunnel. Sierra fell in behind Adan as they carried him through the door.

Shuffling feet whispered sorrowfully down the hallway, sweeping away any last hope that the search party would come back in time. Sierra stared blankly ahead, looking so disconnected Adan might have taken her for an Oasis scientist if he didn't know better.

Complete silence hung over the group of twenty remaining Sentients as they made their way into yet another tunnel. Adan glanced furtively over the edge of the stretcher as they passed into a curved passage. For a brief moment he contemplated jumping off and running out into Oasis to find the missing Sentients. With the yeso covering his ankle he didn't think he could injure himself any further, but he knew it would be pointless. He had no idea where they might be by now and would just as likely end up sharing their fate.

But then a thought, one that was not his own, thrust itself into Adan's mind.

"Someone—open the latch."

It was Von; and he was just outside the entrance to the tunnels.

Adan's eyes darted up at Sierra, but her face remained impassive. *She didn't get the message,* he realized.

Glancing up ahead of him, he could see only Waymen. The former members of the Collective were too far away to have received Von's plea.

Without a second thought, Adan shoved the cutter onto his arm, flipped his legs over the edge of the stretcher, and staggered to his feet.

"I'm on my way," he answered.

The yeso on his ankle made it awkward, but he pounded down the tunnel as fast as he could. The thump, pad, thump, pad, thump, pad, sounds of his odd gait broadcast his exodus to the nearby Waymen, though most of them just kept walking.

"Wait," Sierra called out, chasing after him. "Where are you going?"

"It's Von. I've got to let him in."

Sierra caught up to him and grabbed hold of his arm. "He made it? What about Raif and Nance? Are they there too?" The Waymen carrying the stretcher stopped and stared at the two of them, but the rest passed out of sight, around the bend in the passage.

Adan checked to see if there were any other bioseines within range, but Von's was the only one.

"Von, what happened to Raif and Nance?"

"We got surprised by somatarchs," Von informed him. *"They got captured."* The sight of Raif's unconscious body

hefted onto the shoulder of a white-robed somatarch flashed through Adan's mind.

"They got captured by somatarchs," Adan relayed the information to Sierra. The color drained from her face. "Sierra, you should use your bioseine—Von needs us."

After a reluctant moment, her thoughts at last connected to his. *"Are you sure Von's alone?"*

"Does it matter?" Adan asked, picking up the pace. *"We have to let him in."*

"I'm alone as far as I know," Von's thoughts shot back into Adan's mind.

Sierra hurried after Adan. *"Von, we've sealed the entrance with synth metal to keep the somatarchs out. We can't open it anymore, even from the inside."*

Adan slowed. He had forgotten about that.

The Waymen with the stretcher came running back towards them.

"What's wrong?" one of them asked.

Adan stopped in the middle of the tunnel.

"Wait," he said, ignoring their question and holding up the cutter on his arm. "I think I know how we can get through." His words came out in a jumble as he turned and addressed the Waymen. "Go—tell the others we went to let Von in. He's just outside the tunnel entrance—bring help."

The Waymen nodded and turned back the way they came. Sierra and Adan took off running towards the exit.

"What's going on?" Von asked, desperation pulsing through his thoughts like a warning beacon. *"How are you going to get the door open?"*

"I have a cutter. Don't worry, we'll be there soon," Adan assured him.

"I hope this isn't a mistake," Sierra confided to Adan privately. *"If he was followed we could lose the whole cell."*

The possibility troubled Adan, but not enough to make him turn back.

"Von, are you sure you're alone—no one followed you?" Adan asked.

"Yes. I lost the somatarchs in the storm."

They sped down the long tunnel, soon arriving at the outer entrance. The gap around the edge of the circular hatch was covered by a wide metal strip, fusing the door to the wall in a seamless plane.

The yellow blade leapt from the end of Adan's cutter. Sierra shied away from him as he approached. She pointed at the seal. *"Try to cut the synth metal just along where there's a bit of a dip in it. That's where the gap is between the door and the wall. I have some more synth in my pack. We'll seal it back up when we're through."*

"We're almost there," Adan told Von.

He started in around the swathe of synth metal surrounding the door, but his sling made it awkward.

"Wait," Sierra grabbed his arm. *"You're cutting into the wall. You could bring down the door on top of us if you keep going like that."*

"Sorry. Why don't you cut it instead? I can't even reach the top anyway."

She gave him a dubious look, but nodded and took the tube and shoved it on her arm.

Avoiding the hinges, she sliced through the seal. The yellow blade glided perfectly around the gap. After a few moments, the seal was broken. Adan spun the wheel lock mechanism and swung the portal open.

Air rushed in around the sand covered figure of Von. His eyes shone with grateful relief.

"Thank you for coming. I've got the chronotrace." He reached inside his robes and pulled out the device. He held it out towards Adan, but Adan never got to touch it. A blur of white rushed in at that moment, slamming into Von. It carried him right between Sierra and Adan, sending him colliding with the floor.

Adan turned to see a somatarch, its darting hands latching around Von's throat, already choking the breath from him. Adan leapt on top of the creature, but the somatarch swung its arm back like a club, hitting him in the chest and knocking him to the side. Adan landed on the floor as chips of yeso went flying. He felt the cast around his ribs crack.

The somatarch resumed its grip on Von, who was dazed and barely conscious, but it kept its lifeless eyes locked on Adan, regarding him with neither malice nor care.

As Adan regained his feet, he saw Sierra swing the cutter's blade at the creature's shoulder. But the yellow blade did nothing more than rip his clothing and trace a glowing line through the air.

Adan charged the creature from the side, his sprained ankle a distant memory. The somatarch kicked his legs out from under him and he fell a second time, landing flat on his back. The yeso cracked even more.

"Red," Adan shouted to Sierra, as the somatarch smashed Von's head against the floor. He ceased to struggle. "Flip the switch to red."

"How? I don't know how it works!" Sierra screamed.

With Von no longer a threat, the somatarch leapt on top of Adan before he could get up, covering the distance with a single leap. Its hands latched onto his throat.

Unable to speak, he reached out to Sierra with his mind.

Twist right, swipe up. Twist right, swipe up. His thoughts went out desperately towards her. The somatarch slammed the side of Adan's head into the floor and sparks of light erupted across his eyes and everything went blank.

SIXTEEN
A QUICK HEALER

THE RED LIGHT OF THE CUTTER CAST A HAUNTING GLOW over the room as Adan came to.

The white-robed somatarch lay beside him, its eyes, lifeless even while it lived, now staring blankly in his direction.

Sierra stood over the fallen body, the cutter on her right arm. Beyond her, Von rose up slowly off the floor.

"Are you all right?" Sierra asked, kneeling beside Adan as the blade winked out of existence.

"What happened?" he asked, sitting up. "You killed it?"

Confusion and shock undulated across Sierra's face. "I got your message," she said, looking up and down the length of the tube. "I did what you said and turned the cutter red." She touched the shattered bits of yeso still clinging to Adan's body. "Your casts are ruined."

"I'm all right," he said.

"No, you're not. Look at you." She touched the side of his face and, as he could feel nothing, he checked his bioseine and found he was bleeding from a cut near his brow. The side of his head was also starting to swell. She took off the cutter and pulled out some almamenth from a little pouch in her jumper. After she finished rubbing some of it into his neck, she wiped the blood from his face with a rag.

Von walked gingerly towards them.

"I'm sorry I put you in danger," he said. "If I thought I had been followed, I never would have asked you to open the door."

The blows Von had received to the head looked much more serious than what Adan had suffered. His entire left ear was covered in blood.

"We're just glad you made it back." Sierra rose to examine Von and began treating him with almamenth as well.

"Adan, we couldn't find the shifter," Von said. "We looked as long as we could."

"That's okay, the chronotrace is what mattered."

Adan rose tentatively and stared out through the open door onto the dust-filled ramp leading out of the tunnel. He should have thought through what he was doing. Saving Von was the right thing to do, but he had almost gotten them killed by rushing in without getting anyone else to help.

"We'd better seal the portal back up," Adan said.

"I'll do it. Just let me finish with Von," Sierra replied.

"I can do it," Adan said. "Just give me the synth."

"Adan, you've got two cracked ribs, a broken collarbone, a sprained ankle and just came within a heartbeat of losing your life. Just rest. I'll be done in a moment." She lectured him with her eyes as well as her words.

Adan sat down against the wall. He supposed he wasn't exactly an ideal patient. He touched the yeso around his ribs and some of it crumbled in his fingers. He pushed his fingers through the gaps and felt the bone. It felt surprisingly strong.

Intrigued, he checked his bioseine to see the status of his injuries and whether or not his bones were as strong as they felt.

"Sierra," he said, as he took in the information. "I think you're a better handler than you give yourself credit for. You or Zain, one or the other."

"What are you talking about?" Sierra asked. Finishing with Von, she went over to the door. She got out the canister of synth as Adan rose to his feet—his very stable and solid feet.

"My ribs and my collarbone," Adan said. "Even the wound to my leg. They're almost completely healed. I just checked my bioseine."

Though he had no reason to doubt his bioseine, he reengaged his ability to feel pain just to be sure. All he felt was a stiffness around his neck and shoulders and some tightness across his ribs.

"That's impossible." Sierra half-frowned, as if he were making a bad joke.

"I can let you connect to my bioseine and see for yourself if you don't believe me."

"But the bioseine can't heal our bodies. Not like that anyway."

Adan itched his skin through the cracked yeso. The gel layer was drying out quickly now that it was exposed to the air. "I don't know what's going on either. My bioseine's not telling me anything."

Sierra scrutinized him, looking more concerned now than when she'd been treating his injuries.

Von stepped in. "Whatever is going on with you, we'll figure it out once we get to the new cell. Right now, we have to seal up this portal."

Adan nodded in agreement and Sierra opened the canister of synth. Together they shut the door tight. She ran the nozzle on the end of the container around the edge of the door. A shiny silver paste flowed into the gap and spread around the edges in a thin sheet, about a hand's breadth wide.

Once she finished, Von handed Adan the chronotrace. "Unfortunately, I couldn't salvage the bismine. All of the crystals were either shattered or lost."

Adan's shoulders slumped. Von had risked his life for a useless device.

"Do you have any chips we can use in your supplies?" Adan asked.

"I don't know. We can check."

"I can't believe we lost Nance and Raif..." Sierra said.

Von paused, but Adan could read in his face what he was about to say. "Our only hope of saving them now is to find Adan's friend." He stared at the sealed door, as if he were the one who was the prisoner and the door was the only thing between him and freedom.

It did not take long to arrive at the new safe haven. The new location looked almost exactly like the one they'd left, except that the tunnels were a little narrower. The Waymen and the former Collectives spread out into three branches that met in the middle, each with its own hatch connecting to more tunnels. They began to transform the area into as much a semblance of a living space as they could, unpacking their gear and lining up sleeping mats along the walls. Most had very little: a change of clothes or so for each person, a few bowls and cups made out of clay, and some pinions and shivs. A few lumins were scattered about the room as well, shedding light down the passages.

Bryce had not taken the loss of Nance and Raif well. His face settled into a scowl when Von gave him the news and his reaction shifted into a full-blown tirade when he heard how

Adan and Sierra had opened the door and let in the somatarch. He stormed off with Von following after him.

Adan withdrew into a corner of the tunnel to sulk. His time with the Sentients was not going well and he was no closer to finding Gavin or the extractor. The recovery of the chronotrace was a small victory, but without bismine to power it, it was a hollow one. Zain had gone off to look for some of the energy chips, but had yet to return.

Sierra came over to Adan, bringing a bowl of steaming mosh in her hands. He had watched her prepare it inside a metal crate on top of some white incandescent stones. Though he should have been famished, he was more interested in feeding his guilt and somber mood than his body. Not even the rich smell of it drifting through the passage could rouse his spirits.

"Want some mosh?" Sierra asked, hunkering down. When he didn't answer she waved it enticingly in front of him. "What's the matter? Don't trust my cooking?"

Adan let her plop the bowl of blue green paste in his lap, unable to bring himself to eat. He glared at the lumpy substance as if it were somehow the source of his troubles.

"I messed up back there," he said finally.

"Yeah, you did," Sierra said with a little laugh. "But you saved Von's life. That's what matters."

"No, *you* saved Von's life. I just got beaten over the head." He still felt miserable, but somehow her rare display of levity stirred him enough to realize that he was actually quite hungry. He dipped his hand into the warm paste and put some in his mouth.

"There you go," she said, looking pleased.

The warmth from the paste spread inside of him. The taste brought back memories of his time in Senya's hogar.

"Sierra, this is pretty good," he mumbled.

"Thank Zain," she said, "he's the one who taught me the recipe."

"You still have to show me where you get the ingredients."

"Right, the quarry," she said, "We actually need to go there and get some more soon. We're running low. But it can wait until tomorrow. We've had enough excitement for one day, I think."

"Do you think it's safe, now that they know about the tunnel entrance?" Adan asked, stuffing more of the delicious paste into his mouth.

"I don't know," Sierra said, her mood turning serious again.

At that moment Von came back from his meeting with Bryce. Everyone in the room turned to watch him. He ignored their looks and helped himself to his own bowl of mosh from the crate. Then, noticing Sierra and Adan, he walked over and sat down next to them.

"Aren't you going to have some?" Von asked her.

"No, I'm okay," she said. "Everything smoothed over with Bryce?"

"He'll be fine," Von said. "As long as we can get that chronotrace working and find the Developers. That's what he cares about now."

"I hope this device of yours works," Sierra told Adan in a pensive voice.

Adan stared beyond them to the others spread up and down the passage. Would Gavin really be able to help these people? He hadn't been able to stop the Developers the last time. Even the destruction of Oasis had only seemed to slow them down.

Zain entered the chamber and strode over to them.

"I found three chips," he said. "I had thought there were more, but hopefully this will do. With Numinae, little is much, as we say."

"Thank you, Zain. It's enough to at least try." Adan took the precious yellow chips from Zain. They let off a welcoming glow in his hands.

"Now, tell me about this miraculous recovery of yours," Zain said. "Sierra was trying to explain it to me, but it didn't make any sense."

"I don't know if it's a miracle or not, but somehow everything is back to normal," Adan said.

"But your wounds are less than half a day old," Zain protested, his mouth and brow pinching skeptically.

"Something like this did happen once before. A few days ago, actually. Though I wasn't this badly injured."

"Let me check you with an activator." Sierra pulled out her metal rod and ran the lights up and down his body several times, pausing on the injuries.

"He's right. Totally healed." She shook her head in disbelief.

"Are you certain?" Zain asked.

"It's like the bones were never broken," Sierra said.

She and Zain regarded him with searching looks. Adan could sense their minds struggling to find an explanation for what had happened.

"Well, I don't see what the problem is," Von chimed in. "I'd rather have him healthy than injured, wouldn't you?"

"Let's keep this between the four of us, though," Sierra said. "I don't think the others should know about it until we figure out exactly what's going on."

Zain's eyes brightened. "Numinae walks in the high winds. Far, far beyond what we can see."

Sierra and Zain pulled the last of the yeso off Adan's ribs and let it fall to the floor. They had moved to a small section of the tunnel where the supplies were kept, leaving Von to finish his mosh.

"Praise Numinae," Zain said as the white substance crumbled to the ground.

Adan nodded nervously, still uncomfortable with his accelerated rate of healing. "Well, I better get to work with the chronotrace."

"Yes, your friend," Zain said. "Let me go find a place for you to do your work uninterrupted. People might need to come here later to get supplies."

Zain disappeared around the corner, leaving Adan and Sierra to themselves.

"Zain was right," Sierra said, "there is something special about you."

Adan shifted self-consciously beneath her gaze. "I hope you're not just saying that because I'm a quick healer," he said, offering a feeble grin.

"No, no, it's more than that. You care about people—I mean Zain is like that too, but the way you do it is different."

Adan's level of discomfort only grew. He looked away and tried to compose himself, but nervous energy fluttered all through him.

"I'm sorry," Sierra said. "I didn't mean to embarrass you."

"No, it's all right. I...I appreciate what you said and I, um, I think of you in the same way—as a caring person, I mean—no, really, I mean it. Now that I think about it, I saw it even when I was in the Institute. You were the only one there who acted like I was a real person."

Now it was Sierra's turn to look embarrassed. She blushed and ran her fingers through her hair as the two of them stood in an awkward silence.

Zain's quick return broke the tension.

"I found a place for you in one of the unused tunnels. I told Von to make sure you're not disturbed."

Adan pulled out the bismine chips from inside his garrick. "Let's just pray it's enough."

"We cannot know more than we were meant to know," Zain said. "But I will pray all the same."

"I'll let you get to work." Sierra gave him a nod and took her leave. Adan watched her walk off feeling like there was something more he should have said to her, but not knowing what it was.

Zain and Adan walked in the opposite direction, heading towards a round hatch at the end of one of the tunnels. Von stood in front of it, waiting for them.

"Here we are," Zain said as they arrived at the door.

Von moved to open the latch. With a hiss, it swung open, revealing a dark tunnel beyond. Von pulled out a lumin from his robe and set it on the ground where it glowed with a soft, steady white light.

"Thank you, Von," Adan said, "this will do fine."

"I am glad we found each other once again, my friend," Zain said, placing his hand on Adan's shoulder and looking him in the eye. "I believe it was the will of Numinae. Nothing that comes to pass does so without his consent."

Adan studied his friend for a moment. He was anxious to get started with the chronotrace, but there was something on his mind he had to ask first.

"Zain, do you ever regret coming to Oasis? I mean, it's wonderful the way you're helping these people, but this is not your home. You belong out in the Vast."

Zain gave him a piercing look. "Remember what you told me on the ridge? That this place was not the eternal city told of in the legends. I did not believe you then. I had to see it for myself. I never wanted to follow the Wayman path, but it was the only way I knew. But now, with these people, I feel like I have been given a second chance at life." His eyes grew moist, but he held his tears. "My parents dreamed of this day, my friend—the day when I would be free. They never got to see it, but I intend to live free as long as Numinae wills it."

Standing in the tunnel, his garrick tattered and dusty and his hair and beard unkempt, Zain could not have looked more out of place. He was a man of the desert, a nomadic wanderer who had been brought to this city under the pretext of a lie, but Adan could see in his eyes that he belonged nowhere else other than where he stood at that moment.

"Your parents would be proud of you if they could see you today," Adan said.

Zain was silent, his eyes blinking away the tears which now came.

Von stood solemnly watching the exchange. Adan could read in his eyes the deep respect he had for the Wayman. Adan was certain he would have echoed Adan's own words if he were a different sort of person, but the look on his face said enough.

"I'll take my leave of you now, my friend." Zain straightened himself and, with a wave, he and Von turned and departed down the tunnel.

Adan sat down near the wall and placed the chronotrace at his feet. He shoved the bismine chips into the array beneath the device and closed it back up again. The black half sphere sat there, lifeless and dim, but Adan's mind could sense its presence now, waiting for his thoughts to awaken it. He reached out with his mind and the chronotrace sprung to life, lighting up the passageway with its effulgent glow, its top spinning in a burst of light. As the temporal bubble expanded around him, Adan sat and waited expectantly for the chronotrace to unravel Gavin's fate.

SEVENTEEN
MANX CORE

GAVIN SPIT THE GRAINS OF SAND OUT OF HIS MOUTH AS HE stumbled across the dune. He had landed face first in a steep bank of the coarse gray substance. His chin was mangled and he clutched his arm in pain, but he had not fallen onto any of the jagged scraps of metal littering the ground around him and that had probably saved his life.

His lentes having gone missing, he scanned the landscape around him as best he could. Only a single microslice had passed since the crash, but in that time, the forces converging on the lev seemed to have dispersed. All he could see were two walls of shifting sand as the storms made their way towards him. The one on his right was only about two hundred paces away. Inside it, a mote of white light appeared, growing larger by the moment. Something was coming his way.

Gavin did not wait to find out what it was. He turned and ran in the opposite direction. A low hum closed in on him from behind. A moment later, a white-robed somatarch came flying through the air along two beams of bright light. Gavin ran hard towards a clump of machinery buried between two dunes, but he could not outrun his pursuer. The somatarch swooped down and caught him under one arm, barely slowing as it swept up the hapless Developer and headed into the oncoming storm.

The wind rushed past in steady gusts, but the storm was soon behind them. Though at first Gavin had struggled to break free, the somatarch grabbed his throat and held it like a vice until Gavin grew still. Even if Gavin had not been injured, he was no match for the creature.

The somatarch's skates left a trail of intense light blazing along behind them. It stood out like a tear in the fabric of the dimming landscape of the Vast. They traveled like that for a day and a half, Gavin clamped on top of the somatarch's shoulders, only let down every six slices when the somatarch took a few moments to apply viand patches to the both of them.

Pitch black ruled the night, except for the glowing trail of the skimmers. They raced along, two spans off the ground, progressing relentlessly in the direction of Oasis.

When Gavin awoke on the third day, his surroundings had changed dramatically. Gone were the endless dunes and buried mounds of scrap. In their place lay the cracked and broken expanse of the Desiccant Flats. They had passed the nidor strands and were already about half way to Virid Ridge, though neither the foothills, nor the ridge itself could be seen, lost in the massive storm raging across the Vast.

The giant wall of grayish sand ahead was filled with dark, menacing shadows which swallowed the light. The storm was far worse than the one they had come from. It seemed certain they would be dashed against the rocks of the ridge if they attempted to fly through it.

The somatarch drifted towards the ground just before they

reached the edge of the storm. Re-adjusting Gavin on its shoulders, it strode forward, continuing the journey on foot.

Though they had yet to enter the thick of the storm, the sheer violence of the winds was already threatening to knock the somatarch off its feet. A normal person would have looked for shelter, some sort of protection from the vicious gusts, but the creature plodded inexorably forward, straining against the unending blasts, its body leaning so close to the ground it would have fallen over if not for the force of the wind. The air and sky grew blacker and blacker until at last the light failed completely. Still, the somatarch pressed on, gripping Gavin fiercely in defiance of the tempest.

It wasn't long before the somatarch was forced to crawl, dragging Gavin behind it by his uninjured arm. The savage winds ripped off the band holding Gavin's kaff in place. The sash unravelled in an instant, tumbling off into the void. His face now exposed, nicks and cuts opened across Gavin's bare skin. His injured arm hung uselessly at his side, unable to shield him from the blasts of sand.

Just when it seemed the storm would carry off the both of them, they came up against something large and solid which shielded them from the wind. The somatarch pressed against it and, a moment later, a crack of light opened up along the surface, widening until it was large enough to walk through. The creature drug Gavin inside and the opening snapped shut behind them.

Though the winds no longer threatened them, they continued to beat against the outside of the structure.

The room was empty except for a large black disc floating over a circular shaft in the floor. The walls looked like the ones inside the Institute, but they were nowhere near the city yet; they had not even passed beyond the Desiccant Flats.

When they arrived at the disc, the somatarch forced set

Gavin onto the platform. The creature stepped onto the pad and the disc shot down into a chute enveloped in white light.

The light flashed by in an instant and the disc jettisoned itself into another open space. Descending to the floor, it came to rest in the corner of a large square room. The room was about three times as wide and twice as high as the one they had just left. Strips of light ran around the edges along the floor, similar to the emergency lighting in the Institute and Annex.

A large, semi-transparent cube of white locus energy rested in the middle of the room. The side directly facing Gavin was open. The glowing container hovered just above a square-shaped opening in the platform. Below the cube was a line of light, made up of thousands of tiny, shimmering motes. They stretched downwards and curved away through a wide tunnel. Inside the cube stood two white-robed somatarchs and a grey-robed assessor.

The assessor motioned for Gavin to step inside. Gavin studied the man intently before passing into the cube. The gray-robed man returned his stare, the two regarding each other silently for several long moments.

"If you want to say something, you'll have to speak," Gavin said. "I'm not letting you inside my mind."

"You have no need to fear," the assessor said. His face was a mirror of Gavin's, but his expression was stiffer. "I will not tamper with your thoughts. I am only an assessor."

Gavin stared blankly at the energy wall in front of him.

The somatarch who had brought Gavin through the desert remained outside as the cube's missing wall shimmered into existence, sealing off the opening. The glowing white box plunged into the tunnel below, following the tiny thread of light.

"Where are you taking me?" Gavin asked as white lights pulsed by. The man took a moment before replying.

"To the Processing Room," was all he said.

The cube wound its way through the underground network of circular tunnels. There seemed to be an endless number of them. Though the container sped through the various branches at an alarming rate and changed direction several times, no one inside was the least bit affected by it.

Gavin closed his eyes, concentrating. At last he opened them and said, "Someone's waiting for me. Why don't you tell me who it is?"

The man blinked several times, refusing to look in Gavin's direction. "I'm sure they can tell you anything you need to know once we get there," he said. The energy cube swiveled around a corner and plunged into another shaft along the endless pulsing track of light.

The tunnel Gavin dropped through was the longest yet. Several moments went by before an opening came into view below. The cube rushed towards it and shot through, bursting out the top of an enormous cavern. Smooth walls, forty stories high, enclosed a space almost as large as Oasis. The chamber was about half again as long as it was wide. Immense tunnels opened out of it on every side.

Hundreds of glowing spheres drifted about like bubbles on a gentle breeze near the cavern roof, but Gavin's cube passed through them as if they weren't there.

Buildings covered the left half of the floor below, neatly arranged along paved streets. The right half was occupied by a large fleet of vehicles and ships of all shapes and sizes, the majority of them crafted from a dark gray synth metal. Levs floated along the streets. Half a dozen box-like cargo ships called rakers were in the process of being loaded at the docs.

Towards the far end of the cavern sat a fleet of at least forty trammers used for transporting personnel. They were long and high with paneled sides and no discernible front or back. They looked more like floating crates than ships. Near the trammers sat a sizable group of vapors. These small assault vehicles were equipped with blink thrusters making them extremely difficult to target in battle. Several rows of highly maneuverable lancers were lined up behind them: long, triangular ships with energy shields and locus pulsers. A handful of citus axomvacs sat next to these. They were long like the lancers, but incredibly narrow. They had no offensive capabilities whatsoever, but were the fastest ship yet and were used primarily for picking up and dropping off supplies or recovering downed ships with their axom field generators. Interspersed among the other ships were the wide hovland artillery ships, used for taking out enemy structures. Their gigantic wings were not used for flight. Instead, they served as a place to house a wide array of long range assault weapons. They looked ominous and impressive just sitting there; however, they were not the most daunting aspect of the fleet. Overshadowing the entire armada and docked at either end of the cavern sat a pair of praxis cruisers. With their wings retracted, their bulbous hulls looked like giant door knobs to the center of the planet. The ships bristled with oscillathe cannons and locus pulsers and dozens of antipersonnel guns. These heavy assault ships were so large they looked more like floating buildings than vehicles capable of flight.

"You've got an army down here," Gavin said. "What are the Developers planning?"

The assessor's impassive stare deepened, but he failed to reply.

The cube veered towards the arrangement of one story buildings on the left. The exteriors were all made of the same deep blue, glass-like material. Its appearance was striking, reflecting the floating cube on its polished surface as it descended across the chamber.

Most of the buildings were square, but the one in the center was rectangular and twice as long as the others. When the locus cube touched down on top of it, the roof opened and the cube passed inside.

They drifted down a short shaft before emerging into a wide open room. The locus energy walls surrounding them dissolved away once the cube touched the floor. Four somatarchs stood in front of one of the two exits. The door behind them was made of black metal, the other across the room was made of pure locus energy, like the walls of the cube. It was to this second door that the assessor walked.

The walls of the room, opaque from the outside, were semi-transparent from within. A large contingent of somatarchs walked past the building. The shadow from a large ship, most likely a raker, passed over them as they marched by.

The somatarchs beside Gavin prodded him forward as the group by the black door approached.

"These will escort you to the Processing Room," the man said. "The Assessor Primary awaits you there."

Two of the new somatarchs promptly fell in behind Gavin and herded him towards the energy door. The other two led him towards the barrier, which winked out of existence as they approached and flashed back once they passed through.

The corridor beyond was a long one, but eventually came to an end at a thick metal door. The door slid away, revealing a small room with no visible exits beyond a large circular opening in the floor with a black disc hovering over it. The disc was large enough to hold five or six people. A small group of figures stood beside it.

Two of them were somatarchs, but the third was a man

wearing the gray robes of an assessor. The only difference was that his vestments were tinged with black around the shoulders and the hem. He wore a zoelith strapped to his belt. Dark hair and a beard neatly framed his face. His brooding eyes studied Gavin from beneath a prominent brow. He looked nothing like the rest of the Collective, and yet the ease with which he stood in the presence of the somatarchs clearly showed he belonged there.

The strangest thing about him, though, was the faint shimmer which surrounded his body. It was hard to see, only flashing into view from time to time, as if it were some sort of mirage.

"Welcome back, Gavin," he said, striding forward and grasping Gavin's hand. His voice was deep and rough.

Gavin stiffened, as if to match the posture of the regimented man before him. "Malthus, I'm glad you survived the storm."

"Are you really?"

"Of course. But what's going on with this underground base? The Collective's construction abilities are impressive, but surely you didn't just create this in the few days since the storm."

"It's called Manx Core," Malthus said. "It, as well at the Collective, is strictly a military operation now. No more research unless it has combat applications. The building you are standing in is our Command Center. Would you like a short tour?" He motioned for Gavin to step onto the hovering disc. The pointed look he gave showed that his question was not really meant to be an actual one.

Gavin stepped onto the disc.

Malthus and two of the somatarchs joined him. The disc plummeted through the hole. They sped past three floors until it halted at the bottom of the shaft. A door opened and a long metal walkway stretched before them, suspended above a large room.

As they stepped off the disc, Malthus gestured towards Gavin's injured arm.

"We'll get that taken care of. Don't worry."

"Thank you. But what about the other Developers? What about the Collective? How many died in the storm?" Gavin asked as they stepped out onto the walkway.

"Eighty-nine percent casualty rate. Only a few in the smaller buildings survived." Malthus spat out the information mechanically.

Gavin stopped a few steps onto the walkway. A deep sadness softened his eyes. His lips moved, but no words came out.

Malthus shot him a stern look. "Listen, Gavin, this was Darius' project. Now that he's gone, we've repurposed our time and resources into other areas. What happened in the storm is in the past."

"You say 'we'...How many of the Developers are left?"

Malthus started walking again. The somatarchs nudged Gavin to follow.

"Cyrith, Xander, and I are the only ones who survived."

Gavin faltered, but he kept walking. "I had thought more— I suppose I shouldn't be surprised but, still, I had hoped..."

Malthus cleared his throat. "We can rebuild the city another day. For now, we have other things to worry about."

Malthus, two paces in the lead, marched briskly across the walkway. There did not appear to be any means of reaching the cavern below, but the room could easily be seen, even though it was poorly-lit by what looked to be auxiliary lighting. Hundreds of clear rectangular containers stood stacked in metal racks, five high. Inside each of them rested a human body dressed in white robes.

"Vacants," Gavin said. "This is ten times the number we had in Oasis."

"That's right." Malthus' deep voice resonated throughout the chamber. "Darius planned for every eventuality. Within a few days, we will initialize this force and move up to establish ourselves on the surface once again."

"But you can't possibly need this many. The people of the Vast are no threat to you."

The strange shimmers around Malthus made his expression hard to read at that moment. "Darius hoped that if we kept our presence on this planet a secret, our enemies would not be able to find us. But with Oasis gone we can no longer hide. Now our survival depends upon fighting. There is a war coming, Gavin."

"A war against whom?" Gavin asked, his voice strained.

"The coming conflict does not concern you. Besides, I did not bring you here to ask you to fight." Malthus placed his hands calmly behind his back. "I have something else in mind for you. There is a project of yours which I am interested in."

"A project? Which one?"

"The chronotrace." Malthus licked his lips, as if he had been waiting to say that word for a very long time.

"The chronotrace? What could possibly interest you about that?"

"You are not the only defector we've had from Oasis." Malthus stopped abruptly in front of the door on the far side, the click of his boots echoing in the large chamber. The shadow of his brow had never been deeper. He stood perfectly still for several long moments, his back to Gavin, a chiseled man of stone.

Gavin broke the silence. "You want to use the chronotrace to find someone who escaped?"

Malthus turned, scattering the shadows on his face. "No,

we know where he is. He's building a city out in the desert. The renegade's name is Nolan."

"If you know where he is, then what do you need the chronotrace for?"

"I need it to recover his memories. You see, he erased them, not only from the Repository, but from his own mind as well. So capturing him would do no good."

Gavin positioned himself to the side of Malthus, but the man refused to look at him. "What? Why would he erase his own memories?"

Malthus' facade cracked. His gaze shifted so that he stared back out across the endless rows of vacants.

"I don't know. But it doesn't matter. His memories are what I need." Malthus' words marched from his mouth one by one, a resolute force marshaled against Gavin's questions.

Malthus turned back to the door impatiently. After a brief pause it opened and he moved briskly into the hallway beyond.

Gavin rushed after him. "I'm sorry, but that makes no sense."

Malthus failed to acknowledge his words. His boots beat down the hallway in swift rhythm. They soon arrived at a door made from polished, silvery metal. After another short delay, the door opened and they passed through.

The somatarchs fanned out to either side. The large room was filled with cabinets and equipment. All the cabinets had transparent doors, Inside some could be seen hundreds of vials of remin fluid. In others, large capacity memory arrays were visible. These metal cubes about the size of a man's head could each store enough memories to fill the lifetimes of hundreds of people. In the center of the room, dominating everything, stood a massive cylinder of smooth black stone with bluish veins running through it. It was twice as tall as Malthus and three times as thick.

"You had another Repository," Gavin said in low tones, his expression one of awe. He wandered towards the memory arrays as if he meant to pull one out and begin accessing its information at that moment.

"What better place to recover someone's memories." Malthus spread his arms wide. "Welcome to your new home."

"What do you mean?" Gavin asked guardedly, stopping where he stood.

"I need the memories back," Malthus said. "And I believe that the chronotrace is the only means to achieve that."

"But the chronotrace isn't capable of reading thoughts. Even if it was, the power required would be impossible to achieve."

Malthus spun back around and faced his captive, his eyes burning with a singular purpose.

"I've studied your logs. I know it was still a work in progress when you left, but I believe in you, Gavin. You weren't given the time and the resources before to develop it fully. This time I'll give you whatever you need to see that the technology is perfected."

Malthus' tone seemed almost friendly, but Gavin regarded him suspiciously.

"I'm flattered you think I could actually realize the full potential of the chronotrace," he said, "But given that you've brought me here against my will and haven't told me why you need this information so badly, you'll understand if I'm less than inclined to help."

Malthus' mask of cordiality vanished. "Let me see if I can make you understand, then. The only reason you're alive at this moment is because I have need of you. And if you do not do what I ask—"

"Then what? You'll kill me?" Gavin cut him off, matching Malthus' harsh tone. "Then stop wasting your time and get it over with. Because I will never help you destroy the people of the Vast. Wasn't it enough that we hunted them down and killed them in secret? Now you're going to slaughter them out in the open?"

"Ha!" Malthus sneered, making his bristly beard look like a wrinkled rug. "This isn't about the andros. If that was what we wanted, we could have destroyed them long ago. That's not who we're getting ready to fight." Malthus shook his head, pacing in front of Gavin. "I already told you: the chronotrace has nothing to do with the coming conflict. This project is personal. No one else even knows about it."

Gavin glared at him and appeared about to speak, but Malthus raised his hand, signaling he had more to say.

"But if you care so little for your life, then perhaps I can help make this a personal matter for you as well." Malthus fixed Gavin with a penetrating glare. He regimented his words again, speaking slowly and deliberately. "If you refuse to help me, or if you cannot get the device to do what I ask, then I will target the andros. I could wipe them off the face of this planet in a ten span if I chose to."

The anger and bravado drained from Gavin. "What exactly is it that you want me to do?" His voice came out suddenly quiet and weak.

"I need the chronotrace to bring back the memories from before they were erased—two years ago."

"Two years? But I told you—" Gavin began before stopping to regain his composure. "Not all the bismine in the Vast would be enough to go back that far, especially if you want to utilize the thought mapping algorithms."

"But we have celerium—a great deal of it as a matter of fact." Malthus gestured towards the large pillar of stone. "And I can get you more if you need it."

Gavin walked up to the monolith and ran his hand along

the surface. "This can't be celerium. And a sample of this size? Surely you're mistaken."

"Why do you think Manx Core was built?" Malthus said. "This wasn't always a military operation."

"How long has this place been here, then?"

"That's irrelevant. All I care about is getting back those memories."

Gavin's eyes flitted about the room, taking in the somatarchs, the celerium, the storage cabinets. "And what is this information that you're looking for? What did this memorant erase that's so important?"

Malthus paused a moment, clenching and unclenching his jaw. Whatever was passing through his mind, he seemed to be taking great pains not to let himself get worked up about it. He took in a deep breath, and for the first time since their conversation began, a hint of sadness washed over his face. "I want you to recover the memories of my son."

"Your son?" Gavin blurted out. "Generic heredity was never used in the Collective. How could you possibly..." his voice trailed off, as if he were struggling to recall something that wouldn't quite come to him.

"There is much that you know nothing about—nor do you need to," Malthus said, quickly mastering himself again. "You need to run a trace back to the time before his memories were erased and copy them into one of these arrays. If you do that, I'll set you free. No one will ever even know you were here."

Gavin turned back to the celerium pillar, a frail figure against its immense solidity. "Assuming you actually had a son, I can understand why you would want to get his memories back, but what happened Malthus? How did someone else ever get his memories in the first place?"

Malthus passed a hand over his face, but the gesture failed to mask the pain plainly visible there. "My son died years ago.

Darius helped me bring him back by implanting them into the mind of this fool Nolan. It seemed to work at first, but something went wrong. He rejected my son's memories and erased everything. It was like he murdered Dane all over again." Malthus stared longingly at the memory arrays surrounding him, a wealth of information, but worthless to him because it lacked the one thing he needed most.

He continued to speak, but his voice lost its air of command. "Those memories were all I had left of him. And you're the only one who can help me bring him back. I need those memories, Gavin. I need you to help me resurrect my son."

EIGHTEEN
FALLOUT

THE TRACE ENDED ABRUPTLY. ADAN SHUT IT OFF BEFORE the bismine chips dropped below rechargeable levels. The last image he saw was that of Gavin staring at Malthus, a stunned look on his face. Adan could not get the image out of his mind. Nor could he stop thinking about where Gavin had been taken —the Repository. It existed after all. If he found Gavin, he would find his memories as well.

"Your friend is in a tight spot," said a voice from behind, startling him. He whipped around to see Bryce leaning against the opposite wall.

"How long have you been there?" Adan asked, unnerved by his presence.

Bryce shrugged casually. "Long enough to realize that you'll probably never see your friend alive again."

"What do you mean? Malthus said he'd let him go if he did what he asked." Adan was stung by Bryce's frankness, though inside he had been thinking the same thing. There was no assurance Malthus would keep his promise.

"The entire place is a military facility," Bryce said. "It's probably more secure than Oasis ever was. Malthus would never let someone out who knew about it."

"I don't care. I'm going there anyway."

Bryce shook his head. "They said you were naive."

Adan rose, forgetting Gavin and the chronotrace all of a sudden. "Who? Who said I was naive?" Bryce returned the question with a condescending look. "What do you know about me?" Still he gave no response. Frustrated, Adan flung out one last question. "Why are you even here?"

"Why are *you* here?" Bryce retorted.

"I'm trying to save my friend," Adan said, lowering his tone. So far this conversation wasn't going at all the way he had hoped.

"And I'm trying to save everyone else." Bryce's voice rose defiantly. "Don't you even care what they're going to do with that army down there?"

In that moment, Adan thought he caught a glimpse of Bryce's thoughts, though he hadn't been trying to. If what he saw was accurate, Bryce was telling the truth, at least partly. He did intend to save the Collective, but Adan wasn't sure what that meant. Save them so he could manipulate them like the Developers or something else? There was a brash pride to his intentions that hinted his motives were not altogether pure.

"Saving lives is a good thing," Adan said, choosing his words carefully. "But how do you plan on doing it? Do you really think you can stop the Developers when the storm couldn't?"

Bryce snorted in disgust. "You'll see soon enough." He turned to go, but Adan called after him.

"Wait—Bryce—what about the extractor? I know you took it from the compound in the Vast. What did you do with it?" It occurred to Adan that if the Repository still existed the extractor might not be needed, but there was no telling whether

Gavin's memories were actually there, or if they were that they would be able to recover them.

Bryce half turned and glanced back. He did not look in the least surprised by Adan's question. "I don't have it any more."

"But you know where it is."

It was a desperate effort and Adan knew the moment the words left his mouth he wasn't going to get an answer.

"I don't have to tell you anything. There's a lot you don't know, Adan. I'd have thought you'd be getting used to that by now."

Adan let out a frustrated sigh. He might have missed the one chance he would get to find out about the extractor. He had been too blunt, too direct.

"I don't know who sent you here or why." Adan paused, fumbling for the words to hold Bryce there a little longer, "But I —I think we should work together. If you saw the trace, you saw where Gavin was. He was in the Repository. That's where they keep all the memories. Maybe your memories are there too."

Turning his back on Adan again, Bryce passed through the door. "I don't care about the past," he said, not bothering to turn around. "All that matters is right now. And I'm going to finish what the storm started—whether you help or not. Just don't get in my way."

Adan was left alone in the empty tunnel, staring at the chronotrace and wondering what exactly Bryce had planned.

Zain clamped his jaw shut, his eyes aflame. Adan had never seen him this angry before. Though Zain was still able to restrain himself enough not to interrupt the others, when he spoke his words tumbled out in such a torrent his mouth never seemed to close.

"You yourself said there must have been thousands of the hollow men in that chamber, and that was days ago." He directed his words to Bryce, though the entire cell was present. "Think of it, thousands of them and we can barely defeat one or two. This is foolishness. I cannot believe we are even entertaining such a plan. It would be a leap into sinking sand."

Bryce stiffened. "You are a healer, Zain—a very good one, but a healer. Leave the tactics to Von and me." The discussion had been going back and forth in the hub between the tunnels for half a slice. Though Bryce had maintained his composure up to that point, he was close to losing his patience with the Wayman.

"I've seen too many of my brethren run screaming into battle not to know a fool's quest when I see one," Zain said. "I will not stand idly by and watch while my friends jump into a pit. We've lost enough already."

Bryce threw up his hands. "Then what is your plan, desert man? Sit here in these tunnels until they drag us off one by one? Or would you rather just wait until the storm finishes us off for good?"

"The storm will pass," Zain said, but his voice lacked conviction.

"Zain, Bryce is right," Von put in. "We can't sit here and do nothing. I don't like the thought of going into that base any more than you do, but what Adan saw is what we've been waiting for. We know where the Administrators are—and the missing Sentients have to be there too. We can't just abandon them; we have to try to save them."

"If they haven't had their minds wiped already," someone muttered from the back of the tunnel.

The comment was like the first shot fired in a battle. Angry eyes flashed around the room searching for who had said it, and then everyone fired off at once. The room erupted into a broiling argument, with most of the Waymen taking Zain's side and most of the former Collectives voicing support for Bryce. It went on like that, back and forth for some time. Voices rose, harsh words flew from both sides, and grudges that had gone unspoken scurried out from underneath the resentful rocks they had been hiding under.

Just when Adan feared the two sides might come to blows, out of nowhere the floor of the tunnel shook and the ceiling began to tilt.

The chaos of a moment before was nothing compared to what ensued. Everyone started moving at the same time, and in different directions. Adan, who was still trying to figure out what was going on, got jostled in half a dozen directions before he stumbled into a wall. For a moment he thought he was inside another storm, like the one that ripped apart the Institute. But they were underground. No wind was powerful enough to rip apart the stones of the tunnel.

Whatever was causing it, it didn't stop. The ground writhed beneath their feet. Cracks opened up over their heads. Snapping sounds ripped through the air, sending waves of fear through Adan. Then, like a burst of light in the darkness, Sierra was at his side.

She grabbed his hand and yelled in his ear above the thunderous shaking, "We've got to get out of here!"

Her words shocked him awake. They began to run. Others ran beside them and past them in every direction, faceless figures rushing to safety. But there was nowhere safe to go. Showers of small rocks and dirt cascaded down around them, making it impossible to see much of anything.

They stumbled their way along a buckling wall. Adan prayed it would not collapse on them.

Just where he was about to step, the ground split apart. A shockwave sent both of them reeling backwards. Adan lost hold of Sierra's hand. A deluge of dust washed over him, blinding him so that he lost sight of her as he fell to the ground.

"Sierra!" he called out, choking on the powdery assault. She didn't answer. The only thing he could see was the yawning crack in the floor in front of him. As he watched, it shuddered and grew wider.

His arm shot out to steady himself, but instead of hitting the floor, his hand landed on top of something much softer— someone's foot. He scrambled to try and grab more of the person's leg. Rocks were falling along with the dust. One about the size of his fist grazed his shoulder, narrowly missing his head. Wincing from the blow, and wiping the dust from his eyes, he looked beneath him and finally made out the outline of Sierra's body, covered in dust and debris.

"Sierra!" he cried, pulling at her arms. As he propped her up she came to her senses, looking wildly about the tunnel. "Come on!"

He got her to her feet as the tunnel rippled again beneath them. The crack in the floor loomed ahead. Adan thought about running back the way they had come when two Waymen rushed past and flung themselves across the gap, disappearing into the haze beyond. He couldn't see where they had landed. He and Sierra exchanged a quick glance which told him they had to try the jump.

They sprinted the few steps to the edge and launched themselves into the dust cloud. Adan's arms flailed in the choking air. It seemed like he was suspended in time, waiting to come down. At last something hard slammed into his legs and he rolled into a painful heap.

He tried to gain his feet, but something pegged him in the shoulder blade and he fell down. He struggled again to rise, but pain sapped his strength. He collapsed back down onto the floor.

From out of the dust a pair of hands reached out to grab him. With a quick jerk, he was back on his feet.

Staring into the haze, he thought he saw the outline of a Wayman. It was hard to make out since everything was coated in so much dust, but Zain's eyes flashed at him through the chalky air.

"Thank you," Adan cried. Zain said nothing, only pulled him further into the smothering veil.

"Wait!" Adan cried, pulling on Zain's arm. "Sierra! Where's Sierra?" Rumbling and crashing rocks smothered the sound of his voice.

Zain didn't stop. Nor did he let go. He dragged Adan along in a teetering, reeling run. It was like falling forward, but never hitting the ground. The only constant amidst the madness was the back of Zain's dust-caked garrick. Adan kept focused on that until his lungs nearly burst with dust and lack of air. It wasn't until then that he realized that the tunnel had stopped shaking some time ago. The dust settled and he slowed to catch his breath, noticing for the first time that half a dozen other Sentients had been running along with him. At the sight of Sierra among them, a wave of relief washed over him.

The ache in his chest faded and Zain spoke into the silence. "We're safe now."

Adan said nothing, still not sure whether or not to believe the quake had ended. But as his breathing steadied and the ground remained still, he finally came to accept the fact that the tremors which had rocked the tunnel were over.

NINETEEN

THE QUARRY

The survivors of the quake gathered in the dim confines of an abandoned building somewhere in what had once been Axis Prime, the central district of Oasis. Six Sentients had died in the terrible quake inside the tunnels, two Waymen and four of the former Collectives. Only fifteen people were left, including Adan.

Adan's shoulder and back were bruised from the many blows he'd received, but he had come out relatively unscathed compared to others. Many had suffered multiple cuts and sported ugly, multi-colored bruises. One of the Sentients, a man named Trey, was still unconscious and was only alive because two Waymen had carried him out of the tunnels.

No one spoke, though several sobbed quietly, huddled in the hollows between piles of the scrap. Their dust covered faces were devoid of color. Fear had followed them up from below and hung over them now like a cloud.

Like Adan, Sierra had suffered only a few bruises and nicks. She moved mechanically, occupying herself with tending to the wounded, and perhaps for that reason had not broken down.

In the midst of this hopelessness, with the winds still howling in the streets outside the building, Bryce called for everyone's attention. Of all those gathered, the shock and pain registered least on his steely face.

"The tunnels are no longer safe. We've felt tremors before, but nothing like this one. We have to try and find our way into Manx Core. It's our only choice. And we have to go together." His words were stark, made even more so by the bloody gash running the length of his face.

The winds screeched through the ruins in reply, the only answer he received for some time. No one stirred, though a few of those who were sobbing did look up.

Then Zain, who had been helping Sierra wrap the arm of one of the Sentients, rose to his feet.

"How will we get there? Did you not say that it is deep underground?" His face looked weary, doubly so for the dust still clinging to his skin and beard, but his tone was resigned. He would oppose Bryce's plan no longer.

"The quarry is the deepest place we have access to and it's open enough that a quake there wouldn't be nearly as dangerous," Von said. "I suppose we could try and dig in the direction we need to go and hope we hit an access tunnel."

"All of our tools are still down in our sar," said one of the Waymen, a tall man named Wik, formerly of thral Din. "And even with our tools, we might dig for years and never find anything."

"What about the cutter?" Sierra asked, moving to stand beside Zain. Her words were met with raised eyebrows and puzzled looks from the Waymen. "It's a device that Adan brought with him. It can cut through solid rock."

"And you have this device with you?" Zain asked, turning to Adan.

"No," Adan said, "It's still down in the tunnels with the other supplies."

"Then we have to go back for it," Bryce said. "Everything depends now on how much we can salvage from the tunnels. Those of us who are in the best condition will head back down and bring back whatever we can carry. Our priority will be tools and food first, then weapons. Everything else can be left behind."

Zain nodded. "It is a good plan. But I worry whether or not it is safe to go back underground."

Bryce wiped a fresh trickle of blood from the wound on his face. "We have no other choice but to risk it," he said. No one said anything in reply. It was obvious there was nothing more to say.

Thankfully, they did recover the cutter. They also found the chronotrace, which certainly warmed Adan's spirits. They managed to salvage a handful of other supplies as well: some lumins, an energy disruption sphere, a sack of kern, one of Raif's variance modulators, and two of his makeshift zoeliths. They might have gotten more if they'd spent a few days digging, but Bryce said that would be enough for now.

Not everyone was able to go on the mission to Manx Core. Those still recovering from their injuries and two Waymen healers would stay behind.

Adan and the others made their way towards the quarry, lighting their way with a pair of lumins, one with Zain at the front and one with Wik at the back. They used the variance modulator to scan for somatarchs and traveled through the more intact buildings as often as they could. It took them almost half a slice to arrive at the entrance to the quarry.

Adan had hoped it would be as impressive as the Basin, but the quarry was nothing more than a hollowed out section of exposed bedrock amidst the smashed-in lower floors of the Institute. Errant beams jutted out of massive jumbles of stone. Shattered equipment littered what was left of the flooring. The once carefully ordered layout of floors and rooms now looked more like the inside of Will's scrap barrels than any place ever inhabited by humans.

The climb down through the twisted girders and battered infrastructure involved a great deal of ducking, crawling, and squeezing through difficult spots. They utilized a series of rope ladders which had been tied in place to drop into places too dangerous to jump to. The trip would have been impossible if Adan had been on his own, but the Waymen showed him where it was safe to step and helped him navigate the treacherous patches.

Once they reached the quarry, all signs of the Institute disappeared. It was a cavern of bare rock, roughly eighty paces in diameter and about two body-lengths in height. Adan had never seen how the Waymen and Welkin harvested their powders from the rock, but he got an idea by looking at the various striations along the walls. The rocks ran horizontally in layers of muted shades of purple, green, yellow, and white. These colored rocks were pocked with channels and holes where the Sentients had extracted samples.

After setting down their weapons and gear, Bryce divided the party into two groups. Adan was paired with Zain, Wik, and Bryce while Von and Sierra went with Yor and Ket, the other two Waymen. Each group was to take a turn using the cutter to delve into the rock. Based on the information from the chronotrace, the Core was located down and to the west, running beneath the Desiccant Flats.

One person from each group would do the cutting while the other three would clear out rubble. Adan was given the task of carving out the tunnel for his group since the cutter belonged to him. His group took the first rotation.

He passed by the colored veins and headed towards a smooth, dark section of rock at the back of the cavern. The bright slice of yellow light from the cutter pierced the darkness, giving rise to scattered murmurs from the Waymen.

Adan made a large, sweeping circle at the base of the wall. A few flakes of rock fell to the ground, but nothing substantial. After the deliberateness of his first cut, he decided to try a more vigorous approach. He slashed two times, crisscrossing his cuts. When nothing more came out, he started slicing more wildly, alternating the angle of his cuts with no real pattern. It felt more like he was weaving a brilliant tapestry of light than tearing up the wall. Chips of rock went flying, but little else. Finally, a small, fist-sized chunk tumbled to the floor. It looked like a ball of hardened, gray mosh, but at least it was something.

Soon the rocks began to fall more frequently. Whenever they did, Adan's crew moved in swiftly to pull out the rubble. The dark wall surrendered itself slowly to his incandescent assault.

Carving out the tunnel was draining work. Adan swung the metal tube on his arm over and over again. The tube grew so heavy at times he thought he might topple over. Though he had taken off his garrick before starting, the air in the tunnel was stifling. His shirt dripped with sweat.

As hard as the work was, and as tired as he was getting, his other aches and pains from the quake slowly dissipated. The bruises on his shoulder and back, which had still been sore when he started, felt perfectly fine by the time he stopped.

He'd not even received any almamenth and yet his strange healing ability continued.

Sierra was chosen by Von and the others to wield the cutter for the second group. The tunnel was twenty paces long by the time she started and far enough down that only their heads and shoulders were visible when they stood at the far end.

As Adan sat with the others, Zain took out a piece of kern and began to chew. He looked at Wik and asked in the Wayman tongue, "What do you think? Are we baiting the storm down here? This whole place could fall down on our heads."

Wik eyed the tunnel warily. "The legends say that when the ground trembles, it is because the world is sick, but it is hard to say. I'm not sure I believe the legends anymore."

"May Numinae protect us all," Zain said. He closed his eyes and Adan could tell he was praying.

Adan thought about uttering a prayer himself, but found he could not. The power he had felt in the tunnels seemed so unstoppable, he wondered what good praying for protection would be, especially if it was Numinae who had caused it?

Adan waited until Zain finished praying and caught his eye.

"I've been thinking about what you said," Adan began tentatively, "about Numinae, and how we need to accept what happens to us as his will."

Zain regarded him with an expectant look.

Adan continued, "But if that's so, then why bother to pray? If we're meant to simply accept things, what is the point of asking for help?" Adan felt brash for even asking the question, but he thought Zain would understand.

"A valid question," Zain said, nodding. He finished off his bite of kern. "I do not believe you have spent very much time around children, but if you get the chance it might help answer your question."

"You're saying that children understand prayer better than adults?"

"That may be, but that is not what I meant. I was thinking of the way they act around their parents. You see, children have no reservation when it comes to asking them for advice or seeking their attention or help. They simply let their wants be made known, and sometimes in rather unpleasant ways. If they are tired or hungry or cold they will find a way to communicate this. And often they will receive help, because it is the duty of parents to care and provide for their children. More than their duty, fathers and mothers love them dearly and want the best for them. But sometimes the best thing for children is telling them no. Because often what they want is not good, and a good parent, a perfect parent, knows what is in a child's best interests. Do you see the parallel?"

"That Numinae is like the parent and we are like his children. But the children don't change their parent's mind do they? At least not if the parent is trying to do the right thing like you said."

"Correct. And deep down children know this, but they cannot help themselves. It is in their nature to ask."

"So they ask just because it's natural?"

Zain picked another piece of kern out of his pouch, but kept it in his hand, gesturing with it as he spoke. "There is more to it than that. They ask in order to find out what is good and what is not. They ask because even more than love, they need the truth. They ask to discover the will of their father, to see if their heart's cry finds an echo in his."

Adan's heart felt strangely warmed at these words. He looked into Zain's sparkling brown eyes and at last he thought he understood.

As Adan finished praying, peace spread through him like the sensation he got when drinking a piping hot cup of atol.

He got up from where he'd been sitting to stretch his legs and noticed Bryce standing off by himself. Adan wasn't sure how long he'd been praying, but Sierra and the others had gone far enough into the rock that all he could see now was the glow from the cutter reflecting off the walls.

He wandered over towards Bryce. "It looks like they're making good progress."

"We still have a long way to go," Bryce said, not bothering to take his eyes off the tunnel.

"I worry about them in there. What if something happens?" Memories of the quake played afresh in his mind.

"The tunnel is short. They'll be able to get out quickly if anything happens. Besides, the further down you go, the safer it is. Most of the tremors happen near the surface." A curious look came over Bryce, as if he had just now realized that Adan was standing next to him. "You and Sierra have become friends, haven't you? Maybe more than friends?"

"What are you talking about?" Adan's thoughts scattered. He had no idea what Bryce was getting at.

"She told me that you and she had met before, when you were in the Institute," Bryce said enigmatically.

Adan focused in on him, trying to gauge what he was thinking, but as far as he could tell, Bryce was merely making idle conversation.

"And what does that have to do with anything?" Adan asked at last.

"I'm just trying to gauge your state of mind going into this," Bryce said. "You may not be a warrior, but you know more about the Devs than any of the others. I don't want you losing sight of our mission down there because your emotions get in the way."

Adan still wasn't sure exactly what Bryce was driving at, but there was something about the tone of the conversation he didn't like.

"You don't have to worry about me. I'll do whatever I can to make sure we all get out of this alive," Adan said. "Gavin is down there, remember?"

"Our first priority needs to be stopping the Developers. If we don't do that, we'll all just end up getting captured or killed."

"I can tell you don't trust me," Adan said. He wasn't sure if he should be sharing the impressions he was getting from Bryce, but if Bryce was going to question Adan's commitment to their cause he might as well be up front with him. "I don't have much reason to trust you either. You stole Gavin's extractor. You won't tell me who you are or why you're here. Yet you still expect me to listen to you."

A dark expression flickered across Bryce's face. "If you really care about these people you'll do what I say. I'm ready to give my life for them—unlike some." The pointed stare he gave Adan convinced him Bryce knew about Will and the virus.

"What did Nolan tell you about me?"

Bryce's eyes twitched in surprise at the mention of the Reeve's name. "You've been to see Nolan?" A knowing look crept into his eyes. "That explains things, then."

"Explains what? What are you talking about?"

"That he wants you alive, which I didn't expect. But then again, that man is full of surprises." Bryce gave Adan a thin smile, like a crack in an otherwise smooth stone.

"What is his plan? Why did he send you here?" Adan blurted out, grasping for any information Bryce might give him.

Bryce started walking towards the tunnel. "I think it's finally time we gave them a rest."

"You're not going to tell me what your plan is, are you?" Adan hurried after him, but Bryce stared straight ahead and continued walking.

He's just like Will, Adan thought. Nolan sent them both for the same reason: to destroy Oasis. But this time it wouldn't be a virus. It would be something else, though Adan had no idea what that might be.

The two teams alternated back and forth for more than seven slices, twice shifting the direction of the tunnel based on Bryce's suggestions. Adan's group had only been resting for a few microslices after their most recent stint when Sierra shouted something from down the tunnel.

Bryce shot to his feet and rushed to the opening. "What's going on?"

"I think I found something," Sierra yelled. "It may be just a natural cavern—I'm not sure yet—but it's definitely an open space."

Adan and his team, hurried down the tunnel, joining Sierra, Von, and the two Waymen around a small black opening in the floor. It looked just big enough for a single person to fit through.

Bryce asked for a lumin and shined the light down into the hole.

"It's a man-made tunnel," he said, beckoning Von to take a look. "See the smoothness of the floor. That's not natural stone."

Several smiles flashed in the darkness. A rush of renewed energy pulsed through Adan's tired limbs. Bryce patted Sierra on the back. "Good work. Now let's go get the supplies and jump down."

Tired as they were, the Sentients practically ran down the tunnel to collect their things. The quarry bustled with activity and excited conversation as everyone gathered their equipment.

Despite the grime on her face and the sweat matting down her hair, Sierra's eyes seemed to sparkle brighter than anyone else's. It struck Adan as he watched her finish packing that she had never looked more beautiful. He tried to push the thought out of his mind because it made him uncomfortable for some reason, but he found that for all he tried he could not deny what he saw.

"Aren't you excited?" Sierra asked, walking up to him as everyone gathered near the entrance to the tunnel. Adan stared blankly at her, unable to speak. "Well, I am—and nervous. I can't remember when I've felt this restless—or this hungry. Could I have a strip of your kern?" she asked.

"Oh, yes—sure," Adan sputtered, shoving his hand inside his garrick and rummaging around for where he'd put the kern. For some reason he had trouble finding it; every pocket that he thrust his hand into seemed to be filled with something that wasn't kern.

"What—did you finish it already?" Sierra teased.

"Here, have a bit of mine," Von said, joining them and offering a slice from his own supply. As Sierra took the kern Von gave Adan a gruff look. "I think all this excitement may have gone to his head."

"Sorry," Adan mumbled, looking away, embarrassed. "Maybe you're right." But looking into their eyes he silently wished that he was not a memorant, for he could see that neither of them believed him.

"All right, everybody. Keep your spears sharp and your eyes

and ears sharper," came Bryce's voice, resounding above the chatter. "Today we end this once and for all."

Taking the lead, he marched into the freshly cut tunnel. Adan, still embarrassed about the kern, fell in self-consciously behind Sierra, his stomach in knots. But he could not tell this time whether his nerves were due to the impending descent into Manx Core or the strange things he had begun to feel whenever he looked at Sierra.

TWENTY

CONTINGENCIES

THERE WAS A DROP OF ABOUT TWO BODY-LENGTHS ONTO the floor from the hole Sierra had made. They helped lower each other down to avoid injury, all except for Wik, who went last. He was the most agile of the group and he dropped the distance easily on his own.

The first thing which struck Adan about the new tunnel was the size. It was certainly the widest he had ever been in. The entire group could walk abreast. The walls were also perfectly smooth, forming a half-circle over their heads.

Zain and Yor shined their lumins about. In the steady white light the passage stretched off out of sight in either direction. A thin layer of dust coated the ground.

"No one has been in this part of the Viscera for a while. That is a good sign," Zain said.

Now that Adan was finally here, it hit him that there was no going back. They would follow this tunnel to wherever it led and would not leave this place until they found what they came for. A fleet of ships, an army of somatarchs, and the technology of the Developers seemed an impossible challenge for a few Sentients armed with pinions and a cutter. Would they be able to free the Sentient prisoners? What about Gavin? What had seemed like the only choice after the quake seemed a fool's errand now that they were down here. And what about finding Adan's memories? A hope more foolish still. But such things were all he had to cling to in the enduring dark.

Bryce gestured from them to come in close and he addressed them in hushed tones.

"From here on in, anyone with a bioseine will use the Collective channel to communicate. I'll use hand signals to relay any messages to the Waymen. We need to capture an assessor at some point in order to hard link. That will give us access to the system down here. Most of the patrols will be somatarchs, though, so we'll have to be careful."

Bryce wasn't telling them anything new at this point, just reminding them of what they'd already decided before they started digging in the quarry. The plan was to hard link to the mind of an assessor, giving them access to the esolace, the system the Devs were using to communicate with and control Manx Core. Using that, they would find out where Gavin and the captured Sentients were being held. Hopefully, they would both be in the same place, or at least close by. If they got discovered while freeing the prisoners, Von had suggested they could highjack some of the enemy ships to escape. It was a risky plan, but it was the best one they had.

Although Adan had connected to the minds of the other Sentients before, it had been brief and informational in nature. Now as his mind entered into a more lasting bond with theirs he was able to observe the free flow of thoughts, feelings, and impressions shared amongst the group. He sensed they were just as nervous as he was, even Bryce, but beneath that there was a quiet resolve, the sort of acceptance that comes from facing hard realities and knowing there is nothing else to be done. In this they shared a remarkable solidarity.

Before they set off, Bryce thrust a pair of pinions into Adan's hands. *"Take these. You have your cutter, but you might need these if you have to hit something at range."*

For the second time, Adan reluctantly took the weapons from Bryce. As much as he hated the thought of fighting, particularly with these Waymen spears, there was a good chance it would be necessary.

"What about Sierra?" Adan asked, noticing that she was unarmed.

"She's a handler. We don't want her getting in the thick of things if at all possible. Besides she likes fighting even less than you do."

Bryce gave him a strap to fasten the weapons to his back. Once everyone finished readying their equipment, they set off wordlessly down the gently sloping passage.

As wide as the tunnel was, Adan felt like the walls were pressing in on him, the passage growing smaller and smaller as they went. If another tremor occurred, there would be no way out this time. Though they walked at a brisk pace, it wasn't fast enough. The sooner they got out of this place the better.

They met no connecting tunnels for some time. There was only the long, steady descent through the slumbering rock. But at least they didn't run into any patrols. Adan tried to focus on that and keep his mind off the dangers of traveling underground.

Small bits of gravel and dust coated the floor. Eventually they came across cracks running through the walls and ceiling. They became more and more prominent, as did the debris underfoot. In spots they had to pick their way over the top of large piles of rubble.

The Waymen gestured towards each other, waving their hands and brushing the air with their fingers.

"What are they saying?" Adan asked, hoping the Sentients understood.

"They are saying that this damage looks fresh," Von answered. *"Bryce taught us the signals. You'll need them as well."* Along with his thoughts, Von passed what he knew of this Wayman system of communication.

Adan immediately was able to read Wik's gestures. *"Probably caused by the same quake that hit us this morning,"* he signed to the others.

So much for it being safer lower down, Adan thought to himself, recalling Bryce's assurances.

They continued on through the rubble, step by tentative step. At last the debris started to thin. Then it disappeared altogether. They had been walking for almost a full slice by then. They walked another half a slice after the tunnel cleared without seeing any change.

Finally they reached an intersection with a tunnel that was even wider than the first. The most notable difference between the two was the beam of light running down the center of the new passage, like a luminous cord, as thick as Adan's body.

"This energy rail must be part of their transportation system. Levs and other ships can travel along it without having to use their own power," Bryce explained. *"It should eventually lead us into Manx Core."*

"How do you know this tunnel will lead us there?" Adan asked. Matching information from his bioseine with what he'd discovered in the chronotrace, he knew their location in reference to where Gavin was being held, but he had no idea whether or not this new passage would take them there. *"There might be other transportation systems down here. And besides, we're still too far up. The Core is twice as far down as this."*

"True, but the tunnel we're in now doesn't look like it's being used. This one is much more likely to go to the Core."

With everyone's thoughts connected, it only took a moment for Adan to realize that the consensus was to follow Bryce's suggestion and head down the light rail to see where it led. Adan didn't push the issue.

Bryce signed the decision to the Waymen and they started down the new passage. The round, translucent cord lit up their surroundings with a peaceful glow. This strain of locus energy was harmless to both living and nonliving matter, but everyone kept their distance, walking on one side in case a transport should come whisking through the tunnel.

The new passage had metal supports at regular intervals. These showed no signs of damage from the recent quake, nor did the walls. The path curved downwards at a much steeper incline than the previous tunnel, but Adan could tell from his bioseine they were still quite far from Manx Core. In fact, the direction they were headed in was opposite from the one that they should have been going in.

Adan was about to suggest they consider retracing their steps, or maybe get out the chronotrace to see where this tunnel led, when they arrived at another intersection. The new tunnel ran off to the left and sloped even more sharply downwards, another light rail running down its center as well.

Up in the lead, Bryce paused, looking down the tunnel. It was headed more in the direction they needed to go, but he stood checking his modulator to see if it was safe.

"We should go this way," he announced. Then a sense of alarm gripped his thoughts. *"And let's hurry. There's someone coming down the tunnel we're in."*

He waved the group into the new tunnel. Zain did the same, hanging back until everyone got in.

"I'm tracking six zoetic signals with bioseines and they're

coming faster than I thought," Bryce informed them as they hurried into the tunnels. *"Forget about stealth. Run."*

They sprinted along both sides of the light rail. Hurtling down the steep passage they quickly picked up speed. Adan was near the back with Bryce and Zain, his legs churning as he tried to put as much distance between himself and the last tunnel as possible, but he noticed Bryce falling behind.

Bryce pulled out a black disc from his garrick and tossed it into the middle of the tunnel.

"What are you doing?" Adan asked.

"It's a contingency trigger. Hopefully it will stop them."

Adan recognized it as the same sort of device he had seen inside Nox's coat. This immediately raised his suspicions. What were they both doing with something like that?

Bryce picked up his pace and surged back towards the others. He had barely gone twenty paces when the first of a group of white-robed somatarchs appeared behind them. It ran through the air, streaks of light trailing from beneath the skimmers on its feet. Three more appeared behind it in rapid succession.

Bryce drew a pinion and his shiv, but he had no chance against four somatarchs. Adan reversed course and headed back towards him. He had no idea what he was going to do to help, but he didn't want Bryce facing these creatures alone.

"Are you crazy?" Bryce's thoughts burst into Adan's mind. *"Don't worry about me. Keep running."*

Adan ignored the warning and caught up to Bryce. They were about a hundred paces from the trigger when the first two somatarchs, who were skating neck and neck, reached the black disc. As they passed over it, the tunnel flooded with white light, blinding Adan momentarily. When his vision returned he saw the charred and mangled remains of the two somatarchs hitting the ground. Two of the skates detached from the somatarchs' feet and went hurtling straight towards him. Bryce tackled Adan and the two men crashed to the floor. The skimmers whizzed just over their heads and clattered to the ground, skipping harmlessly towards the fleeing Sentients.

As Adan rolled over, the other somatarchs streaked towards them. This time he remembered to shield his eyes as they glided over the trigger. When the flash faded, he opened his eyes in time to see the latest somatarchs fall. Their skimmers also ricocheted off the tunnel walls, but they petered out a few dozen paces away.

For a moment Adan thought they were safe. Then another somatarch, who must have been bringing up the rear, appeared. Surely it had seen what had happened to the others, but it continued on, though it hugged the side of the tunnel. It twisted its body and swerved to avoid the blast, but the explosion clipped the creature in midair all the same. The somatarch slammed into the side of the tunnel. The crack of its body hitting the stone reverberated down the passage.

The creature bounced off the wall and landed in a twisted heap. It should have been killed on impact, but Bryce held his pinion above his head, ready to strike as he advanced towards the fallen body.

The creature stirred in a weak attempt to rise. Bryce let his pinion fly. It found its mark in the creature's side and the somatarch shuddered, but continued struggling to rise. Bryce's arm whipped behind him and another pinion flashed down the passage before the creature could steady itself.

The second shaft pierced the somatarch's leg, but it barely fazed the creature. It regained its feet and began plodding towards them.

Bryce launched another shaft, but the creature was on its feet now. It sidestepped the throw and continued on. It began to run, the pinions embedded in its body flopping up and down.

Bryce hurled another pinion—and narrowly missed again. Adan reached back and pulled out one of his own.

Before he could throw it, the creature drew a glittering pistol from its belt. *An oscillathe.*

Adan threw his pinion with all his might. It sailed well past the creature. Bryce managed to get off one more pinion—his last—and the shaft plunged into the shoulder of the creature just as it fired, ruining its aim. A haunting whisper rushed over their heads, lifting up the hair on the back of Adan's neck.

With no other weapons left, Bryce drew his shiv and charged the soulless creature. The somatarch raised its oscillathe again, but instead of disintegrating Bryce in a deadly whisper, five spears zipped towards the somatarch from the Sentients behind them. Three found their mark. The somatarch staggered forward, taking one last step before its oscillathe clattered to the ground. Its lifeless body doubled over and fell to the floor, riddled with the deadly shafts of the Waymen.

TWENTY-ONE
DISSENSION

THE SENTIENTS STOOD STARING AT THE FALLEN somatarchs. A hush had descended over the group, but it lasted only a moment before Von stepped forward, his eyes trained on Bryce.

"Where did you get that contingency trigger? Raif never made anything like that." Von's question shot out like an aftershock from the battle; his tone lacked the usual deference with which he addressed Bryce.

Bryce did not respond, but the muscles in his cheek flexed as he clenched his jaw.

"What's going on here?" Von pressed him.

Bryce continued to ignore him, instead walking over to collect the oscillathe that had fallen from the somatarch's hand.

"I think you owe us an explanation, Bryce," Sierra said.

In response Bryce pointed the oscillathe towards Von and pulled the trigger.

Von almost tripped as he backpedalled, but there was no blast and he remained standing, unharmed. Exclamations of disbelief rippled across the group, most notably from Wik, whose cheeks flushed with color as the Wayman word for 'crazy'—*locura* shot from his lips.

"That's what I thought. It doesn't work," observed Bryce, ignoring the stir he had caused and shoving the gun inside his garrick. "These weapons can only be accessed with a connection to the Manx Core esolace."

Von rushed him. It looked like he might take a swing, but Bryce took a quick step back and Von pulled up a hand's breadth from his face.

"Stop playing with us and tell us where you got the trigger you used to blow up those somatarchs," Von demanded.

Zain walked over to stand between the two of them. "Do not let anger take hold. We need to work together if we are going to rescue our people." He gave Bryce a pointed look. "It does seem like a simple enough question, though."

Bryce brushed Zain's words aside, as if offended. "This is not the time. They know we're here now. We've got to get moving—"

"We're not going anywhere until everything is out in the open." Von folded his arms into two rigid right angles. The looks on the faces of the others mirrored his.

"I saved your lives, what does it matter?" Bryce shot back. His outburst prompted Von to start forward again, but Zain held him in check.

Noticing Von's second attempt to rush him, Bryce finally seemed to take stock of what was happening. The fire in his eyes dimmed somewhat.

"Look," he said, "I got the trigger from someone who used to be a Developer—someone who defected, just like Adan's friend Gavin."

"So you lied to us about being sent here by the Waymen." Von's cold stare locked onto Bryce.

"No, that was true. He's organizing the Waymen to fight

back. He wants the same thing we all want—to put a stop to the Developers."

"What *exactly* were you sent here to do?" Von's expression turned more guarded than ever. Adan was on edge, waiting to see how Bryce would respond and whether or not he would tell them about Nolan.

"I told you—to free the Collective," Bryce said, matching Von's stiff tone.

Adan knew enough to know Bryce was not being completely honest with these people. They were trusting their lives to his leadership and he was taking advantage of that trust.

"That's not true," Adan said. It was high time the Sentients knew who their leader really was. If they still wanted to follow him after that, so be it, but they needed to make that decision based on the truth. "Nolan sent you. He wants to destroy Oasis. And this isn't the first time he's tried to do it." Adan had finally been able to see the truth as it flashed through Bryce's mind. And for the first time, he did not doubt the accuracy of his memorant abilities.

Bryce hesitated, taken off guard by Adan's words.

"Who is this Nolan?" Von asked.

"Someone who used to be part of the Collective," Adan said.

Bryce shook his head. His bravado and stiffness vanished. "Look, you're right. Nolan did send me to destroy Oasis. But he didn't know about the Sentients. Neither did I. I still want to stop the Administrators, but I'm fighting for you now. We have to save the Sentients. We have to be free. I want that as much as any of you."

"And just when were you planning on telling us all of this?" Von said, stone-faced.

A shade of Bryce's defiance returned. *None of you understand what's at stake here,* his expression seemed to say.

Before Bryce could reply, the modulator on his wrist lit up. Patterned red lights reflected onto his face from the miniature screen. "There's another patrol incoming." Bryce's nostrils flared in anger. "I told you we were wasting our time here."

"We'll finish this another time, Bryce," Von said in a low-pitched voice. "Don't think you're getting out of this."

"Quick, everyone grab a pair of skimmers." Bryce reached down and scooped up a nearby set. "They don't have a bioseine interface. Click them together to engage the hover plates."

The other Sentients scrambled to collect the rest.

"Pair up with a Wayman—we can carry them on our backs. Four groups of two."

Adan, Von, Sierra, and Bryce each stepped into a pair of skimmers. They were simple to put on, forming a bond with the bottom of their feet in the same way lentes attached to a person's eyes.

"I hope I am not too much of a burden," Zain said, sidling up behind Adan.

"You carried me out of the riot at Sparc's camp. Now I get to return the favor."

Zain hopped onto his back. He was even lighter than Adan expected.

Adan clicked the skates together and slowly rose off the ground. Though the skimmers had been easy enough to put on, he was not prepared for the complete instability of walking on air. Had his bioseine not kicked in and adjusted his balance, he almost certainly would have crashed back down to the floor.

"Hurry," Bryce warned, *"they've already entered this tunnel."*

Standing on nothing more than a cushion of light was the most unnatural thing in the world, but once he got moving, it got a little easier. Before he knew it, he was fifty paces down the tunnel and picking up speed.

The last to start out, Adan trailed the others. Glancing over his shoulder, he didn't see any sign of pursuit.

"How close are they?" he asked.

In response, Bryce projected the information from the modulator on his wrist across the channel. The patrol was still a ways off, but was moving much faster than they were. They would not be able to outrun them.

"Let's just hope they're assessors. We need to make a hard link or we're never going to get anywhere," Bryce reminded them.

"All right, tell us what to do," Von came back. Of necessity the distrust which had dominated the group a few moments before vanished as Bryce's plan came streaming over the shared connection and into each of their minds.

The assessors came flying down the tunnel less than three microslices later. There were four of them, each one piloting an attack skiff. They were coming much faster than the somatarchs had.

"No matter what happens," Bryce instructed, *"just keep going. When the riders lose control of their skiffs they'll come crashing down the tunnel after us."*

"You're sure they won't be killed in the crash?" Adan asked.

"The chances are good that at least one of them will survive," Bryce answered. *"Their bioseines should keep them alive long enough for us to get what we want."*

Even though the plan was only to stun the assessors with the trigger, Adan didn't like the possibility that some of them might die when their skiffs crashed.

"I don't like it either," Sierra told him, in answer to his thoughts. *"But I don't see any other way."*

Catching up to her, Adan caught a glimpse of the fear in her eyes. *"I should be the one reassuring you, not the other way around,"* he thought.

"Remember, these are assessors," Bryce cautioned. *"They're smarter than somatarchs. If for some reason they spot the trigger and destroy it before it goes off, we go to the backup plan."*

The skiffs were getting close enough now that Adan could see the large oscillathes mounted on the front.

"They have to be in range by now," Adan observed. *"Why aren't they shooting?"*

"They want to take us alive," Bryce replied.

The skiffs hurtled on. They would overtake the Sentients at any moment.

"Now, Bryce!" came Von's command.

Bryce was the furthest back, having let the others go by. He reached into his garrick and hurled the contingency trigger onto the floor of the tunnel.

The skiffs came in hard and fast. In a heartbeat the first assessor's ship passed over the black disc. The air around it flashed, exploding in white light, but then something strange happened. The light clung to the assessor's body for several moments, flickering a few times before dying out. Adan couldn't say what had caused the brightness to linger, but it was clear Bryce's trigger had failed. The assessors kept coming.

The next moment the second assessor passed over the trigger with the same results: a flash, followed by flickering lights and the skiff flew on. Two more flashes followed, lighting up the tunnel as the last two skiffs passed over the useless trigger.

"Blanks," Von cursed. *"I didn't think those skiffs would have energy suppression fields."*

Bryce pushed his skimmers to the limit, surging forward, but it was no use, the first skiff overtook him. Two short white bolts of energy shot out from the pilot's hand as he passed by. Bryce and Yor, the Wayman on his back, went limp. They careened into the side of the tunnel upside-down and slid to the ground.

Von and Ket pulled up and spun around in midair while Adan and Sierra went flying by. As the assessor's skiff got within range, Von hurled a tiny black energy disruptor at the incoming ship. It blossomed into an enormous sphere of white energy, filling the passage and consuming the entire flight of assessor ships.

As the light from the blast faded, the skiffs came skidding down the tunnel, sparks showering the air where their bases scraped the floor and walls. All the vehicles were empty, their pilots having been thrown to the floor. The disruptor blast had completely disabled the skips.

Adan, Von, and Sierra slowed to a stop.

"We did it," Adan said.

Von allowed himself a rare smile. "Let's go back for Bryce and Yor."

"Wait," came Sierra's voice, cold with fear. "Look—they're getting up."

Adan didn't understand what she was so alarmed about at first. He thought she meant Bryce and Yor. But they were still lying motionless on the tunnel floor. The assessors were not. One by one, Adan watched in morbid fascination as they rose and advanced down the tunnel. All of them were bruised and bleeding, but none were seriously injured.

Adan suddenly didn't care about getting access to the Manx Core esolace. His whole body tensed, ready for flight. But they couldn't leave behind Bryce and Yor.

"They're not drawing any weapons," Sierra said.

She was right, the assessors held nothing in their hands and had no visible weapons on their belts. Had they lost them in the crash?

"They're not unarmed," came Von's ominous warning. He floated to the ground and let Ket slide off his back.

Watching the hardened stares and deliberate movements of the advancing assessors, Adan had no doubt that Von was right.

TWENTY-TWO
HARD LINKING

Adan and Sierra landed beside Von and Ket. Zain and Wik slid off and had barely touched the floor when Von and Ket hurled two pinions through the air. The pointed shafts zipped towards two of the assessors, but the gray robed men thrust out their hands and a white burst of energy shot forth from their fingers and wrapped around the javelins. The two shafts froze in midair and fell clanking to the floor.

"It's what I thought, neutralizers," Von said.

The Waymen stared at the inanimate spears, their eyes dark pools of disbelief—but only for a moment. The four advancing figures soon recaptured their attention. The assessors did not move in unison the way somatarchs did, but Adan had no doubt they were mentally coordinating their attack.

"We've got to do something," Sierra said. "We can't just wait for them to come at us."

"*The neutralizers have a short range, but once they get close enough, they'll knock us unconscious,*" Von informed them, signing the same message to the Waymen. "*We need to stall until I can think of something.*"

"*I'll try to read their thoughts to see if I can figure out anything,*" Adan shot back, though he knew he had little chance of finding anything in time.

He fixed his eyes on the assessor closest to him, but it took a moment to focus. The man looked so much like Gavin that Adan kept having to fight thoughts of his friend from creeping in.

Von moved to the side. "Spread out," he said. Then he added a mental message, "*Draw your cutter, Adan. I have an idea.*"

Adan pulled the tube from the strap on his garrick, but one of the assessors pressed forward before the Sentients could react, stretching his arm towards Wik. In response, the Wayman rushed to meet him, drawing forth his shiv.

"No, Wik! I told you to—" Von cried out.

Wik slashed at his enemy's hands, but the assessor's gloved fingers flashed with white light and Wik fell to the ground and did not rise.

Von, who was isolated now, made a feint with his pinion, but the assessor in front of him didn't fall for it. Ket rushed in with his shiv to help, but he wasn't quick enough. Von fell to the ground with another white blast. Ket tried to check his charge when he saw what happened, but a second blast dropped him beside his friend.

"*Adan, hurry. Have you thought of anything?*" Sierra's thoughts were scattered and frantic. "*Did Von want you to kill them?*"

"*I can't do that. I need to get a read and figure out a way around those neutralizers.*"

"*I'll keep them distracted.*" Sierra stepped in front of him. "*Just figure something out before they take me down.*"

"Stay back," she called out to the assessors. "We don't want to hurt you."

The gray robed men fanned out to ensure the Sentients did not outflank them.

Adan concentrated, trying to get a glimpse into the mind of the assessor advancing on him.

Sierra and Zain backed down the tunnel.

"Stay close to me," Sierra said, pulling Adan with her. The three of them gave up spreading out and huddled together.

The assessors advanced steadily, but more quickly now. They were closing in.

Adan thought again about running, but it would only delay the confrontation at best. He forced his mind to cut through the distractions and hone in on the assessor before him. At last he caught something. It was like a little thread poking out from the door of the man's mind. Adan rushed to follow it inside before the door shut. He found himself in an unlit room. As his mind adjusted to his surroundings, the dim outline of what the assessor was thinking slowly revealed itself.

"*Neutralize the one with the cutter*," the assessor told the others. "*Just in case.*"

Adan had no idea what the other man replied, but the other assessor responded with "*All right. We charge on my command.*"

At last Adan saw what the neutralizers were. They were the segmented metal bands the assessors wore around their wrists. And he realized what Von wanted him to do.

The cutter's yellow blade leapt to its full length and he lunged forward. At the same time, all the assessors surged forward in unison.

Everything happened so fast it was like someone shook the room. The blade swiped through the closest assessor's arm in a blazing flash.

Zain leapt forward to meet the enemy, striking with his shiv, but jumped right into the white bursts shooting forth from their hands. Sierra hopped backwards, trying to dodge a blast from the left.

Adan dove to the side to avoid the neutralizer blast from the right, but was a step too slow.

A numbing sensation shivered across his skin. The last thing he saw before he went unconscious was Sierra's body slumping next to his to the floor.

***

Adan's body jerked awake as if he had just startled himself out of a dream. His eyes still closed, he caught the soft rustle of fabric beside him. He felt the cutter jerk off his forearm. His first thought was that the neutralizer must have merely stunned his body and that his mind was still aware, like when Will had possessed him at the Institute, but a moment's reflection told him that was not the case. His body tingled a little from the lingering effects of the neutralizer, but he could still move.

He had no time to figure out what had happened because another thought followed quickly after this realization. *They must think I'm still unconscious.*

Adan opened his eyelids a sliver. He waited until the assessor reached towards him and then shot out his hand and yanked the neutralizer band from his wrist. The band worked through the movement of the muscles in the wrist. Adan shoved it on and flexed his fingers before his opponent knew what was happening. A white light flashed between them and the man collapsed on top of him.

Adan shoved the man off. He didn't bother to get up, extending his body in the direction of the other three assessors. Two quick bursts of light caught all of them at the legs just below the knees. Standing so close together, they had no time to react to Adan's sudden attack.

Adan sat up, the only conscious person in the tunnel, though he had no idea why.

———

Adan's heart was thumping so loud he half thought it should be echoing off the cavern walls. What had just happened made no sense, but there wasn't time to try and figure it out. He hurried about the tunnel, pulling off the neutralizers from the remaining assessors. One of the bands had been sliced in two. So he had managed to strike true, though it hadn't done any good. He put on one and shoved the other two good ones into his garrick.

He twisted the one on his wrist, reversing its field. The neutralizers could be used both to knock someone unconscious, or revive them if they'd been knocked out. Since they were powered by zoetic energy, Von's disruptor had no effect on them.

Adan reached Sierra and grabbed her shoulder. There was a short, buzzing snap and her eyes fluttered open to momentary confusion.

"What happened?" she asked.

He took a moment, trying to think of how to explain it. "I used the neutralizers against them."

Confusion etched itself deeper upon Sierra's face. "How did you manage to avoid getting hit?"

"I'm...not sure. Listen, I'll explain later."

He took out one of the spare neutralizers and put it on her wrist. He sent her a quick mental message on how they worked and then added, *"Go wake the others. I'm going to attempt a hard link before the assessors come to."*

Sierra nodded and went over to revive Zain.

Adan rushed to the nearest assessor, knowing he had to

work fast. He had taken over people's minds before using the esolace, but this was different. Hard linking was something he had only heard about. Gavin had described it once in explaining how he had accessed Darius' thoughts after he'd been knocked unconscious. Adan would have to impose his will onto the man's subconscious.

He knelt beside the assessor, absentmindedly touching the small bulge of the chronotrace in the pouch at his belt, as if that could somehow guide him through what he was about to do.

Adan closed his eyes and turned his focus within. He could sense the presence of Sierra's mind, bright with the light of conscience, but the assessor's minds hovered like clouds of smoke, intangible, yet still able to be perceived. Their minds shimmered, trying to grow brighter, trying to solidify them-selves. It would only be a matter of time before they awoke.

He reached toward the mind of the assessor beside him. The moment he made contact, the man's thoughts seemed to fly in a hundred directions at once, like motes of darkness fleeing from the light. Adan grasped for them, but caught only a few. Still, he held onto the ones he did catch and sent his thoughts speeding after the rest, imagining a hundred hooks which tentacled out in every direction. He caught a few more here, a few more there, but they proved frustratingly elusive.

It was mentally exhausting, but after catching a thousand or so stray thoughts he sensed he had them all. He drew them together, packing them tight like a ball of mental vapor. He wasn't quite sure how he managed to keep something so intan-gible together, but he knew if he kept his focus on the gossamer mass it would not be able to escape. He pressed his awareness inside the haze, pushing his mind into the assessor's thoughts, searching for what he needed.

The first thing he found was the man's name, which was Faron. Soon details about his life, his position, his interests, and his memories followed, all rushing by in a blur. Adan ignored all of that and hunted for anything he could find about Gavin or the prisoners who had been taken from Oasis. The haze cleared and the assessor's mind grew more defined. Images of people flitted through his thoughts, ephemeral remembrances he had acquired over the course of his short life. It was clear there were gaps in his memory, but Adan passed over these as well. He concentrated on the people, trying to find out who they were, hoping that some of them might turn out to be Sentients.

He soon discovered that some of these people were real, but some existed only inside the esolace. Faron had come to see the distinction only recently and there was still a great deal of confusion in his thoughts about how this could be. But Faron still held on to the esolace memories as important and needed. In fact, the majority of his identity was built upon the relationships he had formed and the things he had done there. There was a whole world inside those experiences which Adan could not help but marvel at it even as he passed quickly through it. It was a world which Adan had never known existed. He saw oceans and mountains covered in white, palaces and stadiums, swiftly running rivers coursing through sprawling grasslands, with grass blades waving in golden light. And everywhere there were people, walking, running, resting, talking; they came in every shape and size, and wore every type of clothing imaginable, but none of them were the prisoners he sought, no one there was even remotely connected to Manx Core.

Adan burst through the other side of that constructed world, the world of the esolace, and found himself standing in a crowd of assessors inside a large, vaulted chamber. At last he was starting to get close.

His awareness swept onwards until another memory rose before him.

Faron was standing in front of another assessor, but they were not looking at each other. Both of them were staring at a metal wall across the room, their eyes unfocused, their thoughts flitting back and forth in a mental exchange. They were using a channel called the 'quorum'. Adan had never heard of it, but inside Faron's thoughts, he intuitively understood how to use it.

"*How many did you bring to the vault today?*" the other man asked. He had only recently joined the ranks of the assessors, having been a simple technician before the storm.

"*Only two,*" Faron answered.

"*And yesterday we didn't get any.*"

"*It will be all right,*" Faron assured him, "*Malthus has another force of somatarchs awaiting activation in the Command Center. And once we've got enough Collectives in the vault we'll begin training them as assessors.*"

"*I hope so. I don't really trust that many vacants to follow their directives when they aren't under direct control.*"

"*There have been plenty of tests. They've got the kinks worked out this time.*"

"*I sure hope so. I'm tired of living down in this pit. We need to get back up on the surface as soon as possible.*"

"*I'd rather be down here and safe than face an army before we're ready.*"

Faron's thought spun around in the other assessors mind, as if he were waiting for it to stop and make sense to him, but it never did.

"*You really buy all that Delegation talk?*" came the other man's reply at length. "*I think they're just trying to scare us into believing that so they can keep us motivated. The only thing on this sand encrusted husk is us and the andros. All the scans say the same thing.*"

"*This isn't the same Collective, Kaz. The Admins are*

shooting straight with us now. War's coming. The simulation is over. This one's for real."

Though Adan was alarmed by what Faron was telling his companion, he didn't pursue the memory further. There wasn't time. Instead he backtracked to follow the trail of thoughts associated with the Collectives they had mentioned.

A moment later, he found the memory he was looking for.

TWENTY-THREE
THE LIFE OF THE WORLD

FARON TRAILED THE TWO CHROMIUM CARTS AS THEY hummed down the wide ramp into the cavern. In all the crowded complex, this was the one section that remained relatively open. No one came to the vault unless they were picking up or dropping off prisoners. It was a monotonous trek and one of the least pleasant aspects of Faron's duties. It was during times like these he wished he still had access to the Oasis esolace. There had never been any monotony back then. In contrast, the Manx Core system had little to offer. It was functional enough, but far less powerful. It lacked the full immersive capabilities of what they'd had in Oasis.

He arrived at the doors to the vault. They were not much wider than the carts. The carts slid into the opening in the cavern walls and floated into the metallic hallway beyond. He followed the cart past two chambers on either side, each framed by a glowing strip of blue lights. At the end of the hallway the passage opened up to the left and right.

The carts drifted somberly to the last door on the left. Faron commanded the door to open with his mind. Inside, the carts slid the bodies resting on top of them onto the floor next to half a dozen other frozen figures. Their cargo unloaded, the carts floated out of the chamber. Faron stood outside, silently directing them. Even from out in the hallway, he could feel the chill wafting across his skin.

Watching the memory play out, Adan flinched when he recognized the frosted forms of the two men on the floor. It was Raif and Nance.

He severed his connection to Faron's mind and opened his eyes.

All the other Sentients were up and standing nearby, staring at him.

"I found out where the prisoners are being held," Adan said. "And I know how to get into the Manx Core system."

"Good," Bryce said. "You can fill us in on the details while we get moving. Von, get the cutter and start ripping out the bioseine interfaces on those skiffs."

"Right." Von grabbed the metal tube off the ground and headed off to the closest ship. "I'll have us up and running in no time."

Despite removing the bioseine controls so they could not be tracked, the Sentients had little trouble using the manual steering columns to fly their hijacked skiffs. They were far more stable than the skimmers and they had collision algorithms which helped them avoid the sides of the tunnel.

Von piloted one of the ships and Bryce flew the other. The other two ships had been beaten up too badly when they crashed. There was just enough room for four to ride on a single skiff together. Adan rode along with Zain and Sierra in Von's ship.

As they zipped through the tunnels, thoughts flitted back and forth between Adan and the other Sentients. Though Faron's access to the quorum channel had proved helpful, it was not complete. It didn't give them access to high security areas or even the ability to fire Bryce's newly acquired oscillathe. But it did give them access to no military equipment and also provided them a map of the tunnels surrounding Manx Core—at least the tunnels Faron knew about—and that was enough to find out where the Sentients were being held prisoner. They also found the location of the Repository, but as tempting as that was, it would have to wait. Gavin's rescue was vitally important, but he was only a single person. There were many more Sentients locked in the vaults.

Based on the map, the fastest way to get to the Sentients was through a nearby mining cavern. Von and the Waymen had expressed concerns that the mine would be occupied. They didn't have access to the oscillathes mounted on the skiffs to fight their way through, but that was fine. They wanted to avoid conflict if at all possible. Instead, they planned on abandoning the skiffs just outside the entrance and sneaking through the mines on foot.

No one spoke as they sped down the tunnels, but Adan could see from the look in Sierra's eyes that she was still shaken from the encounter with the assessors. Things had not exactly gone well up to this point.

As if Zain were the one who could read thoughts, he placed his hand on Adan's shoulder and, with a meaningful glance towards Sierra, mouthed the word, "pray."

It was the best thing he could possibly do, not only for Sierra, but for himself and everyone there.

He closed his eyes and took a deep breath.

Numinae, if you can hear me down in this dark place, please help us find our friends. We need your help, but I think Sierra needs it especially. I don't know why, but there is something about her. I don't know what it is. There is so much I don't understand. But you do. And I know you will do what's best.

He had no assurance that anything would change because of this simple petition, but it did not matter. He had done his part. He had placed his concerns before the one who alone would know what to do with them. Hope swelled inside him as he opened his eyes again.

The skiffs continued on, following the light rails until a dim glow appeared up ahead. Von and Bryce brought the ships to rest on the tunnel floor, about two hundred paces from the light, and everyone dismounted.

Even though they were not yet in the mine, loud humming sounds assaulted their ears from up ahead.

"We stick to the left wall," Bryce said, raising his voice enough to be heard over the racket as they huddled together behind the skiffs. With all the racket going on inside the mine, there was no longer any need to use the hand signals. "If for some reason we get separated, make your way to the vault on your own. We'll wait there until exactly one slice from now. If you haven't made it by then, we'll have to go on without you."

"But the Waymen don't have access to the map," Adan said. "How will they find their way if they get lost?"

Bryce nodded and took a moment to pull the Waymen aside and explain to them as best he could the layout of the tunnels. Adan remained doubtful even after he finished, but he supposed there was nothing else they could do about it.

"Do not worry about us, my friend," Zain said with quiet confidence. "Most of us have been in the Welkin tunnels before, often with far less information than what has been provided. We will find our way should we get separated."

Bryce motioned for them to head off, single file, down the

hallway. Sierra and Adan lingered at the back of the group, waiting to fall in behind the others.

"I don't know if I can do this," she said.

Adan could sense her mind closing in on itself, curling up in a ball of fear.

"You stood up to the assessors," he told her, trying to draw her away from the edge of panic. "I know when it comes to it, you'll find the courage to face whatever happens. Your friends need you—I need you. We'll get through this."

She nodded stoically and looked into his eyes. He could not be sure, but he thought his words might have had some small effect on her.

Looking at her, the same enigmatic influx of emotions he'd felt at the start of the journey rippled through him again. The only clear part of them was that something inside of him was drawing him towards Sierra in ways he did not fully understand. He was almost grateful to turn his concerns back to the dangers of crossing the mine. At least that was a problem he could comprehend.

From where Adan crouched, he could barely see the end of the cavern. Veins of neophosphorous ran through the ceiling and along the far walls, giving it a haunting blue glow reminiscent of the Basin, but brighter. Machinery crowded the expanse, but most of it wasn't moving. It was only on the far side, some distance away, where any activity could be seen. The noise, however, was everywhere. It ranged from low, droning sounds to loud, whining noises coming from a group of machines working along the back wall of the cavern.

Bryce and the rest of the Sentients studied the mining operation for several microslices, trying to determine the best route to take across the cavern.

Many of the vehicles and equipment here were of types Adan had never seen before, but which, from his bioseine, he immediately recognized. The largest of these were the haulers, massive hovering platforms which held stacks upon stacks of chromium crates. The crates not already loaded onto the haulers floated about the room, waiting to be filled by the tunnelers: long, low cylindrical vehicles which emitted bright yellow cones of energy on one end. This sustained funnel of energy was used to carve through rock in the same manner as a cutter, only on a much larger scale.

Trailing behind the tunnelers were groups of somatarchs, their white robes visible here and there in the cavern's omnipresent light. Whenever they passed near the massive boulders being carved out by the tunnelers, they would touch the rocks with the end of a short black fractal rod. After a moment the boulder would crumble into piles of smaller rubble. Floating discs of locus energy would eventually pass over these piles and suck up the smaller rocks onto their shimmering circular surfaces and deposit them into the nearby carts.

The cones of one group of three tunnelers blazed a bright blue. They were working on a large exposed vein of black rock at the back of the cavern. These tunnelers were twice the size of the others and yet they were having little success cutting into the rock. This seemed mostly due to the fact that they only ever attempted to do any cutting for short intervals before stopping.

"*Why aren't they using the yellow spectrum since it's inorganic material?*" Adan asked Bryce, who was crouching next to him.

"*That's not rock,*" Bryce said, eyeing the formation with intense interest. "*It's celerium.*"

Wik pointed at the rock and muttered something to the

Waymen which Adan missed, but he caught the word *viviendo* in it somewhere, which meant "life" or "living".

Adan nudged Zain, who was hunched down on his other side. "What did he say?"

"The Life of the World," Zain whispered, awestruck. "No Wayman I know has ever seen it. It is only spoken of in the legends."

"What is it?"

"They say there are veins of rock like that running all through the deepest places of this world. The land cannot survive without them. Only a fool would ever attempt to disturb them as these men are doing."

As amazed as Zain and the other Waymen were, Bryce was just as enthralled by the presence of this rare material. The look in his eyes showed clearly that he had something in mind for the celerium, but Adan couldn't tell what.

Bryce turned his attention away from the rocks to the center of the cavern and pointed. "We need to figure out a way across that," he said.

A huge crevice ran through the center of the cavern, cutting it in almost equal halves, the side opposite their group being slightly larger. The scintillating blue light shining up from its depths shimmered hypnotically along the edges of the rock. How far down it reached Adan could not say, but it was over a hundred paces across. A black metal bridge, just large enough for one of the massive haulers to float across was the only access to the other side of the cavern.

"*There is no way we can make it across that bridge unnoticed*," Von told them.

"*What if it didn't matter if they saw us?*" Bryce's mind settled on the nearby machinery. "*Look at all these empty haulers stationed on this side of the cavern. What if we got inside these crates and then floated one of the haulers across the bridge ourselves? We can connect to the quorum channel now so they would think it was just another piece of equipment involved in the mining operation. After they load it up with rocks and ship it off down the far tunnel, we can get off."*

"If we cover ourselves in rocks, how will we get out of the crates?" Adan asked, not liking the sound of this.

"We can use the cutter to slice up some of the other carts and make slats to put on top of us," Bryce suggested.

"That will still be a great deal of weight." Von gave Bryce a distrustful look. He still hadn't gotten over Bryce's dishonesty about his past.

"The slats will keep the carts from getting too full and if anyone gets stuck, we can use the cutter to get them out."

"But are you certain they won't know when we've connected to the hauler?" Adan asked. "When I was in the Annex—"

"That's just a risk we'll have to take. They already know we're here. We can't wait around forever until they float our hauler across. Or would you prefer to just sprint over the bridge, running out in the open? There must be a dozen or more somatarchs on the other side."

"I don't like it," Adan replied. "The Developers wouldn't just let us take the hauler without noticing. Couldn't we rip out the bioseine interfaces and control them manually, the way we did with the skiffs?"

"Those are fully automated vehicles," Bryce explained. "They have no manual overrides. Listen, if the Devs do override the hauler I can use one of the contingency triggers to disrupt them and cover our escape."

Von shook his head, but no one suggested anything else. Sierra just stared at the bridge in gaunt silence.

Reluctantly, Von pulled Zain and the other Waymen aside and explained to them Bryce's plan. Adan could tell Von was hoping the Waymen would object, perhaps even come up with another idea, but when Zain nodded at the end, he knew that would not be happening.

"Very well," Zain said. "We will try these machines. But we will have to leave our pinions. I do not think they will fit inside those crates."

They hid their pinions behind a stack of carts and Bryce gave Adan his extra shiv as a replacement. Adan shoved it into his belt as quickly as possible, not wanting to touch it. The thought of what might happen if the somatarchs found them out loomed unsettlingly in his thoughts.

He wished the neutralizers they had taken from the assessors would have been of some use, but according to Von, they were not strong enough to knock out somatarchs. And they were trying to avoid confrontations anyway.

"*Sierra, I think you should take the cutter,*" Adan suggested. He added privately, just to her, "*I don't want to lose you in there.*"

Sierra didn't want the cutter, but she reluctantly accepted it with a grateful look.

Bryce regarded Adan smugly. He hid his thoughts on the channel, but it was obvious what he was thinking.

Adan brushed it off and walked over with the others to one of the haulers at the edge of a crowd of vehicles. As quietly as they could, they lifted Sierra onto one of the haulers and she began slicing up some of the crates. The flickering light on the end of her cutter was so small it disappeared almost completely as she ran it along the surface of the carts. She worked quickly, cutting out eight sheets. Adan and each of the Sentients took one and and crept into the crates. The containers were wider at the top so the sheets only slid down to about two handspans below the lip. Underneath, the Sentients hunkered down, readying themselves for what Adan hoped would be a quick trip across the bridge.

TWENTY-FOUR
THE CROSSING

THE HAULER HUMMED ALONG, MAKING NO MORE NOISE than the ubiquitous chromium carts, but from inside the crates every bump and jostle seemed to reverberate like someone was hurling rocks against the metal panels. They were on the top row of crates, stacked four high, and there was far too much movement for Adan's liking. Each time his compartment quivered or scraped one of the other crates, his anxious imagination told him the somatarchs had found him out and were about to rip off the protective sheet and reveal his hiding place.

Bryce, who was controlling the vehicle from inside his crate, used his bioseine to determine their position and maneuver them around the stationary machinery on their side of the cavern. Still, the hauler wasn't built for speed and with each passing moment, the tension mounted. When at last they made it onto the bridge, Adan fingered the hilt of his shiv nervously, certain someone would notice what they were doing.

As if in answer to his unspoken fears, the hauler came to an abrupt stop halfway across the bridge.

"*I'm locked out*," came Bryce's warning. "*They're coming to investigate. There are five—no, six somatarchs headed our way,*" he informed them, relaying the information he saw on his modulator.

"*We can't defeat that many.*" Adan was trying to stay calm, but not seeing any way they were getting out of this.

Footsteps pinged on the metal bridge.

"*Make for the skiffs,*" Bryce told them. "*Use the skimmers to get there and make sure to help the Waymen.*"

Adan's panicked muscles jerked into motion. He squirmed inside his cart until he had pulled the skimmers from his garrick. He had to rearrange his legs so he could fit the slats on his feet. In the process, he lost precious time.

The footsteps on the bridge rang out louder and louder.

Once he had the skimmers fastened on, he flipped over the chromium sheet so he could climb out. He tossed himself over the side and landed on a lower row of crates. When his foot hit, it slipped into a gap between two other containers. His leg buckled and he fell. The crates shifted even further as he sank down, wedging his foot deep in between them. He couldn't pull it out.

As the rest of the group popped out of their carts and abandoned the floating platform, Bryce's thoughts came racing over the Collective channel.

"*I'll stay on the hauler as long as I can to try and draw their attention. Now go!*" he ordered.

Snatches of white robes could be seen over the edge of the crates. The somatarchs were almost to the hauler.

Adan engaged the power on the skimmer caught between the crates, trying to force it loose, but it wouldn't budge.

"*I'm stuck,*" he sent his plea for help across the Collective channel.

Someone grabbed him by the shoulder from behind. He

twisted around to see Bryce's outstretched arm reaching towards him.

"Hurry," Bryce urged, *"They're here."*

Bryce grabbed Adan's arms and yanked on them several times before giving up and kicking at the crates to widen the gap. At last he booted one of them so hard Adan's foot jerked free, but the sudden movement jarred his skimmer loose. It fell into the crack and disappeared.

"My skimmer," came Adan's frantic thought.

"Take mine." Bryce slipped one of his skates off and thrust it into Adan's hands.

"But how will you—I can't—" Adan started to protest, but he never finished the thought. At that moment, a somatarch leapt up from below and onto the row of carts with Bryce and Adan.

Adan saw the creature reach for the oscillathe at its waist, but he didn't wait for it to fire. He dove off the crates, jumping blindly off the hauler. He didn't know if he was jumping into the crevice or onto the bridge. A cruel whisper rushed past him as he plummeted into the unknown.

He was just able to catch a glimpse of the metal surface of the bridge before he collided with it, landing awkwardly on his knees. The impact sent a numbing shock through his legs, but he rolled up and onto his feet, his bioseine quickening his reactions. He was standing on the edge of the span, but there was hardly any space to move. The hauler was only an arm's length away. He refused to look over the side of the bridge, knowing it would only deepen the panic which threatened to take hold of him. He looked around for any of the Sentients, but he was alone.

Adan still had one skimmer on his foot, but he must have dropped Bryce's skate during his fall. His eyes darted underneath the hauler, but he saw nothing. He looked up and down the bridge and then he saw it, lying near the edge, half on the bridge, half sticking precariously over the side.

He slipped off the one skimmer he was still wearing so he could run, but before he could take off, something thudded onto the platform behind him. He glanced back, expecting to see a somatarch, but it was Zain.

"Zain," he called out, a surge of hope rushing through him. "Come with me." He motioned to his friend before heading for the skimmer.

He coasted to a stop a couple of steps from the dangling skate. He crept forward, afraid any vibration might send it over the edge, and just as fearful of falling over himself. Every movement felt like a calculated risk. He slid his feet along the surface of the bridge, moving far more slowly than he would have liked. The somatarchs might appear at any moment.

Adan was reaching for the skimmer when a loud crash rocked the hauler floating beside him. He looked up just in time to see the body of a somatarch and several crates come hurtling down from above. One of the containers caught him in the shoulder, sending him off balance. His arms flailed wildly, as if they could somehow generate enough wind to pull him forward, but he couldn't stop himself from going over the edge. The skimmer he'd been holding flew from his hand, but then his bioseine took over and his body contorted itself acrobatically. His arm shot up, grabbing the edge of the bridge and keeping him from falling into the crevice. With his body dangling over the dizzying drop, he gripped the metal ledge with a strength he did not know he had, but the metal was too smooth. He felt his fingers slipping.

His eyes darted towards the great void below. The body of a somatarch tumbled end over end alongside several crates and two tiny slats of metal which flashed in the light—the skimmers. A wave of vertigo washed over him and he nearly lost his grip.

The black walls of the crevice plummeted far below like in the Basin, but here he could see the bottom.

A glowing flow of blue neophosphorous filled the crevice beneath him. The exposed, ichory river glided, ominous and sluggish, towards an opening at the far end of the divide.

Adan closed his eyes, not wanting to see any more. His fingers slipped further and further. Just as he prepared himself to slide into the abyss, a firm hand wrapped itself around his forearm.

"I've got you, my friend," came Zain's heartening voice as Adan looked up into his face. "Just reach up with your other hand," Zain instructed calmly, though his face glistened with sweat as he strained to pull Adan to safety. "A little more..."

Adan swung his free arm up and was just barely able to reach Zain's outstretched hand. As their fingers brushed, the body of a somatarch slammed on top of Zain. White robed arms shot around his throat and Zain was gone.

Adan slipped, but somehow held on. He doubled down on his grip to keep himself from falling and yet the metal continued to slide beneath his sweaty fingers. His hold would not last forever.

"*Please, someone help me,*" his thoughts went flying out across the Collective channel, "*Please—I'm on the edge of the bridge. I can't hold on much longer...*"

"*I'm coming for you,*" came the answer. It was Sierra.

It was too late. At that moment Adan lost his grip and the tips of his fingers slid over the edge.

He felt weightless for the briefest of moments and then the air came rushing past him, his garrick billowing around him as the rushed past. He recalled the last time he had fallen like this, in the storm which destroyed Oasis. But this time, there was no mysterious presence to wrap him serenely in its arms.

The world above flew away even as the light reached up to

embrace him from below. The neophosphorous was strangely forgiving as he impacted on the surface, breaking his fall and saving his life, at least for a few moments longer.

His legs plunged into the thick, gelatinous river. Instantly he began to sink. At first, he fought desperately to keep himself from slipping further into the sludge-like flow, but the more he struggled, the quicker he went under. His hips, and soon his torso and chest, passed below the surface. He was hopelessly trapped inside the lumbering currents of the warm, oozing, river of light. The enveloping flow had captured him and it did not intend to let go.

He thrust his arms above his head as his shoulders, followed quickly by his neck and chin, sank beneath the surface. The ooze covered his mouth. Then his nose. Then the rest of his head. All this in a matter of moments. All he could do was hold his breath and wait for the inevitable.

His forearms, still raised above his head, started to slip below, but then soft sure hands grabbed hold of his own. A moment later he was spitting the metallic neophosphorous from his mouth and gulping desperately for air. Above him was the most beautiful sight he had ever seen, the face of Sierra, pink with effort, but shining brighter than all the glowing river surrounding him. Looking into her eyes, he knew he would be safe.

His chest and hips came free with squelching pops. After that his knees and feet shot out in a sliding rush as Sierra pulled him into her arms.

Buoyed by her skimmers, she flew over to a narrow ledge of rock alongside the river. His entire body was glowing and his clothes were torn, but he was alive.

"You came back for me," he said.

"I guess you were right," she said, breathing heavily. "You needed me after all."

Though the joy Adan felt seemed like it would last forever, it faded all too quickly as he gazed towards the top of the crevice.

"How are we going to get out of here?"

"I don't know. Skimmers can't fly that high."

"We have to at least try." He had not escaped death to stay down here, trapped, until the Developers found them.

Sierra slipped the skimmers off her feet and handed them to Adan. "It would be better if you carried me," she said, "You're kind of heavy."

"All right," he said, grinning.

As Adan finished placing the slats on his feet, a deafening boom from above shook the air around them, echoing off the walls of the crevice.

Sierra and Adan looked at each other, as if to brace themselves for what might come next, but all they could see was the bridge which, from this distance, looked unharmed.

"If that was an explosion," Adan said, "I hope the others got out before it hit."

Sierra's hand went to her mouth. "Wik—I set him down to come after you."

Adan looked up, hoping to see a sign of movement—anything that would let him know what was going on up there, but an eerie silence settled over the cavern. The machines all stopped. "We'll find him," he said. "But we have to get up there first."

Sierra wrapped her arms around him from behind and Adan engaged the skimmers. He was so consumed by the urgency of getting out of the crevice he barely felt her weight at all.

"I know you can do this," she whispered in his ear.

Adan set out over the ribbon of neophosphorous. Skimmers were not designed to fly straight upwards. Like the sand duster ships, they required something solid beneath them to generate the cushion of energy along which they could float.

Adan headed for the far end of the crevice, where the river disappeared into the rock. Flying above the flow, he rapidly picked up speed.

Sierra gripped him even harder. "You do have a plan, don't you?" she asked.

"I'm just going to try this and see what happens. Hold on tight."

He raced along the flow until there was barely any space between the two sides of the crevice. Then he turned abruptly, so that his feet went perpendicular to the wall. For a few moments, they shot up the side, but then their momentum stalled. Before it was gone completely, Adan pushed off the wall and flipped his legs to the other side so that they shot up the opposite wall instead. He kept going up that side until they started to lose speed again and twisted back to the other wall. He repeated the process, each time, rising a little higher, jumping back and forth between the walls until they reached the top of the crevice.

"You did it," Sierra squeezed him tight as they crested the edge of the cliff wall.

Their elation lasted but a moment, cut short by the scene of wreckage and devastation which greeted them as they hovered above the floor of the mine.

The mine was strewn with bodies and overturned equipment. The bodies were mangled beyond recognition. Adan had no way of telling whether they were somatarchs or his friends.

A sickening wave rose into his throat. He fought against it, forcing himself not to give in to panic.

At first he had thought there was nothing moving in the cavern, but he soon realized that was not true. A group of somatarchs were silently advancing towards them from the far side of the bridge, the side from which Adan and the Sentients had come. The vehicles there remained undamaged.

The moment they spotted Adan, all six somatarchs broke into a run.

Since Adan had skimmers and the somatarchs were on foot, they wouldn't be able to catch him, even carrying Sierra, but he couldn't just take off without any idea of where he was going. He quickly compared the schematic in his head with the layout of the mine.

Two of the passages exiting the cavern had caved in and were now impassible, including the one they needed to travel down to get to the vault.

"We need to find a way to get into that blocked tunnel," he said.

"There." She pointed at a tunneler. It was tilted on its side near the entrance to the caved-in passage, propped up by the remains of some overturned carts, but it was not as severely damaged as some of the others.

"Let's hope it's still operational."

Adan skimmed above the wreckage as the pounding feet of the somatarchs on the bridge reverberated across the cavern. He reached the elongated vehicle and sized up its condition. It had been dented up badly, but the hatch was still intact, as was the drilling ring in front. He connected to the device with his mind and saw that it still had power. The hatch whisked open with a thought and they flew to the opening. He let Sierra slide off his back and down into the vehicle. He followed her in and the hatch closed shut behind them.

Inside, there was space for four operators. Adan and Sierra connected to the tunneler's sensors so they could see what was happening outside as if the entire hull were semi-transparent. The somatarchs were picking their way through the wreckage, leaping over large machines and twisted hunks of metal, closing in fast.

Adan planted himself next to Sierra in one of the white plastic chairs, then ripped off his skimmers and tossed them aside. Sierra's eyes glazed over as she brought the tunneler up to full power. Before she engaged the lev generator, she brought up a map of the mine which Adan could see as well. Using the ship's own modulator, they scanned the cavern for zoetic pulses. A hollow feeling welled up inside Adan, but it wasn't from the six red pulses closing in on them.

"There are no other survivors," Sierra announced, her emotions as empty as his own.

"They must have gotten out in time." Adan tried to convince himself. *"I only saw a few bodies in the rubble."*

With the somatarchs almost upon them, there was no time to go back and search for their friends. Sierra engaged the drill cone. It burst into brilliant yellow light in front of them. The tunneler's lev engaged and the vehicle shuddered and shook free, righting itself and plunging forward. It floated to the entrance of the caved-in tunnel as the first of the somatarchs arrived. The locus cone plunged through the remains of a large, overturned hauler blocking the tunnel, ripping it in half. A moment later their tunneler was drilling into the rock-filled passage.

Rocks clanked against the fuselage, but as they passed through them into the open tunnel beyond so did something else.

One of the somatarchs had reached the tunneler. He was running beside them with a rod.

"Those fractal rods—the ones they were using to pulverize the rocks—they must be using them to try and break down the

hull." Sierra increased the speed, but the somatarch matched them. Another somatarch came up on the other side with another rod and did the same. The sides of the vehicle quivered and shook. Pops and hisses came from the paneling.

"We can't outrun them in this. It's too slow." Adan had thought they would be safe inside this giant machine, but now it felt like a death trap.

"Then we'll just have to go where they can't." Sierra drove the tunneler into the debris strewn floor. The locus cone pulverized everything in its path. The somatarchs fell behind, but kept coming.

"What are you doing?" Adan wondered if Sierra still had control of the machine.

"Covering our trail."

They passed deeper into the bedrock. lLoose rocks above caved in on the ship, but the hull held against the weight. Surging forward, the falling rocks filled in the new tunnel behind them, burying the somatarchs and ensuring they could not to follow.

A few moments later the tunneler pivoted back upwards until it re-emerged into the passage.

"Great thinking," Adan told her, *"Now we can get out of this ship and make our way to the vault."*

"Actually, I was thinking this vehicle might be a better way of getting into the vault than following that assessor's map. We could just drill our way straight into the prison cells from below."

"It would save us an awful lot of time," Adan acknowledged. At the same time he wondered what they would do if the Devs seized control of this ship the way they had with the hauler. After mulling it over, he decided saving some time was not worth the risk of being trapped inside this vehicle if it was

taken over. *"I don't think—"* he began, but a flash of alarm in Sierra's thoughts cut him short.

"Adan, we've got to get out of here," she said, disconnecting her thoughts from his.

"What's wrong?" he asked, though the question was more like a reflex since he already knew the answer.

"The Devs have control of the ship."

Adan stared at their position on the modulator as the tunneler rushed forward at ever increasing velocity.

TWENTY-FIVE

CLEAN

ADAN TRIED TO CONNECT TO THE TUNNELER BUT IT WAS nothing more than a moving hunk of metal now.

"How are we going this fast?" Adan asked.

"I don't know, this is way faster than it should be able to go." Sierra pulled on the hatch's emergency lever. "It's locked down. I'll have to open it with the cutter."

"Hurry. There's no telling what they might do next." Adan shoved the skimmers into his garrick and came up beside her.

Sierra put on the cutter and the energy blade shot out from the end. She threaded the beam around the seal of the hatch. In moments the round door came crashing to the floor. The ceiling of the tunnel sped by above them in a blur of blacks and grays. It was not an inviting sight, but there appeared to be enough space for them to crawl out on top of the vehicle.

Sierra shimmied up the ladder and eased herself out through the hole. Adan climbed up after her, crawling out onto the roof with gripping fingers, keeping his head down. They held onto the rim of the hatch to keep from slipping on the curved fuselage.

Adan could feel the tunnel ceiling rushing by above him, suffocatingly close.

"I guess we're supposed to jump?" He hoped Sierra had a less risky idea.

"If we use the skimmers, they should kick in before we hit the ground."

The locus cone had disengaged, but the neophosphorous coating Adan's clothes and body lent a considerable amount of light to the otherwise pitch black tunnel. He could see enough of the floor to tell it was not much of a jump in terms of distance, but the tunneler was going three times faster now than what Sierra had it at before. Even with the skimmers there was no guarantee they would land safely.

"Let's hope this works." Adan let one hand go free of the hatch to hunt for the skimmers inside his garrick. It was an awkward business slipping them onto his feet with one hand while gripping the rim of the hatch with the other. All while the tunneler plowed blindly ahead in the dark, jostling him around on top of the fuselage. Once he got the second skimmer in place he shifted into position for the jump.

"Don't think about it," Sierra advised, looping her arms around his chest. *"Just jump."*

White lights flared out from beneath Adan's feet. He pushed himself over the edge, bracing for impact. His feet hit the cushion of invisible energy generated by the skimmers and his arms shot out to steady himself. His knees buckled and he felt himself start to lose his balance. Sierra squeezed him so tight he could hardly breathe. He pitched forward towards the tunnel wall, but his bioseine kicked in and spread his legs out and righted his torso. A moment later, he was bouncing softly on the skimmers in the middle of the passage as the tunneler sped away in the dark.

"We made it!" Sierra shouted, her words echoing down the

tunnel into the darkness. *"Oops,"* she added, *"I hope no one was listening."*

Adan let out an airless chuckle. *"Could you let go a little?"* he asked.

"Oh, sorry." Sierra realized she was cutting off his air and relaxed her grip. *"Where do we go now?"*

Adan took in a deep breath, enjoying the freedom to breathe again.

"I don't know. Let's skate down this tunnel and we'll figure it out on the way."

Adan skimmed down the tunnel with Sierra holding on not quite as tightly from behind.

"I don't think this is a good idea." Sierra's thoughts came into his. *"They know we're in this tunnel. They're bound to come looking for us."*

"I was wondering if we should go back and try to find the others."

"Part of me feels like we should. But there weren't any signals on the modulator. And the plan was to flee and meet back up at the vault. If we go back and look for them, we might not get to the vault in time."

She was right, but it still felt wrong, like the way he'd abandoned Senya in Hull. *"They'll probably be sending more somatarchs to investigate what happened there. The mine wouldn't be safe to go back to even if we wanted to,"* he added, half-heartedly. It felt like there was no way to salvage the mission now. Too much had gone wrong.

"We just need to get to the vault. Everything will work out somehow," Sierra told him. She was struggling, though, just as much as he was.

To take his thoughts off the mine, he examined the map of Manx Core in his mind. The tunnel they were in ran through the lowest levels of the complex. It looped back around at the end and connected to the tunnel leading to an access shaft where they could reach the upper levels. A water reservoir sat between the tunnel they were in and the access shaft tunnel, but there was no way for them to get in on this side.

"I don't see any way out of this tunnel, except to go all the way to the end, and since that's the way the tunneler went, they'll probably be expecting us."

Sierra was studying the map as well.

"We could cut our way through the reservoir," she suggested. *"The walls aren't that thick and the tunnel we need to get to runs along the other side."*

"But skimmers only work across solid surfaces." Adan reminded her. *"How would we get across all of that water?"* From Adan's time with the Welkin he had formed the idea that falling into deep water was deadly, but as he searched the information in his bioseine he saw this was not necessarily the case. Falling into it from a great height such as the upper reaches of the Basin would prove fatal, but they could carve a tunnel with the cutter that would bring them into the reservoir only a short distance above the surface of the water.

"Your bioseine knows how to swim," Sierra assured him.

*Swim...*This was something else that was new, but she was right, he already knew how to do it. Despite this realization, the idea still made him nervous.

"What about carving a passage to the vault from here so we can avoid the tunnels altogether?" he asked.

"That might work if we started from the other tunnel. It's too far from here, though. The cutter doesn't have enough of a charge left."

"We could try to find some more bismine," Adan suggested,

though he doubted there would be any this far down.

"No time. If the others survived, we have to get to the vault as quickly as possible."

"All right, we'll try swimming, then," Adan acquiesced, shaking his head. The thought of plunging into the water still gave him chills.

Their course set, they skated down the tunnel until it ran parallel to the reservoir. Adan eased onto the ground. He slipped off the skimmers while Sierra engaged the cutter and made her first incision.

She made this hole much smaller than the one she had made in the quarry. It would be big enough for them to crawl through one at a time, but that was it.

Adan popped one of the bismine chips out from the chronotrace to see if he could sense any more nearby, but as he expected there was nothing. He returned the chip to its housing and started helping clear out the rubble from the tunnel Sierra was making.

It took about five microslices before they broke through. The hole came in at exactly the position they were aiming for, but the water level was much lower than expected. The dark water lurked more than three body-lengths below. It was a straight drop.

The reservoir was lit by a or so dozen lumins, but they were only about half as bright as the lumins Adan was used to. This only added to his reluctance to jump. All he could see were the edges of the walls and the endless, night black liquid beneath.

"Ready to lose that glow of yours?" Sierra asked, glancing at his brilliant skin and clothes.

"I suppose so." He had forgotten all about his appearance while obsessing about the water. *"That jump looks higher than I thought it would be."*

"You'll be fine," Sierra said out loud. To prove it, she dove in head first, hitting the water with a grayish ruffle. Her head bobbed up a moment later, pale and dripping. "It's okay. The water is a nice temperature."

Adan knew it was no use waiting on the edge. They had to get to the prison and see if any of their friends had survived.

He closed his eyes and leapt feet first into the darkness.

The water slapped his body like a giant hand, one made of rock. Liquid shot up his nose and darkness surrounded him on all sides. He gyrated every part of his body that would move in an effort to escape the oppressive heaviness surrounding him.

Just when the pressure was starting to build in his lungs, his head emerged above the water. As he recovered his breath and expelled the water from his nose, he found himself treading in place as if it were the most natural thing in the world.

"See? I told you there was nothing to it," Sierra told him, bright-eyed and calm, as if she were enjoying this. "Now are you ready to get going?"

He wanted to tell her he wasn't ready at all, that it would be better if they looked for a way to climb back up the smooth rock wall to the opening and take their chances in the tunnels, but he knew that would be foolish.

"Let's just get out of here as quickly as we can," he said.

Sierra started out across the water. Adan followed, doing a modified breast stroke so that he kept his head perpetually above water. As they slipped through the placid pool, he had to admit the brisk temperature of the water was rather refreshing. The taste of the drops which slipped into his mouth were delicious as well. In the back of his mind, though, he still felt vulnerable suspended in the midst of this dark expanse. Who knew how far down it stretched or what might lay beneath? He kicked a little faster and soon caught up and even moved past Sierra.

They were over halfway across the reservoir when Adan

felt a slight current start to run through the waters. Over time it grew stronger, threatening to pull them off course. They started swimming harder to compensate, but soon even that was not enough as the current picked up speed.

"What's going on?" Adan asked, *"I can't get through this."*

He sensed Sierra's mind struggling to figure out what was causing it as well, but neither of them could unravel the mystery. Along the walls nothing had changed. The lumins stared back at them, lidless and impassive eyes watching their struggles.

Adan increased the speed of his strokes, his hands knifing through the water. His legs were kicking so desperately it seemed as if his own efforts must be causing the waters to churn even more. Whatever he tried it was no use; he and Sierra were being pulled back further and further towards the center of the pool, directly opposite the direction they needed to go.

By now the waters were starting to foam. Adan felt as powerless to stop the pull as if he had been falling through the air. Even worse, the currents were tugging from below, trying to pull him under.

"They must be draining the reservoir," Sierra conjectured. The next moment she was gone, dragged under by the current.

He could sense her position with his bioseine and dove towards her. He latched on to her hand as the current mounted.

"Use the cutter," he told her, *"We have to be able to see what's going on."*

There was no use fighting the current now. It was too strong. Sierra let go of his hand. For a moment fear gripped him at the thought that he might lose her, but then the yellow blade flared to life underwater.

In that flash of light, Adan saw they were only a couple body-lengths from the bottom of the reservoir. He also saw what was pulling them under, a large transparent tube running along the floor, wide enough for a large person to fit through. It was sucking water into it at an incredible rate.

As they rushed towards it, Sierra thrust the cutter below her legs. The next moment she was sucked into the tube. Adan had no time to be horrified. He was sucked in right behind her. His arm and then his head banged against the hard casing. Then he flipped over and started sliding on his back.

Light gashed his vision as his swirling world came to an abrupt stop. Something yanked him upwards. The current shifted suddenly and continued pushing him back up. Sierra was floating beside him, the yellow light from the cutter's blade shimmering beside her in the water. A mangled opening was visible in the tube below them.

"*It's all right,*" Sierra gestured upwards. "*Swim up now.*"

She kicked her feet and shot towards the surface, the cutter flickering like a beacon, beckoning him to safety.

He swam with burning urgency, his lungs dense pockets of pain inside his chest. The two of them broke the surface together. Chunks of the sliced up pipe bobbed in the water around them. The current still swirled, but its grip no longer had sufficient strength to pull them under.

"*You cut your way out of the pipe!*" Adan spit out a mouthful of water, amazed they were still alive.

She nodded. "I'm starting to actually like this cutter." She gave him a soggy smile. She swam to one of the larger pieces of tubing and threw her arms on top of it to get a break from swimming. Adan did the same.

"You're not glowing anymore," she said as she turned off the cutter and slipped it back onto her belt.

Adan couldn't see his garrick all that well under the water, but that was the point. She was right. It was no longer glowing. He was finally clean.

TWENTY-SIX
SHAFT TO NOWHERE

With no more currents to contend with, Adan and Sierra resumed their swim across the reservoir, but Adan's nerves were on edge the whole time. He kept wondering if the current would pick up again. Maybe there was a backup drainage pipe somewhere else? He swam as though another current propelled him, one pushing him to the opposite side of the chamber.

Once they finally reached it, Sierra carved out a little place for them in the wall at the edge of the water where they could rest. Adan lay inside the hollow, catching his breath, hoping he would never have to get into water again.

Tired as they both were, they did not rest long. They soon started carving out a tunnel in the black rock of the reservoir wall. This time Adan did the cutting so Sierra could rest. He worked his way into the rock, crouching low and giving himself just enough room on the sides to toss out the rocks behind him. He carved the tunnel at an incline so most of the rocks slid out on their own accord.

"How much time left before the cutter goes dark?" Sierra asked about five microslices in.

Adan slid away a small panel that showed the power level down to a burnt orange color. "Half a slice, if that." When the panel hit red, the chip would need to be swapped out. "We may have to resort to using the chips from the chronotrace soon."

"How many are in there?"

"Three, but they are all on low power."

"Too bad the skimmers don't use bismine."

"We'll have enough to get us to the vault," he promised, though that was assuming everything went perfectly.

Sierra made a noncommittal sound, indicating she was probably thinking the same thing.

"What about once we get the prisoners, though?" she asked a few moments later. "How are we going to get them all back up to the surface if Bryce and the others aren't there?"

Adan paused from his cutting and wiped the sweat from his brow. "I'm sure we'll find a way. Maybe Gavin will be there, too. If so, he'll know what to do." Adan had almost forgotten about his friend in all the chaos. Gavin had helped him escape the Institute. Adan was confident he'd be able to get them out of Manx Core. If they found him.

Adan started cutting again, working faster than before. His limbs soon grew exhausted. The cutter was like a pendulum that was losing its momentum, swinging with less and less force after each pass, but he kept going to let Sierra recover as much as possible. When he broke through the wall about ten microslices later he let the cutter fall to the ground and took another quick rest until Sierra emerged through the opening.

"You're spent. Why didn't you let me have a turn?" Sierra asked, putting her hands on her hips. Adan felt like her patient all over again.

"You can have it the next round." Though exhausted, he

slurped in a big gulp of air and got out the skimmers. Every moment wasted was one more delay keeping them from reaching the prisoners.

He fired up the skimmers and they sped down the maintenance tunnel on the other side of the reservoir. It was only about three spans across, half the size of the tunnel they'd used to leave the mine. Track lighting ran along the edge of the floor, but the passage was otherwise rather nondescript.

They ate up the distance with smooth, air-cushioned strides. Within two microslices they arrived at the spot which, according to the schematic, was directly beneath the vault.

"All right, my turn to do the cutting," Sierra said. "Pass me the skimmers and I'll start into the ceiling. Once I carve out enough space for both of us, I'll crawl in and you can come up."

"Okay, be careful," Adan said, hoping she didn't get hit by any of the rocks as they fell.

He sat down with his back against the wall, giving himself plenty of distance to avoid the falling chunks himself. Though Sierra was careful to cut at an angle, away from her body, he couldn't help but cringe when some of the larger rocks slammed into the floor. They made a horrible amount of noise. Without a modulator they would have no idea whether or not someone entered this tunnel. If they did, the noise would be sure to alert them.

Eventually Sierra was able to slip into the hole she made in the ceiling. From that point on, all Adan could see were her feet dangling from the lip. Then even those disappeared as she carved out enough space to be able to stand up inside the shaft.

Adan walked over to inspect the hole a couple of times and to see her progress, but he didn't get too close. Each time he asked if she would like to take a break, but she always refused.

She had been carving for almost twenty microslices when

Adan thought he heard a noise somewhere back down the tunnel.

"*Hold on a moment. I thought I heard something,*" he told Sierra, who promptly stopped cutting.

They waited for a while, but heard no sounds, so she went back to work.

Not long after that they ran into a problem with the shaft.

"*I've hit a vein of that black and blue rock,*" Sierra informed him.

"*Celerium?*"

"*Yes. And the cutter isn't doing anything to it. I think I'll have to carve a way around it.*"

Adan remembered how Gavin had used the blue spectrum to sculpt the celerium back in the compound. But even then, it had taken him a long time just to fashion a small coil. It would probably take forever to cut through a large vein.

"*Do you think the cutter has enough energy to carve around it?*"

"*As long as the vein isn't too large,*" she answered, trying to keep her thoughts positive.

"*Right. We're so close.*" Adan did his best to echo her mood. They were almost three quarters the distance they needed to go to get to the vault, but there was no telling how far they would have to dig to get around that vein.

Sierra labored for a few more microslices before she tossed him down the skimmers and Adan finally joined her up in the shaft. Now that she wasn't excavating vertically, she needed someone to help clear the rocks. Adan, who was by now completely rested, was more than happy to assist. He offered to take a turn at cutting as well, but she just shook her head and went back to work.

He took a moment to study the immense bluish vein she had uncovered. He was struck not only by the size of it, but also by how incredibly smooth it was. He had never seen rock as naturally smooth as this. It certainly was beautiful with its cobalt blue flecks scattered amongst the blackness.

Sierra carved out a tunnel a dozen paces long with no sign of the end of the celerium. That was when the cutter finally gave out, plunging the shaft into darkness. Adan cringed when it happened, but refused to panic, reminding himself that they still had the chips from the chronotrace.

He whipped out the device in the dark and removed one of its chips. Reaching out, he placed it in Sierra's hand, sensing her position through her bioseine.

She swapped out the bismine chip and the cutter blazed back to life, lighting up the dark passage once more.

As she turned to face the rocks she'd been carving into, she dropped the old, dead bismine chip and it went ricocheting down the short passage, past Adan and down the shaft that led to the maintenance tunnel, landing with a muffled plink.

The new round of cutting was not long underway before Sierra stopped.

"Are you tired? I can take over for you now," Adan offered.

"No, it's not that. It's just...I'll try one more direction, but even if I guess right this time and we're able to get around the vein, I don't know if we'll have enough to make it all the way up and into the vault. But it's pointless to keep going on in this direction."

"That makes sense. I doubt it's that deep in all directions."

Sierra abandoned the new tunnel and started cutting back the opposite way. Adan could tell she was exhausted; her cuts were coming slower and slower. She had resorted to using her free hand to help keep the cutter up. Once again he offered to relieve her, but she refused to relinquish the device, snapping at him and telling him to stop asking; she would tell him when she was too tired to keep going.

Adan said nothing, but the silence afterwards was palpable. His hopes drained away with each passing moment, as much from her reproach as from the grim circumstances they faced. The two realities intertwined themselves together in his mind, forming an unbreakable bond which, much like the celerium vein, he could not cut through.

Sierra toiled on, slashing at the rocks as if she were taking out her frustration on the inanimate material, but it did little good. She had gone a dozen paces in the new direction when the cutter died again.

Wordlessly, they repeated the same procedure as before and restored the cutter with the second chip from the chronotrace.

This time Sierra didn't bother consulting him, but struck out in a new direction. It was just as well. Adan saw little hope they would get around the vein, no matter which direction they chose. They were trapped here, only a few short spans beneath the prison vault. The time to rendezvous with the others would soon pass.

Despite Sierra's mounting frustration, she did not close off her mind. And there in the stifling rock, as she hacked futilely beneath the vein, he sensed she was close to losing all hope. She slashed her way down the new path like a burning ember melting into the sand. Her will to go on would soon vanish altogether. It was only a matter of when.

Adan was contemplating asking her to give over the cutter one more time, in spite of her warning, when Sierra gave a little cry of surprise, followed by a chuckle.

"*I found it,*" she announced, her thoughts the complete opposite of what they had been a moment before. Hope glimmered brightly inside her once again. The ember had been rekindled. "*I found the end of the vein.*"

She flashed Adan a smile that washed away all the tension

which had built up between them. He sensed her energy quicken as she set about busily carving through the rock around the end of the vein.

The vein proved to be as tall as it was thick, but it was no longer in their way. It was straight up from there on out and she carved so quickly Adan could barely keep up with clearing out the debris.

She burrowed her way through the black rock as if she were just starting out again. Adan's spirits rose with each chunk of debris that fell. From the schematic he knew they were only three body-lengths away from reaching the vault.

And that is when the yellow blade died again. Fumbling over himself, Adan produced the third and final chip, handing it to her with a trembling hand. All their hopes rested on this small crystal half the size of Adan's palm.

They made terrific progress as Sierra seemed to push her way through the rock through sheer force of will. Chunks fell like an avalanche now. Two body-lengths to go. Then one.

They came to within a half a body-length of the vault before the final chip died. Sierra slammed the cutter against the side of the tunnel, whether in frustration or in the vain hope she could jar it back to life, Adan couldn't tell. Utter blackness filled the tunnel. Her mind went dark as well, even darker than the tunnel around them.

There was only a small stretch of rock between them and the vault, but it might as well have been the entirety of the Vast.

Sierra climbed slowly back down the long shaft she had made without a word. Even in the dark her very movements echoed in defeat. As she set foot back in the lower tunnel, Adan heard her begin to weep softly.

"What are we going to do?" he asked at last, his voice just above a whisper.

Sierra didn't answer. After a few moments the sounds of her crying died down and then disappeared. The two of them sat in silence for so long the darkness felt like it was a thing in and of itself, as if it were their real obstacle and not the span of rock which separated them from the prisoners.

Then she at last she spoke. Her voice was barely more than a whisper, but the sound of it gave Adan something solid to hold onto in the dark.

"You know, back in the esolace you could engage in what they called challenges," she said. "They could be whatever you wanted. You could push yourself physically or insert yourself into some mystery that seemed impossible to solve. But if it ever got too hard, if it ever seemed too much, you could just walk away and the whole thing would disappear. I sometimes wish life was like that. Then we could just leave this place and go home and our friends wouldn't be prisoners anymore because they wouldn't even be real. They'd be just another part of the story that was playing out in our heads."

Adan tried to imagine what it would be like knowing you could be free of a problem with a simple thought.

"But then you wouldn't push yourself as far as you could, would you?"

"No, I suppose you're right," she admitted. "It just seems like there are some problems that are impossible to solve. We failed, Adan. We failed."

Adan had no answer this time, for he had the same thoughts himself. Without the cutter, they would never be able to get into the vault the way they planned. They could go back out and take the tunnels into the main chamber. But even if they could somehow reach the front entrance to the vault unde-tected, he doubted the two of them would be able to overcome the guards there by themselves. The others, if they had even survived, would be long gone by then.

"I'm sorry I snapped at you," she said softly.

Her words released a knot he had been holding inside of him, but he didn't know how to respond.

"You're supposed to say, 'apology accepted'," she said. "That is, if you want to."

"Oh—apology accepted, then," he said. Then his mind froze up again. Another awkward silence enveloped the darkness. "Sierra," he said at last, an odd mix of emotions rising inside him, "I want you to know something," he began, but faltered, words failing him once again.

A scraping noise from the shaft interrupted his thoughts. The tunnel was completely dark, but instinctively he looked in the direction of the sound. Then he heard it again, closer this time.

"Someone's coming up the shaft," he warned.

"What are we going to do? We're totally blind in here."

Adan's heart ricocheted around inside his chest. They were at a dead end. If someone was coming to attack or capture them, there was no way out. But he couldn't let his fear take hold. He forced himself to focus in on what he knew, what possible advantages they might have, blind and alone in the dark as they were.

The bioseine. It could dampen his senses. Maybe it could augment them as well. A quick query to his system revealed that to be the case.

"Use your bioseine to focus in on your hearing," he instructed.

He already knew the layout of the tunnel from memory. Now, with his bioseine taking hold of his senses, dampening his vision and focusing all of his mental energy on his hearing and touch, he began to notice a subtle change. While he still couldn't see anything, every sound was magnified. His breathing, his heartbeat, small noises he had simply filtered out before rushed to the forefront of his awareness, clamoring for attention.

The padding of Sierra's feet on the rock sounded like she was stomping down the passage. He felt her body pushing against him in the dark. It was strange being so close to her. The sensation made it difficult to concentrate. Thankfully, she squeezed past him and the feeling passed.

"Wait, where are you going?" he asked, his mind freeing itself from the distraction of her presence.

"The cutter may be dead, but it can still be used as a weapon," she replied.

"I still have my neutralizer."

"If it's a somatarch, that'll be useless."

"Wait, my shiv," he told her, feeling at his belt for the knife Bryce had given him. But it wasn't there. He must have lost it in the neophosphorous or in the water. *"Never mind. It's gone. But give me the cutter instead—"*

"There's no time," Sierra shot back, *"I'm almost to the opening."*

Adan heard her steal towards the lower shaft. He started down the tunnel after her, determined not to let her face the danger alone. The rocks felt more solid than before as he groped his way along the wall. Even his feet were more sure as he edged his way down the roughhewn tunnel.

"I'm at the opening," she informed him. *"The light from the maintenance tunnel is partially blocked. Someone's definitely in the shaft."*

As Adan crept towards her, he could hear her breathing getting louder, but he couldn't hear anything from whoever was coming up the shaft.

He had almost reached her when a white light burst through the tunnel, momentarily scrambling his senses.

Sierra's mind went blank. She'd been hit by a neutralizer.

He went still as the rock around him. For a long terrible moment he couldn't think. If he went forward, he might be hit by the next blast, but if he stayed where he was, whoever was coming up the shaft would eventually come up and take him out as well. He didn't want to count on the neutralizer failing to affect him a second time.

Unexpectedly, the celerium vein nearby pulsed ever so briefly and he got a glimpse of the tunnel. For a brief moment he saw Sierra's crumpled body lying at the edge of the shaft. Beyond her was the opening below, a stretch of blackness from which the enemy approached.

Though he had no idea what had caused it, the light faded as quickly as it came, but Adan could still see the scene in his mind. He could hear the sound of someone coming up the shaft distinctly. The intruder sounded like he was almost to the lip of the lower shaft.

Adan could not let whoever it was reach the upper shaft. He didn't stand a chance in a fight with a somatarch, and he couldn't wait to see if it was an assessor. With no time to consider some other possibility he rushed forward, vaulting over Sierra and tucking his legs up under his body, hurling himself like a human ball down into the shaft.

It only took a moment before he impacted with whoever was climbing up. The collision jarred Adan's body and slowed his descent momentarily, but then the resistance gave way and he continued on, hurtling down through the darkness, tumbling and reeling in a free fall into the unknown.

TWENTY-SEVEN
IN THE FLESH

A HORRENDOUS RUMBLING SHOOK ADAN TO HIS SENSES. The ground trembled. Debris pelted his back. Someone was dragging him by the legs face down along the ground so that he could not raise his head to see who it was. His chest exploded in agony as it scraped along the stone floor. Instinctively, he engaged his bioseine to shut off the pain.

Everything went still. The person dragging him dropped his legs, letting them bang against the floor. Adan rolled onto his side and his bioseine flashed a warning: several of his ribs were bruised, but he dismissed the information as a singular thought seized his mind: where was Sierra?

He sat up and scanned his surroundings. He was in the maintenance tunnel, but the hole in the ceiling was gone. The passage was filled top to bottom with boulders and rocks. A haze of dust hung in the air. Had there been another quake? If so, the rocks had settled. It looked like the danger had passed.

On Adan's side of the fall-in, there was scattered debris, but the passage lay open behind him. Standing with his foot against one of the larger rocks and looking down at Adan with an unsightly sneer was a portly figure dressed in a dusty garrick and kaff.

Adan took in a sharp breath. "Nox?"

The Wayman acknowledged him with a nod and flashed his horrific grin, malicious and gleeful all at once, like always.

"In the flesh," said the Wayman, patting his generous midsection and then choking on the dust clouds which issued forth from his coat. His garrick was torn in several places so that it resembled one of Will's tarps after a storm. He wore a bandage wrapped around his left arm and had several nicks and cuts on his face, but whatever he might have been through since the sand duster crash, he had the same violent look in his eyes. And he'd managed to pick up the shiv on his belt and half a dozen pinions strapped to his back to follow through with whatever aggressive impulses which managed to seize him.

"What are you doing here?" Adan asked, staring at him in wide-eyed fear.

"Saving your life, apparently," Nox said, still coughing.

"There was a quake?" Adan eased back towards the rubble. He knew he couldn't escape that way, but it made him feel safer to put some distance between himself and Nox.

Nox nodded and pounded his chest in reply, his barking cough echoing down the tunnel. While Adan waited for his fit to die down he surveyed the rock pile behind him, hoping in vain to see some sign of Sierra. Seeing nothing, he rose rapidly and began heading towards the rubble. He had to find her.

"Ah-ah-ah." Nox finally recovered his voice. He bounded over to Adan and grabbed him by the arm. "Where do you think you're going?"

"To find my friend." Adan pointed towards the cave-in. "She might be trapped in the rubble." He felt a pit opening up in his throat, sick with the thought of what might have happened to Sierra.

"That female you were running with?" Nox let out a harrumph, shaking his head. "You'll have to hope she's as lucky as you are, then. There's no time to look for her. You're coming with me."

Adan pulled against the Wayman's fleshy grip, but failed to free himself. "You don't understand, she might be—"

"Oh, I understand, all right," Nox said, yanking him back down the tunnel and spinning him around. "And I said, you're coming with *me*." He adjusted the shiv in his belt for emphasis.

A mantle of dread wrapped around his chest. He wanted to scream at Nox, *I don't care what you do to me, I have to find her,* but the bitter liquid of fear gagged him and kept the words from coming out.

"Let's get going," Nox said, giving him a shove.

Adan glared at him. Never had he felt such anger towards another person in his life. But Nox's hand was still on his shiv and Adan knew he would not hesitate to use it. He glanced back over his shoulder at the wall of debris between him and Sierra. Realistically, there was no way he would be able to get through it, even if Nox wasn't there, but he couldn't stand the thought of leaving without her.

"The girl wasn't there when I pulled you out of the cave-in. Get over it and let's get moving," Nox said bluntly.

Adan could only hope the quake had not affected the tunnels Sierra had dug in the ceiling. And if they had...*Oh, please Numinae, don't let her die.*

If only he could find a way to escape from Nox. The neutralizer! He glanced at his wrist. It wasn't there.

"You disarm me, I disarm you. Only fair, don't you think?" Nox's smirk had never been uglier.

That was it. He knew he could never take Nox in a fight. He glanced back one last time at the rubble. *I'll find you some-how, Sierra,* he promised.

Adan dusted off his garrick and gathered his emotions. Nox would slip up somehow, he told himself. He'd let down his guard and then Adan would seize his chance.

"How did you find me?" Adan asked.

"I followed you. And it wasn't easy, I don't mind telling you. I swear I rubbed off more than a little skin squirming through those tunnels you carved out. You could have made them a little wider. And the water! Whatever possessed you? That was the most unnatural thing I've been through in all my life. Almost died half a dozen times. If you hadn't left me one of those floating scraps I'm sure I would have drowned."

"You followed us down from the surface—from Oasis?"

Nox nodded. "Hard to believe isn't it? I'm a tighter swedge than I look." He tapped his head.

"But why, Nox? What could you possibly want down here?" Adan focused in on him, trying to unravel what he was thinking, but as usual it was a jumbled mess. His mind seemed to flit between something like wondering where his next meal was coming from and the most horrific images of blood and death. Adan shuddered and looked away, not wanting to see any more.

Nox rubbed the hilt of his shiv distractedly. He seemed to give his answer a moment's thought, but no more than that. "I suppose it wouldn't hurt to tell you, seeing as how I'm armed and you're...well, not in the best of shape." He let out a laugh, but then clapped his hand over his mouth and glanced down the tunnel. "Ay!" he muttered, "Got to keep quiet. Never know when one of those ghost warriors might be close."

"Right, so you were telling me why you followed me down here," Adan said.

"Ah, yes." Nox nodded vigorously, "Well, I already told you, didn't I? To save your life." He let out another guffaw, immediately stifling it again with his hand.

"Thank you for that, by the way," Adan said. He knew there had to be a sinister motive behind Nox's actions, but from what little he could glean from his thoughts, at least the part about rescuing Adan was true.

"There's nothing to thank me for, really," Nox said, "I couldn't keep following you if you were dead, now could I?"

"I suppose not."

"Look at all the scrapes you've gotten yourself into without Nox to look out for you."

"You've managed to come through relatively unscathed," Adan observed.

"Yes, well, I did have a bit of help with that," Nox admitted, then he pulled out the necklace he wore from beneath his garrick and dangled the metal gear on the end of it in front of Adan. "I don't remember the name of this thing, but it keeps those gear heads from seeing me."

"Where did you get that?" Adan asked.

"Nolan, of course," Nox said, as if it should have been obvious. "He's the only Wayman with any sense when it comes to machines."

"He sent you down here? But what for?" Adan's fears only deepened at the mention of Nolan's name, but he tried not to let it show.

"To kill the leaders of this place, why else?"

"But—but what about Bryce? Why did Nolan send you if he'd already sent him?"

"Well, if you were the Reeve, would you send in one assassin when you could send in two? Besides, when that hammer head left, Nolan didn't know Oasis had already been destroyed. After he found out about the storm, he sent me in just to sweep the rest of the sand under the rug, to make sure the leaders got what was coming to them, that sort of thing."

"So you didn't know they would have this base underground?"

"Did you? I'd wager even Nolan himself didn't know about it—and he's got more gears in his head than the rest of us put together. All I know is that I was sent here to kill the leaders, specifically one named Malthus, and Nolan said you would lead me to him."

Adan's thoughts worked backwards, retracing everything that had happened to him since he left Hull. His mind drifted back to Nolan's words: *You will serve me, whether you choose to or not.*

"So Nolan let me escape. He knew I would hunt down Gavin and that Gavin had most likely been taken to Oasis."

"He's awfully good at guessing, isn't he?" Nox chuckled under his breath. "I really don't know how he does it. There's not a Wayman in the Vast that would cross him now that Sparc's dead, not even me, and I've got no more sense than those rocks over there."

"But he tricked Sparc and the other thrals into attacking Oasis. Why would you take orders from someone who is just using you?" Adan asked.

Nox scratched his eyebrow in dismay, as if what Adan had just said had never occurred to him. Then a sly grin crept over his face.

"Well, you not being a Wayman I can see how you might be confused. But that's the way things work in the thrals. It really doesn't matter which Reeve you serve—your brother, or the one who betrayed him. 'Honor is so much empty breath', as the saying goes. Kill or be killed. That's the only thing that matters. Speaking of which, it's time we stopped jawing and set our hands to the cutting. Can you walk? Or will I have to drag you the rest of the way?"

Adan stared at Nox, so overcome by a mixture of disbelief, fear, and dismay that for a long time he was unable to reply.

Even if Adan and Sierra had still been together, it would have been impossible to free the Sentients without the cutter. He secretly hoped that if they did find Malthus, he would be able to get the Assessor Primary to free the prisoners somehow. It seemed unlikely, but Adan was desperate for anything to help keep his hopes alive. For now, though, he had to figure out how to get away from Nox, or at least get Nox to help him find Gavin. After some considerable explaining, he finally managed to convince the Wayman that finding Gavin would be their best hope of finding Malthus.

From the map of Manx Core, Adan knew that traveling down the other end of the tunnel would lead them to an exit shaft which ran up to a building near the Command Center: the Assessor Barracks. It was hardly an ideal route, but it would be better than trying to walk out across the main base in the open. And since the Command Center was where Adan had seen Gavin's lab in the chronotrace, the nearby barracks seemed the best option.

Adan was surprised that Nox did not push them to move faster down the tunnel. At first, he thought Nox might be taking it easy on him, realizing he had hurt himself when he'd fallen down the shaft. But after a while, Adan came to realize that Nox simply didn't like to move all that quickly. For a Wayman, he seemed strangely averse to exerting himself, calling for regular breaks along their journey. Adan found this odd, for he'd been on long treks with Nox before, sprinting across the desert. Perhaps without his masters driving him, Nox was reverting to his natural tendencies. Whatever the reason for their slow pace Adan was glad for it, even if it did make him a bit nervous they might be discovered.

After they passed the third intersection, Adan thought he heard movement coming in their direction. Nox heard it too and pulled Adan in close, claiming that the bauble around his neck would protect them both as long as they stayed next to each other. Whether the necklace really worked that way or the strangers in the hallway took another path, Adan couldn't say, but they never saw anyone.

When at last they reached the shaft leading up to the barracks, there was a black disc floating at the base of it. In addition, steel rungs ran up along the side. A small lumin shone down from near the hatch the top of the shaft.

Nox asked Adan about the disc and he explained that it could be used to float up the shaft. Adan would have liked to have used it to avoid the climb, but decided against it.

"If I connect to it with my mind, they may detect me in their system," Adan explained.

"Whatever you say. I was taking the ladder either way," Nox said, careful to keep his distance from the platform. "You go first."

Adan gripped the metal rungs. They felt sure enough, but Adan certainly was not. It wasn't just the thought of having to make their way through the barracks. He could not believe he was being forced to work with Nox a second time. He had no interest in killing Malthus. Worse, he doubted the Developer would be the only casualty. He tried to imagine a way in which this would end well, but he couldn't think of any. All he could do was pray an opportunity to part ways would present itself.

He started up the ladder. The climb was long, but not tiring; Adan's bioseine kept him from feeling the effects of his efforts.

When they reached the top of the shaft, he turned to Nox and whispered, "Now keep quiet and stick close to me."

"Of course." Nox gave him his corroded smile. "That's all I've been doing ever since I came down here."

Adan shook his head, wishing the Wayman would do the exact opposite of what he had just said and not stick close at all, but he said nothing and turned his attention to the small manual lever just beneath the top of the shaft. He pulled on it and the circular metal lid above them slid away, revealing a small room lit by a soft yellow glow. The glow came from a collection of bismine cores, stacked three high and almost completely filling the room. The only clear area was a little path that ran to the door.

Nox glanced warily at the array of cylinders, clinging to Adan's garrick with his thick hands.

According to the schematic for the barracks, there was a long hall outside the room which ran into the training gallery. If they made it through that, they could reach the outside via an emergency exit. The other end of the hall led to the living quarters and the front exit via the main lobby. Both exits were supposed to be guarded according to protocol, but the main lobby would be more heavily trafficked. He decided the back exit would be the safest choice even though it would not put them as close to the Command Center as the front entrance.

He dared not use the quorum channel to see if he could sense the presence of any assessors with his bioseine for fear of being discovered, but he could use the limited range of his personal bioseine.

When he didn't sense anyone, he listened at the door, just to be sure. After several moments, satisfied it was safe, he ventured through. As he'd hoped, the passage was unoccupied and they moved down its length as quickly and quietly as possible. They paused at the door to the training gallery, listening again for sounds of activity on the other side. Once again Adan was surprised that he neither sensed anything with his bioseine nor heard anything. He slowly pulled open the door.

The gallery was also empty, both the open floor before them, as well as the balcony which ran around the edge of the room. Relieved to have encountered no one thus far, Adan and Nox hurried to the door on the other side, their feet shuffling across the smooth black floor.

Again at the door he sensed and heard nothing. He was beginning to wonder if the entire building was deserted.

He slid open the door leading out of the gallery. Two assessors stood guarding the back exit.

Adan froze. Why hadn't he sensed them with his bioseine? They were well within in range.

They had their backs to him, but turned when the door opened. The one on the left turned only in time to be speared by the pinion Nox launched through the air. It embedded itself into his chest and he dropped in an instant. The second one rushed forward, extending his hand. Nox stepped in front of Adan and let another pinion fly. This one failed to reach its target, though. White light wrapped around the shaft and it clanked on the floor.

Adan ducked back around the door just in time to avoid the second burst of energy. Nox's body thudded to the floor, his head falling backwards across the threshold and keeping the door from sliding shut.

Adan tensed, wondering if there would be another blast, but he heard nothing but the sound of the assessor moving cautiously down the hallway.

Why isn't he hurrying? Maybe he thinks I'm armed. Or maybe he didn't spot me.

The man's footsteps drew closer. Adan realized he would have to jump him once he crossed the threshold. The element of surprise was the only advantage he had. But when the man reached Nox, he stumbled over the body of the Wayman.

He didn't see him. The necklace must still be working.

While the man was recovering his balance, Adan reached around the corner and swept the assessor's legs out from under him. His head slammed against the metal wall and he collapsed to the floor.

Adan stared down at the unconscious man. He'd managed to knock out his adversary by sheer accident, but this was no time to wonder at small mercies. This was his chance to finally be free of Nox. He stepped over the Wayman's body and then stopped. More assessors would eventually come to investigate. The assessor Adan had knocked out would soon wake up. Nox would be captured and most likely killed. As much as he wanted to, Adan couldn't leave him now, not like this.

He leaned down and dragged the Wayman down the hall away from the assessor so that their two bodies were no longer touching. Then he pulled the neutralizer off the assessor's wrist and jolted Nox back to consciousness.

At the same moment, the assessor groaned and began to stir. Adan hit him with another blast from the neutralizer.

"What—" the Wayman muttered, shaking his head and rolling his eyes in every direction. "You!" he grabbed Adan by his coat, a vengeful look on his face. "You were going to leave me here, weren't you?"

"No, Nox—"

Nox jumped to his feet, never releasing his grip on Adan. He slammed Adan against the wall, scowling. "Thought you could crackle me with your fancy gears, did you? Well, Nox is too well-built to get shankled by that gimcracked scrap. Bah! Worthless relics."

"I didn't—I wasn't going to leave you, Nox," Adan said. He could see from Nox's expression that he didn't believe him.

Nox snorted and laughed derisively. "I've still got a few pinions left in my quiver," the Wayman warned. "If you try that again I'll hunt you down and do you like I did your friend."

Adan shook his head. Nox would never change.

"Come on," Nox said, pushing him again. "Malthus is waiting."

Adan tugged his sleeve down over the neutralizer. At least Nox hadn't noticed it. Adan now had a way out. He just had to wait for the right moment when it would be safe to abandon the Wayman.

Nox rode Adan's heels down the short passage until they hit the door. Once there, he shoved Adan through the opening without bothering to listen if anyone might be on the other side. Thankfully, there was no one in the immediate vicinity of the exit. What Adan did see, however, was not at all what he had imagined.

TWENTY-EIGHT

THE COMMAND CENTER

YELLOW LIGHTS FLASHED ON THE OUTSIDES OF EVERY building in the complex. Far off towards the end of the cavern, humming engines heralded the takeoff of dozens of ships from the docks. A moment later they ascended, all of them attack skiffs. They sped towards Adan's side of the cavern. Adan had the momentary urge to run back into the barracks, afraid he'd been spotted, but they weren't headed for him. They were headed for the vault.

Had Bryce and the others been discovered? Had Sierra made it to the prison? Whatever was happening there, he could do nothing about it now. He had to find Gavin.

He and Nox started to run. The Command Center was just down the street. It rose above the low, flat buildings around it, solemnly reflecting in its shiny blue windows the chaos which had overtaken the cavern.

Ignoring the ships and the flashing lights, Adan and Nox reached the corner of the Command Center, but as they sped around to the back of the building they spotted a large contingent of white-robed somatarchs heading their way.

Nox yanked Adan back around the corner. "Is there another entrance?" he asked in a loud whisper.

Adan shook his head. "The other ways in won't be any safer than this one—worse, actually."

"Okay, let's hope this trinket keeps working." Nox clutched the little gear on the end of his necklace, muttering words underneath his rancid breath. It sounded like a prayer, but Adan doubted that's what it was. Mostly it just sounded like he was mumbling nonsense and his babbling did nothing to calm Adan's nerves.

The first of the somatarchs marched past down the street. A long stream of them followed, all headed toward the docks. The vault was beyond the docks. Was that where they were headed?

None of the somatarchs turned to the side to notice the two figures huddled together in the shadows at the corner of the Command Center.

More than twenty filed past before the line ended. When no more could be heard, Adan peeked around the corner and saw that the entrance was clear. He signaled Nox to follow and the two of them bolted for the back exit.

The back door consisted of two glassy panels identical to the walls around them, but Adan knew from the schematic they would slide away when accessed via the quorum. When they reached the entrance, Nox stood there glaring at his reflection in the glass, as if it had insulted him.

"Where's the door?" he asked. There was no handle or other visible means to open it.

"It's right there. I'll need to use my mind to open it, though," Adan said.

"And you wonder why I don't like mechanical things," Nox muttered.

There was no point in secrecy now. They had to get inside

this building and using the quorum channel was the only way. Adan was just about to connect to the door when the panels slid open on their own. Nox stared at them in astonishment, as if he suddenly understood how mechanical doors worked. But his expression quickly turned to one of alarm as more somatarchs marched through.

Nox snagged Adan by the collar and pressed him up against the side of the building as the somatarchs marched past. As before, the creatures rushed by without so much as a glance towards them.

As the last of the mindless creatures went past, Nox practically hurled Adan through the opening and darted in behind him before the doors slipped shut again.

Inside they found themselves in a wide hallway with metal walls, floor, and ceiling. Using the layout of the building from Faron's map, Adan took off down the passage which led to Gavin's lab. After a couple of turns down different hallways, he and Nox came to a stop in front of a black metal door blocking their way.

"Okay, we got inside undetected, but if I open this, they'll know we're here," Adan said.

Nox squeezed the hilt of the knife on his belt. "Fine. My shiv is thirsty, anyway."

Adan closed his eyes and focused on the doorway. It took him a few moments to find it on the quorum channel since he wasn't used to it, but a moment later the black panel slid open. They rushed across the new room towards a blue sheet of light which blocked the doorway on the opposite side. Nox pulled up several paces from it.

"What's that light?" he asked in a shaky voice. Adan did not bother answering. He found the new door on the quorum channel and a moment later the wall of locus energy disappeared.

Nox followed Adan tentatively through the door, looking it up and down as he went past. Once through, he ran like a man possessed, quickly catching up to Adan. They were on the same path now that Gavin had taken in the trace. It wasn't long before they reached the metal door to the Processing Room.

This door also had no manual trigger to open it. Worse, when Adan tried to connect to it with his mind, he found he had no access to it. Whether it was a high security door or the Devs had simply found out what he was doing and locked him out, he couldn't say, but it was far too thick to force. This was the only means for them to get into the Processing Room and down into the lower levels. They had to find a way through it.

"Are you going to open it or not?" Nox asked as Adan continued to stand there.

"I can't. I don't have access, if that makes any sense."

"No, but it doesn't matter. Move out of the way."

Nox didn't wait for Adan to step aside. He shoved him out of the way and gave the door a swift kick. When it refused to move, he stared at it, his face crimson from anger or perhaps from pain. With a grunt, he wrestled his water pouch from his waist and yanked off the stopper with a flourish. Lifting it up defiantly to the door face, he squeezed and clear liquid poured down the surface. Instantly, the metal began to smoke. Though the liquid looked like water, it wasn't. It was taline acid. The substance ate away at the surface of the door until a hole large enough for even Nox to fit through opened up.

"Why didn't you tell me you had taline acid?" Adan asked.

"You didn't ask." Nox flashed a triumphant grin and sealed the pouch. He walked through the smoking hole like he was stepping over the body of a vanquished enemy.

Adan followed him into the Processing Room. It looked just as it had in the chronotrace except that it was unoccupied. The black disc hovered over the hole in the floor as before, waiting to carry them to the lower levels. Once again Adan hesitated, knowing that not only would using the platform alert the Devs to his presence, but that it was possible they might take it off system while he and Nox were on it, letting them fall to their deaths. But with no other way to get down to the lower levels, there was no use delaying the inevitable. He stepped onto the disc, but Nox held back.

"Are you sure that thing is safe?" he asked.

"Yes," Adan said. "For now, anyway. The longer we wait, the less safe it will be."

Despite Adan's warning, Nox made no effort to get on. He touched the edge of the black disc gingerly with his foot, testing his weight as if he expected it to give way even though Adan was already standing on it.

"Come on," Adan urged, connecting to the disc with his mind. He gestured impatiently for Nox to hurry up, flustered that he was causing a delay. "You're wasting time. They could—"

His words were cut short as the disc fell away beneath his feet. Adan dropped with it, but his fall lasted only a moment. Nox's arm shot out and grabbed him by his coat. The disc disappeared below Adan's dangling feet as Nox deposited him back to solid ground.

"I knew it wasn't safe," Nox said, spitting down the shaft, "Can't trust these relics. Black circles weren't made to stand in the air like that."

"I suppose you're right," Adan said, trembling. "But that was our only way down."

"Down? We need to go down?" Nox asked. "Well, why didn't you say so? Waymen are nothing if not expert climbers. We have to be if we want to get at those crankshaft Welkin settlements in the Viscera."

He pulled out a cord and a pair of rusted spikes from a small pack he wore on his hip and tossed them on the floor.

"I'm not so sure about this," Adan said, as anxious about Nox's rope as Nox had been about the disc.

"What's the matter?" Nox gave him an impatient look, "You climbed out of the pit, didn't you? Going down is easier than going up."

"I don't know," Adan said. "This looks a lot farther." He glanced around the room, trying to think of some other way, but knowing he wouldn't find any.

"This will be as easy as snorting sand out your nose after a storm," Nox assured him, but the malicious look on his face suggested he was enjoying Adan's discomfort.

"It won't work," Adan objected after a long pause, "We don't have any way to secure the rope."

"Nonsense. That's why I brought these." Nox grabbed the two metal spikes and started pounding one of them into the floor with the thick end of the other. It caused a tremendous racket which made Adan wince, but the Devs already knew they were inside the Command Center by now. The noise wouldn't make any difference.

"You pound the stakes then knot her up. I prefer the girdle knot myself," Nox said. The spikes had holes in the thick ends. Once he had the first spike nice and snug, he threaded the cord and tied one end of it to the spike with several quick loops. Then he tossed the other end into the hole. "There we go. Straight down the gut," he said. He grinned and stared expectantly down the hole as if this were going to be a pleasant side diversion. "I should probably go first. Test it for weight. If it will hold me it will definitely hold a flim like you."

Adan nodded, surprised the Wayman would risk himself like that, but Nox looked anything but worried. Adan suppressed a shudder as Nox plopped onto the floor and rolled over the edge. Nox wrapped one of his feet around the cord and slid down, hand over hand. A short time later, he stood on the distant ground below. When he realized he was actually standing on the fallen black disc, he quickly hopped away towards the little niche in front of the doorway at the bottom.

"All right," Nox called up, sticking his head in from the opening. "I've shown you how it's done. I'll wait for you in the passage, away from that...black thing."

Adan took a moment to collect himself. Then, as if each of his limbs had to be moved by a separate mental command, he bent down onto his knees and eased his way over to the edge of the shaft, his heart thumping inside his chest. He could not get over the fact that all that stood between him and serious injury or death was a flimsy looking piece of rope and a rusty metal spike.

He thought back to the rickety cart which had carried him across the endless chasm of the Basin. If he had made it across that large of an expanse, he could make it to the bottom of this shaft. Hands trembling, he eased himself over the side.

Because his bioseine was still repressing his senses, he couldn't get a feel for how much grip the rope really had, but it probably would not have mattered. His hands were so covered in perspiration they started to slip from the outset. He fiddled with the cord, trying to get one leg wrapped around it the way Nox had, but after several frustrated attempts, and with his grip slipping by the moment, he started to let himself slide down using just his hands.

He might have slid all the way down if he had not accidentally banged his feet against the side of the shaft and kicked away in a panic. This made him swing away from the wall, and also checked his momentum. When he drifted back towards the wall, he got his feet out in front of him and managed to brace himself. From that point on, he was able to walk himself down while holding onto the rope. He was almost to the floor when he heard sounds of movement up above. Footsteps beat against the metal floor, approaching quickly.

Panicking, Adan let go of the rope and dropped the rest of the way. Though he only fell about a body length and managed to land on his feet, he wondered if the impact would have any effect on his ribs. He didn't bother to check, though, he was too terrified at the thought of getting caught.

"They're coming," he said as he rushed towards a burned out door which the Wayman had already destroyed with acid. The moment they stepped through, the black disc flew back up the shaft.

"All right." Nox shoved Adan towards the bridge beyond the doorway, glaring at the disc as it jettisoned up the shaft. "You keep going. I'll take care of these shims."

Adan paused, giving the Wayman a questioning look. Nox was perhaps the most irrational man he'd ever met, but even he could not possibly think that he would be able to defeat a group of assessors or somatarchs single-handedly. Nox just grunted and gave him another shove. "Get going," he growled.

Realizing that even if he stayed, he wouldn't be much help, Adan took off running across the bridge. Glancing down, he saw endless rows of transparent blocks below. Unlike when Gavin had passed through a few days before, at least half of the containers were empty. The chill in the room ran down Adan's back. Had all those somatarchs been activated?

Looking back as he reached the other side, Adan saw that Nox had stopped in the middle of the bridge.

"What are you doing?" Adan shouted. "Come on, I need your help getting through the door. I can't access this one either."

Nox waved him off. "I'll be there in a moment."

Adan thought about going back for him and trying to coax

him across the bridge, but knew Nox would never listen. All he could do was stand and watch as a group of three assessors rushed out onto the opposite side of the bridge.

As far as Adan could tell, none of them had oscillathes, so perhaps Nox might have a chance against them. But the Wayman wasn't drawing any of his weapons either. He just stood there as if waiting to be captured. In fact, he even beckoned them forward with his hand.

The first of the assessors was no more than twenty paces away when Nox flipped the stopper off his taline pouch. He sprayed the bridge in a line, all the way across, then turned and bolted towards Adan.

The metal span shuddered as he ran. Within moments, it snapped in half where the line of acid had been laid down. The assessors on the other side plummeted to the floor, landing in the stacks of empty containers below and toppling them over with a thunderous crash.

Nox was shrieking and still running like a madman. The bridge was falling out from under his feet, pulling him towards the floor. When it became clear he wasn't going to make it to the other side in time, he flung himself onto the slanting walkway, thrusting his fingers into the grated surface. The bridge bounced as it crashed against the cubes below, nearly jarring him loose, but somehow the tenacious Wayman held on. Once the bridge stopped falling, Nox began clawing his way back up bit by bit, his pudgy face bulging from the effort. It looked like his eyes might burst, but somehow he made his way to the top.

"That was close," Adan said as he helped Nox over the edge and onto the floor.

"Out of my way." Nox pushed past Adan without so much as a glance. He pulled out his taline pouch again and doused the door with the acid.

Nox let out a subversive chuckle as the door melted away, but his laughter was cut short by the sounds of stirring below.

Adan looked down to see that the assessors, whom he had assumed were dead or at least unconscious, were on the move again. One of them had reached the base of the fallen bridge and started climbing up. Adan considered waiting for them to reach the top and using his neutralizer, but guessed the assessors had neutralizers of their own and he couldn't count on getting off his blast first.

Nox whipped out one of his pinions and flung it at the first assessor. The throw was on target, but the assessor saw it coming and waved it away with a gesture and a flash of light.

"More demon tricks!" Nox shouted. He pulled out another pinion and was about to hurl it as well when Adan grabbed him by the arm and pointed across to the opposite side of the room. Three more assessors had appeared in the doorway.

"There's no point. We have to find Gavin. He's our only chance to get out of here."

The acid had by now burned a hole in the doorway large enough for them to fit through. For once, Nox heeded Adan's advice and turned and squeezed through the opening. Adan darted after him and they took off down the hallway.

They were half the distance to the Repository when Adan glanced back to see the first of their enemies step through the opening they'd made in the door. The assessor did not seem to be in much of a hurry.

Adan and Nox stopped in front of Gavin's door. As expected, Adan could not access it. He turned to Nox.

"Do you have any more acid?"

Before he answered, Nox turned and fired one of his pinions at the lead assessor. The weapon flew straight for the man's chest, but again a white light sent the shaft harmlessly to the floor.

"Cursed relics!" Nox muttered under his breath.

"Forget about them," Adan said, "The taline—do you have any left?"

Nox nodded, "Sure, sure, sure—here," he jabbered, thrusting the pouch into Adan's hands.

The pouch was awfully light. Adan doubted it had enough taline left to get them through, but he had to try. This was the last door. If they could get in and free Gavin, hopefully he would know how to deal with these assessors. They were still some distance behind. In fact, it looked like the leading assessor had actually stopped to wait for the others to catch up.

Why weren't they moving any faster?

Out of the corner of his eye, Adan saw Nox pull out another pinion to throw, but for the first time, he hesitated.

Adan searched the room mentally for signs of anyone with a bioseine, but nothing came back. Was Gavin even inside?

He stepped towards the door and heard a click. He looked up just in time to see a small contingency trigger pop out of a panel in the ceiling. White light streaked in every direction and both of them slumped to the floor.

TWENTY-NINE
SECOND THOUGHTS

Dane walked towards the elevator, measuring each step, trying to compose in his head exactly what he would say to his father. He had arranged the meeting yesterday; it was one of the rare times they would both be off duty at the same time.

As expected, his father was waiting for him. He rose to meet Dane as he entered the room, wrapping him in a warm embrace.

"Greetings, Father," Dane said.

The dark haired man studied him for a moment. Dane knew those lines in his father's face better than the lines in his own hands. They were full of worry, and regret.

"You're troubled," Malthus said. "I thought as much when I received your message, but I see it's worse than I imagined."

"I could open my thoughts and just share them with you directly," Dane offered.

Malthus waved his hand dismissively. "You know what I think of thought transfer. The only reason I'm part of the Collective is for you, Dane. I have no interest in sophisticated tricks when simple words will do. Besides, you think I don't know my own son? I know you better than you know yourself, young man."

Dane nodded, though he knew it wasn't true. He could read his father well enough to see he had no idea what was going on with him. Dane had changed, but his father refused to see it. He wasn't the same person he had been growing up, or even the soldier who had fought under his father's command in the Delegation's wars. He just didn't know how to tell him that in a way that would make him understand.

"But there are all these new things—things that don't make sense...I feel like something's wrong with me," Dane said.

Malthus rubbed his chin the way he often did when he was upset. "What has Darius been telling you?"

Dane did not want to upset his father, nor did he want to increase the rift he sensed developing between them, but he had to get this resolved before he went mad or did something he'd regret.

"It's not what he's been telling me. It's the memorant abilities," Dane said. His father's jaw stiffened at the mention of the word 'memorant', but he went on. "I don't feel like I should even have them. It doesn't feel right."

"I agree," Malthus snapped. "You shouldn't have them. But you do. And since Darius thinks we need mind melters to keep the Collective in line, we don't have much choice. You'll just have to do what he says."

"I feel like I'm seeing *too* much. And I don't like what I see."

Malthus shot him an accusatory glance. "Like what?"

"I don't know if I should really be saying this, actually—"

"You are my son." Malthus threw his hands up. "We do not keep secrets in this family."

Dane caught one of his father's thoughts as it flashed

through his mind. *I knew this wouldn't work. I'm losing him all over again.*

"You're not losing me, Father," Dane said reflexively, giving away the fact that he'd been reading Malthus' thoughts. He could have pushed further to see what his father meant by the idea of losing him "again", but he held back. He wasn't sure he wanted to know.

Malthus' eyes widened. "I told you never to read my thoughts," he bellowed, taking his son by the shoulders.

"I'm sorry, father," Dane said. "I can't help it. That's why I'm so worried. I thought I caught a glimpse of Darius' thoughts yesterday. When he looked at me the name 'Nolan' flashed through his mind. For just a moment, it seemed like that's who he thought I was. But then the thought vanished and we went on with our lesson. I felt like he was suspicious of me for some reason during the whole time after that, though, like he knew what I had seen."

Malthus turned his back to his son. His fists clenched and he cursed under his breath. Dane had witnessed his father's fits of anger before. He knew it was best not to say anything when he got like this. He just had to let the storm blow over.

After a long silence, it looked like the winds had finally died down. Malthus turned back around.

"Everything is going to be all right, Dane. You know that the memorant abilities don't always show you the truth. I'll schedule an appointment for you with Cyrith's staff. They'll have a look at you and we'll sort this out."

And I'll have a word with Darius, Malthus added privately to himself, though Dane caught that as well.

Dane was about to caution his father not to be too hard with Darius, but he checked himself. He had provoked his father's wrath once already through the display of his memorant abilities.

At that moment, Darius walked into the room. He was glaring at the two of them with a cold smile, though neither of the two men acknowledged his presence.

"I don't want to cause any trouble," Dane went on talking to Malthus as if Darius wasn't there.

Then, though Malthus' lips did not move, his voice echoed across the projection from the chronotrace, reverberating in all directions. "Stop the trace," he ordered. "Darius was never there. Something must have gone wrong."

The trace of Dane's conversation disappeared and the Repository returned to normal.

"It must have malfunctioned," Malthus said. "Perhaps you let it run too long."

Gavin heard him, but he didn't answer. His mind was still lost in the chronotrace, trying to determine if indeed there had been a malfunction. He stood in front of the massive sphere he had built next to the celerium core. It was almost a full body-length in diameter and was still spinning. The golden light from the ring between the two halves flooded the room so the locus cube imprisoning Gavin could barely be seen.

Malthus paced outside the cube, walking back and forth between the two somatarchs standing guard there. He had been pacing back and forth between them with the regularity of a metronome throughout the last portion of the trace.

"This is taking far too long," he muttered under his breath, stamping his foot as he pivoted and marched back towards the other somatarch. The strange shimmering light surrounding him rippled briefly and then faded, like a tiny pebble plopping into still water.

At a gesture from him the two creatures sprang forward,

passing through the cube and laying hold of Gavin, whose eyes shot towards Malthus. "How am I supposed to work like this?"

The light from the chronotrace faded and the spinning of the sphere died down.

"I may be a vacant when it comes to technology," Malthus said, "But I've been around mind melters long enough to know when one is trying to deceive me." The distracting shimmer glinted again.

"Connect to my mind, then. See if I've been doing anything beyond what you've asked."

"Bah!" Malthus set his jaw at a stubborn angle. "I don't need to resort to that worthless mind linking to see you're stalling. That trace didn't go back nearly far enough. I need Dane's memories *before* they became corrupted."

"You saw the trace—" Gavin tried to explain.

"And it failed. The conversation with Dane was accurate up until that part where Darius came in. But that was wrong. He was never there. I am absolutely certain about that."

"I would caution you when thinking you know exactly what Darius did and did not do," Gavin said, but then he caught himself. He doubted Malthus knew about the miasma channel, and if he didn't, it was best not to mention it. Though Malthus was not a memorant, just knowing about the channel could do a great deal of harm.

Malthus searched Gavin's face. For a moment Gavin feared he might press him on the subject.

"I know Darius was using us," Malthus said at length. Gavin folded his arms, bracing himself for what would come next. "But this is not about Darius, it's about the chronotrace. Don't try and distract me from the fact that it has failed again by changing the subject."

The tension in Gavin's shoulders eased. He gave Malthus a

deferential nod, as if acknowledging he'd been caught in the sort of subterfuge Malthus was accusing him of.

Malthus placed his hands behind his back imperiously, locking eye on Gavin.

"You only have ten slices left to resolve the issue," Malthus reminded him. "Even if the device did not malfunction, you could clearly see that Dane's psyche had already been corrupted with the influx of Nolan's thoughts at that point. You have to go further back."

Even with all the improvements he had made, and even with the almost limitless power offered by the celerium core, that what Malthus was asking was impossible. The further back the device went the longer the trace took. It would take at least two more days, most likely three or four, to get back as far as Malthus wanted, but he could not let Malthus know that.

"Of course," Gavin said, not daring to say more for fear of giving himself away.

"If it were up to me, I would give you all the time in the world," Malthus said, his voice shifting to a friendly tone. "But this complex is going to be shutting down soon. Things are moving much faster than expected. I'm afraid this is out of my hands now."

"I understand."

"You always were a reasonable man." Malthus opened his mouth to say something more, but stopped. The easy-going expression on his face vanished, replaced by one of concern. His eyes glazed over and Gavin sensed he was connected to whatever system the Developers used to control Manx Core. The shimmering barrier kept Gavin from reading his thoughts, but Malthus' expression shifted to one of alarm.

He said nothing and Gavin dared not inquire what was happening, but he was certain that the Assessor Primary must be attending to some important matter which required his attention. He often did so during his visits with Gavin.

When at last Malthus came out of his trance, he addressed Gavin once more. "Finish the trace. I'll be back shortly." With a stern look, he turned on his heel and walked briskly towards the exit. The alloyed door slid away and Malthus paused at the threshold. "Remember what will happen if you fail, Gavin. I would hate to have to punish the andros for your incompetence."

He turned and disappeared into the hallway.

Gavin knew he could never make Malthus' deadline, but with the unexpected appearance of Darius in the trace, perhaps he might not have to.

THIRTY
LESSONS OF A MENTOR

THE CHRONOTRACE SPUN BACK TO LIFE. THE EFFUSIVE glow gave off no heat, but seeing it warmed Gavin's heart. There was much that he had to do and little time in which to do it, but for the first time since he had arrived at Manx Core, circumstances seemed to be shifting in his favor.

Gavin glanced at the somatarchs to either side of him. He still was not sure how he was going to deal with them, but he would have to figure that out later. He had to work quickly before Malthus returned.

He closed his eyes and connected to the chronotrace. The somatarchs, along with the rest of the laboratory, melted away, replaced by the scene he had just finished watching. Dane, Malthus, and Darius stood frozen in time. Gavin resumed the trace and the conversation between the father and son resumed. Darius continued to stand, unnoticed, observing them.

Gavin wasn't interested in what Malthus and Dane had to say anymore. All of his attention was focused on his former mentor: Darius. Gavin had only just gotten the thought-mapping algorithm working yesterday, but he had not had time to use it unsupervised until now.

Focusing in on Darius' thoughts he saw that he was merely biding his time, watching the two men before him, vaguely amused at their struggles to resolve Dane's worries and concerns.

This has been an interesting social experiment, Darius mused, *but it is clear these sorts of relational structures can only harm the efficiency of the Collective. Malthus' performance has been slipping due to his constant worries about his son. It may have been a necessary consolation to get him to join us, but the time has come to end this.*

Using the miasma channel, Darius took over both their minds at once. The two men froze where they stood, Dane's mouth agape in mid-sentence. A thrill shot through Gavin's weary frame. This was what he had been waiting for. He shadowed Darius' thoughts, studying the means which he used to ransack the minds of Dane and Malthus, absorbing everything his mentor did.

With Malthus, Darius inserted a memory that Nolan had discovered his true identity and rejected that of Dane. It would have happened eventually anyway; Darius was merely accelerating the process. He would have liked to have erased the man's memory of Dane altogether, but he had learned from experience that slow changes were the ones that took hold best. It might take several iterations to restructure Malthus' thoughts in the proper manner and he was too valuable to risk destabilizing with a sudden change. He may have been a sentimental old fool when it came to his son, but he was the most brilliant military mind in the Collective.

When it came to Nolan, Darius had no intention of letting him keep anything, not the memories from Dane, and certainly not what he had learned from his time as a Developer. They would have to do a complete mind wipe. As a memorant, Nolan's mind was much stronger and could withstand the mental trauma better, but this also meant that he would be more difficult to break down. It would require several days of intensive work. Darius briefly entertained the idea of simply killing him, since he had proven so difficult to control, but he quickly rejected it. Killing memorants was inefficient. They were far too valuable a resource, and far too rare. He would just have to work harder at keeping his former mentor under control. He could not afford to allow Nolan's true personality to resurface.

Darius was not able to expunge Dane's memories then and there. That would require a remap, and he had several post-flatline Collectives he had to process at that moment. He certainly could not entrust the task to the other memorants. Nolan's reaping would have to wait for a day or two. For the time being, he walked up to the two men and deactivated them with his zoelith. Then he used the esolace to send for a pair of somatarchs and chromium carts. After giving them their instructions, he walked out of the room, ordering the somatarchs to take Malthus to his quarters where he would awake to grief over the death of his son for the second time in his life. Darius decided it would be best to also erase Dane's memories from the Repository, lest Malthus stumble upon them at some point and attempt to revisit this failed experiment.

Darius had Dane's body sent off to the vault. He shuffled down the Annex hallway, barely making a sound, satisfied with what he had accomplished. Being the guardian of humanity was tiresome, thankless work, but he preferred survival to oblivion.

As Darius finished his work, so too did Gavin. By the time

the trace ended he had gained the advantage he was looking for. He once again had access to the miasma channel.

Gavin turned to face the somatarchs. The miasma channel allowed him full access to any human mind he could connect to, but it was useless against these vacant creatures. Both of them had zoeliths a their belts, but no other visible weapons. Still, he was no match for them physically, he would have to find some other way to get past them. But first he had to escape the locus field surrounding him.

"I've found what Malthus is looking for," he announced, "but I'd like to make a backup of what I recorded first."

He had no idea just how autonomous this version of somatarch was. When Malthus had been there, he had ordered them to bring Gavin whatever supplies he needed and they had readily complied. Out from under the Assessor Prime's supervision, Gavin was unsure whether or not they would be quite so helpful.

The somatarchs remained silent.

"If something happens to the chronotrace, we'll lose all of this information and I don't think Malthus would appreciate—"

"We cannot help you," one of them interrupted, its lips barely moving.

Gavin sighed. "Well, couldn't you at least relay my request to someone in this building who could? All I need is a memory array. There are dozens of them right over there."

Once again, the somatarchs gave no response.

"What about that assessor who delivered those zoetic isolators two days ago? Could you relay the message to him and see what he says?"

He waited a long time for another response, but never got

one. The longer he waited, the more his thoughts turned to what would happen when Malthus came back.

He wondered if even the miasma channel would be able to break through the mysterious shield which seemed to guard Malthus' thoughts. Gavin had not been able to read them during any of their encounters thus far. He walked over and ran his hands along the top of the chronotrace. For all his abilities as a scientist, and for all the enhancements he had incorporated into his device over the last few days, none of that offered a way out of his prison.

But as he stood there, staring at his handiwork, trying to think of a way out, unexpectedly he became aware of the presence of three people with bioseines outside in the hallway.

This was his chance.

Using the miasma channel he closed his eyes and sent his thoughts towards one of them. After a brief moment of fuzziness, he found himself staring through the man's eyes down the hallway outside his room. He was still some distance from the door, but he wasn't moving, and neither were the two assessors behind him.

Gavin scrambled to check the security directives which had been issued to the assessors. They had been sent to investigate the presence of foreign entities accessing devices on the Manx Core esolace. They had engaged them briefly on the bridge in the somatarch lab and even made visual contact with one of them, but there were at least two involved and they suspected the other was using a pallium generator to mask his presence.

The assessors were waiting for clearance to do a deep scan, which would involve disconnecting from Com and using unguided visuals to get around the generator. No sooner had Gavin accessed this information than the permission was granted and the hallway shifted focus and Gavin saw things through the man's natural vision.

Two figures blinked into view in front of the Repository door. Both were wearing desert gear. One was of average height and build and the other short and squat. Gavin recognized them at once. One of them was Nox, the Wayman who had killed Will—and the other was Adan. Gavin's surge of joy at seeing his friend disappeared the next moment when a contingency trigger on the wall above the door fired and both of them dropped to the floor.

As the other two assessors moved past Gavin's host, he searched the man's mind to discover what sorts of weapons he had. Since he was merely a facility guard, all he possessed was a static neutralizer, but that would do. He caught up to the one trailing behind and grabbed him by the shoulder. A short burst from the neutralizer on his wrist shocked the assessor into submission. Before the first man hit the floor, Gavin's assessor was reaching out towards the second. The man flinched and recoiled, but he was too late. Another quick burst caught him and he went down as well.

Gavin's host sprinted over towards Adan, arriving just in time to see his eyes flutter open, a look of alarm registering on his face.

"Relax, Adan," said his assessor, stepping over Nox's body. "It's me, Gavin."

He was surprised to find Adan already up, but he could see the confusion etched on his face. He didn't understand what was going on.

The assessor sent a reverse field static burst into Nox's body. "You see," he said. "I'm on your side."

He reached down to pull Adan up, but before he could grab his hand, someone landed a vicious blow to the back of the assessor's head from behind. He collapsed unconscious to the ground, expelling Gavin from his mind.

THIRTY-ONE
CALCULATED RISKS

Adan watched the assessor fall, revealing the figure of Nox standing behind him.

"Nox!" Adan shouted through clenched teeth, "You shouldn't have done that. That was Gavin."

"The friend you're looking for?" Nox asked, dumbfounded. "You could have fooled me. He looked like one of those gray shims that was chasing us just now."

"Well, he was, but—actually, never mind. Just—don't attack anybody else unless I tell you to, all right?"

Nox shrugged lightly. "Well, I can't promise anything. It's second nature." Then he started off towards the other two fallen assessors.

"Nox," Adan called after him. "What are you doing?"

"Don't boil your kern, I'm just checking," Nox said. "No harm in being prepared. Don't tell me these two are friends of yours as well?"

"No, but don't kill them."

As Nox walked away, Gavin's thoughts flashed into Adan's. *"You're here! How did you find me?"*

"*With the chronotrace—and some help from some people I met. I'm so glad you're alive, Gavin.*" Through their mental connection he sensed Gavin's location inside the room. "*We need to get through this door and get you out of there.*"

"*But what about Nox? Is he with you?*"

"*Yes. Sort of.*"

"*Okay, well just make sure to keep your distance from him for now. Did you know he's using a pallium generator? It interferes with certain bioseine connections.*"

"*Ah, his relic—that's why I couldn't sense you before.*"

Gavin's mind whirred for a moment, calculating. "*I think I can open the door if I take control of one of these assessors. But you'll have to use one of their neutralizers to wake them up first.*"

"*No problem,*" Adan answered. "*I've already got one.*"

He hurried over to the closest assessor and told Nox to stand aside. After a brief protest he left off, shuffling towards the other one.

Keeping his distance from Nox, Adan used the neutralizer to jolt the assessor awake.

"What are you doing?" Nox rushed back, in a rage. "Those are our enemies!"

The Wayman flew at the assessor before Adan could react. The assessor flung up his hands in defense.

"Don't attack, Nox," the assessor said. At the mention of his name, Nox hesitated. "I'm on your side. I'm here to help you and Adan."

"Right, and I'm a Welkin's whistle," Nox said. He raised a hand to strike the assessor.

"Nox, wait!" Adan yelled.

But Nox swung anyway. Adan's words must have distracted him, though, because he only landed a glancing blow.

When Gavin's assessor didn't fight back, but kept insisting he was a friend, Nox eyed him warily, but allowed him to rise to his feet.

"Now let's get Gavin out of this room," Adan said, pointing towards the Repository door.

"What in the Vast are you talking about?" Nox asked, throwing his hands in the air. "I thought he was right here." He pointed at the assessor.

"No, I'm still inside. I'm just using this man to open the door," Gavin's assessor said. "Beware—there are two somatarchs in the room which I have no control over."

"What language are you speaking?" Nox asked. "If you're really on our side, could you use words that all of us can understand?"

"What he means is that there are two guards holding Gavin prisoner inside," Adan explained. "We have to find a way to defeat them."

"Fighting. Now that I can understand." Nox scratched his chin. "Hmm, will this help?" he asked, digging around in his garrick until he produced a small black disc.

"A contingency trigger? That's perfect," Gavin's assessor said. "That's extremely advanced technology for a Wayman."

"So?" Nox said. "You can use it, right?"

The assessor nodded.

"Are you sure you trust him?" Gavin's thoughts came back into Adan's mind.

"No," Adan answered. *"He's been sent here to kill Malthus. I don't think he'll hurt us though unless we get in his way."*

"All right," Gavin replied, his thoughts moving quickly, *"I have an idea, then."* He sent the details of his plan to Adan in a swift deluge of information.

"It seems a bit risky, don't you think?" Adan asked once the exchange was complete.

"Yes, but we have to hurry or they may send in reinforcements before I can get free."

"Okay, Nox, you'll have to give him the trigger," Adan said.

Nox raised an eyebrow. "You're sure this will help us get to Malthus?"

"Without me, you have no hope of finding him," the assessor stated flatly. Nox glanced back and forth between Adan and the assessor several times before handing over the disc.

"You have to attack the guards when we go in," Adan told Nox as the two of them hung back.

Gavin's assessor went up to the front door. His eyes went glassy as he accessed it on the quorum channel.

"The guards will be wearing white robes," Adan said, moving to the side of the door and motioning for Nox to move to the opposite side.

"Ghosts, eh?" Nox cracked his knuckles. "Been wondering when I'd get another crack at them. You're sure it will be okay to attack this time? None of them will be your friends in disguise?"

"No," Adan said. "The ghosts are what you need to focus on. Be careful, though. You've fought them before. You know what they are capable of."

Nox chuckled. "Flesh and blood, fast or slow, it all dies the same."

Adan took a deep breath, wondering whether even Nox could be so dense as to believe that. Maybe it was just false bravado. Whatever the case, he hoped the Wayman's recklessness and apparent fearlessness would work to their advantage.

The door opened and Gavin's gray-robed assessor walked in. Through Adan's connection to Gavin, he could see what was happening in the room, though he remained hidden around the doorway.

The assessor approached the somatarchs, halting a few steps outside the locus cube. The somatarchs failed to acknowledge his presence in any way.

Beyond them, inside shimmering walls of blue light, Gavin stood in front of a large, dark cylinder and a metallic sphere. He was as motionless and as glassy eyed as the somatarchs.

"I've come to move the prisoner," Gavin's assessor said. There was a long pause.

"You do not have the authority to override the Assessor Primary's directives. You may gain this access by utilizing the proper Core protocols," answered one of the somatarchs, still staring blankly at the wall.

"I see," the assessor said. "Well, I do know what the protocol requires if I do this—" With that he launched the contingency trigger across the floor towards Gavin. The moment it came into contact with the energy field, a white flash engulfed the room and the locus cube vanished.

"Now, Adan!" Gavin shot him the mental command.

Adan rushed forward, Nox close on his heels. As they ran, Gavin's assessor dove towards one of the somatarchs. The creature reacted in time to avoid the lumbering attack, but the assessor's hand managed to get close enough for the white burst from his neutralizer to connect. The shock of the blast rippled through the creature's body and it staggered to the side. It was not enough to knock it out, but the blast dazed it long enough to allow the assessor to leap on top of it and bring it to the ground.

Whatever slight advantage Gavin's assessor had gained was erased the next moment when the other somatarch rushed in to help. It grabbed the metal band around the assessor's wrist before he could raise it for another blast and snapped it clean off.

The neutralizer may have been next to useless, but Gavin's host had managed to snatch the somatarch's zoelith. He thrust it towards his prone enemy, but again, the other somatarch reacted too quickly. It pinned the assessor's arm to the floor with its foot before Gavin's man could lift it, drawing its own zoelith at the same time.

Gavin's assessor tried to wriggle his trapped hand loose, but he was not strong enough to overcome the full weight of the somatarch pressing down on it. A moment later, the somatarch's zoelith slammed into his temple, incapacitating the assessor.

That same moment Nox unslung one of his pinions and hurled it at the white-robed creature with a guttural shout. His cry must have alerted it, or perhaps the creature was just that quick. It ducked and the streaking shaft clanged off the celerium core.

The somatarch on the ground sprang to its feet. Though Nox charged forward with an even more riotous shout, the two creatures appeared not to notice him.

Adan lagged behind. In the aftermath of the Wayman's cry, he sensed several people with bioseines coming down the hallway outside, but he maintained his focus on Gavin, waiting for his moment.

No longer inside the assessor's mind, the real Gavin rushed at the somatarchs from behind as Nox charged from the front. The savage Wayman came growling and snorting like he meant to paralyze them with the sheer clamor of his assault.

For a moment it looked as if Nox's attack would connect. The somatarchs never bothered looking his way, but at the last moment, the one in front tumbled to the side and rose up behind the startled Wayman like it really was a ghost, materializing out of nowhere. The creature delivered a blow between Nox's shoulder blades, dropping him to the floor.

While the creatures were focused on Nox, Gavin raced towards the contingency trigger near one of their feet. Once again, the somatarch reacted too quickly, tripping him up and knocking him to the ground. It followed this up by plunging its zoelith at Gavin's forehead. He only just managed to duck in time.

As Gavin fought off the somatarch bearing down on him, he kicked the trigger towards Adan. It skated across the floor where Adan stopped it with his foot.

Though Nox had gone down, he was still conscious and fighting for his life. The somatarch which had struck him had pinned him face down to the floor and was raining down blow after blow upon his back.

Gavin strained to keep the somatarch's zoelith at bay, but his arms crumpled and the device crashed through his defenses, slamming into his forehead. He toppled to the floor beside the fallen assessor. A moment later, the somatarch attacking Nox landed a blow to his head that knocked him out as well.

A group of five assessors came rushing through the door as Adan picked up the trigger. His fingers jittered across the surface of the black disk as pulses of light appeared beneath them. It only took a moment for him to drag them into the pattern he needed and then the lights faded.

He tossed the disc onto the floor so that it landed in between the two somatarchs. A crackling sound erupted around them and a flash of light engulfed the two creatures, blanketing Nox and Gavin as well.

THIRTY-TWO
SPECKS OF DEBRIS

ADAN DID NOT WAIT TO SEE IF THE SOMATARCHS WENT down. The first of the assessors was only a few steps away. He closed his eyes and reached out towards the man's mind. It was his first time connecting to someone else's thoughts using the miasma channel. Gavin had shared the knowledge of how to use it with him in their exchange in the corridor.

Unlike the other times when Adan had attempted to seize control of someone else's mind, there was only a brief period of disorientation. And instead of chaos and a confused, unfamiliar mental landscape, everything inside the assessor's mind was perfectly still. His thoughts were frozen, even the subconscious ones. The assessor could not resist Adan or even think at all while Adan was there. In fact, if Adan did not re-engage the assessor's other bodily systems, the man would soon die. The world for him, both internally and externally, had stopped, and it would not start up again until Adan allowed it to.

Adan was terrified by the absolute power he held over this man and quickly restarted the normal operation of his body. He had little difficulty in controlling his host's movements. He raised the man's arm and, with two quick bursts from the neutralizer on his wrist, caught the other four bunched up assessors by surprise and sent them the floor. Adan turned the neutralizer on his host, lancing him in the leg with a static blast. This thrust Adan back inside his own body.

He hurriedly scooped up a zoelith and used it to deactivate the somatarchs. He then pressed the device's silvery disc onto Gavin's forehead and waited for it to take effect. Since Nox was close by, he flicked the wrist of his free hand and revived the Wayman with a neutralizer blast.

Nox gave a groan and began to stir. He rolled over on his back, cradling his head like it was a delicate vessel that would shatter to pieces if he dropped it.

"Are you okay?" Adan asked.

"Sharp as a Reeve's blade," Nox said, wincing as he wobbled to his feet. Pulling one of his hands from the back of his head, he stared at the blood coating his palms and fingers. "Ah, my favorite color," he snickered, but the laughter seemed strained even for him. He thrust the same hand into a pouch on his belt and came out with a small metal tin. Flipping the lid, he took out a daub of greenish almamenth paste and smeared it into his neck.

Still grimacing, he wandered over to one of the fallen men and began rifling through his belongings. He shuffled around, examining each of them in turn and growing more flustered with each search.

"Why don't these shims carry any weapons? Welkin children are better equipped than these empty shafts."

"The leaders of this place don't trust them," Adan said, "There have been...uprisings in the past." Though he hadn't realized it at the time, Adan had absorbed this bit of information from the assessor he had taken control of, and a great deal more besides.

"Well, no wonder we defeated them. An unarmed warrior is like a storm without wind."

"And yet, they would have beaten us if Gavin had not been here."

Nox glanced at Gavin's unconscious figure. "Him? All he did was take a nap. Didn't even put up much of a fight from the looks of it."

Adan shook his head. He was about to respond when the floor quivered slightly. Glancing up, he saw the ceiling panels shift like something was crawling beneath the surface. Just as suddenly as it came, the tremor passed.

"Curse Nolan for sending me down here," Nox exclaimed, "We've got to get out—now."

Adan stared at the zoelith, as if doing so would somehow speed up the process of reviving Gavin, but he just lay there, as immobile as ever.

Another tremor shook the lab. This time, the floor rocked up and down. A few of the ceiling panels came loose and crashed to the floor. Half a dozen cabinets shook open, sending memory arrays and vials of remin fluid tumbling and shattering across the room. Adan cringed, wondering if any of those memories belong to him or Gavin. Would their even be time to search for them once Gavin came to?

The ground heaved upwards and cracked beneath Nox's feet. It was not a very wide crack, about a finger's width, but the Wayman scrambled away from it, screaming.

"If we don't get up to the surface, it won't matter if that lazy dreamer wakes up or not," Nox shouted, panic etched across his face.

All Adan could do was hold on to Gavin and the zoelith and pray the tremors would pass. He looked around for a cart or something to transport Gavin out of there, but there was nothing, just memory containers, the celerium column, the giant chronotrace, and a few tables. He tried to pray out loud, but all that came out was, "please, please, please..."

A ceiling panel crashed at Nox's feet, narrowly missing his head. "I'm leaving!" he shouted. "I don't want to be buried in this Welkin tomb."

Adan thought it was best to let him go. There was no point in all three of them dying down here.

Nox wagged his head and gave Adan a look which clearly told him how much of a fool he thought he was. Then he turned and sprinted off through the quivering doorway, scooping up the contingency trigger from the floor as he went.

The ground near Adan jerked and the massive column of celerium in the center of the room began to totter. Fear melted his resolve. His heart bubbled like liquid in his chest. He was just about to release the zoelith and drag Gavin away when he felt his friend stir at last.

Gavin looked around the room, his eyes unfocused. "What's happening?"

"It's a quake," Adan said as calmly as he could. Gavin's revival restored to him some measure of hope. But was it too late? "We have to get out of here."

Adan pulled Gavin away just as the celerium pillar toppled over and smashed into the floor where they had been. It rolled past them, crushing scores of memory arrays before it collided with the wall.

He felt Gavin's mind connect to his, but he was still in something of a daze. *"But the Repository. There's so much data here—your memories—my memories; they have to be here somewhere. If we leave this place..."*

Adan stared out at the rows of memory cubes and cabinets full of remin fluid. How many lives were contained in those shelves? How much knowledge? How much history? He thought about what it would mean to have his identity back, about what it would mean for Gavin—a thousand questions answered, their lives restored, their world made whole.

His eyes darted to the ceiling caving in around them. A massive sheet of rock fell away and crashed near the door, burying the five assessors there and sending shockwaves throughout the lab. Dozens of cabinets opened, sending more memories cascading to the floor. Almost nothing remained left in the shelves.

It would be madness to stay.

"We have to go." With that thought, Gavin snapped out of the daze he was in; he realized the same thing Adan had: if they stayed here they would die.

They took off running towards the door, dodging the falling debris. Adan stumbled once, but kept on his feet, as they shot out into the hallway. The corridor buckled and twitched as they sprinted down its length, like a giant arm seized by spasms.

They caromed down the passage, tossed from side to side so that Adan thought there was no way they would ever reach the doorway. The tunnel was closing in around them. He was running as fast as physically possible, heedless of the waves of cascading debris and pummeling rocks. Was the end of the tunnel already closed? He couldn't tell. There was barely any light. Then, like a break in a storm, they somehow burst through onto the edge of the bridge.

The chamber before them was buried in so much rock, metal, and dust it was barely recognizable. The carefully arranged stacks of containers were all toppled and broken, most of them filled with rock and bits of metal from the ceiling, which crumbled apart as they watched.

The chances of them making it across this room were no better than they had been for making it down the hall, but there was nothing for it. Adan flung himself onto the wrecked bridge and slid to the bottom, landing awkwardly on his ankle, but feeling nothing because of his bioseine. Gavin managed to get down more smoothly, though he lagged a few steps behind.

They clambered their way through the jumble of crushed containers, rocks, and debris, stumbling every third or fourth step as the landscape shifted and changed beneath them. A few rocks pelted Adan in the head, but nothing large enough to knock him down.

When they reached the remains of the bridge on the opposite side, Adan glanced up. All he could see was a dusty haze drifting across the threshold of the bridge. He could only hope Nox's rope was still hanging from the shaft above. Even if it was, they had to get up the fallen bridge to reach it and the twisted steel girders were shaking so violently he didn't know how much longer they would hold.

Adan and Gavin hurled themselves onto the bottom of the bridge and began scrambling their way up the trembling latticework. They had barely begun their ascent when the bridge jerked so wildly it shook both of them loose and sent them tumbling back down into the morass below. A fist-sized rock grazed Gavin's head as he struggled to his feet. Adan feared he might black out, but he grimaced and rushed back towards the bridge. Adan grabbed hold of the span alongside him and they launched their ascent anew. The framework had snapped from its moorings in several places. It was dangerously close to detaching from the wall altogether. Seeing this, they climbed all the more recklessly, knowing that if they fell back down, the bridge might not be there for a third attempt.

And then, just like that, the bridge stopped shaking. The room was still rumbling, but the beams only quivered slightly. Not wanting to miss their chance, they shimmied up the last few sections of the skeletal frame like they were being pushed from below by invisible hands.

Adan reached the top first, but instead of climbing onto the solid ground, he bent down to make sure Gavin achieved the ledge as well. As he grabbed the arm of his friend, from the shaft above him came a noise that drowned out all other sounds in the room. It sounded like a terrible explosion was ripping through the upper floors. The noise was brief and soon died away, but was replaced by another, more ominous sound. A primordial hum rattled through the building, racing through the structure above them, as if the building itself were howling in a mad protest against the devastation being wreaked upon it. The clamor intensified by the moment.

He pulled Gavin up onto the ledge as the rushing sound shook the air around them. It vibrated through the core of Adan's being, reducing whatever courage he had left to rubble. Fear was the only thing which animated his limbs now. He and Gavin shambled into the shaft. For one brief moment Nox's rope fluttered before them, the single strand which held all the world together. Then the cord shivered and went slack, dribbling onto the floor into a useless pile, their hope of ascending the shaft falling with it. As if the rope had been the building's last defense against the noise, an ear-splitting roar descended upon them.

His gaze drawn irresistibly upwards, Adan watched as a bluish glow stifled the opening and a massive flow of neophosphorous spilled down the shaft. It slapped the ground in front of Adan with a punishing boom and then paused for half a moment, the bulbous shapes inside it like hungry eyes searching for victims upon which to feed.

Its prey in sight, the swarming brightness poured over Adan and Gavin unchecked. It swept them over the ledge and back into the somatarch chamber, enveloping their bodies before they even hit the ground. They became one with the luminous flow of death. They bounced in a violent slosh along with the garbled wreckage, their bodies merely two more bits of debris sucked into the churning maelstrom.

Somehow, in the pandemonium swirling around them, Adan felt Gavin clutch his hand.

"Just keep holding your breath," came the strangely unpanicked thoughts of his friend. *"Your bioseine will keep you alive until we find a way out of this."*

Despite Gavin's attempt to stir his hopes, Adan felt nothing but terror in face of the beautiful, suffocating glow seething around him on every side.

His mind went to Sierra. She would not be there to save him this time, but that was not what mattered. What mattered was that he would never see her again.

THIRTY-THREE
AWAKENING THE SENTIENTS

Sierra opened her eyes in the darkness. Shaking off the last bit of haziness still clouding her mind, she felt her way up the wall and onto her feet. Her first thought was of Adan. She reached out to him with her mind, but could not sense him anywhere.

She whispered urgently into the dark, "Adan..." straining to listen for an answer.

Using her bioseine to guide herself up and down the tunnel, she felt along the floor to see if perhaps he was lying there unconscious, but found nothing. She was alone.

With no sign of him in the passage, she crawled back to the edge of the shaft leading down. A faint light glimmered from the maintenance tunnel below, not nearly as bright as it had been before.

She grabbed the cutter and carefully made her way down the shaft, placing her hands and feet into the notches she'd carved out. All the way down she mentally prepared herself for the long drop to the floor below, but when she got to the end, a pile of rubble had been amassed in the tunnel. It was so high she could almost step down onto it from the shaft.

Easing down onto the jumble of rocks she saw that the passage had suffered extensive damage. It was completely blocked by a cave-in on one side. It looked like the tunnel up in Oasis after the quake.

Bits of the track lighting poked through from beneath the rocks and also ran further down the tunnel. She began her search for Adan at once. She climbed over the rubble for several microslices before she spotted a bit of grayish clothing peeking out from between the rocks near the floor. As she drew closer, she saw that it was attached to an arm. Fighting back the urge to break down, she crept closer. But even after she reached it, the light wasn't good enough to tell whether or not it was Adan. With trembling hands, she removed some of the smaller rocks on top of the arm. She sent them tumbling down the pile until at last she glimpsed a face, staring up at her in death. She sighed a deep sigh of relief, recognizing the mangled visage of a dead somatarch. Its clothes were gray from the dust and debris which had buried it.

She started to turn away when she caught sight of something glinting beneath the rocks near the creature's shoulder. Digging until she could reach it, she uncovered the shattered remains of an oscillathe. The outer casing was crushed and broken, but as she pulled it free from the rubble and peeled off one of the panels, she noticed a snatch of bright yellow hiding underneath some cabling. Wedging her fingers into the weapon's guts, she worked it back and forth until it slipped free.

It was a bismine chip. As she examined the crystal she could hardly believe it. It was completely intact and nearly at full charge.

The cutter, though dented and banged up, was still functional. She hurriedly swapped out the old chip for the new one.

Placing her arm back inside the recharged tube, she twisted her wrist and smiled as the yellow blade returned to life.

A thrill of excitement ran through her momentarily, but she was still no closer to finding Adan. She could carve the whole pile of rocks into little pieces, but doing so might bring the whole thing crumbling down on her if she wasn't careful, and it might make it impossible to get back up in the shaft. There had to be a better way to find him. She sat down amongst the piles of rock and stared out into the long, dark tunnel, wondering what had happened to him and whether or not she would be able to go on without him.

I've lost everything, she thought to herself, *everyone I know and cared about is gone.*

Memories from her life in the esolace flooded back as they often did. She had lived through loss and pain there as well. It had felt so real then, but this—this made all those experiences seem like nothing.

Adan, where are you? I need you, she called out in her mind, wishing there was some way he could hear her now. The memory of their last exchange inside the shaft came back to her. *I want you to know something,* he had said, but he hadn't finished.

If I ever do find you again, Adan, Sierra told herself, *I'll listen, I'll find out what you wanted to say. I promise you that.*

That thought crystallized her resolve. If Adan was buried under that rock, he was most likely dead. But he wasn't buried here. Somehow he had escaped. She was sure of it. She would find him, and she would find the others. She had the cutter, and she knew the location of the vault. It was time to stop feeling sorry for herself and do what she came here to do: save her friends.

Sierra clawed her way back up to the top of the rubble pile. Pulling herself through the opening in the ceiling, she tackled the ascent with renewed purpose. It was not long before she got back to where she had last been carving, just below the vault.

Whipping out the cutter, she plowed through the last section of rock until she was just outside the wall of the vault. She left the rock so thin, she probably could have smashed through with her foot.

Sitting on the little lip she had carved at the top of the shaft, she cut a small hole in the wall. A waft of cold air blew across her face, letting her know she had broken through. She took a moment to collect herself. Though the assessor's map had proven accurate down to the last detail it didn't say anything about which prisoners were in which cells.

The opening gave her a view along the floor of an alloyed room. From her vantage point she could see at least a dozen bodies, all stiff and frozen, lying in various positions. Though she could see some of their faces, she did not recognize any of them. Then again, they were so lifeless and pale they barely looked human at all.

As far as she could tell there were no assessors and that was the most important thing. She widened the opening further, scraping metal and rock back into the shaft behind her. When she judged the hole large enough, she pushed herself into the chamber.

Crouching beside a nearby body she withdrew Raif's makeshift zoelith from a pouch she wore on her belt. It was a silver strip about the width of her thumb with two small bismine crystals the size of a fingernail on either end. Not enough to power something as large as the cutter, but sufficient for a zoelith. She attached the device to the forehead of the closest person she saw and moved to the chamber door and waited for it to revive him. If someone came in and saw what she was doing, she had the cutter on her arm, ready to defend herself.

"Who are you?" came a voice, startling Sierra out of her thoughts.

She snapped back around to see the person she had been trying to activate holding the zoelith. She had been so intent on watching the door she hadn't noticed when he came to. He rose stiffly from the floor, rubbing his bluish arms. His movements were jerky and slow, but his eyes were alert.

"My name is Sierra," she said. "I'm here to get you out."

"What is this place? Where am I?" he asked.

"It's a storage vault underneath Oasis. I came down here with some other Sentients to rescue the ones the Admins captured. We got separated, though. I'm the only one who made it as far as I know. But we're going to get out of here—we're going to get everyone out of here."

"I'm Halerin," he said, nodding with some difficulty. "I was in the Sentient cell in block A-12."

"Listen," she said, taking care to keep her voice low. "I don't like using my bioseine, but it would be best if we communicate on the Collective channel from now on. I can tell you everything much more quickly that way. I'm a Sentient like you from the surface. You can trust me."

Halerin surveyed the frozen bodies around him. After taking a moment to think things over, he opened up his mind to hers. Sierra gave him everything he would need to know about the plan to free the others, as well as everything that had happened to her up to that point in her journey into Manx Core.

"*I noticed in the information you retrieved from the assessor that there is an emergency panel on each one of these doors,*" he told her. "*If they're triggered, it will cause a zoetic stimulant to* be released into the air which will re-activate everyone in the cell."

"You're right," she replied. "I hadn't noticed that. But won't it also alert the Admins to our presence?"

"Yes, but we'll be discovered the moment we open that door anyway."

"Good point."

"Why don't you trigger the panels while I keep watch in the hallway. I'll alert you if any assessors come."

She took the cutter and traced the outline of the door with the yellow blade. There was a flash of light around the edge as the door jerked away from the wall and tilted towards her. The two of them grabbed the metal slab from either side and leaned it up against the wall. It was so cold, it burned her hands. She rubbed them together fiercely and the feeling returned.

Out in the narrow hallway the floor was made of smooth stone. The walls and ceiling were covered in metal plates. Halerin stayed by the entrance while Sierra found the emergency panel. Not surprisingly, she lacked access to connect to it, but she simply sliced away the protective housing and reached inside. She connected the inner activation panels manually to trigger it. A pale blue cloud issued forth from the walls near the floor and quickly enveloped the room. It had a sharp, sterile smell.

She found the panel on the door opposite the first one and did the same thing. After that, she traced the outline of the door and caught it before it fell. As before, Halerin helped her prop it against the wall. The room beyond was already filled with smoke.

Sierra moved automatically now, urgency driving her to finish her work, certain the security forces would arrive at any moment. They repeated the same process with the remaining two doors and panels along that passage. She ran to the T-intersection at the end of the hall. Taking the left side first, she triggered the emergency panels and broke the seals around two more doors before doubling back down the other branch. With Halerin keeping watch in the first hall, she had to let the slabs she cut from the doors fall to the floor.

She had just flipped the final trigger and finished tracing the outline of the last door when Halerin's thoughts flickered back into her mind.

"Two assessors just entered the passageway. They've spotted me. I'm heading your way."

"Run," she shot back, but if he received the message, she couldn't tell. His mind vanished. Off down the hallway a flash of white light was followed closely by the thump of a body hitting the floor. Booted feet thumped against rock, pounding their way down the hall. She hurried to the corner of the intersection and pressed her back against the wall. An icy chill seeped through her skin. She held her breath and clamped her teeth to keep them from chattering.

Cradling the cutter with her free hand, she swiped the middle switch inside. The blade flickered from yellow to red. She dreaded what she was about to do, but she didn't have a choice. She held her breath and waited for them to come.

But the sounds of pursuit ended abruptly, replaced by a different set of noises. There were grunts, cries of pain, and something slamming against the wall. It sounded like a scuffle, but she had no idea if the assessors were being put down or if it was the other way around. She sensed four bioseine signatures down the corridor. She risked a glance around the corner and saw four people, their skin still bluish-white from the vault, standing over the bodies of two assessors in front of the first room, the one Sierra had tunneled into.

One of them pointed at the fallen assessors and said, "How

are you feeling now, Mr. Assessor?" His frozen skin obscured his features, but Sierra recognized his voice.

She powered down the cutter, ran towards him, and threw her arms around his frozen neck. "Raif!"

"Sierra, is that really you?" Raif said, hugging her back.

"And what about us? Is Raif the only one you came to rescue?" Von broke in from behind her.

She let go of Raif and turned to see Von and Nance standing there. She embraced them both, hot tears cutting fleshy channels down her frigid cheeks.

"Von, you're here! What about the others?"

"I don't know, I got knocked out as soon as I hit the bridge." Von's confusion somehow got lost in the moment.

"How did you make it, Sierra?" Raif asked. His color seemed to be coming back faster than the others. Maybe it was from the fight with the assessors or maybe it was the excitement of finding Sierra, Nance, and Von there. Maybe both.

"I just—" she began, but found she couldn't finish. Joy washed over her like the frosty clouds slowly dissipating inside the cells, but there was sadness there as well, a cold, icy sadness that the joy could not entirely banish. She had found her friends, but she didn't see Adan among them.

"You can explain later," Von said. More of the Sentients were wandering out of the vaults, half dazed.

"Yeah. What's the plan?" Raif asked. When Sierra stared anxiously at the assembled Sentients, he added. "You do have a plan, don't you?"

"There are ships outside," Von said. "We need to commandeer some of them."

"Ships? Oh man, this almost makes me glad I got caught," Raif quipped.

Sierra brightened at his remark. They were going to make

it. Somehow she'd find Adan before this was all over. Somehow.

She sensed Raif's mind connecting to hers. *"Tell me everything I need to know."*

With more half-frozen Sentients streaming into the hallway by the moment, she opened up her mind and shared all that she knew about Manx Core and how they were going to escape.

THIRTY-FOUR
COLLECTIVE NO MORE

"YOU'RE SURE YOU CAN RIG THOSE LANCERS TO FLY?" SIERRA asked as they finalized their plans. By now all six cells had been emptied. They were ready to head towards the exit and into the hangar located outside the vault.

"Lancers are not much different from levs," Raif assured her. "If you rip out the bioseine interface then anyone can pilot them manually."

"Do you really think we'll be able to outmaneuver the Collective? They'll have the advantage of thought controlled flight and we'll be forced to use our own reflexes." The question came from Halerin, who had only just reawakened after the assessors' attack.

"It's not as easy as using your bioseine, but that doesn't make them better. It all comes down to making the right decision, not just who can react the quickest," Raif replied.

That might be true for you, Sierra thought privately. Raif was a natural with anything mechanical. But she wondered about the rest of them.

"Couldn't we just go back through the tunnel Sierra made?" Halerin suggested.

"They know we've been awakened," Von answered, impatient that they had not yet left the vault. *"Going single file through that shaft, they would catch up to us and pick us off one by one, or head us off in the tunnels below. The ships are the only real chance we have of getting out together."*

Von placed his hand on Sierra's shoulder.

"You take the lead, Sierra," he said, "You've got the only weapon we have right now."

Sierra pulled back. "No, Von, I'm just a handler. Let me give the cutter to someone else. I really don't want to do this anymore." She stared down at the cylinder encapsulating her right arm. She was no fighter. Killing a somatarch had been one thing, but she wasn't ready to lead these people into battle.

"You're the only one who made it here without being captured," Von said, "I think you've got more in you than you realize."

Sierra met his steady gaze. She knew she wasn't the best choice, but the look in Von's eye made her realize she would be letting the others down if she didn't do whatever she could to protect them.

"All right," she said, swallowing hard. Hopefully they got to the ships before it ever came to a fight.

"One last thing," Raif said. "What happened to the rest of the group? You said there were eight of you who came down, but Von's the only one who got sent to the vault."

"Like I said, I don't know." Von's expression was grim, even for him. "When the somatarchs showed up in the mines, we scattered. I jumped off the hauler and I remember landing, but then I blacked out. The next thing I remember is waking up in the vault."

Sierra felt the old sadness seep back in at Von's words. She had grown close to the Waymen, especially Zain. Her stomach knotted up at the thought of what might have happened to them. Were they killed in the explosion? Did they escape? There was no way of knowing, and no way of resolving the emotions churning inside her until she knew for sure.

And then there was Bryce and Adan. Bryce could take care of himself and somehow she felt no sadness at the thought that he might have perished in the mines. It was not that she didn't care about him, but he had always seemed like someone who wanted to go down fighting.

But though she had known Adan only a short time, she felt closer to him even than the other Sentients. Of all the people in the group, his absence was the hardest to take. She knew that if she let herself dwell on it her emotions would paralyze her. She took a sharp breath and tried to shake it off, but the slight quivering of her lips betrayed her.

"Adan and I escaped together. But I lost him in the tunnels. Something knocked me out and then..." She hesitated, unable to finish without losing it completely.

"I understand," Von said quietly. "You did what you could."
Had she?

Sierra turned and walked towards the main doorway leading out of the vault, trying to be strong, but feeling weaker with each step.

The chunk of the door Sierra had carved out crashed onto the stone floor outside the vault, announcing the Sentients' presence to anyone on that end of the cavern. The chamber which stretched out in front of her was made entirely of stone, smoothly carved away to create an arched ceiling. The floor sloped downwards and the walls gradually widened until they opened into an ample bay on the edge of a much larger cavern. Dozens of ships rested on the ground near the edge of the bay. Beyond that, yellow lights flashed in warning from the buildings in the main chamber.

Half a dozen somatarchs and a pair of assessors were coming towards them from the other end of the chamber. The Collective forces stopped advancing once they spotted Sierra and the others emerging from the vault.

One of the assessors called out to them from down the stony slope.

"You are not permitted to leave this area. You must stand down immediately."

The Sentients continued to fan out to either side of the opening. Von gave them a mental command not to move forward until everyone was through.

"We're not part of the Collective anymore," Von said as the last of the Sentients emerged. There were over sixty of them in all. "We don't want to hurt anyone, we just want our freedom."

"I warn you that we are armed with oscillathes," the assessor shouted back, "And we have been authorized to use lethal force. Do not do anything foolish." The somatarchs and assessors drew their silvery pistols.

Sierra's resolve wavered in the face of the assessor's threat. She glanced down the line at Raif, Von, and the others spread out along the wall in front of the vault. None of them were armed, but they had all been instructed by Von about what to do if it came to a fight. Individually none of them would be able to overcome even a single somatarch, but together, they had a chance against the small security force before them.

"*They're stalling,*" Von told the others, "*Waiting for reinforcements. We need to go now.*"

"*But you heard what he said.*" Sierra still was not sure they should go through with this. *"If we move forward, people will die."*

The rest of their group wrestled with the same fear, but slowly, one by one, their minds came to be of one accord. Going back to the vault was not an option. Whatever it was the Admins had planned for them, life in the Collective was no life at all. It was time to break free, no matter the cost.

"We charge on Sierra's signal," Von declared.

Still unsure why Von had chosen her, she nervously raised the cutter in the air. A crimson razor flamed to life on the end of her arm. She stared down at the small force of somatarchs and assessors.

"You have no right to keep us here," she shouted. "We are Sentients now. We choose our own path. Even if some of us fall, we will have our freedom or die fighting."

She thrust her arm in front of her and charged down the slope. The rest of the prisoners rushed after her, the sounds of their feet hitting the stone in a rumbling rhythm which reverberated across the cavern. Their lines widened as they picked up speed so that their enemies would have to pick them off one by one.

"Sierra, keep your blade out in front of you. If you do, it will interfere with the evanescence and protect you," Von instructed her.

So that's why he wanted me to have it. She did as Von instructed her, grateful for the kindness of her friend.

The whispers came, swift and deadly. They were not close to Sierra, but she could still make them out as the invisible evanescence waves washed over the line. Eight people disappeared, their empty gray clothes shriveling to the floor in their place.

The Sentients never faltered. The awful whispers rippled across their group once again. This time, one of them came close to Sierra, sweeping between her and Von and erasing the life of another Sentient.

How many more would have to die. Memories of the dead pulled at her, begging her to abandon this hopeless charge.

They had covered more than half the distance to the enemy. More oscillathe blasts poured over their lines. Each time the shots fired the results were the same, more Sentients disappeared. Their attackers never missed, but the Sentients still outnumbered them four to one.

After each blast, the somatarchs and assessors fell back, but the Sentients were closing the gap.

"Stay strong," Von told those still running.

Sierra was not as fast as most of the other Sentients. About a dozen of them had sprinted past her, desperate to reach their enemies before they fired again. The lead vanguard was almost on top of the somatarchs, who stood a few paces in front of the assessors. A heartless murmur consumed one of them, brushing past Sierra as it went.

As she closed in on the enemy, her stride faltered. Was she ready for this? But her momentum and the slope kept her hurtling forward. It was the only thing left to do; fight until they won or she was consumed like the others.

The somatarchs and assessors got off one more round of oscillathe blasts before the first of the Sentients reached them. There were only six Sentients, and they had no chance at defeating their enemies, but by engaging the somatarchs they kept them from firing again.

Sierra and Von rushed one of the somatarchs. The first Sentient to attack it had already been knocked to the floor by a brutal blow to the head. As Sierra reached the creature, it swung at her head. Instinctively, she brought the red blade of her cutter up to deflect the attack. The creature's fist connected with the side of her face, but the blow's impact was barely felt as the somatarch's forearm disconnected from its body and dropped to the floor.

The loss of its arm did not even faze the creature. It pummeled her with its remaining hand. The blow would have been devastating if it had landed with full force, but Von deflected the strike.

Afraid of cutting Von, Sierra shut the blade off and swung it like a club at the creature's head.

The somatarch jerked its one good arm and caught the cutter in the air. Before Sierra knew what was happening it ripped the tube off her arm and sent it clattering across the floor. Sierra jumped back in shock, just in time to avoid the creature's follow-up kick.

Von dove at its waist while another Sentient rushed in to take a swing at its head. The somatarch twisted as it fell, avoiding the blow and landing a jarring counter strike to Von's chin. As the two dropped together Von's head rolled to the side and he brought his arms up to guard his face.

The somatarch's blood drenched its robes, but somehow it kept fighting. Realizing they were not going to be able to take it down on their own, Sierra took off running for the cutter.

The creature kicked the other Sentient in the face, knocking him senseless, and bolted after Sierra. It tackled her from behind, a step before she reached the cutter. The two went down hard on the rocks. Her chest pulsed with pain like the yellow alarm lights pulsing off in the distance.

Another Sentient came rushing in, probably saving her life. He landed on top of the somatarch, but the creature snapped its elbow back and smashed the side of his head.

The maneuver forced the somatarch to let go of Sierra momentarily. She scrambled over the rocks, reaching for the cutter.

Her enemy slipped free of the dazed Sentient and knocked

her legs aside, sending her once again to the rocky floor. She landed on her shoulder this time. The creature rolled her onto her back, its grave-like gaze boring into her and draining her will. She had no hope of defeating it. The dead bodies she had seen in the aftermath of the storm flashed before her eyes. She knew that she would soon be joining them.

Out of nowhere, Von blind-sided the somatarch, knocking the creature clean off her.

She lunged for the cutter, grasping the cold metal and ramming it onto her forearm. She turned and saw Von wrestling the somatarch on the ground. Though the creature was on top of him, its blows did not have nearly the force they once did. Von was able to deflect them with one hand while he held the creature at bay with his other.

The loss of blood must finally have taken its toll.

"Let it go," she told Von. "I'll finish it."

Timing her blow perfectly, Sierra thrust the red blade into the creature's back as Von rolled away.

Freed from Von's grasp, the somatarch struggled to stand for a few moments, but fell back to the ground dead.

The moment it stopped moving, Sierra turned to see another of the horrible creatures staring at her with hollow eyes and a pitiless face. It stood not ten paces away. Three Sentients lay dead or unconscious at its feet. Sierra watched, frozen in horror, as it pointed a silvery pistol at her.

Her body tingling with terror, she forgot all about the fact that the cutter would protect her and turned to run.

Instead of the lethal murmur, a splitting, popping noise roared from behind. The heart-pounding whisper came next, but it flew over her head. Glancing back, she saw a great crack erupting from the ground beneath the somatarch's feet. Then the whole world shifted and she went sprawling to the ground.

'Up' seemed like an indecipherable riddle. She could just as easily have been laying on the wall or the ceiling. Somehow amidst the revolutions, she found her feet and the spinning stopped. She saw that the somatarch had fallen as well, and that its leg was wedged into the crevice which had opened up underneath it. Large chunks of rock fell from the ceiling, exploding into shards as they hit the floor. In moments the creature was buried.

Everywhere she looked, the chamber shook uncontrollably. The ground convulsed and splintered. Chunks of the ceiling assaulted the floor, raining down on those struggling to escape.

A quick scan of the cavern told her all of the somatarchs had been overrun or killed. The assessors were nowhere to be seen. A few dozen prisoners lay on the ground, unconscious or dead, but at least a dozen were still standing. The floor was still wobbling, but there was a lull in the intensity of the quake.

"Raif, where are you?" Sierra asked, her thoughts skittering out across the Collective channel.

"I'm okay," he replied. *"I just finished off a somatarch. The assessors have fled."*

"We've got to go," Von told them, coming up beside Sierra, trying to hold her steady on the trembling floor.

"What about the unconscious ones?" A sickening chill washed over her as she thought about the Sentients still on the ground. *"If we leave them here the quake will kill them."*

"If we stay here we'll all die too," Von shot back.

"But we can't—"

"We'll come back for them once we get the ships," Von promised.

Sierra wanted to resist, but she knew he was right. With the whole cavern collapsing around them, the only thing to do was escape and come back when they could.

Raif and about half a dozen Sentients stumbled towards them, dodging the falling rocks. Sierra joined them. The hollow-eyed rabble staggered through the deluge towards the open bay. The chamber crumbled apart behind them, but up ahead lay a vast array of ships, for the most part unaffected by the quake. They sat there unattended, beckoning them forward, just waiting to fly them to safety.

THIRTY-FIVE

THE STAGING AREA

WITH RAIF BESIDE HER, SIERRA RAN FROM SHIP TO SHIP, her yellow blade piercing the sides of the thick metal hulls where the bioseine controllers were located. The lancers were long, sleek, triangular ships with dark gray exteriors that seemed to swallow the light. As soon as Sierra cut the controllers out from the ships, the prisoners came in behind her, activated the outer doors and jumped inside. Each lancer could hold ten people, but they spread themselves out into four ships to make sure they'd have room to pick up any survivors.

The tremors had stopped shortly after they'd left the ramp to the vault. A cloud of dust now hung over the area behind them.

"We'll fly back and pick up any survivors," Von informed them. *"Raif, Nance, and I will go. Halerin, your ship is already full so you stay here and watch for trouble. Let us know if they send reinforcements—which they certainly will. Only use the ship-to-ship communications if you have to. The Admins are sure to be monitoring them."*

"Got it," came Halerin's response.

One by one, the ships took flight. Sierra was onboard with Raif. They soon lost contact with Halerin and the others as they moved out of bioseine range. Raif's eyes sparkled with delight as the lancer's controls moved deftly in his hands.

"This thing floats like a cloud," he gushed to Sierra, who sat beside him. "The controls are so intuitive, who needs a bioseine?"

Sierra looked out one of the view panels and spotted an open section of the ramp where the dust had begun to dissipate. "Let's land there," she said, pointing.

Von and Nance had spotted it as well and the three ships lit down near one of the cavern walls.

"*I'm picking up twelve survivors on my ship's modulator,*" Von informed them as their bioseine connection was reestablished.

"*So, four per ship,*" Sierra replied, confirming the locations on her own ship's modulator.

"*Let's do this quick,*" Raif added.

They left the lancers and fanned out to the positions from the modulator. It was tiring work bringing back the Sentients one by one. Some were able to walk on their own, but most had to be carried or supported in some way.

Sierra and Raif were bringing back the third of their four passengers when Halerin's voice came over the ship's sound system.

"We've got ships incoming," came the strained message. "A dozen attack skiffs, piloted by somatarchs. They'll be here any moment."

Von and Nance were already done and were just waiting for Raif and Sierra to finish.

"Take off without us, Halerin," Von said. "We're not ready. Nance and I will stay back and run interference for Raif if we have to."

"No," Raif objected. "You've got your passengers. Don't let us hold you back."

"We're staying," Von said flatly. Sierra had heard that tone many times before. It meant discussion on that topic was over.

"Fine," Raif said. "Let's hope your shield hold."

"We're scattering," Halerin informed them, "We'll see you on the surface." Sierra saw the lights from his engine flare in the haze above the docking bay and disappear. Nance and Von's ships lifted off, but they remained hovering in the middle of the cavern, ready to protect Raif and Sierra while they went for the last survivor.

Raif and Sierra rushed towards the back of the ramp, near the door to the vault. Sierra trampled an empty pair of clothes as she ran, all that remained of one of the Sentients.

She shuddered, but kept running. They soon found the last of the prisoners, a woman who looked a lot like Sierra.

"Let me take her," Raif said, scooping her up. "She doesn't weigh that much. It will be faster if I carry her by myself."

Sierra nodded and took off running for the lancer, reaching it well in advance of Raif.

"Is Nona going to be okay?" one of the Sentients waiting on the ship asked.

"She'll be fine. Get inside and strap yourselves in. We're taking off."

Sierra kept the door open, watching Raif lumbering towards her out of the haze.

Come on, hurry.

It took forever for him to reach the ship. When he did, Sierra helped him strap the last Sentient down.

"They're here," came Von's voice over the ship's audio. "We'll try to keep them occupied."

Through the still open door, Sierra caught sight of Nance and Von's lancers disappearing into the haze-covered bay. She could hear the hum of new ships arriving. She glanced back at Raif just as a yellow light flashed through the air above them. Sierra tackled him to the ground and they hit the floor as a beam ripped through their lancer.

There was a hiss and then a loud snapping sound. When Sierra looked up, the lancer had been cut into two disproportionate pieces. The pilot's compartment tipped forward until the nose of the ship touched the ground while the back section, where everyone was, tilted up in the middle.

"Pulsers!" Raif slammed his fists on the controls. "Man, why didn't I get the shields up in time?"

"Is everyone okay?" Sierra looked over the Sentients in the back of the ship. Everyone was still strapped in.

"We're fine," one of them said. "Should we get out?"

"Everyone stay here," Raif said. "Pulsers only affect inorganics. They weren't trying to kill us, just disable us. Unfortunately, they did a pretty good job of that."

"But why stay? The ship's useless," Sierra said. At the same time there were too many of them to fit into Von and Nance's ships and escaping on foot was out of the question. They were stranded.

The glint in Raif's eye told her he'd already come up with a new plan. "Wait here while Sierra and I look for another ship," he told the Sentients. "You'll be safer if you stay inside."

Through the dense haze, more lights flashed above them, white ones this time.

"Nance and I will try to hold them off with the lancer's disrupter bursts," Von promised over the audio. "Are you about ready to take off?"

"Not exactly. This ship has...issues," Raif said. "We're going to have to jack another one. We'll be back in a micro."

Von didn't reply. He was probably too busy fighting for his life.

Sierra and Raif leapt out of the now gaping hole in their broken ship and sprinted into the haze of the bay. The scuttling sounds of an attack skiff grew louder as one of them burst out of the haze, nearly clipping their heads.

The skiff doubled back. They'd been spotted.

Sierra and Raif plunged into the endless rows of docked ships. The skiff, heedless of the danger, skimmed the floor behind them, zipping under the wings of the larger vessels.

As Sierra ran underneath the massive wing of a hovland assault ship, she jammed the cutter onto her arm and sprang into the air, straining to reach the wing with her yellow blade. She only just cleared the distance, managing to slice through most of the wing. The excessive weight pulled it crashing to the floor.

The skiff came in too fast to adjust its course as a section from the enormous span collapsed on top of it. The skiff and the somatarchs piloting it were crushed beneath the massive wing. Sierra barely managed to avoid getting caught herself.

Her maneuver put her slightly behind Raif. As they turned the corner around the front of the hovland they came upon another row of lancers. They raced over to them, but Raif shot right past.

"*What was wrong with those?*" Sierra asked.

"*Nothing,*" he replied, "*But I didn't see these before.*" He ran past the lancers to a group of six narrow, low-profile ships. "*Citus axomvacs.*"

"*They look like reconnaissance ships. Do they even have weapons?*"

"*No, but they've got what we need: speed.*"

They slowed down in front of the new row of vehicles. The ships barely came up to Sierra's chin and were even more narrow than the lancers. They did have two large lev propulsors attached to the back of each one, but little else to commend them as escape vehicles.

"*There is no way one of those can hold all of us.*"

"*It has an axom field generator underneath it for lifting things. The ship's propulsor engines are big enough for it to haul a ship twice its size. It only seats two crew, but we can use it to pick up the remains of the lancer and we'll be faster and more maneuverable.*"

Sierra had never questioned Raif's judgment before when it came to technology, but even if they could haul the remains of the lancer with this tiny ship, it looked like a disaster waiting to fly.

"*Are you sure about this?*" she asked.

In answer, Raif simply raised his eyebrows and pointed towards the bioseine interface panel.

Sierra scrunched her mouth disapprovingly. "All right, then," she mumbled.

Yellow and white lights glittered through the upper reaches of the cavern, the sound of pulser fire peppering the air with discordant whines. Even with shields, Von and Nance could not last long in that.

She sliced out the bioseine panel and tossed it underneath the ship. They slid inside the vehicle, leaning forward on their stomachs, their feet behind and slightly below the rest of their bodies.

Raif's mind jittered with excitement, oblivious to the attack skiffs whizzing above their heads.

"*This machine uses an adaptive steering system. We both have input into the controls and the vehicle will choose whichever input it deems to be the best course to take.*"

"*You're kidding, right?*" Sierra asked, though she knew he wasn't. "*So we're both going to be flying this thing?*"

"*With help from the ship itself. If we hadn't ripped out the interface it would be a lot easier, but you and I know each other well enough that it should work out."*

"Let's hope so," Sierra answered, liking Raif's choice of ship even less than before.

Raif didn't give her any more time to second guess his decision. He engaged the accelerator and the ship jettisoned into motion, vaulting them above the docked ships below.

They shot above the thicker parts of the haze. Nance and Von's lancers were still airborne, but Von's wing had been badly damaged. Part of it was blackened and bent, causing the ship to fly erratically. Skiffs swarmed around them, pelting them with pulser fire, but most of the blasts got absorbed by the lancers' energy shields, which shimmered into existence whenever they absorbed an attack.

Raif turned sharply into the area in front of the vault, bringing the citus to a sudden halt above the severed lancer.

"Make sure everyone's strapped in snug under the covers," Raif warned the lancer's passengers. They were hovering only three or four spans above the wrecked ship, allowing for bioseine communication.

"We're ready for you to get us out of here," came the relieved reply.

Raif engaged the ship's axiom field and the remains of the lancer floated off the ground. As the two sections from the hull clamped onto the bottom of the citus, Raif's voice went out over the ship to ship channel. "All right, Von, Nance—time to trek."

"Couldn't be more ready," was Von's reply.

"Same here," added Nance.

Raif punched the accelerator controls, thrusting Sierra back in her seat. They shot under and past all the skiffs and most of the docking bay. It was like someone slung the ship out into the middle of the cavern.

Raif slowed down to let the lancers catch up.

"*That's what I mean, see? I'll take speed over fire power any day.*" Raif told Sierra.

Ahead of them three hovland cruisers rose from the docking stations to test Raif's theory. The heavily armed ships climbed so slowly into the air Sierra knew they wouldn't be able to catch them, but the array of disruptor canons nestled beneath their wings made her wonder whether that really mattered. Involuntarily, she moved the steering controls so that the citus swerved out of their firing arc.

"*We shouldn't have to worry about those,*" Raif assured her, "*They may be nasty, but they're slow as cryo.*"

The citus, with Von and Nance following, streaked towards the upper reaches of the cavern on its way to one of the many exit tunnels. They did not get far before the hovlands wheeled around and opened fire.

A single shot erupted from each ship at the same time, all aimed at the citus. They were slow pulses, but Sierra thought from the way Raif was piloting, he only spotted two of the three. He was steering them directly into the path of the third pulse. Sierra pushed down hard on the steering levers. Their ship dipped at the last moment and avoided the hit.

"Oops," Raif acknowledged his mistake. "*I owe you one.*"

As they sped towards the exit, the cruiser closest to them laid down a swath of locus disruptor fire, along with another emitter blast, in an all-out effort to bring them down.

Raif and Sierra reacted to avoid the blasts, both of them piloting simultaneously. In the end it wasn't clear who was actually controlling the ship as it whirled on its side and back level to avoid the cluster of lights swarming around them. Then the ship shot straight up, spinning through a second wave of beams which neither of them had noticed. Sierra's stomach was doing similar maneuvers, but they were alive.

"That was...interesting," came Raif's thought. *"Was that you?"*

"I thought it was you," Sierra answered as she glanced below, amazed the lancer was still attached to them.

"Are you okay down there?" Raif asked.

A chorus of affirmatives came back. There was dizziness, and some touches of nausea, but the seat straps had held during Raif and Sierra's escapades.

Nothing but open space now separated them from the exit tunnel. Sierra glanced back to see if the others had made it through.

Von's ship had sustained more damage. Part of the tail had been clipped off and ragged gashes scored both wings. It was a wonder the ship was still flying. Nance's ship had pulled back and was laying down cover fire to protect Von from the hovlands and skiffs. The skiffs were more of an annoyance than anything, but there was only so much one lancer could do against three fully loaded assault cruisers.

"We've got to go back and help them," Sierra told Raif.

Raif took one look at the scene and sent the ship doubling back around.

"You know we don't have any weapons," Raif reminded her.

"We don't need to take down the cruisers," Sierra told him. *"Just get near that damaged lancer."*

"The citus won't hold two lancers," Raif informed her, like a teacher trying to put an overly ambitious student in her place.

"Will it hold two halves?"

"Yes, but—"

"Just get us close and I'll take care of the rest," she assured him.

She let go of the steering column as the citus joined the fray. Disruption beams and locus pulses flew everywhere. Von's lancer avoided most of them, and the ones that did hit were absorbed by what remained of his shields.

"Don't worry about us," Von's voice came over the audio. "Save yourselves."

"Not a chance," Sierra said. "We've got you. Just hold tight."

"Everyone down in our ship," she addressed the Sentients in the sliced up lancer they were hauling, *"Hold on tight. We're about to take on some additional passengers."*

Once everyone was in place, she adjusted the axom field so that the unoccupied section of the lancer they were hauling fell away and crashed into the buildings below in a shower of metal and sparks.

She flipped the citus so it was flying upside down and maneuvered the ship beneath Von's struggling lancer.

"I see what you're up to," Raif commented.

He manipulated the citus so that it dipped down, dodging more incoming pulser beams from the attack skiffs. He brought it back up a moment later and slid up under the lancer.

"Von, get yourself and your passengers to the forward part of your ship, as far as you can—and hurry," Sierra instructed. "We're going to grab onto your vessel with our axom field."

"But your ship won't hold—"

"I'm going to cut you in two. Just make sure everyone is forward of the exit and let me know when you're ready."

Nance's ship continued to fire its feeble disrupters at the hovland cruisers while Von's passengers got into position. Nance was now drawing the bulk of the fire. His own ship's shields were failing in several places and the nose of his lancer was charred and falling apart.

"We're ready," Von said.

"You'd better make it quick." Nance's voice popped in

across the audio. "I don't know how much longer I can hold out."

Raif nudged the citus so it was almost touching the side of Von's lancer.

"*Okay, Sierra,*" he told her, "*Time for a little remodeling.*"

Sierra pushed the manual release on her window and flipped herself onto the underside of the upturned citus' wing, hanging upside down with her legs from the safety handles embedded there. It was bad enough that Raif and Von had to continue maneuvering their ships to avoid enemy fire, being upside down didn't make things any easier.

As Raif guided her over the top of the lancer. She engaged the cutter and shoved it into the fuselage below.

"*Go, Raif!*"

The citus shifted, swooping beneath the battered lancer, rolling so Sierra's blade stayed thrust into the guts of Von's ship. As they popped out on top, the lancer below split in two. The citus dove after the forward half of the plummeting ship until the axom beam caught it, a few spans before it crashed into one of the buildings below.

"Got you," Raif told them. A mixture of exhilaration and relief flooded his thoughts.

Sierra crawled back along the wing and down inside the ship.

"*You know, to be honest, I really didn't think that was going to work,*" Raif admitted.

"*Don't ever let me do something like that, again,*" she told him, her heart pounding in her ears so loud she could barely hear the sounds of battle outside.

"Okay, next time, you drive," he said, laughing.

Sierra took in several deep breaths. They were not out of the Core yet, but she was beginning to think they might have a chance. All they had to do was reach the exit tunnel ahead.

The skiffs behind them no longer seemed to be firing directly at them. In fact, it seemed like they were merely laying down fire on one side in order to keep them from reaching the tunnel. The hovlands were holding off any direct fire as well.

As much as they needed to make for the exit, there was nothing they could do. The citus was too weighed down to outmaneuver the skiffs.

Soon Sierra saw what the harassment fire of the skiffs was doing. The somatarchs had only been buying time for the rest of the ships to mobilize. Up ahead of them, it seemed as if half the fleet was rising off the cavern floor. There were dozens of skiffs, an entire flight of the smaller vapor ships and another half-dozen hovland cruisers all going airborne at the same time.

What filled Sierra with dread, though, was the ship in the center of the pack. It was one of the praxis assault ships. Though the citus would easily be able to outmaneuver it, even in its overburdened state, the power and accuracy of its weapons far surpassed any other ship in the fleet, especially at long range.

Beyond its imposing bulk and the almost uncountable number of weapons clinging to its burgeoning frame, there was something else about it which gave Sierra pause. She had seen the strange glass-like material which covered it in many of the buildings below. Why the Administrators had used the same material here, Sierra had no idea, but whatever the reason, she had a feeling it would not turn out to their advantage.

THIRTY-SIX

THE PRAXIS

Ten pulses of white light sliced towards the Sentient ships from halfway across the cavern as the praxis let its first volley fly.

Every single one hit Nance's ship. Nine were absorbed by the shields, but that was all they could take. The tenth pulse passed through as if no damage had been done, but disruptor beams weren't designed to destroy a ship, only disable it. The lancer plummeted.

"*Eject, eject, eject,*" Raif sent the mental message, though Nance was too far away to receive it.

Eight figures burst from the roof of Nance's ship and floated towards the cavern floor, the speed of their descent minimized by the small lev pads they clung to. Most of them did not reach the ground before skiffs swooped in and captured them, carrying them away. Nance's lancer slammed onto one of the pathways below, bursting to pieces with an echoing boom.

"*There's no way we're going to make it out of this, Sierra. There are too many ships. We can't possibly outrun them all.*" Raif's thoughts were dark and desperate. Through all the

dangers they had faced in Oasis, this was the first time she had
ever known him to give in to panic.

But Sierra was not ready to give in. *You were not meant to
die like this,* she told herself. She had no idea where the thought
came from, but it galvanized her courage.

"We don't have to outrun them," she told Raif with a
private thought. *"We just need to take out one ship."* The image
of the praxis flashed from her mind to his.

*"What? The praxis? You're insane. That thing has more
weapons on it than it's got places to put them. You saw what it
did to the lancer."*

*"Yes, but if you can get me inside that ship, I can take
control of it and use it against the rest of the fleet."*

"Take it over? By yourself?" Raif asked, incredulous, *"That
ship is probably crawling with somatarchs and assessors. There's
no way you'll take them all out by yourself."*

*"I have to try. It's the only chance we've got. Get me over
there before it shoots us down."*

Raif paused, wrestling within himself as dozens of ships
closed in on them. He and Sierra steered the ship in wild,
unorthodox patterns, trying to make it as difficult as possible for
the praxis to target them, but it was only a matter of time before
one of the locus beams or disruptor pulses hit them.

*"I suppose I could blow the propulsors and get there in one
shot, but I don't know how long I can keep this thing in the air.
You'll have to be quick."*

"If you've got a better idea, I'd love to hear it."

Raif's mind spun, but came up with nothing. *"I hope I don't
regret this."*

The decision made, Raif engaged the burst cycle on the
propulsors. The citus shot across the cavern straight for the
praxis, threading a single, tight line through the floating mass of
Collective ships.

As their ship pulled alongside the enormous hull of the praxis, Sierra slid her window open again and sat up in her seat.

"I'll stay close," Raif told her. *"If this ship has one weakness, it's got almost nothing for close ranged attacks."*

"I'll send you a message once I've secured the ship," she told him.

Raif brought the citus' wing within a hands-breadth of a maintenance ladder that ran up the side of the praxis. *"I'll just hang out and chew the kern with my friends. Take your time."*

"I'll be in and out before you even notice I'm gone," Sierra promised.

With that, she leapt from the citus onto the ladder. The glassy outer surface was too smooth to climb, but the rungs on the side allowed her to scale her way up to a little ledge below a square maintenance hatch. It was sealed tight.

As the citus dipped underneath the praxis, Sierra pulled out the cutter. The yellow blade flared out from the end of her arm. She traced around the hatch, hoping to break the seal, but the cutter left no visible mark in the bluish material of the ship. She blinked in disbelief. There must have been a glitch. She tried it again. Nothing happened. Panic set in. She made several quick slashes into the hull but it remained untouched.

This can't be happening, It's the celerium vein all over again.

Instinctively, she looked around for Raif and the citus, but he was gone.

This was a bad idea.

The citus may have disappeared, but three skiffs were now speeding towards her. She gripped the rungs tighter, her legs weak and unsteady. For the first time she noticed just how high up she was. Thoughts of what would happen to her if she fell raced dizzily through her mind.

She started to climb. She had to get off the side of this

thing. What she was going to do about the skiffs she had no idea, but she couldn't stay where she was.

Ten rungs to go from the top, one of the skiffs pulled up alongside her, mounted by two somatarchs. The gunner reached out to grab her while the pilot stared blankly ahead.

Sierra locked her elbow around one of the rungs just before the creature latched onto her feet and started to pull.

She slashed with the bright yellow blade, cutting off the front of the skiff. The ship lurched to the side. Pain shot through her legs as the somatarch's fingers dug into her feet at the ankles, trying to hold on. The skiff torqued to the side and her boots were ripped from her feet. The somatarch flailed about in the tetherless air, still holding her empty boots. The skiff spiraled out of control and plunged towards the ground, crashing into one of the blue glass buildings. It shattered into pieces, but the windows did not show so much as a scratch.

Sierra strapped the cutter to back on her belt and raced up the ladder. The cold and unforgiving metal was jarring to her bare feet, but she didn't care. The other two skiffs were right behind her.

Perhaps seeing what had happened to the first ship, the other two landed on top of the praxis instead of attempting to grab her mid-flight. Their ships had barely stopped moving when the somatarchs, all four of them, jumped out of their vehicles and took off after her.

Sierra jammed the cutter back onto her arm and flipped on the red blade as she turned to face them. The somatarchs stopped and waited to see what she would do.

Only five or six paces separated them, but before either side could make a move, a tremendous cracking noise exploded down the length of the cavern. A multitude of fractures popped out along the walls, slithering down like infected veins. A low rumbling shook the chamber, but the somatarchs ignored it, never taking their eyes off their quarry.

Seeing she didn't advance, the somatarchs moved forward, approaching with caution. She thought about trying to run around them and get to the skiffs, but knew she wasn't fast enough. Her only hope was the cutter.

As they closed they made no move to grab her. Taking a risk, she lunged at the one on her far right, but the creature reacted in time to avoid the streaking blade. In perfect synchronization, the somatarch beside it kicked her legs out from under her. She slammed down on the impenetrable fuselage. Before she could get up or even roll away, a third somatarch leapt on top of her and the fourth one pinned down the arm with the cutter.

She struggled to break free, but the somatarch on top of her had little difficulty keeping her down. The cutter was jerked off her arm and shut down as they wrestled her hands behind her back. She felt something clamp shut around them. They had her.

Wrenching her to her feet, they marched her towards one of the skiffs. She had failed before she ever got inside the praxis.

From somewhere above the ship, another timpanous crack reverberated through the air. Sierra felt certain it was another tremor, but then a burst of blue light pierced the ceiling and came blazing down onto the praxis. The force of the impact sent a shudder through the entire ship and knocked Sierra and the somatarchs off their feet.

Looking up from where she'd been thrown, Sierra saw that a tunneler had carved its way through the ceiling and penetrated the roof of the praxis up to the drilling cone. As she watched, the brilliant blue color surrounding the front end of the tunneler faded and disappeared. The vehicle stood straight up where it had landed, rising from the surface of the cruiser like some monument to impossibility.

The somatarchs paid no attention to the new arrival, springing back to their feet and grabbing hold of Sierra once again.

The hatch to the tunneler could be heard sliding open behind her. This, at last, made the somatarchs pause. They turned and stared at the range up vehicle as several figures emerged from behind it. There were four of them, all dressed in garricks and kaffs.

"Let go of that woman," Zain commanded as he drew a pinion from the bundle on his back. The others did the same.

The Waymen had survived! Amidst the tremors, the battle, and Sierra's failure, this realization was like finding a pocket of calm inside a raging storm.

The somatarch holding Sierra yanked her to her feet and took a step back, but Sierra knew it was not out of fear. The other three somatarchs surged forward.

The Waymen focused their attacks on a single somatarch. They were at such close range they could hardly miss. The creature nimbly dodged one of the spears, but three of them struck home. One pierced straight through the heart. The somatarch sank to the ground and did not stir.

The other two charged ahead, but the Waymen dashed behind the tunneler so that their enemies would not have a straight shot at them. The somatarchs disappeared behind the machine after them, splitting to either side.

Loud cracking noises erupted all across the cavern, drowning out the sounds of the struggle behind the tunneler, but not entirely. Someone cried out in pain and one of the

Waymen was flung beyond the edge of the vehicle. He landed like heavily and stayed where he fell, motionless.

The somatarch holding Sierra began dragging her back towards the skiffs. She dug in her feet and tried to squirm free but it was useless. With her hands tied behind her back and no weapons, all she could do was slow down its progress a little.

As she glanced over her shoulder, she saw another Wayman stagger backwards, this time from the other side of the vehicle. A white leg shot out and connected with his face and the man sank to the ground.

At last, a single somatarch emerged from behind the tunneler, its robes torn and blood trickling from its mouth, but otherwise unharmed.

"Raif, where are you?" Sierra wondered, reaching out to him with her mind. But the only answer she received was the quaking rumble of the cavern getting ready to fall down on top of her.

THIRTY-SEVEN

NUMINAE STAYS HIS HAND

The two somatarchs strapped the clamp around Sierra's hands to a silver cord in the floor of their skiff and took off.

As they cleared the hull of the praxis, a howling yell ripped through the air. It sounded like something between a wail of pain and a shout of triumph. A skiff came hurtling straight at them from behind, spinning out of control. It was spinning so fast Sierra could not tell who, if anyone, was piloting it. The somatarchs maneuvered their ship out of the way, but the incoming skiff swerved unpredictably at the last moment and rammed into them.

The somatarchs flew from their skiff as the two ships locked together and barreled into the tunneler. Sierra blacked out, but woke up a short time later to the sound of someone groaning loudly. Pain shot through one of her arms and half a dozen cuts throbbed on her face. She shut off the pain at once and forced herself to stand. Looking at her arm, she thought it looked sprained, but not broken.

The silver cord was still attached to her clamps, but it had snapped in two and was no longer connected to the skiff. She pulled the clamps under her legs so that her arms were back in front of her.

Looking around, she saw what was left of the somatarchs. The other skiff must have clipped them both, one at the neck, the other at the waist for they now lay bloody and still on the shiny blue surface of the praxis. The fact that she had been sitting down and tied to the floor was probably the only reason she had not suffered the same fate.

The two twisted skiffs, now fused together, were embedded into the side of the tunneler which had tipped over, exposing an enormous hole in the surface of the praxis.

As Sierra stared at it, a chubby Wayman stumbled out from behind the wreckage, moaning and bleeding.

"You...look like you know something about this place," the man said, addressing Sierra in a rough, gravelly voice.

It was not any Wayman she had ever seen before. For a moment she was so shocked by his presence she couldn't think how to reply.

"I'm a bit lost," he blathered on, clearing his throat and wiping the blood from his face with his filthy sleeve. "Looking for a shim named Malthus, ever heard of him?"

"No—I mean yes. Look, I don't know who you are, but we can talk later," she said as he reached her. "My friends are hurt."

She brushed past him, rushing towards the tunneler, careful not to step on any of the shrapnel with her bare feet. For the moment, she forgot all about her mission to commandeer the praxis, her only thoughts were of what had happened to Zain and the other Waymen.

"Wh—Where are you going?" the stranger asked, taking a jagged path after her, looking only half conscious. Sierra ignored him.

As she ran, she spotted the cutter the somatarchs had taken from her. She could not hold it very easily with her hands still bound and she didn't want to stop so she asked the Wayman to pick it up for her. He grunted in acknowledgement of the request, but she didn't stop to see if he fulfilled it, she just kept running.

The moment she reached the other side of the tunneler she let out an involuntary cry. Scattered around the edge of the gaping hole in the praxis lay the bodies of two somatarchs and the four Waymen who had fought against them. When she spotted Zain her heart went into her throat. His head was bleeding badly and one of his arms was twisted at an odd angle.

"No," she murmured, kneeling beside him. She leaned in to find a heartbeat. After a few moments she calmed down enough to detect a faint rhythm inside, feeble and fading, but still there.

"You're alive," she said, breathlessly.

Zain stirred at her words and opened his eyes. "Is it you?" he asked.

"Yes, yes, it's me, Sierra."

"You're safe now?" He mumbled feebly, his eyes unfocused.

"Yes," she said, breaking into tears. "You saved me."

He did not seem to hear her answer. His face looked so very still. Sierra sensed she was about to lose him. She had seen that look in others many times before.

Another rumble echoed across the cavern. The rocks of the ceiling were pulling apart. More cracks opened up along the roof. Chunks of debris pelted the buildings and ships. Rocks, some of them nearly as large as the skiffs, pounded the praxis, but they shattered on impact, leaving the massive hull completely undamaged.

The thunderous tremors seemed to rouse Zain. His eyes

flew open wide, as if he'd been awakened suddenly. His gaze fell upon the large Wayman coming up behind Sierra. His face clouded over, but his gaze shifted towards the ceiling of the cavern.

"It has begun," Zain said. "You must leave this place."

A head-sized rock shattered a few paces away, peppering the other Wayman with debris.

"The man is right," the Wayman said, pulling on Sierra's arm, "This ship is the only thing big enough to protect us from these rocks. We've got to get inside."

The Wayman didn't wait to see if Sierra would follow him, but turned and jumped into the yawning hole in the praxis' hull.

"Are you strong enough to help me get the others?" Sierra caressed Zain's bloody face, trying to keep him conscious.

"Bryce is the one doing this." He spoke dreamily, unaware of what she'd said. "He wants to break the Life of the World."

"What? What are you talking about?"

"I saw him...after all these years—I saw him."

"Who, Bryce? You know where he is?"

A large rock pummeled the tunneler. It swayed and the paneling groaned. Sierra feared it might roll on top of them, but it held for now.

"No, an eidos—he appeared to me out of the rocks in the mine." Zain's voice grew more faint. He was struggling for breath. "We should have died in the blast, but he saved us, protected us. He told me to get into this tunneler and warn the others. He said that Bryce was going to destroy this place—"

"But how? How could he possibly—" Sierra interrupted, but Zain waved weakly for her to be silent.

"You don't understand," he wheezed. The air was becoming hard to breathe from all the dust and debris. "The Life of the World was not meant to be exposed in this way. But the eidos said that it was the will of Numinae to stay his hand. 'The veins of the land will open and its blood will wash away the evil of men', he said."

Another boulder slammed into the tunneler, shards of rock flew all around them. One of the larger ones zinged into Sierra's shoulder, but she felt nothing.

"Go, Sierra," Zain said. "I am beyond help. I go now to the Eversky...where there is no pain, no sorrow..."

"No!" Sierra sobbed. "I won't let you go!"

But at that moment, the Wayman who had dropped down into the hole reached up from inside and pulled her down into the ship as the air erupted in a shower of jagged stones.

"Why did you do that?" Sierra knifed the words at him, her face plastered by a mixture of dust and tears.

The heavyset Wayman ignored her, dragging her further away from the edge of the hole which was rapidly filling with rubble and debris.

The air was so choked with dust it swallowed the lights of the cavern, leaving them in total darkness.

The hole was gone, and with it her access to Zain. Sierra moved as if in a dream, fumbling through the dark and choking on the dust as the world around swayed in every direction.

And then, as if they passed through a curtain, the darkness parted and they found themselves in a hallway sealed at the end by a locus energy door.

"I just saved your life, you know. Are you ready to take me to Malthus now?" the Wayman asked impatiently.

Sierra looked into his bloodshot eyes and scruffy face. He seemed to be leering at her, as if he had a dozen intentions at that moment, and none of them good. The overwhelming impression she got from what she saw there was that this man was not to be trusted. "I don't care!" she screamed, pulling at her hair. "Zain's dead! He was—that was my friend up there."

She doubled over and began to sob again.

The Wayman took two steps to her and slapped her in the face. Though she felt nothing physically, the action jarred her emotionally, snapping her out of her grief in an instant.

"Why did you do that?" she said, angrily. But when she caught sight of the savage look in his eyes, her anger quickly turned to fear.

"Death is no big deal," he said coldly. He leaned in close, the javelins on his back rattling. "Now you can either help me kill Malthus or I can send you off to the same place your friend went to, eh?"

He was so close she could smell his loathsome breath even with her bioseine dampening her senses. All he had to do was slip the knife from his belt to follow through with his threat. And she had no way to defend herself. He was holding the cutter as well.

"Who are you? And what are you doing here?" she asked, trying to steady her nerves.

"Name's Nox," the man said, "and as I said, I'm here to take out the leader of this place and I figured if he was going to be anywhere, he'd be in this flying fortress. It's the one I'd pick if I was the Reeve of this place." He let out a seditious little laugh.

Sierra was about to tell him she had no idea if Malthus was on this ship or not, but then realized that perhaps he had a point. She had no desire whatsoever to help him in this task, but it occurred to her that if Malthus was in charge of this ship, Nox might actually be willing to help her in commandeering the praxis. And considering his threat to kill her, at this point she really didn't have much choice anyway.

"If he's in command here, I might be able to help you find him, but we need to take control of this ship or it won't matter what you do to Malthus. It's the only chance we have of getting out of this place alive."

Nox shrugged indifferently. "Fine. But we kill Malthus first."

Sierra gave a reluctant sigh. "Before we do anything I need you to get me out of these clamps." She pulled her hands up and showed him the black clasps.

"Hmm," the man scratched his forehead. "I left my pincers back at the sar. Guess I'll have to shiv you out." He pulled out a jagged knife from his belt.

"No, wait. That will take too long," Sierra said. "Just use the cutter you picked up."

"The what?" Nox asked.

"That metal tube. The one I told you to pick up."

Nox's eyes lit up with recognition. "So that's what this thing is, a cutter. I like the sound of that name. How does it work?"

"Just reach inside, grab the handle and flick your wrist to the left. Then swipe the middle panel up to extend the blade."

Nox eyed the tube with suspicion, inserting his arm into it slowly, as if he were expecting it to hurt him. After several moments in which the level of consternation grew steadily on his face, a long red blade of light finally appeared, shining out from the end of the cylinder.

"No, left, not right," she corrected him. "And watch where you're waving that thing."

Nox stifled a grunt and the blade shifted from red to yellow. "Interesting," he remarked.

"Now slice the binders on my wrists," Sierra told him.

She heard a subtle hiss as the binders split in two.

"I didn't nick you, did I?" the Wayman asked with a nervous giggle.

"It won't cut living things," she informed him, starting to make her way towards the locus doorway, "Not when it's yellow."

"Well, what good is that?" he asked, looking at the object in sudden disgust.

"The red is for cutting living things," she explained, though the moment she said it she wished she hadn't.

"Ah..." Nox's eyes lit up. "Yellow for made stuff, red for bloody stuff. Got it."

"All right," Sierra said, reaching out her hand. "You can give me back the cutter now."

Nox gave her a shifty look. "What, this?" he asked, then wagged his head, grinning. "Well, I'm not one for gears usually, but I think I'll keep this trinket for the moment. I have a feeling I might need it in the near future."

Sierra did not like his response, but the malevolent gleam in his eyes told her that arguing would be a mistake. This man was dangerous. Extremely dangerous. She shrank back from him, wishing there was some way she could escape and doubtful whether or not he would even help her on her mission in the end.

Nox appeared not to notice her reaction and instead turned his attention to the glowing door, giving it a puzzled look. He tried slicing through the sheet of energy with the yellow blade. When nothing happened he tried the red.

"That won't work," Sierra told him, staying well back as he took another wild swing at it.

"How do we get through this...light or whatever it is? This thing isn't working." He banged the cutter against the metal wall beside the door.

Sierra stared at the door, the thrumming of rocks on the hull turning her thoughts back to Zain, Wik, Yor, and Ket. They had given their lives to save her, but she would gladly have taken their place.

"Useless machines!" Nox blurted out as he turned to her. "I thought you were going to help me find Malthus." The glowing red blade on his arm and the menacing expression on his face startled her out of her thoughts.

"You know, it would probably be best if we went straight down, actually," Sierra said. "Just cut through the floor. It will be much quicker and they won't be expecting it."

Nox let out a shout of excitement. "Ha! I knew you'd be good for something."

He started to cut a hole in the ground, but when nothing happened, he cursed and shook the cutter and the blade flickered back to yellow. He then proceeded to trace a wobbly shape in the floor. When the paneling fell through, he stepped back, admiring his handiwork.

"I think I might like this cutter of yours," he said and Sierra could not fail to miss the cruel light simmering inside his eyes.

That light only seemed to grow more sinister as they carved their way through the next two levels, burrowing down until they had dropped into the central passage which ran outside the control room. They had managed to avoid meeting anyone up to that point, but this time when Sierra landed, she immediately spotted several somatarchs heading towards them.

There were six of them in all. Nox let out a howl and charged with the cutter blazing red. The lead somatarch paid no attention to him, instead mechanically drawing the oscillathe it wore at its hip. Sierra turned around to hit the floor and ran right into the white neutralizer blast of an assessor who'd come up behind her.

THIRTY-EIGHT

AN UNSTOPPABLE FORCE

A FOUL ODOR ASSAULTED SIERRA'S SENSES JUST BEFORE she regained consciousness. When she did open her eyes, she found herself staring at Nox's hideous face. As terrible as his breath was, it was distinct from the odor pummeling her senses at the moment. This new smell did not feel like anything that would come from a person. It was more like hot iron, and it was all around her, breaking through the filter of her bioseine.

"Ah, the beauty stirs," Nox said, chuckling. "It's about time. I was starting to think I might have to leave you behind."

Sierra sat up and looked down the wide hallway and at once understood what the smell was: blood. Everywhere she looked the passage was strewn with disfigured somatarch bodies. Though she knew they were not fully human, in death, it was all the same. She tried to look away, but the carnage was everywhere.

Her gaze swung back to Nox. She regarded him with a look of disgust. He must have been even more brutal than she thought.

She knew from her bioseine that she had only been unconscious for a little over a microslice. It was unusual that she had regained consciousness from the neutralizer so quickly, but it was baffling how Nox could have killed so many somatarchs in such a short time; there must have been over fifteen bodies all lying in close proximity to each other, far more than the few she had first seen.

"How many did you kill?" she asked numbly, her brain attempting to make sense of the scene.

"Oh, I'm no good with numbers," Nox said, his eyes lighting up with glee. "They streamed in here like Welkin running to water. Must have been twenty, thirty, maybe more by the time they finally stopped coming. I guess ghosts die as easy as men when it comes down to it."

"But how—" she began and then stopped, realizing that she didn't want to know. The details would only make her more afraid of him. "Well, thank you all the same. I suppose this is the second time you've saved my life."

Nox's chin rose vainly. "I used my last bit of almamenth on you, too," he said, pointing at her arm. One sleeve was rolled up and the arm was moist. She had missed that fact, as well as the wonderful smell, because her bioseine was masking her pain. "You better be worth it."

"Well, we still have to find the control room. I think it might be behind those doors over there." She pointed towards the double doors in front of them, but Nox, on hearing the word 'doors', headed off towards the ones at the end of the passage instead.

"Wait," Sierra called after him, "not those. They're too big. They probably lead to a cargo bay or something. I mean these two, over here by me."

"Is that where Malthus is?" Nox asked.

"I think so." She rose to her feet, stepping around the carnage. "At least that's the first place we should look."

Nox snorted giddily. "I guess it's time to do what I came for." He walked up to the doors and tried the handles. As Sierra expected, they didn't budge.

He flailed at them with the yellow blade of the cutter, chopping the panels into a pile of scrap in quick fashion. Once the opening was big enough, he leapt through like he'd been shot from a spring.

By the time Sierra followed him in, he was already halfway down the ramp leading to the control bridge. A massive window composed of a single curved surface surrounded the chamber looking out onto the base. Her gaze was drawn to the scene of devastation which had overtaken the cavern of Manx Core. Half of the buildings were covered beneath mountains of rock, while others looked as though they'd been ripped to shreds from the inside out. Crushed ships littered the ground. Not a single one remained aloft. They had all either fled or been battered into wreckage by the endless torrent of rocks cascading down from the ceiling.

Where was Raif? Had he made it out alive?

The praxis was the only ship left. It hovered in the midst of the catastrophic scene defiantly, as if it alone had the power to weather the devastating rain.

The praxis' behavior was puzzling, but there was some-thing even stranger. Just below the ship, a fountain of neon blue sludge bubbled up from between several buildings, gushing forth from the cracks in the ground like an open wound. Rivers and pools of glowing neophosphorous formed around the crack, illuminating the hazy ruins with a haunting light. Within moments, streams of it began pouring down from the ceiling as well, pillars of light suspended amidst the immense amphithe-ater of destruction.

Why was the praxis still here?

A solitary figure dressed in the dark gray robes of an

assessor stood near the window, looking out across the devastation, oblivious to the arrival of Nox or Sierra. Though the man had yet to move, Nox had stalked up behind him as quietly as he could, his red blade glowing menacingly.

Was he really going to just kill him without first finding out who he was? And was the control room really only occupied by a single person? It couldn't be this easy. Something told her the man in gray was not as vulnerable as he looked.

Nox passed the long black tables and empty polymeric chairs at the base of the ramp and still the figure did not move. There was only open space between Nox and the assessor now.

Nox abandoned all pretense of stealth and sprinted the last few steps, his red blade swept back for the deadly blow which would end his opponent's life in quick and bloody fashion. Sierra winced. It felt so callous, so wrong to kill someone like this. She wanted to scream at Nox to stop, but the cry froze in her throat.

The thin blade of light fell, passing through the assessor's body, but with absolutely no effect. The only thing it did was invoke a shimmer of light across his frame. The assessor's arm shot out and grabbed Nox by the throat as calmly as if he were picking up a cup to take a drink. The Wayman's body was enveloped in an intense white light. Nox shuddered once and dropped from the man's grasp, crashing to the floor and failing to rise.

A deep voice sounded from the dark robed figure. "I prefer not to be bothered just now," he said, never taking his gaze from the enormous wrap-around window and its panorama of falling rock, sinking buildings, and glowing sludge. "I am trying to save my son."

His son? Was such a thing even possible? Sierra thought that had been forbidden in the Collective. Surely this had to be Malthus, but there was no time to think about that now.

She had to get control of this ship. Escaping the Collective fleet was no longer a priority. All the ships had either been wiped out by the quake or fled. But the cavern was coming apart before her eyes. The praxis, with its impenetrable hull, was the only hope she had for getting out of Manx Core alive.

"We need to fly this ship out of here," Sierra said. There seemed to be no other choice but to try the direct approach.

The man said nothing. His gaze remained fixed on the scene before him. The deadly beauty of the glowing fountain below lit up his face like he was watching one of the firework shows she had seen in the esolace.

She followed his gaze to what he was staring it. Though it lay mostly in ruins, she could see from the bits of blue glass and tall beams that it was the remains of the Command Center. Adan had shown it to the Sentients when he shared the scene with Gavin from the chronotrace. Flows of neophosphorous smothered the remaining buildings, pulling them down into the glowing lakes like huge chunks of salt dissolving in the rain.

From the praxis five bright yellow beams shot across the open space below, etching odd patterns into the flows and carving out chunks from the writhing slime in a desperate attempt to keep the building from collapsing altogether. But the neophosphorous pools grew far more quickly than the beams could cut it away.

Sierra reached down and quietly removed the cutter from Nox's arm. It wouldn't be of any use against this man, but it might allow her to wrest control of the ship from him by other means. Nox remained insensate, his bulky frame sprawled awkwardly across the floor.

"*Raif, are you there?*" She reached out to her friend, feeling a surge of hope when he answered.

"*Sierra, you're alive!*" he replied. "*Sorry, I had to duck out there for a while. This cavern is having a serious case of indigestion."*

"What's your status?"

"Feeling pretty lonely at the moment. I was the life of the party until the tremors hit. But for some reason all the other ships zipped off down the tunnels when the world started to fall apart. They just don't know how to have a good time, I guess. I've been hanging out underneath the praxis' wings since then, but I'm not sure how much more even this ship can take."

"I'm on the control bridge. I just need to find the bioseine interface," Sierra informed him.

"You're amazing." Raif's mind buzzed with ideas. *"There are two interface panels on the ship. A main and a backup. The main is on the bridge and the backup is in the cargo bay."*

"Okay, I'll take out the one in the cargo bay first since I'll have to be on the bridge to fly this thing once the panels go down."

"There's a manual steering column in the control room. Just remember to open the cargo bay doors once you get control of the ship so I can get out of this nasty weather we're having out here, okay?"

"Got it." Sierra was already running up the ramp and out of the control room. As she had hoped, the assessor took no notice of her departure, remaining fixated on the crumbling Command Center.

She sliced through the cargo bay doors in the next room, barely pausing as she burst into the wide open chamber beyond. There were half a dozen skiffs docked there, but most of it was empty space. She spotted the bioseine control panel at once. It was much larger than the other ones she'd removed, but it looked essentially the same, a series of parallel gray interface strips.

Sierra slashed the seal around the controls and they crashed to the floor. Her task complete, she turned and sprinted back to the control room.

When she returned, the assessor was still in the same position, consumed with his tireless vigil of the Command Center. Nox still had not stirred. The main bioseine interface was at the back of the room. Sierra ran over to it and began to slice it up.

"Hey," came Raif's thoughts in the midst of her work, *"Are you getting a visual of what's going on outside?"*

Sierra glanced over her shoulder at the showers of falling rock and the bright streams of neophosphorous pouring from the ceiling.

"What is the praxis up to?" Raif asked.

"Give me a moment. Kind of busy here." She had to go carefully around the edge of the panel this time, taking care not to damage any of the sensory and environmental panels on either side. A few moments later, the second interface clanged onto the floor. Sierra turned to see what the assessor's reaction would be.

The man pivoted on his heel, his dark eyes no longer distant, but aflame with anger. His beard framed his face at unforgiving angles. He must have been handsome once, Sierra thought, but he was no longer. She had no doubt now that this was Malthus, the Assessor Primary from the chronotrace.

"You!" Malthus said, his hands trembling in the air as if he wished to choke her from afar, "What have you done?"

He leapt through the air, covering the half dozen paces between them in an instant. Instinctively, Sierra lifted up the cutter's blade to ward off his attack, but the yellow beam did nothing to deter him.

He landed on top of her, pinning her to the ground with one hand while raising the other above his head as if he meant to strike her, but instead of bringing it down, he held it there, blazing in the air like a red lumin.

"I almost had him," Malthus cried, shaking her, causing her head to jerk from side to side. "You killed him. You killed my son!"

"I don't know what you're talking about," Sierra cried, gasping for breath, "We need to get this ship out of here."

"Were you jealous of his love and devotion to me? Is that why you took him from me?" the assessor raged, his expression devoid of all sense and reason.

The praxis list to the right, no longer flying level.

"You're losing altitude," came Raif's warning.

"I can't do anything," she answered, her thoughts drowned in terror. *"There's a madman trying to kill me!"* She opened her vision to Raif so he could see what she was seeing.

"If one of us doesn't do something, this ship is going to crash." She gasped out the words.

Her message pierced through Malthus' blazing wall of rage. His head snapped back towards the window. Seeing the ship's tilting trajectory, he let out a howl, his eyes bulging from their sockets. Sierra could feel her throat collapsing in on itself under his crushing grip.

"Please," she reached out to him with her mind, no longer able to talk. *"Please just let me go and I'll help you find your son. I'll do whatever you want,"* she pleaded, but she could not tell if he received the message.

The mad light in his eyes flared brighter. "I should cut you to pieces," he said, his voice low and guttural.

His grip grew tighter and tighter.

"You'll kill us both," she implored him.

Sierra fought against him with everything she had, prying at his fingers with both hands, but his grip was fast as stone.

Her bioseine screamed at her in warning. It would be shutting her down at any moment.

Just when her breathless body reached the brink of collapse, Nox appeared out of the corner of her vision. From the edge of the room he tossed a black disc along the floor. The assessor turned toward the scraping sound. A flash of light blinded her and then everything exploded in an avalanche of noise. Sierra flew through the air and crumpled to the ground on the other side of the room.

When she came to, she was bleeding from a deep gash in her right thigh and multiple cuts on her legs and unprotected feet.

Nox was standing near the window, a look of terror on his face. His eyes were riveted on the assessor, who stood in the middle of the mangled control room, completely unharmed. Strewn all around him, tables and chairs had been alternately torn apart and fused together in a tangled mess.

"You're a demon," Nox shouted as he drew a pinion and fired it.

The assessor made no effort to avoid the weapon as it struck him squarely in the chest and splintered into fragments. The dark robed assessor advanced methodically towards Nox, his right hand encased inside a red sheath of light.

"You are Malthus, aren't you? No wonder Nolan wanted you dead," Nox said, firing another pinion which shattered after slamming into the assessor's shoulder.

"So you are friends with the man who destroyed my son?" Malthus asked. "All the more reason to kill you."

The assessor marched forward, shrugging off a third pinion and coming to a halt a step away from the horrified Wayman.

Nox darted to the side, but as quick as he was, Malthus leapt in the same direction and caught him by the arm, tossing him to the ground like a piece of scrap.

"The ship," Raif called out to her, *"Sierra, do something!"*

Sierra clawed her way to her feet using the wall. The crazed assessor ignored her. All he saw now was Nox.

As the ground loomed before them, Sierra rushed to the steering column, leaving a bloody trail. She yanked it back as hard as she could.

The sudden shift in direction knocked the assessor off balance. Sierra risked a glance back towards him and saw Nox scrambling to his feet. Malthus recovered and pounced on him, knocking him again to the floor.

Sierra brought the praxis around further, narrowly missing the top of what was left of the Command Center.

"So you're Nolan's assassin? That's who sent you?" Malthus asked, his hand a crimson light once again. "Perhaps one day I'll get to do to him what I'm about to do to you."

The glowing hand flared like a falling star and plunged into Nox's belly. With a dismissive gesture, he sliced to the left and then back to the right, his hand passing as easily through Nox's body as a cutter's blade.

Nox stared at the cauterized gash where his midsection had once been, a cruel grin on his face. "Kill or be killed," he said, and then slumped to the ground, dead.

Malthus arose, his face lit up like it was consumed by red fire. In that moment Sierra knew that he would kill her too.

But as he stepped towards her, something caught her eye from the window and she shouted.

"I see them! There, on top of that building!"

She pointed to the gutted framework of the Command Center where two men covered in glowing blue light clung to a crumpled platform of steel.

"That's Adan," she said, barely able to voice the words. "And that must be Gavin. They're alive!"

"Gavin?" Malthus muttered, his rage vanishing. "Gavin's

alive?" He pushed Sierra aside from the steering column and took control of the ship. "Then my son is alive as well! I can still bring him back!"

Sierra moved over to the ship's auxiliary system controls, including the one for the axom field. She didn't bother to try and understand the change which had come over Malthus, but focused instead on pulling the twisted platform holding Gavin and Adan out of the quagmire surrounding it.

It rose slowly, still covered in a thick blanket of bluish sludge. As powerful as the axom field was, it seemed uncertain whether or not they would make it. The flows in which the platform was mired were unwilling to release their victims, but with a sudden jerk the platform broke free and Adan and Gavin began to ascend towards the ship.

"Thank you," Malthus whispered as the platform pulled closer and closer. He motioned towards the exit. "Open the cargo doors."

Locking the steering column so that the praxis would remain hovering in place, he bounded up the ramp and out of the room.

"*Raif, the ship's been stabilized,*" Sierra told him in an exhilarated rush. Her fingers danced across the auxiliary controls, triggering the cargo bay doors to open. Then she hurried after Malthus. "*And we found Adan and Gavin—they survived! We're pulling them out of the wreckage. The cargo bay doors are opening now.*"

"*Are you sure? I saw two figures being pulled up on a platform. Was one of them really Adan?*"

"*Yes*", she answered, joy flooding her every thought.

"*Well, he's a lot shinier than I remember him, then,*" Raif added, her friend's words only adding to the elation she felt.

THIRTY-NINE

THROUGH THE VISCERA

Adan and Gavin pulled themselves from the wreckage of the bridge, which lay, still dripping with neophosphorous, near the circular opening in the floor of the cargo bay. Moments before, they had floated up out of the ruins and into the enormous praxis cruiser as if lifted by the hand of Numinae himself.

As they set foot on solid ground once more, Malthus, and then Sierra, rushed into the large room. Malthus's presence was troubling, but when Adan saw Sierra, he forgot about everything else. His joy was too complete to have anything overshadow it at that moment. Sierra was alive. She had terrible wounds on her legs, but she was alive and he had never been happier to see anyone in his life.

"Gavin," Malthus said, throwing his arms wide and embracing the haggard scientist. "I thought I'd lost you."

Gavin returned the embrace wearily. "Thank you for saving us. We owe you our lives."

Sierra ran to embrace Adan at the same time, tears spilling down her face.

"I can't believe I found you," she said in his ear.

Adan could find no words to express what he felt. He simply held onto her, feeling for the first time that this is what arms were made for.

"I thought you might have been...I'm sorry I couldn't go back for you. Are you all right?" he said.

"I am now."

The reunion was broken up by the arrival of the citus through the large opening in the floor.

"What is this ship?" Malthus asked. "I gave the order for everyone to evacuate."

"Just more survivors from below," Sierra said.

"It's the pride of Oasis, my friends, the last line of defense, the man of the moment, the ace of the fleet..." Raif's thoughts bubbled out across the Collective channel.

"And his sidekick, Von," added the former assessor, surprising everyone with the uncharacteristic remark.

The same delight and relief at being alive and together radiated through the thoughts of everyone gathered, everyone that is, except Malthus. His thoughts remained closed off from the others.

"Now that I've found you," Malthus said, regarding Gavin intently, "we can get out of this place. We'll build another chronotrace—a better one this time. There is a lab on this ship with everything you'll need to get started." His face formed something like a smile, but the sheen surrounding him distorted it, making it look more like an agonized grimace. When Gavin did not reply, it looked like his expression morphed again, to something more akin to worry or impatience. "Is something wrong, Gavin?"

Gavin remained silent. Like Adan, he was a strange sight, his skin, hair, and clothing shone a bright turquoise blue, making him look like some otherworldly being. The only thing that betrayed his emotions were his eyes. They looked sad and somewhat guarded, two patches of darkness within a shining countenance.

Malthus' eyes scanned Gavin's expression, as if looking for something he had lost. On the other side of the cargo bay Raif maneuvered the citus so that he set down the remains of the two lancers. He floated the citus gently down beside it.

Though everyone else turned to watch the landing, Malthus just kept staring at Gavin.

"I realize that my threats before may have hindered our relationship," Malthus said, his tone warm and yet forced. "But when I saw the Command Center crumbling into ruins, I realized what a fool I'd been. If I lose you, I've lost everything. You are the one hope I have of getting back my son."

Gavin's gaze fell. Adan could tell he did not want to say what he was about to say, but that he felt compelled to say it nonetheless.

"I'm sorry, Malthus," Gavin said, "but you've been lied to."

Malthus gave him a startled, angry look, as if Gavin had just slapped him in the face. "What do you mean?" he thundered, his cheeks flushing.

"There is no way to bring back your son." Gavin spoke slowly and deliberately, "Darius was lying to you about bringing him back. He only told you that it was possible so that you would join the Developers."

As quickly as the color had rushed into Malthus' face it drained away. He stared at Gavin with hollow eyes, the silvery sheen flickering across his face as if it represented his vacillating thoughts. He looked unsteady on his feet all of a sudden, ready to stagger or faint.

"No, you're wrong, Gavin," he said, recovering slightly. "Dane was here. You saw it in the chronotrace. That man may not have looked like my son, but outward appearance is irrelevant. I know my son. It was his thoughts, his memories."

"That is what Darius wanted you to think. He manipulated your mind so that you would be happy, so that you would help him protect Oasis. But Nolan's personality started to take back over almost from the start. Darius knew the memory transfer would never take hold permanently so he ended it when it no longer served his purposes. It was Darius who erased Dane's memories from the Repository, not Nolan."

"No." Malthus exhaled the word like the first rattling winds signifying a storm. "You are the one who is lying. No one can change my thoughts. I am protected, even from memorants." His voice seemed sure and deep, but at that moment the sheen around him faded. His eyes darkened and locked with Gavin's and suddenly Adan, who was standing next to Gavin, could read Malthus' mind for the first time.

Adan realized that Gavin was using the miasma channel to break through the shield protecting Malthus' mind. The variance field had protected not only his mind, but his body as well, making him almost invulnerable to harm. But the miasma channel operated above this shield, or perhaps below it. It was as primitive as it was advanced, something that technology had "unlocked", but which had existed from the beginning of time. Darius had no more invented it than scientists had invented the law of gravity.

Malthus' mind was a rigid framework of knots and cords which bent at sharp angles. The strain between them was so great it was a wonder they didn't break. The lines became smaller and smaller the closer they got to the center until they disappeared into a small black hole. But as Adan became accustomed to the mental landscape, he could see that the hole was growing larger.

"*What is happening to him?*" Adan asked Gavin privately,

realizing that something was not right, but not able to grasp exactly what it was.

"That hole is his relationship to his son. And it's eating up everything inside of him. His hope that he can bring Dane back to life is the one thing that's keeping him alive, the one thing that has kept the hole from devouring him up until now. Darius saw this as well. In a twisted sort of way, by lying to Malthus and stringing him along with false hope, he kept this man alive. If I take away that hope, he may give up on life altogether."

"I didn't want to have to do this, Malthus," Gavin said. Adan could see the conflict raging in his friend's face almost as clearly as he could sense it in his mind. "But I can't let you live your life based on a lie, no matter how precious it is to you. Your son is dead and you will never get him back."

The words, though spoken softly, sent a tremor through Malthus' body.

"No!" Malthus shouted and started for Gavin, raising his hands as if he meant to strike down the man he had so desperately been trying to save a few moments before. But Gavin stopped him with his words.

"There is no way to bring him back, Malthus. We are more than our experiences, a succession of events and choices. There is something transcendent within us that no technology can capture or replicate. You need to let him go," Gavin whispered. His eyes looked empty and sad, as if it were his own hope he was crushing as well.

Malthus tensed, like a spring winding up to be released, but Gavin stopped whatever he had intended to do, overtaking his mind completely with the miasma channel. Though he could have made Malthus believe at that moment whatever he wanted him to, he did not use his abilities to manipulate Malthus' thoughts as Darius had done. Instead, he removed the barriers which Darius had created, barriers which kept him from seeing the truth. Thoughts and lies fell away and all the sharp angles and twisted corners of Malthus' mind cracked and crumbled under the weight of that truth. Gavin travelled through Malthus' thoughts, breaking down these barriers and setting him free at last to see reality once again in all its cold harsh light, and all the while the black hole at the center grew.

In the time it took the first of the passengers from the newly arrived ships to disembark and begin wandering towards Adan and the others, the lies gripping Malthus' mind had been undone. When Gavin released him back to his own thoughts, Malthus finally saw the truth for the first time.

The shimmering shield surrounding him was gone, and with it Malthus' hold on life as well. He looked hollow, exposed, lost. He said nothing, but the emptiness in his eyes said all that needed to be said. In the space of a few moments, Malthus looked to have shriveled in stature. He was no longer the imposing man he had once been. He was broken, wretched, and alone.

"He's gone isn't he?" Malthus muttered, the color utterly drained from his face. Indeed, the contrast between Gavin's glowing countenance and Malthus' pale one could not have been greater. Malthus stood there staring at Gavin for the longest time, as if he no longer recognized him.

Raif and Von arrived, embracing Sierra and Adan excitedly, but when they noticed the solemn air which had settled over the group their excitement evaporated and their smiles were replaced by puzzled looks.

"Who is this?" Raif whispered.

"*Someone who's lost,*" was all Adan had the heart to reply. For he could feel what Malthus felt at that moment and it was the exact opposite of all the joy Adan had experienced the moment before. It was a sadness that no joy in the world could ever fill because Malthus's world was too overcome by pain and loss to allow any other emotion to enter.

Malthus slipped a segmented black band off his wrist and handed it to Gavin. As he did so, the flickering sheen around him vanished for good.

"Here," he said. "I won't be needing this anymore."

"No, Malthus," Gavin pleaded. "You don't have to give up. You can come with us. You can leave the Collective. You can start a new life."

But the vacant look in Malthus' eyes made it clear he gave no thought to Gavin's words.

"Thank you," Malthus told Gavin, placing a hand on his shoulder. "For helping an old man die in peace."

"No, Malthus, don't—" Gavin said, reaching out for his hand. But Malthus raised it in a rapid salute. Then the assessor stepped backwards and vanished into the broad opening in the cargo bay floor. Gavin stretched out, but grasped only empty air. From the edge of the wide hole, Malthus' body could be seen plummeting into the glowing morass below. It buried itself in the sprawling sea of neophosphorous and was gone within a matter of moments.

"I wish..." Gavin began, but he could not finish. And though his mind clouded over, Adan saw what he had meant to say: *I wish the truth were not so hard to take.*

"We've got to get the praxis out of this cavern."

The thought was Von's. And though everyone present was still in shock, they realized that now was not the time to try and process what they had just seen.

"Right," Raif replied, *"let's get to the control room."*

Everyone marched off after Raif and Von, but Adan and

Gavin took a short detour and passed through one of the ship's decontamination chambers so that they could get the neophosphorous residue removed from their skin.

A chalky mist settled in around them, filling the translucent chamber. In a matter of moments, their skin and clothes had been cleansed of any trace of neophosphorous. Then they hurried on to the control room, but Gavin did not go as quickly as he might have and Adan sensed the weight of Malthus' death laying heavy upon him.

Just as they arrived, Adan caught sight of two Sentients sealing Nox's body in a black bag. The unexpected sight made Adan stop where he was.

Despite the cruel way in which the Wayman had spent his life, Adan took no pleasure in his death. Though Nox had never given any indication that he might somehow change his ways, Adan wanted to believe that if he had been given more time, he might have chosen a different path. When Adan asked Sierra what he was doing there, she gave him a brief summary of what had happened. Sadly, it seemed that Nox had died the same way he had lived: cruelly, and violently.

Adan sat down next to Sierra on the ramp, leaning against the railing. She had bandages on her legs, and her feet were wrapped up in a gauze-like material. He knew she had been treated with almamenth, but he was still worried about her.

His own injuries, even his bruised ribs, once again appeared to be mysteriously mending themselves. Though he had not yet completely healed, he knew from his bioseine that he was not in any serious danger. Once again, this realization troubled him and he wondered if he would ever learn what was going on inside of him. For now, he shifted his concerns to the helm of the ship where Raif stood scrutinizing the viewing screen.

Guided by Raif at the steering column, the praxis navigated

its way through the spilling falls of neophosphorous and cascading rocks. By now the cavern was so completely consumed by the eruptions there was barely any sign left of the military complex which had once occupied its entirety. The landscape was one bright, churning blanket of bluish ooze sprinkled with showers of rock.

As they approached the exit tunnel, the opening shuddered as if daring them to enter. But it was the only exit large enough for them to fit through. Von operated the auxiliary controls and retracted the wings so that the ship would be able to navigate the narrow passageway. A moment later they plunged through the curtain of sludge and debris covering the tunnel, giving the ship a glowing bath.

Inside, the praxis increased in speed and, while it was only a marginal change, it seemed to Adan to be moving dangerously fast through such tight quarters.

"Is it safe to be going at this speed?" Adan asked Raif.

"Von just gave me a glimpse at our backside and it looks like the neophosphorous is rising quicker than before. This ship can handle a lot, but I don't want to plow through any more shiny goop than we have to. It might ruin her paint job."

The tunnels rushed by as the ship rose ever upwards through the Viscera. Von kept a view of the tunnel behind them in one section of the screen. They soon distanced themselves from the morass which had consumed Manx Core. Eventually, the tremors lessened as well, becoming quieter and less frequent as they ascended, until they disappeared altogether.

Once the danger had passed, Adan and Sierra settled in and shared their memories of everything that had happened since they'd been separated. Of all the struggles Sierra had gone through, the one that was the most difficult for Adan to face was the death of Zain. As Adan experienced the memory of his passing, he felt something break inside of him, as if the world no longer made as much sense as it had before.

"He gave his life for me," Sierra said.

"He saved my life many times, too." Tears rushed down Adan's face. *Zain, why did it have to be Zain?* "I don't think I ever met a truer friend."

Sierra grew even more thoughtful. "Something about the way he died struck me, though. As terrible as it was to watch, somehow I thought to myself afterwards that this is how a man is supposed to die."

"It's hard watching someone you care about die," Adan said, his thoughts turning to Will. The two men could not have been more different, but their deaths both gripped him with the same sort of despair. Why was it that men had to die? All the answers seemed to run away from him, carried out through his tears and onto the floor.

"I've seen many people die," Sierra said. "But it never hurt like this."

Adan swallowed his tears, wincing at the bitter taste. "Sometimes I think it would be better not to know certain things," he said, glancing over to where Gavin sat in the corner of the room. He had disconnected his mind from the others, but Adan could sense the hollow emptiness he felt. *There are different kinds of grief, just like there are different kinds of fear, but the response is the same—it makes you want to run away.*

"Adan, there was something you said before we were separated in the tunnel," Sierra put in gently. Adan sensed a quiet intensity in her words, a tenderness in the midst of sorrow. He turned and regarded her, looking her earnestly in the eye, forgetting for a moment his grief. "You said, 'I want you to know something.' What was it you were going to tell me?"

He recalled that moment in the tunnel, living it once again with his memorant mind. He realized that he probably would not have been able to articulate what he was thinking then, even if their conversation hadn't been cut short. But now, in the face of Zain's death and his separation from Sierra, he had no doubt about what he wanted to say.

"Just this: I want to protect you, Sierra. I don't even know that I can or that you would want me to, but I would like to be there for you in whatever troubles lay ahead. I've lost two people I cared about already. I don't want to lose you as well. You matter more to me than anything in this world."

She placed her hand in his. All was quiet in that moment save the gentle background hum of the ship's engines. "I feel the same way." She leaned her head against his shoulder.

Adan closed his eyes and shed one last tear. He couldn't say why, but his grief and happiness were one and the same in that moment. Treachery, triumph, sorrow, friendship, he had experienced so much in the short part of his life which he could remember. But he needed to know that there were times when the curtain was rolled back and he could see the truth, see what really mattered in life. And somehow Sierra had just given him that.

She brushed the hair from her face, looking up at him with wide, clear eyes.

He would never forget this moment, he promised himself. And as a memorant, he felt certain that was one promise he could definitely keep.

GLOSSARY

Acretian \ah-CREE-shun\ Stone: A stone that is poured out in liquid form. It sets quickly but can easily be formed and smoothed for some time even after it sets. It is similar in function to synth metal and char.

Almamenth \AHL-muh-menth\: Compound in the form of a paste which provides nutrients and strength to the user. Meant to be applied on the skin and absorbed over time into the body.

Ancillary Rim: Outermost district of Oasis.

Andros \AN-drohz\: Derogatory term used by members of the Collective to refer to people lacking a bioseine.

Annex: A building connected to the Institute in the central district of Oasis from which the Developers administer the esolace.

Assessors: The security force of Oasis. They have more access to control of the esolace than typical members of the Collective, but are themselves controlled by the Developers.

Atmos \AT-mohs\ Array: This powerful battery of

machines keeps the environment of Oasis at a constant level and protects it from the storms that afflict the rest of the planet.

Atol \AH-tol\: Hot, grainy drink consumed by the Werin.

Axis Prime: The central district of Oasis. This is where the Institute and the Annex are located.

Axom Field: Localized field used to attract objects from a distance.

Azanya \ah-ZAHN-yuh\: Large tent used for Waymen dwellings, typically housing an eclectic group of Waymen who are not necessarily related.

Beacon Portal: An interstellar gateway, allowing for instantaneous traversal of near infinite distances. Each portal requires a matching one at the point of origin.

Bioseine \BAHY-oh-sahyn\: An organic augmentation grafted into the people of the Collective which regulates their health and allows them to access the esolace. It can also allow people to communicate mentally with each other even when the esolace is not present.

Bismine \BIZ-mahyn\: Yellowish crystals which absorb light and produce inordinate amounts of energy for their size. This is the main power source for all Oasis technology.

Blank: Term referring to someone or something without a bioseine or the ability to connect to the esolace.

Canter: Religious leader amongst the Waymen.

Celerium \suh-LEER-ee-um\: Mineral that is capable of increasing the power efficiency of any machine to incredible levels. It is black with blue flecks and is nearly indestructible.

Citus Axomvac: Long, narrow, two passenger ship with no offensive capabilities, but extremely fast. Used primarily for picking up and dropping off supplies or recovering downed ships with their axom field generators.

Click: Measurement of distance, roughly equivalent to about 2km or 1.25 miles. A click is composed of a thousand spans (see 'span').

The Collective: Name for the general population of Oasis.

Compa \COM-pah\: General word of familiarity used by Welkin to refer to someone with whom they are on friendly terms.

Developers/Devs: Also called Administrators, they run and maintain the esolace and the entire Oasis infrastructure. They have control over the lives of everyone connected to the esolace.

Deton: Compound of various rocks dried together. When struck with sudden force it explodes producing a concussive effect.

Esolace \E-soh-luhs\: The molecular, city-wide network which connects everyone inside Oasis, allowing them access to all of the communication and informational resources of the Collective, including the ability to interface with all esolace enabled devices.

Extractor: A small device that mimics some of the functionality of the esolace such as information storage and retrieval. Usually worn by assessors in the form of a torc about the neck.

Fero \FAIR-oh\: A hollow metal tube, used as a club and also a horn of warning by the Welkin.

Garrick \GAIR-ik\: Coat with many hidden compartments typically worn by Waymen for desert travel.

Hard Link: The act of connecting to someone's bioseine when they are unconscious.

Hogar \ho-GAHR\: Multi-chamber tent-like structure, used by the Welkin for living quarters.

Ishto \EESH-toh\: Welkin word for children. Could also be translated "rascal". Feminine form is 'ishta'.

Kaff \KAF\: Turban wrapped around the head and worn by Waymen for desert travel.

Kindred: Name of the language spoken by both Welkin and Waymen, though they use different dialects.

Knit: Societal organization amongst the Welkin consisting of groups of families; a tribe.

Lentes \LEN-teyz\: Small circular lenses with polymeric padding around the edges which forms a seal around the eye so they can stay in place. They allow a person to see in the dark and to magnify what is seen.

Locus energy: Energy source which holds together nonliving matter. It can be focused into various strains to be used in weapons, as energy sources, or to create barriers of various sorts.

Lucine \LOO-sahyn\: A gel used to augment the range at which a bioseine can connect to other minds or esolace enabled devices. Its development was abandoned due to potentially deadly side effects.

Lumin \LOO-min\: A small device, usually round, which functions as a light source.

Maneusis \muh-NOO-sis\: Religious leader amongst the Welkin who passes on the traditions and beliefs about Numinae.

Memorant: Someone with the ability to probe the thoughts of another person. Memorants also have the ability to absorb and process vast amounts of information when connected to the esolace, far more than ordinary people.

Microslice: Unit of time roughly equivalent to 54

seconds. There are 100 microslices in a slice. (See also slice, nanoslice)

Mosh: A lumpy paste eaten by Werin, made from sere powder mixed with water. Tastes like a mixture of peas and rice.

Nanoslice: Unit of time roughly equivalent to 0.54 seconds. There are 100 nanoslices in a microslice. (See also slice, microslice)

Oscillathe \AH-sil-ley*th***:** A class of weapon which comes in various sizes and forms, but which shoots forth an evanescence wave which dissolves or disintegrates living, organic matter by disrupting the zoetic forces which hold it together. The wave frequency can be diminished so that it merely stuns its victim.

Pinion: Short javelin; principle weapon of the Waymen.

Praxis cruiser: Largest class of ship in the Collective fleet, armed with oscillathe cannons, locus pulsers, and dozens of antipersonnel guns. The praxis cruisers are the largest in the fleet, but not capable of interstellar travel.

Raker: Large, floating cargo ships which have locus energy barriers on top of them to protect their contents.

Reeve: Title for the leader of a Wayman thral (tribe).

Remin fluid: Liquid capable of storing memories. The memories can be recovered by drinking the fluid.

Sar \SAHR\: A Wayman camp.

Sere \SAIR-ey\: A soft, chalky rock that grows slowly over time in certain environments. It can be turned into a powder and if prepared properly, later reconstituted in water to use as food. The principal ingredient in mosh.

Service Ring: The district in Oasis between the Ancillary Rim and Axis Prime.

Sentients: Name of the survivors of the storm that

destroyed Oasis who chose to try and break free from the Collective.

Shiv: Term used by Waymen meaning roughly "warrior" or "soldier". Also refers to the knife-like weapons these warriors use in battle.

Shim: A derogatory term for another person used by the Waymen. Roughly translated it means someone of little worth or importance.

Slice: Unit of time roughly equivalent to 1.5 hours. There are 20 slices in a day. (See also microslice, nanoslice)

Solec: Drug with restorative and metabolism increasing properties. Very powerful but with negative side effects including extreme weakness and tiredness once it wears off.

Somatarch \SOH-muh-tahrk\: Mindless, soulless being which looks like an ordinary human but is controlled by the Developers and has no will or personality of its own. Used primarily for military and intelligence gathering purposes. Also referred to as "ghosts" or "the soulless" by Waymen and "hollow men" by the Sentients.

Sopor \SOH-pohr\: Also referred to as 'naptrap'. A powder made from combining the powders of griff and pheus rocks which will make a person unconscious nearly instantly if enough of it is inhaled. A handful of the powder can put an average size person to sleep for several.

Sovos \SOH-vohs\: Also known as a 'sand duster'. A small, open-topped ship which is faster than a lev and may also be outfitted with weapons. Seats around eight to ten people.

Span: Unit of measurement roughly equivalent to about 2 meters or 6.5 feet. A thousand spans is equal to a click (see 'click'). Also used in the expression 'a ten span' which is the way weeks are denoted (though obviously weeks are ten days instead of seven. Months are also only twenty days, so two ten spans, and there are only 200 days in a year).

Sunder: A Wayman with authority over a group of shivs. They are chosen by the Reeves from amongst the most brutal and ruthless members of the thral. It is not unusual for the next Reeve of a thral to come from amongst the ranks of the Sunders.

Taline \TEY-leen\: A rock that can easily be turned into powder and mixed with water to form an acid that eats through most forms of metal.

Tasada \tuh-SAH-duh\: Name for the eternal city in Waymen lore.

Thral: Societal organization of Waymen with fairly fluid membership held together by a powerful leader (the Reeve).

Throng: A Wayman raiding party.

Vacants: Fully grown adult bodies with no memory or personality. They are used by the Developers for creating somatarchs.

Vadi \VAH-dee\: A geographical formation of living rock which accumulates water over time. Waymen usually make their camps close to vadis.

Vapors: Round, fast assault vehicles which have blink thrusters which allow them to seem to teleport over short distances. They use oscillathe pulses as their primary weapons.

Vast: Term used by the Werin to refer to the planet's surface.

Viand \VAHY-and\ Stream: A molecular distribution system responsible for the sustenance and health of everyone connected to the esolace. When connected to this, a person has no need to sleep or eat and is protected from all forms of disease.

Virid \VEER-id\ Ridge: Elevated area on the perimeter of Oasis where the atmos generators are located.

Viscera: Name the Welkin use for the underground cavities of the planet in which they live.

Waymen: General term for the people who live on the planet's surface. They are nomadic and often raid others for supplies and goods. Though they claim to be distinct from the Welkin, they often absorb members of the Welkin into their numbers.

Welkin: Name of the people living beneath the surface of the Vast.

Werin \WAIR-in\: Name used by the Welkin to refer to all people, whether Welkin or Waymen. The Welkin believe that the Waymen and Welkin are simply two groups of the same people, but most Waymen do not share this view.

Yeso \YEHS-oh\: Made from cretan powder and umor oil, it is used by the Werin to set broken bones until they heal.

Zoelith \ZOH-uh-lith\: A small tool used to 'turn on/off' someone with a bioseine and also to perform 'maintenance' on their bioseine.

Zoetic \ZOH-eh-tik\ pulse/source: Detectable energy signature given off by living creatures.

ABOUT THE AUTHOR

DJ Edwardson always wanted to invent the hovercraft. Not some floaty balloon contraption, but the real McCoy, with levitation and jump jets and cool track lights down the side just because. But he found that not being a scientist or an inventor or a multi-billion dollar venture capitalist put a bit of a damper on that career path so he settled for the next best thing, writing fiction.

But he doesn't just write about exotic gadgets. He's invented all sorts of things that will probably never make it out of that "what if" stage, at least not in his lifetime. He also writes about things that aren't "things" at all, like friendship, courage, love, and faith. And those are even more exciting than hovercraft.

To find out more about his writing visit:
www.djedwardson.com

THE ADVENTURE CONTINUES

Adan's journey continues in the next volume of
The Chronotrace Sequence.

The truth has a way of resurrecting itself.

With the Developers' plans to reengineer the human race in
disarray, this may be the one chance Adan and the Sentient
renegades have of saving the desert world of the Vast.

The third and final book in the series brings the series to its
thrilling conclusion as threats long thought buried emerge from
across the vagaries of time and space.

Available in print and e-book formats

ALSO BY DJ EDWARDSON

A hero is measured by the size of his heart.

Every century a motley is born. Though only children, their patchwork skin marks them as dangerous, especially to those who know about the first motley. That one nearly destroyed the world.

But a chance meeting with Roderick the tailor may hold the key to breaking the curse. Roderick has no sword or armor or power of his own. He's not even rich. But what he does have is a heart moved by compassion for a hunted boy.

Will this be the last motley?

Available in print and e-book formats